PRIZE STORIES
from LATIN AMERICA

PRIZE STORIES
from LATIN AMERICA

Winners of the *Life En Español*
Literary Contest

DOUBLEDAY & COMPANY, INC.
GARDEN CITY, N.Y., 1963

LIBRARY OF CONGRESS CATALOG CARD NUMBER 62–15886
COPYRIGHT © 1961, 1963 BY TIME INC.
ALL RIGHTS RESERVED
PRINTED IN THE UNITED STATES OF AMERICA. FIRST EDITION

TABLE OF CONTENTS

The authors of the following stories won Honorable Mention.
The order in which they appear was established by the editor.

About *LIFE EN ESPANOL's* Literary Contest

"Premio LIFE EN ESPAÑOL"—$10,000 in prizes for the best Spanish-language short novel written by a Latin American—was an unprecedented literary event. It was designed specifically to encourage the production and appreciation of present-day Latin American literature, and marked the first award ever of a Literary Grand Prize specifically for Latin America. (Such awards as the Pulitzer Prize in Letters and Le Prix Goncourt are national awards, and the Nobel Prize for Literature is, of course, worldwide.) Some suggestion of the importance of this contest to Latin Americans may be seen in the fact that following the publication of the names of the prize winners, Argentine newspapers (Argentine writers took a plurality of the prizes) suggested that their showing more than compensated for their athletes' Olympic performance.

In announcing the contest originally, LIFE EN ESPAÑOL's editors estimated that perhaps 1000–1500 entries might be received during the year-long competition. In all, an overwhelming 3149 short novels were submitted, with writers representing every one of the Latin American republics and Puerto Rico. Faced with the monumental task of reading, analyzing, and judging these manuscripts were a panel of five of the most distinguished names in current Spanish American literature: Octavio Paz of Mexico, Hernan Diaz Arrieta of Chile, Emir Rodriguez Monegal of Uruguay, Federico de Onís of Spain, and Arturo Uslar Pietri of Venezuela.

Marco Denevi's *Secret Ceremony* won the $5000 grand prize. Of it, Arturo Uslar Pietri wrote: "Denevi, using apparently direct realistic methods, is able to create a poetic climate around the mystery of personality mutation in this tale of extraordinary technical skill. The handling of the dialogue and situations is extremely sure and uncompromising. Nevertheless, the author sacrifices none of the necessary stuff that makes for real storytelling —neither the spontaneity of his characters nor that mysterious something that brings them alive as people."

PREFACE

One judge analyzes the value of *LIFE EN ESPAÑOL's* Literary Contest

A contest of this kind, as well as fulfilling its obvious purpose, offers the opportunity to explore, albeit rapidly and haphazardly, the present-day situation and trends in narrative literature in Latin America. In statistical terms, the 3149 originals can be considered a reliable sampling of the predominant literary trends in Spanish-speaking America. It is possible that many of today's best-known writers did not enter, but on the other hand, these thousands of manuscripts, both good and bad, excellent and mediocre, reflect the notions of a vast group of people spread all over the continent about what is, or ought to be, fiction. Even the bad tale, clumsily put together by an amateur with no aptitude for writing, mirrors what the average reader looks for or wants to find in a good story. Social psychologists might find in this unexplored and revealing field a rewarding ground for probing and gathering data, and perhaps they could tell us the exact meaning of the predominance of stories about violence and death, the extraordinary abundance of sentimental themes, the preference for themes of fatality, loneliness, injustice and desperation, and for the feeling of man's insignificance before fate or nature. In this sense, the avalanche of manuscripts sent in comes to constitute a kind of chaotic and even contradictory outpouring of what the Spanish American soul looks for in literature.

If we limit ourselves, as elementary common sense dictates, to the winners of prizes and honorable mentions, we will find some interesting characteristics. Young people abound. Most of the winners are under forty, and some of them are in their twenties. All earn their livings from some activity other than creative writing. There are government workers, like Marco Denevi, who works in the Postal Savings Bank in Buenos Aires; others are lawyers, and there is even a simultaneous translator for international conferences. Among the others are a farmer, a sheep-raiser, businessmen, and, of course, journalists.

The professional writer is the exception in Latin America. There are very few who can or dare live from their pens. Literature never has been a career for the Spanish-American, but rather a somewhat heroic vocation, a way of surrendering himself to a divine mission or passion involving the acceptance of an arduous, difficult life. The Spanish-American writer, unlike his U.S. counterpart, has no chance for lucrative best sellers, fabulous book-club dividends, high pay for contributions to great magazines, or even the mirage of Hollywood with its contracts for tens of thousands of dollars for screen adaptations.

None of this is within his reach. Thus he rarely becomes a professional writer in the U.S. sense, but, on the other hand, through his dedication to a kind of priesthood, he acquires a prestige and influence that the professional writer of North America has rarely enjoyed. The prestige of the intellectual and the writer in Latin America is immense: it converts him into a kind of spiritual adviser, truth-teller, and trail-blazer, conferring upon him a unique function in the eyes of his countrymen, a function that all too often carries him into politics. This explains the important roles of Sarmiento in Argentina, Martí in Cuba, Vasconcelos in Mexico, and Gallegos in Venezuela. Not one of them could have considered himself a professional writer, but, in a larger sense, in the realization of their human destiny, they were even more than that.

Latin American literature has always been very receptive to outside influences. In this sense, it is one of the least provincial literatures in the world. Nevertheless, none of her great writers has blindly and unquestioningly followed the European or North American model.

Many of the stories entered in the contest contain traces of the narrative technique of some of the great universal masters of the contemporary novel. There is nothing wrong with this, so long as it doesn't destroy the writer's creative instinct or his own personality, for in every age there are prevailing trends and styles.

Receptive to world influences, sensitive to novelty, drawn simultaneously by aesthetic and social considerations, moved by the desire or the anguish to express the quintessence of Spanish-

Americanism and also to contribute toward its discovery, Latin American literature merits more attention than it receives from the world at this time. The Nobel Prize awarded to Gabriela Mistral did not really completely break down the wall of isolation and ignorance. This wall exists not only between Latin America and the rest of the world but also to a great extent among the Latin American nations themselves, still very much unaware of their mutual cultural, artistic, and literary life.

If the difficult voyage that I undertook as a judge, over the vast sea of so many written pages, has contributed in any way to a better recognition of the literature of the Latin American countries, I am content to have embarked on this adventure of the creative spirit.

ARTURO USLAR PIETRI
Paris, September 1960

SECRET CEREMONY
by Marco Denevi

MARCO DENEVI, who has been honored in numerous competitions before winning the first prize here, was born in Sáenz Pena, Argentina, in 1922. He is best known abroad for his novel, *Rosaura a las Diez* (Rosaura at Ten), one of the most successful of recent Latin American literary works, which has, since its first appearance in 1955, been made into a motion picture and translated into a number of foreign languages. He has also written many short stories and several plays, among the latter *Los expedientes* (The Proceedings) and *El emperador de la China* (The Chinese Emperor), the first translated into German, the second into French. His prize-winning story, *Ceremonia Secreta,* has already been adapted for television, its presentation being a major event in Argentine broadcasting. It has also appeared in an Italian translation.

It was not yet light when Miss Leonides Arrufat left her house. There was not a soul in the street.

Miss Leonides walked hugging the wall, her eyes low, her body stiff, her step quick, almost martial, the way a woman should walk at such an hour if alone, and decent, and, in addition, single, even though fifty-eight. For you never can tell.

(But, who would have ventured to accost her? Dressed in black from head to foot, on her head a liturgical hat in the form of a turban, under her arm a handbag which resembled a huge, rotted fig, the tall, gaunt figure of Miss Leonides took on, in the dim light, a vaguely religious air. She might have been taken for a Greek Orthodox priest who, under cover of darkness, was fleeing a Red massacre, if the smile that distended her lips had not indicated, on the contrary, that that priest was hurrying to officiate at his rites.)

She walked so quickly that her fleshless, angular knees hit

against her skirt, against the hem of her coat, and dress and coat swirled around her legs like troubled waters in which she was wading and from whose splashing she seemed to be trying to protect the bouquet of leaves and flowers which she was holding reverently with both hands at breast level.

When she reached the house of that paralytic child who had once smiled at her she laid on the doorstep a passion flower, bent her head, and prayed aloud: "Oh Lord, at whose will all the moments of our life transpire, look with favor on the prayers and offerings of your slaves who implore you for the health of the sick, and heal them of all suffering."

She kept on walking.

In the balcony of the house of Ruth, Edith, and Judith Dobransky she laid a spray of periwinkle tied with a pink ribbon, and prayed: "May the God of Israel be the tabernacle of your virginity, oh maiden, and save you from the serpent's snares."

She kept on walking.

She tossed three leaves of cineraria into the garden of a house where, several days before she had seen a funeral procession setting out, and murmured in bold Latin: *"Requiem aeternam dona eis, Domine,"* and *"lux perpetua luceat eis."*

She kept on walking.

Now Natividad González's turn was coming. For months now every day she had been leaving that hussy a big bouquet of nettles. Miss Leonides had decided that the bouquet of nettles should serve as a notice to its recipient whereby, without using dirty words, but dotting the *i's* and crossing the *t's,* she was urged to move to another neighborhood. But it would seem that Natividad González was illiterate in the language of nettles for she showed no signs of moving. So Miss Leonides found herself under the tiresome obligation of insisting in her nettling hints.

But that morning when she stopped in front of Natividad's house, as she opened her handbag, holding her breath (with the object of keeping herself immune to the nettle's bane) and took out her message, just as she was about to lay it on the doorstep, a bolt of lightning flashed out and fell upon her. The lightning bolt was Natividad.

And this Natividad, looking as though she had not slept, as though she had spent the entire night on the watch, pale and disheveled, squared off to Miss Leonides and began to insult her loud and thoroughly. She called her names that bristled with *R's* and *B's* like shards of broken glass; she conferred upon her unsuspected origins; she attributed to her professions sometimes classified as sad, sometimes as gay; she upbraided her as the worst sinners of us shall be upbraided on the Judgment Day, and finally, she invited her to employ the poor nettles for the most heroic and least accustomed purposes. It was as though Natividad had been multiplied a hundredfold and the hundred Natividads were all screaming at the same time. Where did the woman get all those words? Miss Leonides had the terrifying feeling that a wave of lava was moving toward her and that if she did not make her escape in time she would be engulfed forever like one of the residents of Pompeii. To save herself from the river of molten fire, she turned and with all the dignity she could muster, took her leave.

(What I mean is that she ran like crazy, for blocks and blocks, until she could go no farther. When her legs buckled under her like wires, she stopped. She was gasping. The drumbeat of her heart deafened her. Under her clothes her whole body oozed a cold glue. Her feet were throbbing like pulses. Her eyes crossed and she felt like throwing up. It took her forever to calm down.)

She made a long detour to get to the streetcar, for there on the spot she swore she would never again pass before Natividad's house. Never. And as though to emphasize that solemn oath, she threw to the ground the rest of the flowers she was still holding in one hand, all of which seemed suddenly to have withered, blasted undoubtedly, by the sulphurous fumes of the insults.

Meanwhile a kind of steady lightning flash made its appearance in the sky, and propelled by this storm, there appeared, as though emerging from some house, the first streetcar.

Miss Leonides took it, sat down next to a window, and an infinite street, made up of pieces of many streets, began to unroll before her eyes. She knew it by heart, that route. But no matter, she always found some way of entertaining herself. Like counting the trees that lined the sidewalk (skipping an occasional one whose looks did not appeal to her), picking out the letters of her name from the posters on the walls, trying to guess how many people wearing mourning she would see before coming to the sixth cross street. A person who has imagination never gets bored.

(The truth of the matter is that these games had wound up by becoming obsessions. Miss Leonides could not sit down in her bathroom without counting the tiles on the wall. In the kitchen she ran the scale up and down the eight panes of a window. As she walked along the street, she arranged the mosaics of the pavement in crosses, stars, big polygonal figures. At times the design became so complicated that she had to stop until she had worked it out. And when this happened it was a sight to see her, standing in the middle of a river of pedestrians, sweeping the ground with a fantastic pattern of glances that aroused the curiosity of all passers-by.)

But that morning Miss Leonides was in no mood for games. As soon as she had settled herself on the wooden seat of the streetcar, the zephyrs of thought caught her up and carried her far away, transported her to the house of Natividad González.

Dear God, the language that cockatrice had used! Miss Leonides could not recall any word concretely, for all were fused in an inseparable gibberish. But that the stew was seasoned with the most shocking insults, of that she had no doubt. Just imagine, a strumpet like that daring to insult, in the middle of the street and at the top of her lungs, Miss Leonides Arrufat! And she, why on earth had she stood for it? Oh no, things would have to be put in their proper place. And mentally she began to insult Natividad. She did not have the other's vast repertoire, but what difference did it make. She was satisfied with one word. A terrible word. *Slut*. And she repeated it like a magic formula, like a spell, like a person hammering a stubborn nail. She repeated it to the point of ecstasy, vertigo, and angelic intoxication. It seemed to her that that word, intoned in that way, went flying over streets and housetops, to Natividad herself, knocked her down, threw her to the ground, and there sucked all her pride, her youth, her beauty, that vicious strength she had employed toward Miss Leonides, and finally left her the way a swarm of locusts leaves a devoured tree.

(And as she was thinking up these delightful fates for Natividad, Miss Leonides quivered in her seat and gave little starts and twitches, so that anyone sitting beside her might have thought that the lady in the abbatial turban was not quite all there. Or might have thought, as someone did, that she had recognized her and that all this pantomime was due to emotion or added up to a secret code message.)

Suddenly Miss Leonides remembered something. Yes, a little incident in the big scene with Natividad. At the time she had taken it in, and then terror had hidden it beneath its flood. But now that the muddied waters had receded, the little incident re-emerged. What had happened was that Natividad, while she had been riddling Miss Leonides with indecent words, had, without noticing, moved her bare foot close to the nettle, and the nettle had stung her. As though saying to her: "Caw all you like, I'm going to stick my claws in you, for that's what my mistress told me to do. And I obey her, not you." Natividad had started back, had pulled her foot away from the nettle as though it were a live coal, and enraged more by the humiliation than the pain, she had begun to howl like a madwoman. As she recalled it, Miss Leonides had such an attack of mirth that she choked and had to put her handkerchief to her lips. But she could not keep her shoulders from shaking and a ripple of laughter from spurting noisily out of her nose.

Frightened by the noise, the zephyrs dropped Miss Leonides back on the car seat. Miss Leonides squirmed a little, coughed, put on an expression of offended dignity and turned toward the person sitting beside her.

It was like turning around and running into the point of a knife. Because the person seated beside her was a young girl (vaguely she made out that she was blonde, rather plump, and wearing mourning) and this girl, huddled in her seat, with her hands in her coat pockets, motionless and as though her soul had departed her body, had her face turned straight toward Miss Leonides and was looking at her. But she was looking at her, not with the momentary surprise with which one looks at a person who is laughing to himself, but like one who was expecting this laughter, knowing that after it something terrible was going to happen, and was now waiting for this terrible thing to happen.

Miss Leonides looked away (with difficulty, as though to do so—what an odd thing!—she had had to disengage gears) and began to stare out of the window. She waited awhile and then looked ahead of her. That was all she needed to know that the girl had not changed her position.

She looked out of the window again and then straight ahead. The girl had not moved.

"She's a poor crazy creature," she thought.

But thinking that she is a poor crazy creature is not much help if the poor crazy creature happens to be sitting next to us and is staring at us hypnotically. Miss Leonides did not know what to do. She had a vague feeling of danger. It seemed to her that that girl had begun to get a hold on her, to compromise her. From the moment their eyes met the girl had ceased to be a stranger. She was taking possession of her, invading her. She was transferring to her a responsibility, a burden, a danger. The very coincidence that they were both wearing mourning created a mysterious bond between them which set them off, separate and apart from the others.

Miss Leonides' eyes shuttled between the window and the front door of the streetcar, and back again, and thanks to these shifts she could watch the girl. And the girl kept on looking at her.

Miss Leonides repeatedly opened and closed her bottomless handbag, cleared her throat loudly, hummed in a low voice, began to read the fascinating small print on her ticket, showing in all these ways that she was not intimidated.

And the girl went on looking at her. Looking at her. Looking at her.

"If she goes on looking at me like that" (Miss Leonides moaned mentally) "I'm going to ask her if I've got a picture painted on my face. But doesn't she realize how ridiculous she is? Or is there something wrong about me? Have I got something in my ear? Has my face turned purple? Am I getting ready to die?"

Surrendering to a kind of dizziness, she turned toward the girl. Why did she do it? She hastily withdrew her glance. For that crazy creature kept on looking at her, true, but her eyes, which had seemed to be waiting for something terrible to happen, had now broken into pieces. The girl was crying. Crying silently, without a gesture, without making a motion. She was crying with her hands in her pockets. Huddled in her seat, she was crying. Crying and looking at Miss Leonides. Looking at Miss Leonides and bitterly reproaching her for not fulfilling the pact.

The pact? What pact? Miss Leonides lost her head. Hurriedly she stood up, stepped over and on the girl, literally trampling her as she stepped on her feet. It seemed to her that the girl tried to stop her, that she was mumbling something, but she did not listen to her, for if she did she would be lost, lost forever. She rushed down the aisle, bumped into a passenger, yelled to the conductor to stop the car, and when it came to the corner she plunged out of the unoffending vehicle as though it were a burning building, stumbled, almost fell, and hurried off down the street as fast as her legs would carry her. She did not once look back.

She was on San Martín. From the intersection of San Martín and Córdoba she heard the bells of the Blessed Sacrament. The church opened its arms to her as all churches always received her, like a secret sanctuary which put her out of the reach of the infinite evils of this world.

Afterward everything happened as in a game, with one counter advancing slowly, capriciously, moving here, stopping there, along a zigzag path traced upon a multicolored board, while another counter, in the rear, follows it, also moving at intervals, until suddenly, and when chance so wills, the second counter overtakes the first, and then the two, the pursued and the pursuer, abandon the path and meet in the square where they are enclosed as in a fortress.

Miss Leonides went into the Blessed Sacrament, heard Mass (absent-mindedly, alas), went out again, cautiously surveyed the street from the portico, did not see the girl dressed in mourning (who was inside the church, standing between two confessionals, in a dark corner), stepped into the street and turned north along San Martín.

Crossing the square brought her two unpleasant experiences. The first was that couple. How is it possible for people to feel like hugging and kissing each other in a square at eight o'clock in the morning? She passed by the disgusting spectacle as though she did not see it. But she heard. She heard the woman's laughter. Miss Leonides compressed her lips. Slut. Slut. *Slutslutslut.*

The second unpleasant experience: the boys. There is nothing, in the whole universe of galaxies and nebulae, nothing so fearsome as a gang of boys. Nobody can say how they gather, where they come from but there they are, more compact than the tubers of a plant, intertwined in a web of indecent words and gestures, linked together like a single coralline mass. Just look at them. They greet one another with cuffs. They hardly talk. They communicate by means of snickers, winks, secret codes. They assume a sly, wary air as though plotting God knows what scheme. And if a woman passes by, they all look at her, sometimes menacingly, sometimes insolently, as though they knew some secret of hers and were threatening her with exposure. But they are never more ferocious than when standing on corners like a bunch of Indians. One has to be a woman and have crossed this mine field to know the meaning of scorn and derision for one's sex. Take Miss Leonides' word for it.

Fortunately, her sharp eyes identified the danger in time. A gang of boys was coming in her direction. Miss Leonides turned and retraced her steps. She had to pass the couple again (and again the woman laughed provocatively). "Drop dead," Miss Leonides thought to herself, and descended and climbed stairs, walked several extra blocks. But anything was preferable.

It was nine o'clock when she got to the cemetery. She visited the three identical tombstones of gray marble. She read, as she always did, by way of greeting, the inscriptions that were growing blurred: Aquiles Arrufat, d. March 23, 1926; Leonides Llegat de Arrufat, d. March 23, 1926; Robertito Arrufat, d. March 23, 1926.

"I did not bring you flowers today," she explained aloud to them, "because that hussy, you know, that Natividad, dirtied those I was bringing."

She strolled about for a time among the vaults and mausoleums. As she turned a corner she saw her.

There she was, a few yards off, as though barring the way. Miss Leonides stopped and the two stood looking at each other.

Now she could size her up better. She was short, plump, with short, stocky legs. Her head, which was too big for her body, seemed bigger still because of her shock of blonde hair. Her face, which was broad and somewhat coarse-featured, radiated innocence and kindliness, like that of a peasant, and this resemblance was emphasized by a kind of flush, a curious congestion which thickened her already flabby features, as though she were carrying a huge weight on her head. On the other hand, her clothes were of good quality but she wore no jewelry. Nor gloves, purse, or hat. And that was all.

"Gracious," Miss Leonides sighed with relief, "she's just a poor harmless girl. She gives me the impression of being a stranger who is lost and wants to ask me how to get home. Honestly, I can't imagine why I had all those queer ideas in the streetcar."

That was all and yet it was not all. Someone has looked at us fixedly and has cried. One doesn't cry for nothing. Afterward she has trailed us halfway around the city, until she came face to face with us again. Then she has looked at us all over again. Now she's not weeping silly tears. Now she's just standing there, in an attitude of offering and renunciation, of imploring and resignation. And leaving the next move up to us, she waits distressfully to see what we are going to do. One would have to be made of iron to reject her and pass by. That presence there is a question that demands an answer, yes or no. One must make up one's mind. And Miss Leonides was not made of iron, but of wax and butter. So Miss Leonides, without further thought, made up her mind.

What I mean to say is that she smiled. And as though that

smile had suddenly opened a crack in her soul, she plunged head-
long into the abyss, and, unable to control her movements, she
made several gestures by way of greeting. That was enough. A
dizzy mechanism went into operation. As though flung by some
giant's hand, the girl threw herself on Miss Leonides and hugged
her, clasped her arms around her neck, rested her head on Miss
Leonides' flat spinster's bosom, while her whole body shook as
though she were being whipped. And while this was taking place,
from beneath the blonde mop of hair there came a whimpering,
or convulsive laughter, the panting of a terrified small animal, an
inarticulate muttering which slowly became transformed into a
word, a single word, repeated in a tone of frenzied delight:
"*Mom, mom, mom, mom, mom.* . . ."
Miss Leonides blinked in amazement.

Until finally the muttering died away, the shock of blonde
hair moved and drew back from Miss Leonides' breast; from beneath the hair, timidly, like some wary little animal, appeared
the face of the girl. In a kind of terror Miss Leonides looked at
it. She looked at it, and did not see there the silky furrow of
tears, nor the forehead shiny with sweat, nor the spectral smile,
now sorrowful, now gay, which incessantly appeared and disappeared from the lips, nor the throat distended like a pigeon's crop.
Miss Leonides saw nothing but the eyes. Like that, with those
very eyes, Robertito had looked at her that twenty-third of
March of 1926. An immense pity and an infinite tenderness came
over her. She knew that she could no longer escape. She had
fallen into a snare. She was caught, trapped, betrayed. Now
they would take her wherever her captor ordered.

The girl took her by the arm and the two of them left the
cemetery.

Once more they crossed the city. They walked side by side,
linked to one another, like intimate friends or like mother and
daughter. They did not exchange a single word. Miss Leonides
moved with her soldier's stride, her eyes on the ground. She felt
bewildered, excited, confusedly happy. The turn her adventure
with the girl dressed in mourning was taking produced a kind of
intoxication in her. What was going to happen to her? But she

did not even want to guess. Come what would, she was ready for it. For often, sick with loneliness, she had dreamed that in this crowded world there was someone who was aware of her existence, who needed her, who was waiting for her, looking for her, and that sometime this person would find her and take her away. And now this dream was no longer a mad fantasy. But one must never interfere with the delicate workings of magic by seeking explanations. One must yield and let oneself be guided: Miss Leonides did not even dare to glance at the girl out of the corner of her eye for fear the spell might be broken.

But the spell was not broken, the dream continued, the fair chubby doll went trotting along beside her; she could feel under hers the plump arm continually twitching with electric shocks. And she went on, and on. Where was she going? She did not know, nor did she want to.

In this way they came to Suipacha Street. They came to that stretch of Suipacha which runs from the Diagonal Norte to the Avenida de Mayo, and has nothing but shops, shops, shops, and women sniffling around the show windows.

There, in the shadow of the large modern buildings, stood a big old house which nobody ever noticed. It bears (or at least did until a short time ago) the number 78. It has two grilled windows on the first floor, a double door, with two funereal bronze knockers. On the second floor there is a large overhanging balcony, and that's all it has, unless you count a huge crack that crosses it like some evil scar or like the reproduction of a flash of lightning in some naïve water color. On its left there is a store; on its right, another. Across from it, the wall of St. Michael Archangel. The house does everything in its power to avoid calling attention to itself, as though it were ashamed of its ugliness and decrepitude. But it is not necessary, for nobody notices it. They pass over it as though it were a vacant lot. If they do look at it, they've forgotten it the next minute. Perhaps some pair of lovers takes shelter there at night, but it is to kiss, and not to observe its architecture. So the house is there, and is as though it were not there; it is there by oversight, as if through a crack between the two buildings which flank it an excrescence had

risen to the surface, a bit of rubble of the colonial city, which
now lies buried under the skyscrapers and towers. If the store on
the right and the store on the left were to move a little closer to
one another, they could obliterate this growth, as with a pair of
pincers.

Miss Leonides, moving swiftly along Suipacha, stood openmouthed when the girl stopped in front of that relic. She saw her
take a key out of the pocket of her coat, unlock the stubborn
door (whose knockers frightened her as though they were two
barking dogs) and then step aside to let her in. But Miss Leonides could not quite make up her mind.

"Who's here, who's inside?" she asked, peering into the house's
vague shadows.

The girl shook her big head back and forth.

"Nobody, nobody," she said, and her face suddenly became
overcast, and she looked at Miss Leonides in distress.

With throbbing heart Miss Leonides Arrufat then walked into
the house at 78 Suipacha Street.

A smell of dampness, of stale air, medicines, decay and death,
a smell which was the sum and product of all the bad smells in
this world, was the first thing that came out to meet her, ruining
the emotion she was feeling. She would have preferred to turn
back. She would have liked, at any rate, to cover her nose with
her handkerchief. But the girl had already taken her by the hand
and was dragging her toward the bottom of that fetid abyss.

They crossed several darkened rooms crowded with furniture.
They came to a narrow vestibule illuminated by the murky
gloom that filtered through a remote skylight. They ascended a
black wooden staircase that squeaked and creaked under their
feet. They reached another still smaller vestibule. They went down
a hall. They crossed an anteroom. They stopped in front of a
door. The girl opened this door and Miss Leonides found herself in a sumptuous bedroom.

At first she saw only the awe-inspiring double bed, covered
with a white satin spread; the huge triple wardrobe with its long
mirror; a motley of small tables and armchairs, and, in the rear,
a long French door veiled by a curtain of macramé lace. Behind

the curtain she could make out the light of morning, and in it
the ocher silhouette of St. Michael, and this sight, seen from a
perspective so unusual for her, frightened her without knowing
why. Suddenly the whole business struck her as being so absurd
that she did not know how to go on with it.

She took a few steps around the room. She felt the girl's eyes
behind her. She heard her uneven breathing. It even seemed to
her that she could hear again that wheeze, that moaning. She
was embarrassed. They had dragged her, she had allowed herself to be dragged, on to a stage, and now they were waiting for
her to begin to play her part. What part? She had no idea. And
the girl, there, like a curtain going up, like a call bell, like a pointing hand.

Trying to find some way to fill this awkward vacuum, Miss
Leonides did something very funny. She began to examine with
fierce interest the photographs which adorned the bedroom walls.
She exchanged glances with a rosy man who had a long mustache,
with faded ladies wearing hats very similar to hers, then again
with the man with the mustache, with newborn infants, dressed
and naked, once more with the man with the mustache. Suddenly she gave a start. A woman who looked amazingly like her,
who looked a little like her, who had a remarkable, or perhaps,
a faint resemblance to her, was looking at her out of one of the
photographs. Standing beside her a little girl exactly like the
young woman dressed in mourning was leaning her head on the
shoulder of Leonides Arrufat's double, and both of them, through
the lens of the camera, were looking at her steadily, with guarded,
stubborn eyes.

Miss Leonides was so astounded that her head swiveled mechanically toward the girl. She was evidently awaiting this move.
And waiting for it as a warm invitation to give rein once more
to her demonstrations of affections. For, running toward the visitor, she clasped her arm, rested her head on her shoulder, repro-
ducing the posture of the child in the photograph and babbling
again that strange word:

"*Mom, mom, mom, mom. . . .*"

For several minutes the four women scrutinized one another.

"It is a fact," reflected Miss Leonides looking at her double, "it is a fact that she has some of my features. What a pity she wears her hair parted in the middle like that. It makes her look so old-fashioned!"

(A woman who looked as though she had stepped out of a photograph album of 1920 was looking at the picture of a woman who looked as though she had stepped out of the year 1920, and found her old-fashioned. And that is as it should be. For, if this were not the case, there would be no judges or critics in this world.)

"On the other hand," Miss Leonides mused, "the girl hasn't changed at all."

(Not at all, except for the puffiness of her face.)

"So that's the key to the whole thing. She has taken me for this woman, who is undoubtedly her mother and has undoubtedly just died. That clears everything up."

This simple explanation left her with a feeling of disappointment. She had expected something different, less trite, more involved. And now what was she supposed to do? Say to her: "My dear, I am not the person you think. So, please, let me go," and go?

She freed herself from the girl's arm, bore left, then right, like a person looking for an exit, and who, not finding it, stops and rests her hand on a piece of furniture. Suddenly she saw her reflection in the wardrobe mirror. A mixture of fright and anger came over her. And turning toward the girl, she burst forth in a torrent of words which she could not hold back:

"And now what? Now what? What are you waiting for? What do you want of me? Why don't you do something? Why don't you say something? Have you swallowed your tongue?"

She bit her lips. Why had she talked like that? And why had she used that harsh, loud tone, as though she were angry, when she wasn't? On the contrary. Her outburst was, at most, a call for help. When one can't find the exit, one screams and lashes out. And then she had found herself so ridiculous in the mirror, so graceless and grotesque in the luxurious surroundings of the bedroom! And now what? The girl would undoubtedly start crying.

But no, she didn't. Paradoxically, she not only did not start crying but gave a shrill little laugh and mumbled:

"Breakfast, breakfast."

She made a gesture as though asking Miss Leonides to wait, and rushed out of the room.

Standing there in the center of that big bedroom, Miss Leonides blinked her eyes. Had she heard right? Had the girl said "Breakfast, breakfast?" Well, she would wait a little while longer to see what those words and that protective gesture meant. And why not? After all, she wasn't doing anything wrong. If someone, a relative, a friend, say, were to appear, what could they reproach her with? Nothing. Breakfast, breakfast. All right, let's wait.

With a sudden feeling of well-being, Miss Leonides ensheathed herself in a close-fitting chair of indigo velvet. But no, we must make better use of the moment we have to ourselves. She got up, stole a glance out of the window, turned back to the room, riffled the leaves of several books piled on a kind of desk (books of poetry, some of them in a foreign language, and all with a sprawling signature on the first page: *Jan Engelhard,* and a flourish underneath like the tail of a comet and three dots like three stars), opened the wardrobe (a thousand dresses), opened a little door hidden behind a screen (the door opened into a huge bathroom with a sunken tub), and closed it quickly, as though she had surprised a man there with his pants down; she admired the stone fireplace (with its andirons piled with wood, ready to be lighted), a pendulum clock (Heavens, a quarter past ten already!), innumerable statuettes of ivory, jade, strange iridescent substances, and was stroking the satin spread when the girl reappeared.

Miss Leonides straightened up instantly and blushed as though she had been caught doing something wrong. (How silly. Because, as far as the girl was concerned, she was in her own home and in her own bedroom.) But the sight that met her eyes instantly drove from her mind blushes, satin bedspread, statuettes, the clock with the hour of a quarter past ten, the bathtub of the Emperor Caracalla, the thousand dresses, Suipacha Street, the room, the house, the world, everything. For the girl had come in carrying in her hands a gigantic tray. And on this tray there stood, in silver and porcelain, the most sublime breakfast service anyone in his right mind could imagine. The girl set that monument on a little table, pulled up a chair, and then turned toward Miss Leonides, as though inviting her to sit down.

Everything began to whirl around Miss Leonides, and her eyes did not focus. The voracity of a cannibal awoke in her like a fury. Her stomach, her lungs, her heart, her head became sensitized, the same scorpion was stinging them all. Without taking off her hat, tottering, she approached the table and sat down.

Her hands were shaking. She had one last moment of hesitation. She looked at the girl. But she was standing there beside her, with the respectful air of a trusted servant waiting on her mistress. With this Miss Leonides waited no longer. Hunger was stronger than good breeding, than shame, than dissimulation. Like a Hindu god, ten arms sprouted on her left, on her right, and with these tentacles all moving at the same time, she fell upon the tray. For a long time consciousness disappeared. An astral Leonides Arrufat manipulated spoons which buried themselves in pink jellies, in transparent marmalades, in fragrant tea with milk, and then rose radiantly to her mouth; she maneuvered, like little cranes, knives laden with preserves and butter; she crunched toast that filled her head with noise, croissants as tender as boned spring chickens, slices of cake that melted in her mouth and filled it with the most surprising, unexpected, delicious flavors. At times she raised unseeing eyes, eyes of mica, to the girl, who smiled at her, and she mechanically returned the smile and went on devouring.

Until the moment when all that monument was reduced to ruins. Then Miss Leonides and her spirit came together again, she leaned back in the chair, gave a mighty sigh which halfway out was metamorphosed into a belch, looked timidly at the girl, and murmured, apologetically:

"Delicious. Thank you so much."

And she felt suddenly drawn to that girl.

The girl, who looked more and more like a decent Polish or German servant, took the tray with the easy movement of someone performing a daily chore, and left the room with it. Miss Leonides stood up, took off her hat, took off her coat, loosened her belt, and went back to the velvet chair. (On the way she exchanged a glance with the Leonides in the wardrobe mirror, the two of them shrugged their shoulders, tittered, and, completely in agreement, separated.) Miss Leonides felt a sudden optimism without knowing why. Waves of abnegation and kindness laved her body. She felt like talking. Talking with the girl, with someone, any one. The world is beautiful. People are nice. One must live. This is how profound the effects of a splendid breakfast are.

When the girl came back, Miss Leonides, swinging one leg and running her tongue over her teeth, asked:

"My dear, are we really alone?"

The doll nodded her floppy head.

"And did you prepare that breakfast all by yourself?"

Again the head moved up and down like a puppet's.

"Nobody helped you?"

A sly smile rose to the fleshy lips.

"Don't you remember? Don't you remember, mama?" she blubbered in a cottony voice, as though her mouth were full. "Don't you remember?"

"Don't I remember what, dear?"

"We fired Rosa and Amparo. Don't you remember, don't you remember?"

"Oh yes. But isn't there anybody else downstairs?"

"Nobody, nobody."

But Miss Leonides wanted to make absolutely sure.

"And later on, this afternoon, or tomorrow, or the next day, who's coming? Are you expecting visitors?"

"Nobody, nobody."

All right, nobody. Apparently, the poor creature had no relatives or friends, she lived all alone in that big house, she was alone in the world. Miss Leonides felt an inner satisfaction.

"Dearie," she asked in an insinuating voice, "would you like me to stay here and live with you?"

The words were no more than out of her mouth than she regretted them. She had made a slip. As her only answer, the girl knelt before Miss Leonides, took both her hands, looked her straight in the eye, while an expression of violent distress spread over her flaming face; and as at the same time that hateful sly little smile began to play over her lips again, this sinisterly dual face terrified the idol of whom benevolence was thus besought.

"If you want me to," stammered Miss Leonides, "if you want me to stay . . . I'll stay as long as. . . ."

And as the kneeling figure went on staring at her like a sleepwalker, she screamed:

"Forever, forever, I'll stay forever!"

At this the girl began a kind of frenzied contortion. The distress disappeared from her eyes, the perfidious smile began to well up, to spread to the corners of her lips, and burst like a paludal bubble. Miss Leonides found herself hugged, squeezed, kissed. A revolting hiccoughing clicked beside her mouth. Two damp hands stroked her hair. Miss Leonides could not bear to have anybody touch her hair. She struggled under those repulsive caresses. Then with an impulse she was unable to restrain, she gave the girl a slap in the face, and screamed:

"Let me be, let me be!"

The girl immediately fell back, let her hands drop, and turned very pale, very white (and white, like that, her face seemed a copy in pale marble of her other face, red and tanned, a peasant's face), her pupils trembled, but the ghost of the crazy smile went on dancing behind her lips.

Miss Leonides was no less pale. What had she done? Why had she given in to that attack of hysterics? Was that any way to repay that poor innocent creature for her breakfast and her devotion? Was that silly mania about not having her hair touched more important? Poor little girl, poor little doll. And when she saw the mark of the slap begin to show on the girl's cheek, she was on the verge of tears. Poor little doll, poor crazy little thing.

"Excuse me," she murmured, and stretched out her contrite hand imploring forgiveness.

(Yes, forgiveness, forgiveness. But was it impossible for her to stop smiling?)

The girl took that veined, fleshless hand and put it to her cheek, holding it there as if it were a poultice (her face was burning. "I wonder if she's got a fever, if she's sick?" Miss Leonides thought to herself). Her color quickly returned, and the cowardly trembling moisture disappeared from her eyes. Once more she was the peasant coming back after gathering grapes all day in the sun with a loaded basket on her head.

Then she sat down of the floor at Miss Leonides' feet. They sat like that, the two of them, motionless and silent, for a long time, as with lazy eyes they followed the cockchafer of their thoughts and dreams.

Every now and then Miss Leonides turned her head to look out of the corner of her eye at the big double bed. That bed fascinated her, drew her like a magnet. How wonderful it must be to lie in it, not to sleep, but to spend hours and hours resting, reading, or having tea. Often, in her own house, she had planned to spend several days in bed. For no special reason. Because when she got up, she had asked herself: What am I getting up for? Why am I repeating this meaningless routine? What for? But in her house this prospect was not at all alluring. To look at the patches of mold on the walls, to see them as monstrous diseased organs, to run the scale along the rosettes of the ceiling, to think: "In ten minutes I am going to die; in five minutes; in one minute; now," to scream, and then start all over again. But here it was different.

Finally Miss Leonides could stand it no longer. She got up, approached the bed, and stood there looking at it as though she were watching somebody lying there. Then she felt two hot hands resting on her shoulders and beginning to undress her. A minute later she was floating on the bosom of that huge bed as though in clear water, swimming between sheets of embroidered linen, with her head resting on a feather pillow, while warm blankets covered her like a down comforter of sand. And a girl who bent over her and kissed her on the forehead and then went and lighted a splendid fire.

Miss Leonides closed her eyes. Tears of happiness gathered
under her lids. A thousand frozen buds melted in the depths of
her soul and burst into bloom. Old paralyzed mechanisms lost
their rust, and began to move, to run again. She felt herself drifting on the vortex of a thousand opposing currents but all of them
equally delightful. Dear God, at last she was shielded from loneliness, poverty, women who let themselves be embraced in public
places, gangs of street louts, and Natividad González. If only nobody would snatch her from that paradise. If they would let her
stay there at least a day, even a few hours. And as though
asserting her claim to it, she caressed with her feet and hands
that enormous bed fit for an empress.

That first day went by quickly, hastened and as though criss-
crossed by the surprises, the novelties, the continual tension. In
any case, Miss Leonides did not have a bad time. The girl
prepared a lunch for her which was breakfast multiplied by ten;
then she served her a glass of some powerful liqueur which
burned her throat and made her laugh for a long time (although
the girl did not taste the liqueur, she accompanied her in her
laughter); then Miss Leonides talked her head off, without giving
a hoot whether the girl was listening or not, because she was
talking to limber up her tongue, not to be heard by a poor
madwoman. Then came the afternoon, and Miss Leonides, not to
offend, gobbled down an abundant tea; then the girl sat down
at the desk with books (which turned out to be a kind of archaic
piano) and drew from it a tintinnabulation like that of a music
box which moved Miss Leonides deeply; then all sounds died
away, night came, the girl lighted a lamp which colored the whole
bedroom pink; then Miss Leonides decided she wanted to look
out of the window for a minute and see what Suipacha Street
looked like from above at night; then she had dinner; then the
girl read out loud (with gestures) a poem in which someone
kept calling for a certain Anabel Anabelí; then, lulled by the
litany, Miss Leonides fell asleep.

She could not understand how it was, if the window was always
on her left, she now saw it on the right. And what in the devil
was that reddish reflection that glimmered like tortoise shell where

the chest of drawers stood? She sat up bathed in sweat. Several minutes must have elapsed before she realized that she was not in her own house, but in the house at 78 Suipacha Street. The adventure she was living suddenly struck her as being a fantastic nightmare, a dream which, now that she was awake, she would dream all over again. She felt about with her hands until she found the lamp and turned it on. She was alone. A last ember smoldered in the fireplace. The clock showed three.

She got up like a sleepwalker and went out of the bedroom. Downstairs, far in the distance, a light shone. She made out the stairway, went down it to the accompaniment of muted creaks, and reached the hall. She walked with her eyes fixed on that remote light. It was not she who moved it, but the light that came to meet her. Under her feet she could feel carpets, wooden floors, tiles. She struck her ankle against a sharp object. Another, as light as a cobweb, brushed her forehead. The light came nearer, broadened, and turned into the opening of a door. Behind the door she could hear the rattle of dishes and a woman's voice muttering unintelligible words. Miss Leonides stopped and waited, her heart pounding. Then, furtively, she took several steps and stood where she could see into the room where the talk was going on. She saw that it was a large kitchen, and that the enigmatic girl dressed in mourning, wearing an apron and with her hair falling over her eyes, was moving about it. What was she doing there at this time of night? Didn't she sleep? Whom was she talking to? And in what language? And that voluble voice, modulated, changing tone, like that of an actress, was it hers? Miss Leonides stood there for a time watching her. She seemed very busy. She was putting away piles of dishes, opening and closing cupboard doors, scouring pots, sitting down at a marble table and writing, with a pencil she kept wetting against her tongue, in an oilcloth-covered notebook. And all this without interrupting her barbarous gabble. As she never stopped, as nobody answered her, Miss Leonides realized that she was talking to herself.

Miss Leonides shivered. She turned to go back as she had come, but now there was no light to guide her. She moved with-

out knowing where she was going, bumped into the wall, stumbled
over furniture. She did not know where she was, she was lost,
she screamed.

There was a noise of running feet, two hands grasped hers,
and a voice murmured in her ear:

"Come, Mama, come."

The girl guided her slowly through that dark labyrinth; she
soothed her with a kind of cooing, as one does a child; she
clasped her hand tightly.

Miss Leonides groaned and allowed herself to be led.

For two days nobody came to cast her out of paradise.

Miss Leonides was enchanted, really enchanted. But her situation was not yet assured. She was walking the tightrope of an
hallucination. And the victim of the hallucination at moments
kept staring at her steadily as she had done in the streetcar.
Miss Leonides was waiting for an explosion: "Who are you?
And what are you doing here in my mother's bedroom? Get out,
get out of here, fast," and then she would have to leave this
Eden. At other times the girl smiled as though to herself, with
that sly smile which aroused Miss Leonides' darkest suspicions.
"Can she have something up her sleeve?" she wondered. "She
may have brought me here God only knows with what intention."
But what intentions could there be? Except in those rare moments
when she seemed to lose herself in her own aberrations, the girl
was so docile, so hard-working, so anxious to please. One only
had to say to her: "My dear, my dear," and the doll was running
about on her stumpy legs as though she had been wound up.
And the way she looked after her! Like a queen.

But, just in case, Miss Leonides was on the alert. Just in case,
she treated the keeper of paradise with the greatest politeness,
asked her no questions, did not pry into anything. Just in case,
she combed her hair with a part in the middle. She did not leave
the bedroom again. That was her domain, her fortress, her refuge.
No matter what happened on the lower floor, it was all one to
her. Where did the girl sleep? She didn't know. Where did the
money come from? She didn't know that either. She did not know
and she did not care. There was no need for her to venture into

those labyrinths which might shatter her hypostatic identification
with the dead woman. She hardly left the bed, except to exchange
it for the bathtub, which she filled with warm water and quan-
tities of perfume, and where she lay for hours and hours with the
water up to her neck, sighing with pleasure. When she recalled
her house it was like something in a remote, sordid world to
which, later on, she would have to return. But in the meantime
she was living a long holiday. And, as for the bad odor, what
bad odor? She didn't smell anything. Miss Leonides was enchanted, really enchanted.

The girl had served her another glass of that diabolical drink.
Then she had brought in the bottle, and they both drank. A sudden spurt of energy came over Miss Leonides.

"Darling," she said, raising her shoulders and wrinkling her
nose, as though about to propose some mischievous trick, "what
would you think if I were to try on some of those dresses?"

The girl gave a shrill laugh (which left Miss Leonides somewhat disconcerted), moved her puppet's head from side to side,
and rushed to open the wardrobe. Miss Leonides leaped out of
bed and, standing before the mirror, began to try on, one after
the other, the dresses which, it was apparent, had belonged to the
false Leonides of the photograph. They did not look bad on her.
A little short, perhaps, and a bit loose. But how pretty they were!
Miss Leonides gazed at herself in the mirror, turned herself
about, trying to see herself from the back and in profile, repeating
over and over the same thing: "Why, it's an original!"

The girl had seated herself on the floor, watching with an
ambiguous expression the successive transformations of Miss
Leonides. From time to time (for no reason? or when the dress
was especially becoming? or especially unbecoming? how could
one tell?) she laughed screechily. She laughed stupidly. Like what
she was. Like a crazy thing. "Can she be making fun of me?"
Miss Leonides asked herself, with uneasiness and a touch of
anger.

They poured themselves another glass.

Now Miss Leonides began to wriggle into an evening dress of
black silk. Then she added to it a fur stole. Whereupon the

girl, strangely excited, got a box of make-up out of a drawer, and Miss Leonides painted her lips and rouged her cheeks.

They poured themselves another glass.

"Jewelry," Miss Leonides suddenly shouted. "Where is my jewelry? I need a necklace, a bracelet, earrings."

The girl looked feverishly everywhere, Miss Leonides helped her, they searched the room. They found an empty jewel box, several cases, empty too, but not even a modest ring turned up.

It did not matter. With a willowy walk Miss Leonides returned to the mirror and admired herself again. Was she that woman with her hair parted in the middle, all made up, with eyes like a tiger, her body squeezed into a skin-tight silk dress and wearing a fur cape that barely hid her bare shoulders?

She downed another glass.

Suddenly she began to cry. She didn't know why, but she cried. The tears ran down her cheeks, washing away the make-up, dropping down her bosom, wetting the silk of the dress.

(Now the marionette was not laughing. She stood motionless, watching Miss Leonides, her forehead puckered.)

At that moment from the distance, on the ground floor, there came the sound of knocking.

The alcoholic haze vanished like a bubble from inside Miss Leonides' head.

"What's that? What are those knocks?" she asked in a low voice.

The girl had got swiftly to her feet and ran to peer out of the window.

"Who is it? Please tell me, who is it?" Miss Leonides repeated, without venturing to move from the spot.

"Encarnación and Mercedes," whispered the girl, drawing back from the window and running across the bedroom.

"Please, please," Miss Leonides implored, "don't tell them I'm here."

But the girl had already disappeared.

Miss Leonides stood rooted to the floor. Dressed for a party, with the cape over her shoulders, and her face completely raddled, she was offering, in return for not being discovered, the sacrifice of complete immobility.

But after half an hour this corpse came back to life, and curiosity took the place of panic. She slipped off her shoes, put down the fur scarf, and doing everything she could to make herself incorporeal, she began the descent to the Inferno. Now it was not a light that guided her steps, but the voices of several women chattering in one of the front rooms. She came to a little parlor and then to a breakfast room. From there, through a glass door covered with a net curtain, she could make out the visitors, comfortably settled in armchairs. They were two old white-haired women. The girl was sitting on the edge of a chair, her eyes stubbornly fixed on the floor, with the air of a criminal at the bar.

"Cecilia," said one of the old women, whose voice, hoarse and with a strangely metallic quality, paused after every syllable, recalling the bleating of a goat, "we were at the cemetery yesterday. There was not a single flower on your poor mother's grave. It must be a long time since you were there. Do you think that is nice?"

The other voice, slow and mellow, like a trickle of oil dripping on sand, added:

"Your poor mother is dead, Cecilia. You must realize that and not go about the streets looking for her. Are you listening to me?"

"Mercedes," the first voice rebuked her.

"But it's that. . . ."

"Be still."

A silence followed. Cecilia (so her name was Cecilia!), who was fingering her skirt, shook all over. Was she crying?

The goat stamped her hoof on the floor and bleated:

"Now what are you laughing at? Don't laugh. I order you not to laugh, Cecilia. Good Heavens, it seems to me you smell of liquor. Have you been drinking? That's all you needed. To take to drink."

"You're like your parents," growled the other old hag.

"Mercedes!"

"But it's that. . . ."

"Be still."

Another silence, and the bleating started up again:

"And what has happened today that you haven't offered us tea? Come, Cecilia, get a move on."

The girl leaped up and ran to the rear of the house, just as if Miss Leonides had said to her: "My dear, my dear." "Apparently," Miss Leonides thought to herself, "anybody can wind up my doll." And she felt a twinge of jealously.

For a while there was no sound from the dining room. The two old women sat as stiff and silent as statues. But all of a sudden this immobility was shattered. And Miss Leonides witnessed in amazement a scene so perfectly acted that she realized at once that those two actresses had been playing it for a long time. Mercedes, chunky and flat-footed, got up and went to the dining-room door, alert for Cecilia's return. A pause, and now it was Encarnación who got up, raising a long reptilian body, and went straight to a glass case, opened it, and, with movements as deft as the passing of a magnet, picked something up, stowed it in her handbag, closed the case, returned to her chair and sat down. In a moment Mercedes had joined her. Once more the two women transformed themselves into sphinxes. Not even the buzzing of a fly broke the silence.

From her hiding place the single spectator of that pantomime boiled with indignation. She took advantage of the rejoicing of the two old women when Cecilia appeared with the tea to slip out of the breakfast room. For more than an hour she paced the bedroom. And if they heard her downstairs, so much the better. She didn't give a hoot. "Thieves, thieves," she growled. Now they were stuffing themselves on the tea the poor child had fixed for them. And a little while before, like two angels of justice, they had been showering her with reproaches. Who were they to talk! *Sluts. Sluts. Slutsslutssluts.*

She seated herself in the velvet chair and waited. She must have waited nearly an hour for the wretched old women did not go until it began to get dark. Out of prudence Miss Leonides had not lighted the lamp. She was staring absent-mindedly at the fire, whose reflection, lighting her from below, turned her face into a scarlet winking skull.

Cecilia came into the bedroom, sat down on the floor, and, as seemed to have become a habit, rested her head on Miss Leonides' knees. She gave the impression of being strangely happy. Apparently the words of the visitors had bounced off her without leaving a dent.

"She's still drunk," Miss Leonides thought to herself. And she said: "Have they finally left, those two?"

The shock of blonde hair moved up and down and hatched a giggle.

"And you had told me that nobody would be coming. . . ." Miss Leonides went on.

New twitters of hilarity came from under the blonde plumage.

"Did you say anything to them about me?"

Silence.

"Cecilia, did you talk to them about me?"

The plumage swelled, shook, raised up, tossed itself back, revealing the egg of a face.

A demented smile curved those lips. The eyes glittered. She looked at Miss Leonides with terrifying scorn, as though making her an accomplice of some hideous jest.

And in a viscous, molluscous, warped voice, she slobbered: "They think you're dead."

Miss Leonides, terrified, averted her eyes.

Cecilia had gone out.

She had gibbered a mysterious word, something like *danerban,* and had left. Miss Leonides followed that vanishing black point with her eyes through the mesh of the curtain until it disappeared. Then she turned, looked at the other Leonides who, from the mirror, gave her back a conspiratorial gaze; they took counsel with one another, they encouraged one another, and at the same time, in different directions, the two left the bedroom.

There was the house, subdued, prostrate, for her to do her will. A feverish impatience burned in her. She descended on the lower floor as though it were a garment in whose seams she was

looking for a hidden diamond. She switched on and turned off
lights; she opened and closed doors, drawers, windows; she
searched the furniture, piece by piece, so carried away that she
hardly noticed what she picked up and had to go over the things
again; she made sure she had examined every nook, looked behind every curtain, every picture, under the rugs. In sudden panic
it seemed to her she heard a noise, Cecilia's returning footsteps.
Her hands tingled. Her cheekbones stood out. She was sure that
as she turned a corner, as she opened a door, as she switched on
a light or looked inside a cupboard she would make some marvelous or macabre discovery, she would find some fabulous thing
for which all the rest was nothing but the setting. But there was
no trace of fire in the cold ashes.

The only thing that became clear was that that house, with its
sumptuous furnishings and fittings, lay (except for the bedroom
on the second floor) in a state of total neglect. The furniture was
thick with dust. Suspicious gaps were visible (due, without a
doubt, to the depredations of Encarnación and Mercedes). A disgusting fluff had gathered on the floor. It was not hard to imagine
that at night cockroaches swarmed about. Perhaps some rat even
dragged along its damp sinister tail. And the kitchen was like the
rest of the house. To think that she nourished herself on the
meals prepared in the midst of that dung! She noted once more
the stench of putrefaction, medicines, death.

She came to the street door. She found it locked. A post-
humous illusion led her to slip her hand into the mail box. She
found there two envelopes, both addressed to Miss Cecilia Engelhard. One of them was small and seemed to have a visiting card inside. The other larger one bore the engraved address of the *Danish
Bank*. The canceled stamps showed that the first envelope had
been mailed five months before, and the second, two weeks. She
looked at them for a while, shook them in her hand, put them in
the pocket of her dressing gown, and returned to the inner rooms
of the house. "I'll give them to Cecilia later on," she thought.
And without knowing why she had the feeling that she was lying,
lying to herself.

She went up the stairs. On the landing she noticed a door

which she had overlooked before. She opened it and found herself in another bedroom. She saw an unmade bed; she saw a
desk; she saw a shelf, and on it a collection of Dutch dolls;
she saw the film of dust over everything; she saw a window
whose shutters were open; she went over to it, and saw the roof
of the rear of the house, covered with trash, and farther back,
the high side walls of the neighboring buildings; she made several
turns through that gloomy room; her fingers, almost mechanically,
began their search of the furniture; inside the desk she found
photographs, postcards, a letter.

It read:

"Dear Cecilia: I have just managed to get Monday off, and so
I can come. I beg you to tear up this letter. The harpy now
living with you might get hold of it. You're not angry, I hope.
Yesterday I waited for a while on the corner of Suipacha and
Bartolomé Mitre to see if you would come out. But you didn't.
On the other hand, I saw the harpy looking out of the window.
You can expect me on Monday for sure. I'll be on the sidewalk
in front of the church. If everything is O.K., you come to the
window and give me a sign. If I don't see you it's because there's
been some difficulty. Yours, Fabian."

Miss Leonides felt a twinge at the base of her spine. She threw
the letter back in the desk and fled to her room. For a long time
her mind was a blank. Her whole soul was a black pit where a
black wind howled.

Then she began to run the scale over the books, the pictures,
the pheasants in the lace curtain.

Finally wisps of thoughts began to appear amidst these random
notes like fish flickering through foam.

Doremifasolatido. So, the harpy . . . *Dotilasolfamiredo*. The
harpy now living with you. *Dore*. With you. Yours, Fabian. *Dore*.
So she is a cheat, a fraud. Just when she had begun to *dore dore*.
And she shut up here, with that impostor. Under lock and key.
A prisoner. *Domisoldo*. So she had dates with men. Yours, Fabian.
At that very minute she was probably with Fabian. Where? And
doing what? She knew very well what. The hypocrite. Maybe the
two were cooking up something. Something against her? That was

why she had dragged her here, and was treating her like a queen.
A scheme. To kill her. *Solfasol solsol.* But why did they want to
kill her? Why, why? But with a crazy thing and a street lout,
there's no need to ask why. They wanted to kill her and that
was all. And then they'd bury her in the back yard, at night.
And who would be any the wiser, who would notice the disap-
pearance of Leonides Arrufat, who would know what happened
in that cursed old house? Nobody. Nobody. Ah, no, she would go
to the window and call for help. But, no, wait a minute. We
must be calm. Now let's see. *Dear Cecilia. I have managed to
get Monday off.* Monday? When is Monday? What's today? Thursday. Or Friday? Wednesday. It's not Monday, for if it was Monday
yesterday would have had to be Sunday, and it wasn't Sunday,
for all the stores on Suipacha were open. And when had Fabian's
letter come? Had the mailman brought it? Or maybe . . . Letters.

Letters. She put her hand in the pocket of her dressing gown
and brought out the two envelopes. Yes indeed, she would open
them. Now she would open them. She was free, free from obligations, free from scruples. She would open them. Yes, sir.

The small envelope held, as she had guessed, a calling card.
And there was a name engraved on the card, *Andrés Jorgensen,*
and below it, in writing, three words: "My deepest sympathy."
In the other envelope there was a note. "Miss Cecilia Engelhard.
Account Number 3518. We beg to inform you that your balance,
as of July 31 last, unless there are any exceptions taken in the
next ten days, your balance is 4 . . . 4315 . . . 4315276 . . .
4,315,276 pesos. . . ."

Stupor paralyzed all Miss Leonides' muscles, obfuscated her
brain. She could not grasp, she could not take in the meaning of
that monstrous sum. She read it again. Four million. She had a
choking sensation. She had to sit down.

After a time the anesthesia of her stupefaction began to fade,
and little by little she could grasp it. She felt overpowered. She
felt vaguely humiliated, derided, offended. So everyone was plotting behind her back. Cecilia, Fabian, the Danish Bank, the whole
world, everybody. And she was a poor fool. She felt like crying.
(But, at the same time, deep down in her soul, vague desires to

avenge herself began to stir, a general ire, the determination to be henceforth implacable and sly.)

Until she heard the unmistakable steps of the doll. She picked up a book, the first one she could lay her hands on, and leaped into bed. She pretended that she did not see her, as though she did not realize that she had returned. She was so engrossed in that book! She smiled, sighed, frowned, and concentrated her gaze, as though she had not quite understood what she had read and had to read it again.

Cecilia took a few steps in one direction, then in another, approached the bed, went away from the bed, picked up a statuette, put it back in its place, went over to the window, played with the fringes of the curtain, all this without taking her eyes off those of Miss Leonides. But Miss Leonides was a thousand miles off. Miss Leonides was galloping along the bridle paths of poetry. Miss Leonides looked and looked again at certain signs which said (if they said anything):

> *"Du liebes Kind, komm, spiel mit mir,*
> *Gar schöne Spiele spiel ich mit dir . . ."*

Cecilia sat down beside the window as though prepared to wait as long as necessary for Miss Leonides to return. But a person can't read like that. Nobody can read while being watched. The absorbed reader of Goethe rolled over on her side, turning her back on that tiresome creature, and with a regal gesture turned the page, encountering new hieroglyphics, as fascinating as the preceding.

> *"Es war ein König in Thule,*
> *Gar treu bis an das Grab,*
> *Dem sterbend seine Bhule*
> *Einem goldnen Becher gab . . ."*

She, too, was prepared to wait.

But nearly a quarter of an hour went by like that. She had come to the last page of the book, and that idiot sat on without opening her mouth.

"Maybe you think I don't know where you've been," Miss Leonides suddenly shouted without interrupting her reading.

Cecilia got up as though she had been jerked by a string, but she made no answer.

"You think I don't know?" Miss Leonides repeated, throwing her a contemptuous look. Cecilia came over on the side of the bed toward which Miss Leonides' face was turned, fumbled in her pockets, and pulled out a sheaf of thousand-peso bills, holding them up, like a trophy, a safe conduct.

Miss Leonides began to see daylight, but she would not give in. She would go on kicking, just for fun, among the strings of the net.

"I would like to know who gave you that money."

Cecilia's eyes swallowed up her face. She stammered:

"But Mama . . . but Mama . . . I went to the bank . . . to the bank . . . to the bank. . . ."

Miss Leonides' soul was a kaleidoscope turned by brutal hands. One blow, one picture; another blow, another picture.

"Do you swear to me that you did not go out to meet some man?"

Cecilia turned pale, trembled, seemed overwhelmed by that accusing question.

"But Mama, but Mama," she protested weakly, "what are you saying? What man?"

The kaleidoscope formed the reddish pattern of pain that seemed to spread in every direction, to consume the whole world, to devour itself.

"Who is this Fabian? Answer me. Who is he? Where do you meet? Answer me, don't pretend that you don't understand."

"Mama, Mama, calm yourself," sobbed Cecilia.

"I don't want to calm myself, I want you to answer me. I have asked you who Fabian is."

"I don't know. I don't know. . . ."

(Good Heavens, that tortured face, those eyes, those wringing hands, can that all be make-believe? But let's go on torturing, torturing ourselves. And then, by way of compensation, the joy of forgiving, making up, weeping together.)

"Hypocrite. I don't believe you. You are lying. Just so you'll know, I have found Fabian's letter and read it."

"Mama, Mama," Cecilia sobbed, "what letter?"

"So you're still denying it." She could not stand it any more, she was crying, too. "Now you just wait."

She burst violently out of the cocoon of sheets where all her chrysalides were ensheathed, but not a butterfly, an eagle took wing. And she was running like one possessed to the near-by bedroom when, all of a sudden, she stopped. For a memory, a tenuous thread of recollection, a bare sliver, a shaving, had caught fire amidst the rubbish of her disordered thoughts and had set them ablaze. The bonfire of the revelation enveloped her like a martyr. Ah Leonides, Leonides Arrufat, you fool, a thousand times a fool. What was she about to do? Why, Fabian's letter was not recent; a film of dust covered it like all the other objects in that room undoubtedly closed months ago. So the idyll with Fabian was not a recent one, the meetings with Fabian were not now, next Monday was a bygone Monday. And the harpy was not she, but another.

She passed in front of Cecilia again, and took refuge in her cocoon once more, ashamed and wildly happy. It seemed to her that she had been saved from a mortal peril. She closed her eyes. She stretched out her arms. Under the sheets her fingers came upon the two envelopes addressed to Cecilia.

"My dear," she murmured in the suffering voice of a convalescent. "Dearest."

And when Cecilia was at her side, with a sigh of unconditional surrender she handed her the envelopes. But the girl did not even look at them. Her liquescent eyes were fixed on the huddled cocoon. The hateful smile was mirrored again on her lips.

"Mama," she stammered, "who is . . . who is Fabian?"

Miss Leonides blushed and did not know what to answer.

"Daughter," she said in confusion, without knowing what she was saying, to change the subject, "daughter, I'm hungry."

When she was alone she turned things over in her mind.

Who is Fabian, who is Fabian. In the letter he called her "Dear Cecilia," and the contents implied familiarity, an intimacy

dates, meetings, that arrangement about Monday. "Yours, Fabian." But, apparently, this Fabian had been expunged from
Cecilia's memory. Perhaps the idyll had come to a tragic end,
strewn with deaths, partings, suicides. And that was the cause of
the unhappy girl's derangement. Miss Leonides promised herself
that, given time, she would get to the bottom of it. Ah, yes, the
coming Monday she would be on the lookout. For, in any case,
one could not trust this strange girl too much.

In a word, she was staying.

The next Monday nothing happened. Cecilia hardly left her
side, nor gave any sign of uneasiness. Whenever she left the bedroom, Miss Leonides hurried over to the window to peer out.
Nothing. No sign, no young man waiting on the opposite sidewalk. When evening came Miss Leonides breathed a sigh of relief.

But two days later Encarnación and Mercedes turned up again,
and the implacable spiral which was to drag Miss Leonides to
desperate measures began to whir.

Miss Leonides was shut up in the bedroom waiting for the
two old hags to leave. What would they steal this time, she
wondered. And suddenly she heard the voices of the visitors close
by. She barely had time to lock herself into the bathroom. From
there she could hear everything.

She heard them come stomping into the bedroom, their voices
raised, as though they were mad. Encarnación's bleating rose
above the tumult.

"And why, may I ask, are you trying to keep us from visiting
your poor mother's bedroom? Don't forget that we were her best
friends. Her sisters, you might say. Or even closer. Oh, how nice.
You have lighted the fire. And why a fire, when it's not cold?
What a silly idea. What was I saying? Ah, yes, don't forget. Instead of letting all these dresses—excuse me—all these dresses—
just look, Merceditas—hang here until they fall to pieces, you
might give us a few of them. This one, for example. It's just
right for me. Or this otter stole, which the moths will get at before you know it. What do you want it for? And Merceditas needs
it so much. Not another word: I'm taking the stole for Merce-

ditas and the dress for me. And I just wonder about this other
one. . . . What's that? What did you say, Merceditas? What's
the matter with Guirlanda's bed? It's warm? Who's warm? The
bed? But how can it be warm, when it's over an hour . . . ?

A deep silence followed. Then out of this silence came an unrecognizable voice (Encarnación's? Mercedes'?), a murmur
steeped in the blackest suspicion:

"Are you alone, Cecilia?"

And on the heels of this, the same voice, or another, equally
turgid with suspicion, excreted these words, which aroused in
Miss Leonides a kind of prickling of horror:

"Are you alone, or are you up to your old tricks?"

Several soundless minutes elapsed, without the old women or
Cecilia either talking or, apparently, moving. But suddenly Miss
Leonides noticed with terror that the knob of the bathroom
was turning, that a hand was trying to open the door, that the
owner of the hand guessed that someone was locked in there.
(At that moment Miss Leonides might have made a spectacular
appearance. But she did not think of this until much later. Just
then she was suffering a kind of giddiness. The tiles began to
glow. The bathtub came loose and rocked in the air, like a gon-
dola in the water. The bidet disappeared. Amidst all these optical
illusions she heard again the sound of hoofs moving off. Then
silence once more.)

She must have waited a good half hour before she made up
her mind to come out of her hiding place. When she opened
the door she stumbled over Cecilia's stare. She must have been
there, standing in the middle of the bedroom, waiting for her to
emerge. They looked at one another. Miss Leonides' eyes would
have made those of a saint from heaven drop abashed. But the
girl stood there, as cool as a cucumber. She even smiled. She
smiled that sly smile, of an accomplice, which had already on
one occasion given Miss Leonides goose pimples of repugnance.
More than once. But now her revulsion had grown a hundredfold, it impregnated her whole soul, it made her feel almost sick.
She could not get that phrase out of her ears: "You're up to
your old tricks." She sensed an abyss of abjection beneath those

words. And she would not, she could not look into the depths of that abyss.

She walked past Cecilia with her body as tense as though she were walking through a snake pit. Going to the other end of the room she sat down, picked up a book, pretending she was looking through it. She was thinking.

After a good while she gathered the late-blooming fruit of her meditations. With an air of indifference, still turning the pages of the book, she asked:

"Where do Encarnación and Mercedes live?"

No answer. Miss Leonides, making a great effort, had to turn around and look at her. Only then did the girl mutter between her teeth:

"On Cochabamba Street."

The peasant girl's face had a strange look, a rictus, a set expression which was new to Miss Leonides. She was afraid, and to cover this up, she feigned impatience.

"I know they live on Cochabamba Street. What I am asking is the number. I don't recall it. It's been such a long time. . . ."

She made a vague gesture, and not knowing how to continue, she became silent and looked out of the window.

Cecilia went out and came back at once, taking a position alongside Miss Leonides. Miss Leonides looked at the shoes of that suddenly frightening doll, saw out of the corner of her eye that she was holding out a piece of paper to her, took it and read: "Address of E. and M., Cochabamba 1522, Buenos Aires." The handwriting was clumsy and enormous. Miss Leonides croaked out a "Thank you," and went on turning the leaves of the book.

An awkward silence, like an invisible third presence, established itself between the two of them, and prevented Miss Leonides from uttering a single word that whole day. Cecilia, too, remained silent. (But what torture, what torture that of eyes avoiding each other, seeking, separating, pursuing, watching, lurking, spying, tiring, drowsing, awakening, coming to life, studying, provoking, defying, clashing, fighting, attacking, succumbing, asking forgiveness, fleeing, returning to seek one another to begin all over again.)

The next afternoon, after her nap, Miss Leonides began to study the pheasants in the curtain as though they were a map or a timetable, and suddenly in a determined voice which admitted of no argument she stated:

"Cecilia, I am going out."

She heard behind her that panting, eager, uneven breathing, just as that first day in the cemetery. She waited for a minute, and then added:

"I'm going out by myself, Cecilia."

She waited another minute. Nothing? No question? No objection? She wasn't going to stop her? Then, up and at them.

It was at the door, just as she was about to say good-by, that Cecilia, who had been following at her heels with a somber, taciturn air, suddenly said, in a voice so low she could barely hear her:

"Mama, come back . . . come back. . . ."

And ulcerated eyes clutched at her, while the smile seemed to give the lie to the suffering of the expression. Miss Leonides felt a tug at her heart. As best she could she improvised a calm visage and laughed.

"But, of course, I'll be back. What an idea!"

She had walked a few yards along Suipacha heading south, when Cecilia let out a scream. Good God, now what was wrong? Miss Leonides turned around, and with her, two hundred passersby. And the reason for all this? So that poor devil could wave good-by to her with both hands. All right, good-by. Miss Leonides walked on and soon was lost in the crowd.

The farther away she got, and as, free from the beleaguerment of Cecilia, the old Leonides Arrufat came alive once more in the feigned Guirlanda Santos, her spirit took on strength. She felt increasingly intrepid, lucid, and sure of herself. She had dressed herself like the dead woman, had combed her hair like hers, so she was disguised. And like all those who put on a disguise, this gave her boldness and at the same time impunity. Moreover, she had everything all thought out.

1522 Cochabamba. A one-story house, with the front painted
an olive green asperged by rain and dogs. The street door was
open, revealing a passage at the end of which was another door,
closed. Miss Leonides rang the bell. Nobody answered. She
walked in and rang another bell beside the second door. Inside,
far away, she heard a bell, barkings, a voice which Miss Leonides recognized at once, singsonging:

"Coming, coming. . . ."

The door opened, and that simple soul of a Mercedes, beatifi-
cally munching a piece of cookie, suddenly found herself, without warning, face to face with the beyond. Her jaw dropped; the
half-chewed piece of cookie slid off her tongue and fell to the
floor, out of her throat came a strangled gasp. She turned around
and ran, lurching like a bear and screaming:

"Encarnación! Encarnación!"

This initial triumph emboldened Miss Leonides who, without
waiting to be asked in, crossed the threshold and made her way
into the house. She found herself in an enclosed veranda which
ran along two sides of a rectangular patio, on to which successive doors opened, all alike and equally decrepit. One of these
doors opened and—Encarnación leading, Mercedes following—
the two culprits appeared before that figure from the other world
who had surely come to settle accounts with them.

But as soon as she came near, Encarnación's face dissolved
in a smile which looked like a repressed yawn, and, turning to
Mercedes, she said something to her in a low voice. Then she
spoke to the apparition:

"What can I do for you, madam?"

Miss Leonides half-closed her eyes and said:

"I am Guirlanda Santos' cousin."

Encarnación turned again to Mercedes:

"You see?"

And again to Miss Leonides, holding out a languid, flabby
hand:

"Pleased to meet you. As you look so much like the deceased,
this silly thing was frightened."

Mercedes came forward, cowed and smiling, and she, too, stretched out a fat batrachian of a hand:

"Pleased to meet you. Yes, when I saw you, I took you for the departed."

"Except that Guirlanda was a little shorter than you," observed Encarnación with the air of a person who likes to get everything straight, "and her eyes were a different color."

Now the two of them began to itemize the differences so the stranger would not think them a pair of fools whom anybody could take in.

"Guirlanda was thinner," said Mercedes, "especially toward the end."

"That was the sickness. But Guirlanda was not thin," added Encarnación heatedly, as though being thin were a crime, and then went on amiably: "Besides, you've got less hair than Guirlanda had."

"No, now that I take a good look at you, you're very different."

"Of course. I don't know how you came to make such a mistake."

"It was that at first sight. . . ."

Until they realized that they were keeping their guest standing there on the porch.

"Come in."

"Come in."

They went into a dark room that smelled of cat, Mercedes opened the shutters, the afternoon light threw into harsh relief a small parlor furnished in abominable taste. And the first thing Miss Leonides saw was a Dutch doll with its mouth open, its eyes open, its arms open, shrieking to be released from the horrible sofa where it had been seated and to be returned to its sisters, to a shelf, to a lifeless, closed bedroom where there was a desk in which there was a letter that bore a name, Fabian.

The caller and the two ladies of the house sat down on chintz-covered chairs, looked at one another, smiled, sized each other up, the doll seemed to stop her crying and listen, and a juicy conversation began between the self-styled cousin and the two best friends of the late Guirlanda Santos.

ENCARNACION: So you are poor Guirlanda's cousin.

POOR GUIRLANDA'S COUSIN: Second cousin.

ENCARNACION: On her mother's side?

COUSIN: On her father's.

ENCARNACION: So your name is Santos, too, I mean your last name.

COUSIN: Naturally.

ENCARNACION: Then you must have some outlandish name, like all the Santos women. Papa used to say they took them from novels.

COUSIN: Ah, yes, From novels? But not mine. They got mine out of a book of poems. I am called Anabelí.

MERCEDES: Didn't I tell you?

ENCARNACION: Mercedes! It's a beautiful name, Anabelí. And what relation does that make you to Belena?

ANABELI: Me? To Belena? Why. . . .

MERCEDES: Aunt. For if you are a cousin of Guirlanda's, and Guirlanda was Belena's aunt, then you, too, are an aunt of hers.

ANABELI: Of course. Not a real aunt though, but twice removed.

ENCARNACION: I wonder why Guirlanda never happened to mention you.

ANABELI: My dear, you are not doubting. . . .

ENCARNACION: No, of course not. One only has to look at you. But how odd, for Guirlanda said that, aside from Belena, there were no other Santos. And as Jan had come to America by himself, she said that she and Cecilia were alone in the world. For she did not count Belena, you know.

ANABELI: She did not count me either, my dear.

ENCARNACION: Ah.

MERCEDES: Ah.

ANABELI: There were several misunderstandings, family matters, which I'd rather not talk about.

ENCARNACION: Because of Jan? That was just what happened with Belena.

ANABELI: Can you imagine? They didn't even let me know that Guirlanda had died.

ENCARNACION: That was just what happened with Belena.

MERCEDES: Belena found it out from the newspaper.

ANABELI: To be sure, I was living in Córdoba. But, anyway, Cecilia knew my address, and she could have sent me a card. You see, I had to come to Buenos Aires. Because as I was left a widow. . . .

ENCARNACION: Dear me! You have my sympathy.

MERCEDES: You have my sympathy.

ANABELI: Thank you very much, thank you very much. As I was left a widow five years ago, I decided to come to the capital. And naturally, after such a long time, I'm not a person who bears a grudge, the first thing I did was go to see Guirlanda. And I found out that she had passed away.

ENCARNACION: You can't imagine what she suffered, poor Guirlanda. I don't know if Cecilia has told you.

ANABELI: Very little.

ENCARNACION: She died of cancer. She spent her last three years shut up in that house. She didn't want to see anybody, not even us. That gives you the whole picture. Not even the doctor. She even fired the servants. She said they were trying to poison her.

ANABELI: And who took care of her?

MERCEDES: Cecilia.

ENCARNACION: Cecilia. She was nurse, cook, housemaid, everything. She couldn't leave her alone for a single minute, because when she came back she would find her crying her eyes out and screaming that she was dying. Believe me, that girl deserves a front seat in heaven.

ANABELI: And did Cecilia know that her mother . . . ?

ENCARNACION: How could she help knowing it! And for that reason she devoted herself to making Guirlanda's last years as pleasant as she could with an abnegation that brought tears to our eyes.

ANABELI: Until she died.

MERCEDES: Until she died, poor Guirlanda.

ANABELI: It was really a blessing for them both.

ENCARNACION: It was. But, nevertheless, it was a terrible shock

for Cecilia. She idolized her mother. I remember the night of the
wake. She sat there beside the coffin, and the expression on her
face was frightening. In my opinion it was then that she became
unbalanced. I may tell you that the only persons at the wake
were my sister and I. For they didn't have any friends; you
know how odd Jan was, with his manias, his occult sciences, his
Rosicrucianism. As for Guirlanda, I don't have to tell you. And
the few they had left, what with shutting herself up and her queer
ways, they drifted away. We were the only ones who stood by
her. Relatives, there was you. . . .

ANABELI: In Córdoba, without knowing a thing.

ENCARNACION: . . . and Belena. We never thought that Belena
would come to the wake of her mortal enemy.

ANABELI: But she came.

ENCARNACION: She came. When I saw her come in, I was
speechless.

ANABELI: And how is Belena?

ENCARNACION: As beautiful as ever, so distinguished. . . .

MERCEDES: They can say what they like about Belena,
but. . . .

ENCARNACION: Mercedes! The trouble with Belena is that she
is too attractive, and that always arouses envy and gossip. And
excuse me, I am not referring to Guirlanda, God rest her soul,
but in spite of all they have said about Belena, and they've said
plenty, I have no proof of it. If you could have seen her that
night. She kissed Cecilia, she kissed both of us, she looked for a
long time at poor Guirlanda, she wiped her eyes over and over
again. If she had been what they say she is, she would not have
shed a tear over Guirlanda.

ANABELI: And you haven't seen her since?

ENCARNACION: How could we? Don't you know?

MERCEDES: Don't you know?

ANABELI: No. What?

ENCARNACION: Didn't Cecilia tell you?

ANABELI: Not a word.

ENCARNACION: It was like this. As Cecilia had been left all

alone, and as Belena was alone, too, because she lost her husband some years ago. . . .

ANABELI: Like me.

ENCARNACION: Like you. That's life. And as, when all is said and done, and in spite of the quarrels, Cecilia and Belena were first cousins, and as Belena doesn't bear a grudge. . . .

ANABELI: Like me.

ENCARNACION: Like you. Belena went to live with Cecilia.

ANABELI: Did she? Belena? She went to live with Cecilia there, in the house on Suipacha? But she's not there now.

ENCARNACION: No. Not any longer.

ANABELI: What happened? Did they have a quarrel?

ENCARNACION: You ask what happened.

MERCEDES: God in Heaven!

ANABELI: Gracious, you are frightening me.

ENCARNACION: There are some things it's not easy to talk about, madam.

ANABELI: Remember, my dear, I'm one of the family. And it's as though you were, too. You are more than relatives.

ENCARNACION: Well, with your permission. After Guirlanda's death, we often went to see them. Belena received us cordially.

MERCEDES: Whereas Cecilia. . . .

ENCARNACION: Mercedes!

ANABELI: Go on. What about Cecilia?

ENCARNACION: What she is trying to say is that Cecilia never spoke, she didn't open her mouth even to ask how we were, or how Mama was. For you know Mama is paralyzed.

ANABELI: How dreadful!

ENCARNACION: Never! Not a word.

MERCEDES: She takes after her father. You must have known Jan. We couldn't stand him.

ENCARNACION: Mercedes!

ANABELI: But Belena. . . .

ENCARNACION: I was coming to that. We noticed that Belena looked worried. One afternoon she walked us to the corner and told us several things. First, how stingy Cecilia was. She counted out every penny she gave her. Mercedes is right about that. She takes after Jan. But the other thing was more serious. Yes, Cecilia's going out. For instance, she would go out in the afternoon and not come back until night. Belena would ask her: "Where've you been, dear?" and she wouldn't tell her. Naturally, Belena began to suspect that she was up to no good. But what could she do?

ANABELI: Well, if I had been in Belena's place. . . .

ENCARNACION: Sure you would have, my dear. But you were not living on Cecilia's bounty the way Belena was. For poor Belena doesn't have a penny to bless herself with. Besides, you're her aunt, you're a mature woman. . . .

ANABELI: And what about Belena? She's no child, is she?

ENCARNACION: No, but. . . .

ANABELI: It was her duty to look after her cousin who is a minor.

ENCARNACION: Cecilia?

MERCEDES: Cecilia a minor?

ANABELI: Isn't she? I can never remember ages.

ENCARNACION: Cecilia is past twenty-three.

ANABELI: *Doremifa.*

ENCARNACION: Excuse me?

ANABELI: No, I was just thinking.

ENCARNACION: To be sure, she doesn't look it.

MERCEDES: Crazy people never look their age.

ENCARNACION: Mercedes!

ANABELI: Go on, my dear.

ENCARNACION: One day when we went to see them Cecilia was not at home. I, this one, and Belena were talking as calm as you please there in the dining room. When all of a sudden Belena began to cry. You can imagine us. She told us that as she was going over Cecilia's clothes, she had found a photograph —"this one," she said. And she showed us the picture of a young, blond fellow, not bad-looking, but with such eyes. . . . On the back of the photograph there was written: "F. to C."

ANABELI: And was that why Belena was crying?

ENCARNACION: Naturally.

ANABELI: It was nothing to take on about. Any girl can have a boy friend.

ENCARNACION: Yes, but Cecilia is not any girl. Think of her fortune. Think what she is like. Can't you see the bait she is for some adventurer? And if he was the kind of boy friend he should be, why did she hide him? Why didn't he come to the house so Belena could meet him?

ANABELI: That is true.

ENCARNACION: Remember that Belena had never been able to get out of Cecilia where it was that she went in the afternoon. Besides, once Cecilia had got mad and had called her a harpy.

ANABELI: A harpy! What a nice thing to do!

ENCARNACION: Nice, indeed.

ANABELI: And what about you? Didn't you try to talk with Cecilia.

ENCARNACION: But that girl is always in another world. You try to get something out of her, and it's like talking to the wall. Besides, we didn't want to make things bad for Belena by giving away that she had confided in us. Belena herself had asked us not to say anything. And if you don't mind my telling you everything, Cecilia has a kind of dislike for us, I can't think why.

MERCEDES: Between Jan and Guirlanda they had got it into her head that we. . . .

ENCARNACION: Mercedes! The trouble is that Cecilia already was not quite right in her mind. At times people like that, a little touched, take a dislike to certain people, for no good reason, just because.

ANABELI: That's true. And afterward?

ENCARNACION: Afterward?

MERCEDES: Oh, Lord!

ENCARNACION: Afterward what we were afraid would happen, happened. It was one afternoon. We had arranged that I would go with Belena to Dr. Criscuolo's office—you must have heard of him, he's a famous heart specialist. Yes, poor Belena thought there was something wrong with her heart. She asked me to go with her because I had told her that we had known Criscuolo since we were children. I was to come by for her. And so I did.

It was four in the afternoon. I remember that before we left Belena said to Cecilia: "I hate to go off and leave you alone." Can you imagine, it was as though she had a premonition, poor Belena. And I laughed and said to her: "But we'll be back in no time. Nobody's going to eat her." Dr. Criscuolo took Belena around six. He told her there was nothing the matter with her heart. After that we went to have tea at *Los Dos Chinos*. We were sitting there, as pleasant as could be, when Belena began to get nervous, and tell me that the day before Cecilia had received a letter, and that she was terribly worried, because she suspected, from various things she had noticed, that her cousin was carrying on a love affair and so on, and so forth, and that we had made a great mistake in leaving her alone for so long. The long and the short of it was that, having barely swallowed my tea, I had to get up and go back to the house with Belena. When we got there it was dark. The street door was standing ajar. We went in. It was all dark. Belena turned on the light and we saw furniture with the drawers pulled out, an overturned chair, and cigarette stubs on the floor. Belena began to scream: "Cecilia, Cecilia," but there was no sign of Cecilia. I was scared out of my wits. "Let's call the police," I said. But Belena went on screaming: "Cecilia, Cecilia." We searched the whole first floor, and not a sign of Cecilia. Belena dragged me up the stairs. I didn't want to go with her, for I was sure we would find her in a pool of blood, her throat cut, stabbed to death. But Belena made me. The door of her bedroom was locked, and the key was in the keyhole on the outside. We opened the door, and there was Cecilia.

MERCEDES: Alive.

ENCARNACION: What a piece of news! Of course she was alive. But the state she was in! She was shaking like a mad dog, her eyes had a wild look, her hair was all in disorder, and her clothes were torn. And so was the bed, if you see what I mean. All tumbled.

MERCEDES: Tell her about Belena.

ENCARNACION: When she went into Cecilia's bedroom and saw that sight, Belena underwent a transformation. I won't forget her face as long as I live. She became ugly—I don't know if I am making myself clear. Such a hideous face that Cecilia shrank away and began to scream, as if she was afraid that Belena was going to punish her or kill her. It was all very strange. But aside from the expression on her face, Belena did nothing. She just stood there. And then she flew out of the room like a whirlwind. I followed her. She crossed the anteroom, and went into Guirlanda's bedroom, and I behind her. She began to go through all the drawers, and I too.

ANABELI: What were you looking for?

ENCARNACION: Guirlanda's jewelry, the pounds sterling, the Peruvian soles, the Mexican gold, all the coins that Jan had collected, a veritable fortune.

ANABELI: They were gone.

ENCARNACION: The whole lot. Belena stopped searching. She was beside herself. She bit her lips, her hands shook, sparks shot out of her eyes. How did I tell you she went, Mercedes?

MERCEDES: *Uuuh, uuuh,* like that, as though she was blowing through something.

ENCARNACION: After that, without so much as looking at me, she rushed down to the first floor. I didn't know what to do. For a while I wandered around Guirlanda's bedroom and through the anteroom. I didn't venture to go into Cecilia's room. Finally I made up my mind and went to look for Belena. I found her in the kitchen, crying as I have never seen anybody cry in my life. When she saw me she stopped crying instantly, turned her back on me, and said sharply: "Encarnación, I beg of you, nobody is to know what has happened here. I ask it for Guirlanda's sake. And now go. Go and leave me alone." It seemed to me that grief had made her rather rude. But I forgave her. And as I don't need to be told a thing twice, I left that very minute.

ANABELI: My dear, let me ask you a question. Do you happen to remember if that day when whatever it was that happened, happened, was a Monday?

ENCARNACION: Let me think. Criscuolo has office hours on Mondays and Thursdays.

MERCEDES: It wasn't a Thursday, for if it had been a Thursday, I would have gone to the Mission, and as it was I stayed at home.

ENCARNACION: In that case, it was a Monday. How did you know?

ANABELI: No matter. But go on, my dear.

ENCARNACION: There's not much left to tell. When I went back the next day with this one, we found a Belena that was like a stone image; she hardly spoke to us, and when she did open her mouth it was to ask us again to say nothing. It disturbed us to see her like that.

ANABELI: Like that? How?

ENCARNACION: Limp as a rag. She who was so proud. Oh yes, and when we asked how Cecilia was, she screamed at us that she didn't want to hear her name, and began to sob. I repeat, we were terribly upset.

ANABELI: And what about Cecilia?

ENCARNACION: We didn't see her that afternoon. Two days later we went back, but Belena was no longer there. As for Cecilia, she had such a deranged look when she asked us in that we were horrified. She was talking utter nonsense, saying that her mother had gone out, and was taking a long time getting back, and that maybe she was lost and she ought to go out and find her . . . It broke your heart to listen to her.

ANABELI: So Belena deserted Cecilia when the girl needed her most.

ENCARNACION: Yes, we, too, thought it very strange.

ANABELI: And you haven't seen her since?

ENCARNACION: No, never.

ANABELI: Do you know where she lives?

ENCARNACION: No.

MERCEDES: No.

ENCARNACION: We tried to find that out from Cecilia, but it was useless.

ANABELI: So neither you nor Belena informed the police?

ENCARNACION: My dear, what would we have gained by it?

ANABELI: You? On the contrary, you would have lost.

ENCARNACION: What's that?

MERCEDES: Lost?

ENCARNACION: What do you mean, lost?

ANABELI: You would have lost the opportunity to keep on going to Cecilia's house to steal things.

MERCEDES: What?

ENCARNACION: I don't know what you mean, madam.

ANABELI: On the contrary, you know very well.

ENCARNACION: Let me tell you that if that crazy thing has gone to you with tales. . . .

ANABELI: No tales. Cecilia has told me nothing.

ENCARNACION: If that's the case, come to the point, what are you talking about?

ANABELI: To come to the point, I'm talking about a number of ornaments from the dining room. To come to the point, I am referring to an otter stole. To come to the point, I'm talking about several of Guirlanda's dresses. I was the person who was locked in the bathroom yesterday.

ENCARNACION: You?

MERCEDES: You?

ANABELI: Finally, to come to the point, I am talking about that doll.

ENCARNACION: Oh, no, I beg your pardon. Belena gave me that doll.

ANABELI: And what right had Belena to give away things that belonged to her cousin without the latter's permission? So, excuse me. And that buddha.

ENCARNACION: That I will not allow. That buddha was one of my mother's wedding presents.

ANABELI: I'm taking it anyway. In place of the fur stole.

ENCARNACION: Oh, no. I'll call the police.

MERCEDES: The police.

ANABELI: Call them. I'll call them first. We'll see what you have to tell them and what I tell them.

ENCARNACION: Don't raise your voice. My mother may hear you.

ANABELI: Then you set an example by lowering yours. And tell your sister to stop her sniveling.

ENCARNACION: Mercedes, keep still.

ANABELI: And now, let's see: what else?

ENCARNACION: Is there anything else?

ANABELI: Money, the money you stole from the poor thing. Or you've made her sign a will in your favor, forced legacies for which you can be sent to jail.

ENCARNACION: But what are you saying?

MERCEDES: What is she saying?

ANABELI: Now, you listen to me. I forbid you to return to Cecilia's house. I'm going to be there, on the lookout. If you come back, on any excuse whatsoever, I'll have you arrested.

ENCARNACION: That's enough, madam. For pity's sake, that is enough.

ANABELI: Have you understood me?

ENCARNACION: Go, I beg of you.

MERCEDES: Go, go.

ANABELI: I am going. But let me repeat what I said.

ENCARNACION: You don't need to.

MERCEDES: You don't need to.

ANABELI: In that case, good-by.

Still in the disguise of Anabelí Santos, exhausted, racked, all her strength drained away by the long performance she had put on before those two old hags (especially that last scene, when she felt as though she was smashing countless clay images with a rod of iron), Miss Leonides collapsed on her narrow bed, and without even the strength to blink, stared with glazed eyes at a rosette in the ceiling. On the floor, disjointed in an incredible posture, the doll whimpered. Farther off, the buddha smiled and meditated.

The afternoon slipped by, night came, the darkness wiped out the rosette in the ceiling, and Miss Leonides lay there as motionless as a felled tree.

Until—perhaps it was a dream, perhaps it wasn't—it seemed to her that Anabelí Santos was not a figment of her imagination, but was acquiring real dimensions, was there, alive, and conveying to her a kind of long admonition.

Yes, Anabelí Santos said to her: "All right, Leonides. You

have discovered that Cecilia had one of those entanglements that disgust you so. Did you hear them, those two old parrots? And now you draw a line and tot up the sum: Cecilia is this, Cecilia is that, she doesn't deserve my affection, and, therefore, I'm washing my hands of her, just the way Belena did; I'm not going back there any more, the game is over. Leonides, you're doing like the others. Like her mother, like Fabian, like Belena, like all of them. They go to Cecilia, they take advantage of her (some in one way, some in another) and then they run away (the mother left for the other world, but basically it's the same thing). And you, why are you doing it? That business with Fabian has hit you hard. I understand it. You thought that the ruination of that house, that the derangement of Cecilia were the result of her angelic grief, and now those two mummies have come and whispered in your ear that that's not true, that you were mistaken, that it was all a ruse of the beast, a filthy mixture of sex, lust, rape, and robbery. And you shrink away in disgust from that mangy monkey. All right, but let's think things over. You're not going to compare Cecilia, I hope, with those women who kiss and carry on with men in public places, and when they see you go by in your loneliness and that hat of yours laugh insolently. Those women are always beautiful, tall, always sure of themselves (just the opposite of Cecilia). Those women don't shut themselves up in the house to nurse sick people, they don't shackle themselves to the bed of a dying woman who takes three years to die (not three weeks or three days). Their dead die alone, cursing them, while they hurry to embrace some nice-looking young fellow in a park, in an automobile, in a luxurious apartment. Whereas Cecilia is your fellow being, your sister in timidity and suffering. After those three years with her dying mother, what do you think the world holds for her? The same snares as for you. For you, to run the scale along the tiles, talk to yourself, and put a bunch of nettles at Natividad González's door. And for her, to walk along the street looking like a Polish immigrant, and some street lout to see her and follow her. And then it's done. The trap opens and, before Cecilia realizes it, has snapped on her foot. She thought she had finally

found a comrade, a smiling young friend, with whom to walk
hand in hand under the trees, as she had seen so many boys
and girls her own age do. And above all, someone well, someone
strong, someone free from the bite of the horrible crab, and who
did not smell of medicines, or age, or death, but of clean flesh
and youth, and health. All this was what Fabian probably meant
to Cecilia. And when Belena, that handsome, mature woman
(one of those who embrace in public places) tried to interfere,
she defended herself with her only weapon: silence. Silence and
keeping Fabian away. For if Fabian met Belena, he would fall in
love with Belena, and forget her. But in front of him she laid
down all her arms. All of them, even her nails. And she confided to him that her father had left her a collection of gold
coins, and that her mother had jewelry which nobody used now,
that they were put away in cases, and even that there was money
in all the drawers. And another day she said to him: 'On Monday I won't be able to come out. My cousin, who is old, and
very bad' (she was lying, or maybe she wasn't) 'has to go to
the doctor and I can't leave the house alone.' Fabian probably
inhaled cigarette smoke, looked at his nails, and let a whisper
out of the corner of his lips like a trickle of saliva: 'If you'd like,
I can come to see you.' Then all of a sudden he slapped his
leg, took off the mask of playmate, and with his lout's face bare,
muttered: 'Jeez, I forgot. Not Monday. I'm on duty Monday.'
For a day or two he tried to get around it, finally managed, and
wrote that letter: *'Dear Cecilia. Yours, Fabian.'* Cecilia imagined
that they would have tea together, they would look out of the
window over Suipacha; perhaps, if he asked her to, she would
recite the verses about Anabel, Anabelí. But inside the deep,
soundless house Fabian became transformed into another man, a
livid man who roared, threw himself upon her, dragged her to a
bottomless pit, cut her to pieces, dissolved her like a particle of
earth in water, and then left, went away, disappeared forever.
And she lost her mind (those women who are your enemies
do not lose their mind). And mad and lonely, she built a walled
nook where sex cannot enter, where the beast of the flesh cannot slip through. It is a city consecrated to the angel. A sanctuary

where no other rite than the purest love can be celebrated. And it is to you, to you alone, that she has unbarred the entrance. What more do you want? For thirty years you wandered from rejection to rejection. And now that you had been admitted, as soon as you found out the foundation of dross on which the city had been built, you turned up your nose and left. Leonides, you are stupid. Apparently you prefer this jail cell of a room. You prefer the company of the periwinkle. Go look for Natividad González. And in the meantime I can see Cecilia, standing at the door of her house, waving good-by with her hand. And on that hand I see the short, broken nails, I see a blister, the stigma of a burn, just a little red, nothing.

Anabelí Santos, that will do. Don't you see that the sheets are beginning to burn under Miss Leonides. Don't you see that she thinks she heard a noise, sits up, and only after a few minutes have elapsed, does she realize that it's her own sob she heard. Now she gets up, turns on the light, looks at the alarm clock (but the alarm clock, unwound for so many days, no longer tells the time, it tells eternity), opens the door, and forgetting you and the meditating buddha and the doll on the rack, rushes out like a cyclone.

Miss Leonides crosses an unknown city in the streetcar. What time is it? She doesn't know. Nobody knows. Maybe it's eleven at night, maybe it's four in the morning. Impatience gnaws at her like a termite. She looks out of the window without recognizing anything that she sees. The streetcar reaches a corner that copies, with various old props, the corner of Sarmiento and Suipacha. Miss Leonides gets off. Now she hurries down a long deserted corridor. In the distance she can make out the mass of the church. And across from it the house. And in the door, Cecilia. Cecilia, huddled on the doorstep like a beggar. Arms and legs interlaced as though embracing herself. She is looking toward Rivadavia. Looking toward the vast south where, hours before, Guirlanda Santos disappeared from view. It is very late, the city has gone to bed, but Cecilia waits on. Guirlanda Santos promised to return. And she waits for her.

Miss Leonides could not bear it any longer. She felt huge with love. She cried: "Cecilia!"

Her cry spread, bounced back from the walls of the long deserted corridor, awoke the doves of echo.

The knot of legs and arms comes undone as though slashed by a scimitar, the beggar gets to her feet with one bound, whirls around, sees Guirlanda, Guirlanda who has returned, runs toward her, toward Guirlanda with her hair coming loose, her cheeks glowing, her eyes gleaming, looking like a girl, looking a thousand years younger, looking well and lithe and beautiful. A store (closed) to the right, another store (closed) to the left, across the way the wall (sleeping) of St. Michael Archangel; there is no witness to see how these two pitiful creatures rush toward one another, how they embrace, weep, and enter the house, Number 78, closing the door behind them, nor how the gargoyle faces of the bronze knockers beam and seem to smile.

Leonides Arrufat, Anabelí Santos, Guirlanda Santos, the three of them simultaneously and in turn laugh and cry and kiss Cecilia and exclaim:

"You'll never guess where I went. To see a famous doctor. And you'll never guess what he told me. That I am cured. You realize what that means, Cecilia? That now we don't have to live shut up in the four walls of this house. Now we can go out for walks, go to the movies and the theater. We'll have tea every day at a different tearoom, where there is music. And we'll buy ourselves things, lots of things, everything we want. But, what's the matter, Cecilia? What's wrong, Cecilia?"

Cecilia sways, a change comes over her face which seems to split up into several identical faces superimposed on one another without coinciding. Bent double, she throws up on the rug.

Miss Leonides picks her up in her arms (Guirlanda and Anabelí help her), carries her to the bedroom, lays her gently on the bed, undresses her, tucks her in, and is about to tell her that from now on, from now on. . . . But Cecilia, as though struck down by accumulated fatigue, has fallen asleep as soon as her head touched the pillow.

Guirlanda, Anabelí, and Leonides look thoughtfully at that

yeasty face, that face like a loaf of bread that has fallen in the water and swelled without, at the same time, losing its shape.

Suddenly the three of them understood.

Several months went by. The constellations moved in their changeless orbits. Spring was followed by summer.

Miss Leonides would say: "Cecilia, my child," and she no longer felt as though she were using an artificial language. Cecilia would call out: "Mama, Mama," and Miss Leonides no longer noticed, beneath this call, the vacuum which before left it whirling in the air like a dry leaf. For the spirit, as well as the flesh, more than the flesh, makes it adjustments.

They went out walking, arm in arm. They sat down at a sidewalk table of one of the tearooms on Avenida de Mayo, slowly sipping their refreshments, watching the people go by. Or they went into one of the movie houses on Lavalle, watched the procession of those images which always passed too fast, came out as though they were drunk, and for the rest of the day talked about nothing but what they had seen. (To be sure, Miss Leonides realized that many times Cecilia had not made head nor tail out of the picture. But what difference did it make? She looked so happy sitting there, laughing and eating caramels!)

Together, always together. Now Miss Leonides wore gray, white, blue. Her cheeks filled out. She had put on weight. She looked more than ever like Guirlanda Santos ten years back (when Belena saw her alive for the last time). And beside her, neat, obedient, a pearl, the little doll with the face of a peasant and that blonde mop of hair trotted along on her mechanical stumpy legs.

"Dear Lord," prayed Miss Leonides, "don't take this happiness from me."

The house shone like a mirror. The smell of decay and medicine had been aired out. Between the two of them they prepared complicated, unheard-of dishes which they gaily gobbled up in the kitchen.

They celebrated Christmas with a banquet. Miss Leonides, giving free rein to long-repressed fantasies, decorated the dining room beyond recognition. On the table an imposing relief map of

dainties was spread. They drank champagne. They laughed up-
roariously. Miss Leonides whirled through the measures of a
dance by herself, throwing kisses to an imaginary audience. And,
as always, they wound up crying.

"Dear Lord," Miss Leonides implored, "don't take this happiness from me."

But inexorable rust was already gnawing at that gilded structure.

Cecilia's face revealed, like the obverse and reverse of a
coin, at times infinite happiness, at times a mute despair, and as
these two expressions went with that sardonic smile which never
left her lips, her countenance soon took on a tinge of shrewdness
and malice, like those Roman emperors whose severe air is in
contradiction to the sly mouth which seems to reveal a kind of
perfidious inner gaiety. But at other times both sides of the
coin became effaced, and in their place there appeared fleetingly
the profile of a little girl who, alone in the night, hears the sound
of approaching footsteps.

Every time this pathetic child took Cecilia's place, something
clutched at Miss Leonides' heart.

"Dear God," she would pray, seized by a deep distress.

By the end of the summer, Miss Leonides' almost sole company
was this terrified little girl who heard the noise of steps. It was
useless for her to take her hands, press them against her breast,
say to her:

"You wait and see, you wait and see, everything will be all
right."

What was it that would be all right? Cecilia clutched desperately at the hands holding hers, with terror in her eyes at the
same time that the hovering smile became more pronounced;
she moaned in a kind of hoarse wail:

"I'm afraid, I'm afraid."

Perhaps in her dream she knew what Miss Leonides still ignored in hers.

She knew that, when the steps stopped and the visitor knocked,
she must awake, emerge from her dream, open a door and go

out. And that when the door closed behind her she could never come in again.

She knew that the doctor, a stranger whom Miss Leonides had found thanks to a bronze name plate on the door, would say in a sententious and final tone:

"We'll have to choose between the mother and the child."

And that Miss Leonides, horrified, would stammer:

"But, doctor, who's to make the decision? My daughter (dear, beloved Leonides Arrufat), my daughter is not in a state to make such a decision, you can see."

"I see, madam, I see," the doctor would answer, annoyed because they were making him enter into explanations. "But we can't save the two of them."

Perhaps she already knew what the doctor did not know. She knew that, contrary to his pedantic assertions, there would be nobody to save and nobody to condemn.

And she would have liked to tell Miss Leonides so, but she could not find the words, she could not find the way to decant, from one irreality to the other, the subterranean water of that premonition. And for that reason, with growing frequency, she moaned, she twitched with convulsive jerks, that repulsive little smile hovered about her lips as though trying to break through.

And all poor Miss Leonides could think to do was to repeat monotonously:

"You wait and see, you just wait and see, everything will be all right."

Until one night, during carnival, the footsteps halted, the big door swung open, and Cecilia, with a scream, emerged from the dream.

She was sleeping in her mother's bedroom, in her mother's bed. Beside her a strange woman, dressed like her mother, wearing her hair like her mother, was looking at her with eyes that seemed bursting from their sockets.

"Who are you?" she asked weakly, trying to sit up. But her strength dissolved and she had to let her head drop back on the pillow.

From a distance there came a noise that was like a stream of

water running into an empty tank. And at the same time the
stream of water produced a strident music.

"What is all that noise?" she asked, turning her eyes toward
the window through which came a reddish glow.

She heard the stranger's voice answer:

"It's the parade up Avenida de Mayo, Cecilia."

She called her Cecilia, just Cecilia. The girl looked at her.

"Why have you done your hair the way she did? Why have you
put on her blue dress which she was so fond of? Why did I
try to make myself believe . . . ? Or perhaps I myself asked you
to, and I can't remember."

The stranger said nothing, folding her arms over her breast,
as though trying to hide herself, bowing her shoulders with the
air of a servant effacing herself before an imperious mistress.

"I know. You are my nurse. I have been sick all this time."

She touched her abdomen with her hands.

"Why is my body so swollen? Am I going to have a baby?"

Suddenly she seemed to enter a familiar landscape. She recognized it. Everything was in its place. And in this landscape,
that gilded shadow, that frightening shadow, where was it?

"Where is Belena?"

She looked searchingly at the stranger, and the stranger stammered:

"She's not. . . . She doesn't live here any more. . . ."

Belena. There was something that had to do with Belena.
Something unfinished. But she could not remember.

"Where has she gone?"

"I don't know, I don't know, Miss."

"And Encarnación and Mercedes?"

The stranger shrank still more into herself, huddled up, hunch-
ing her head between her shoulders.

"They don't come any more either."

The familiar landscape. The solid ground underfoot. And overhead the sky like a pledge of eternity. Suddenly she remembered.

"Do you know?" she said, in a voice so abruptly adult that
the stranger started and looked around in fright, as though she

suspected it was some other person who had spoken to her. "Do you know why I got sick? Do you know everything?"

"Yes, Miss, I do. And I can't tell you how I pity you!"

She raised a hand. Pity her! This woman did not know that she was the daughter of Jan Engelhard, the sage, the wizard, the saint. Daughter and pupil. At his side she had learned to suffer and keep silent, and to purify herself in suffering like silver in the fire. But the time had come to reveal all.

"Who told you?"

"Encarnación and Mercedes, the last time they were here."

"No, they don't know it all. Listen to me. I don't want to die without first. . . ."

"Miss Cecilia!"

Die, yes, die. Chunks of rubble that fall to the ground like dry husks. And the living kernel, glowing in the light like a diamond.

"I know that I am going to die. I don't have much time. And you are the only person here with me. Listen to me."

The stranger heard this tale:

She was alone. Belena had left, with Encarnación, to see a doctor. Suddenly three men appeared in the dining room, where she was folding some tablecloths. They were young. Two of them didn't look to be more than twenty. The third one, tall and dark, was about twenty-five. They were wearing black leather jackets. And gloves. One aimed a revolver at her. She started to scream and they hit her. They dragged her through the house. They raided the pantry. They ate, they drank, they smoked. Then they took her upstairs. They seemed to know the layout of the rooms perfectly. In her room the two younger ones said to the other: "O.K., brother, it's your show." The other one laughed and then turned and looked at her. She struggled, she defended herself. She buried her teeth in a gloved hand. Then everything collapsed. The roofs, the walls, the bed, the shelf with the dolls. They had left. They had locked her in and had left. She could hear them talking. No, not she. Her head. But her head had come loose from her body, had rolled far away on the floor, cut off, detached. That head which was no longer hers had heard. Now that it was back on her shoulders again, now she knew

what that guillotined carrion had then overheard. The three men
were talking in her mother's room. One of them said: "Look,
seventy pounds sterling." Another: "What time is it?" Another:
"Five of six. Belena said that she wouldn't be coming back with
the old woman till after seven." The same voice added. "When
she gets back and sees that I stopped after the first act and
didn't finish off the cousin for her, she's going to be as mad as
hell." The first one: "Jeez, won't she squeal on you?" The
other: "Let her, if she wants to. For I kept the photo. And
let her explain to the police why she told the two old women
that she had found it in one of the kid's dresses, and that she
suspected that it might be the photo of some boy friend of the
kid's, and that she was worried, and she even squeezed out some
tears, and the photo is of her husband, who died a natural death
a couple of years ago. Ah, no, she'll have to excuse me, but
when it comes to blood, I'm out. I am sorry to deprive her of in-
heriting the cousin's property, which she planned to enjoy in
my honorable company, but I'm satisfied with these leavings."
The second one: "We, too." The third one: "Sure, kid, sure.
We're in this share and share alike. As I said, if there's any
killing, count me out. But she—what guts! But I'm tired of
that bag. Not to mention the fact that she is forty-two, and I,
unless there's been an error or miscount, am twenty-five." The
first one: "Say, and what about the kid?" The other: "What
about her?" The first one: "Won't she talk?" The other: "Let
her. What's she going to say? What clue has she got? Nobody
is going to suspect us. And anyway, Belena will take good care
to queer her pitch. Because she knows that if they catch me,
they'll get her, too. So she's going to take good care to cover
up for me. And let her find herself another sucker. For she's not
going to see hide nor hair of me again."

Her head had heard all this at the time. But not she. She lay
mutilated in a corner of her bedroom. Until after she couldn't
tell how long, the door opened and Encarnación and Belena
came in. On her neck an artificial head was grafted, a vibratile
head of a fetish which moved and talked of itself. With this
automaton wedged between her shoulders, she could no longer

think or reason. All she could do was to hide away in her warm, numb entrails, curl up like her own fetus, drift off in a deep morbid sleep in which Guirlanda Santos was alive. And it was from this sleep that she had just awoken.

But why was the stranger looking at her with that frightening face? Why did she rush out of the bedroom? Why did she come right back with a letter and say to her:

"Miss Cecilia, read this."

And she read: *"Dear Cecilia. I have just managed to get Monday off, so I can come . . . Yours, Fabian."*

She did not understand, she did not understand any of it.

"Where did you find this letter?"

"In your room, Miss."

"But I never received it. I don't know any Fabian."

The eyes of the stranger did not let go of hers. And those eyes were screaming a frightful revelation at her. Those eyes had a name tattooed on them.

It was hard for her to breathe, her head was whirling, a thundering storm was brewing in her womb.

"Belena," she managed to bring out.

The stranger bent over her.

"Where does she live?"

"I don't know. I don't know. But find her. Bring her to me."

The stranger seemed turned to stone.

"Belena," Cecilia's pale lips repeated, "Belena."

A lightning flash burst in her eyes. Now would be when the stranger would call that doctor.

But she was already leaving. She was floating down a murmurous river, full of birds, flowers, algae, fish. A cool clear river that carried her farther and farther away toward a plain as blue as the sea. Before sinking into this sea she turned and made out the stranger who, from the distant bank, seemed to follow her like a faithful dog. She smiled at her, stretched a translucent hand toward her which overcame the distance and reached that maternal face, and asked her again, this time in a tone of inexpressible sweetness:

Who are you, madam?"

But she did not hear, she would never hear, the stranger's answer.

Everything was now clear.

If her face and the face of Guirlanda Santos had been cast in the same mold; if Natividad González, that morning, had covered her with insults; if she took that streetcar, and gesticulated and laughed to herself; if Cecilia, sitting beside her, saw her and saw her making those gestures; if she then stubbornly followed her through the city streets; if no accident, no chance prevented their meeting in the cemetery, and the flight to the house at 78 Suipacha, and the episodes that followed, it was because everything formed part of a vast ceremony, everything made up one of those intricate mechanisms of which we will never know who was the artificer—God or ourselves.

But fate never beckons to anyone gratuitously. If she had been included in the ceremony, it was because, at some determined moment, she was to pass from acolyte to minister and officiate at the final ritual act, the one with which the ceremony would end. She understood that this moment had arrived. Cecilia had laid her hands upon her, and she was now consecrated for the horrid rite.

She looked at Cecilia's face lying upon the pillow.

She looked at it with a kind of voraciousness, as though to impregnate herself in it. Stamp it on her soul like a tattoo on the skin. That face minute by minute became more beautiful. Death, wiping out its fatigue, gradually brought it to life. Until, wide-awake, it glowed like a jewel. Just as in the old fairy stories, the peasant girl had been turned into a princess. And Miss Leonides sank to her knees.

Afterward she got up. She was possessed by an icy calm. She remembered:

ENCARNACION: Just like Belena.

MERCEDES: Belena found it out through the newspaper.

First she would try that scheme. And then others, many, all, until she found her.

She went to an undertaking establishment. She went to the newspaper offices. She arranged for a notice to be published saying: "Cecilia Engelhard, R.I.P. Her bereaved family announces the passing . . . Funeral services at: 78 Suipacha."

The employees of the undertaking establishment prepared the funeral chapel in one of the downstairs rooms, laid out Cecilia in a black coffin, the infant in a tiny white one, placed close by the street door a mahogany urn, and fled from that somber mansion where there was nobody to be seen but the two corpses and a woman who was not weeping but in front of whom, without knowing why, they had to lower their eyes.

Then Miss Leonides took up her position beside a window and waited.

Outside, in the carnival afternoon, Suipacha drowsed.

Several hours went by, as long as days. Night came. Along Avenida de Mayo rainbows of lights sprang up, the music struck up, the procession began its uproar.

And Miss Leonides, standing beside the window, went on waiting. Only her lips moved, as though in prayer. The rest of her body had the lethargy of a crocodile. But from the depths of their orbits, her eyes gave off a gleam of silica. They did not take in the groups of people moving toward the procession. They were aimed, across the city, at a single spot, unknown and divined. And that glance instantly recognized the woman who had stopped before the door.

The woman hesitated for a second. Then she came in. She saw the mahogany urn. She saw, farther off, an open door and the gleam of the candles. She walked over to the door and went in. She saw the two coffins. She approached first one, then the other, she looked into their depths observing them as from a parapet. She seemed perplexed and a little frightened. At that moment she heard someone behind her call:

"Belena."

She turned around.

Her fine eyes, with their firmly etched contours, opened wide with amazement. She was about to cry out when she felt as if a wound had burst open between her breasts, and a burning, sticky liquid was running down her skin under her dress. A sudden drowsiness came over her. She tried to move her head, wave an arm, rid herself of that absurd sleep that was weighing her down, but was unable to, and fell heavily amidst the joyful flickering of the candles.

Miss Leonides then straightened up. A drop of sweat was running down her cheek, which she wiped away mechanically with her hand which was trembling convulsively, looked at Cecilia for one last time, smiled at her, and went out.

In Guirlanda Santos' bedroom she laid the stiletto on the book shelf, took off the blood-stained clothes, put on her black dress, her black coat, the liturgical black turban, slipped the handbag which looked like a huge rotten fig under her arm, went down to the first floor, and without turning off any light, without closing any door, went out in the street and walked away.

A group of masked revelers greeted her with the dry lugubrious laughter of their ratchets.

—Translated by HARRIET DE ONIS

THE ABORIGINES
by Carlos Martínez Moreno

CARLOS MARTÍNEZ MORENO was born in Colonia, Uruguay, in 1917. A newspaperman by profession, he has worked as a theater critic and editorial writer. Since 1948, he has also been a practicing lawyer, specializing in criminal cases. His writing has brought him several literary grants, one of which permitted him to make his first trip to Europe. Among his books are *Los días por vivir* (*Days Left to Live*) published by *Editorial Asir* in 1960, and *Cordelia* published by *Editorial Alfa* in 1961. His most recent novel, *El paredón* (*Against the Wall*), was chosen for publication in a competition sponsored by the Spanish publishing house, *Seix Barral*, and will appear in the near future.

Sitting on one of those famous stones, he watched the stream of cars skirt the Coliseum and then turn to enter Via Cavour or move straight ahead toward Piazza Venezia, where gradually they jammed together. In one direction the column of Trajan, in the other the smooth ridge of the Palatine. He came there often to see the evening fall from the Farnese Gardens or on the top of the stairs of Antoninus and Faustina, between the ancient parentheses of the two arches: Septimius Severus on his right, Titus on the left.

The obliging employees of the Direzione Generale delle Antichità e Belle Arti knew him already. *"Eccellenza"* or *"Signor ambasciatore, prego,"* they would say, bowing, after they had refused to collect his ticket of admission or stepped forward to accept his tip. Massimo usually drove him this far, knowing beforehand that he had a free evening, unless he had to convey the *signora ambasciatrice* to tea or cocktails. If he was going to be free, Massimo would drive the huge Cadillac exuberantly with an agility and dashing *cantabile* spirit that led him to slither into every available space amid the chaotic Roman traffic. The prospect of tea or cocktails, on the other hand, visibly depressed him. For Massimo was "temperamental" and the idle humdrum conversation of the other embassy chauffeurs bored and disgusted him; he felt superior to them in every way as the provider of a range of diplomatic services that was not confined to the steering wheel.

Now, even more, the sun was flaming on the red brick of the Basilica of Constantine, and it was easy to imagine that in a few minutes it would descend over the Tyrrhenian Sea, down there facing Ostia, while here the guards began to inspect the Via Sacra, the ruins of the Vestal temple, and the half-buried, almost intact house of Livia, on the lookout for the last stragglers, phlegmatic errant lovers inspired by paganism and prostitutes.

The uniformed employees walked by him and looked at him with a respect that, unlike the first times, was in no way inquisitive. What was he doing (they must have wondered a year ago), this chubby, copper-skinned foreigner who seemed to contemplate all those columns, all those temples and public baths and gardens, in a withdrawn, absent-minded mood? Could they have imagined that he was stilling his homesickness there for other temples, other arches, other stones, equally ancient and far more removed from the prying of men?

His familiarity with the place would have made it superfluous to consult any guide, any little catalogue of classical antiquities. Only one small book appeared at times, open across his knees and glanced at occasionally, fleetingly, as though to remind him of an uncertain word in the text of an already well-known litany. It was Leopardi and, as if to evoke a previously exhausted pleasure, he always returned to the same lines which—in some mysterious way—made up a part of his feelings on those evenings.

> *Roma, antica ruina*
> *Tu sì placida sei?*

Leopardi's lines were allusive, applicable to the moment; they also referred to the swift and silent flow of cars in the twilight, the harmonious gesticulations with which the artistic policeman sorted out the traffic of the Piazza, channeling it toward Caracalla or turning it aside toward the Trastevere; they epitomized the shaggy, sweet, golden-fruit quality of Rome in this limpid autumn with its high, burning, desiccated skies. Leopardi sang in the strength of the morning sun on Porta Pinciana, visible from the balcony during the first months at the Excelsior; he bestowed his cadence on the deadening circle of dry leaves spreading around the iron grill in the Viale de Villa Grazzioli, over the driveway which led to the pink building of the embassy.

Tu sì placida sei?

And what is certain is that they seemed to him to have sent him, with marvelous understanding, to find repose in the calm of things, to take up his dwelling there for his own autumn so he might squeeze out the flavor of that other slightly bruised fruit which his heart seemed to be, or the time of his old griefs, or the American soul; the American soul which had the habit of afflicting him unexpectedly, which threatened or assaulted him each time more gently and humbly, each time more perceptibly chilled, even when, as now, he was looking at the surface glitter kindling the walls of Santa Maria in Aracoeli, neck bare to the sun of Europe, shoulders haloed by that eternal light which had shed its illumination, before the Roman had gone, on business and rituals and languid embraces turned to dust.

He was already sixty-two years old; his name, its abbreviations and extensions, had been the target of the witticisms of the political caricaturists, who portrayed him squat and swarthy, as though he were a plume on a funeral carriage: *that primitive courtier, that courteous primitive* had remained as the equation of his contradictions—his chunky Indian-like build, his slowly acquired doctor's deference. Son of Primitivo Cortés—doctor, professor, deputy, and minister—grandson of Serapio Morillo, with a statue in one of the squares of his native city (as martyr, protomartyr or whatever he was), they had wanted to christen him all-inclusively Serapio Primitivo.

The aesthetic horror which his first Christian name had always caused him surpassed by far the sense of strangeness, of incon-

gruity irrationally inspired in him by the second. But the awareness of a tolerable inheritance had obliged him to compromise,
and his activities as a company lawyer—and even before that, as
a university hero with black forelock, defiant with a glove—had
made him known as S. Primitivo Cortés M. Abbreviated to two
letters, the heroic lineage had served him as a crutch and thus
had helped him to triumph.

S. Primitivo Cortés. There was a harsh and slightly disturbing pleasure in thinking of the dusty plains city where he had
gone to high school, now that Rome held him as a brooding
guest, welcome at the Quirinale, a reader of unfathomable
Vatican libraries.

Massimo—with one of those open, benignly dissipated faces,
lively and vulgar, dissolute and pleasant, which Italians often
have—was about to appear, getting out of the car on Via dei
Fori. He would take off his blue cap with the thin gold braid
and wave it in an attractively humorous and pompous greeting,
bumptious without lacking grace, gracious without lacking respect,
to let him know that he was there.

At times, in his self-absorption he did not see him arrive.
But Massimo was well known to the employees and would enter
the Forum. The ambassador always got around to ending his
stroll in the last glimmers of daylight—like a nocturnal bird
in its tree—near the panel of public sacrifices inside the Curia,
where night closed in early. Massimo would then appear at the
gateway to the cattle frieze, without going up to it, making an
obsequious gesture, admiring and indulgent all at once, as from
one who respects stubbornness he cannot understand.

But today he would not find him there. The Roman air de-
lightfully cooled what he felt quite literally as the throbbing in
his weary temples. He was enjoying that mild breeze which traveled from his forehead to the bushy hair, the dark, stiff mane
that confined to his sideburns the few white threads that sought
to invade it.

He felt in his pocket for the little newspaper clipping he had
kept when he went out. He was idle enough to look at it again.
In an obscure corner of the *Messagero,* in the surfeiting enjoy-

ment of breakfast, his eyes had happened upon the meager information about the fact and its foreseeable denouement. General Lafuente had suppressed another plot. Students' sedition, playboys' conspiracy, miners' uprising, scorching march of country people over the plains. In prison (if it happened in the cities), with machine-gunnings in the mine tunnel or on the prairie, the revolution someone had incited always failed. And the final destiny of those rebellions, the dampness of those dungeons, the bitter stench of those bodies decomposing under the sun and flies, the fistful of earth in the mouth, the hand clutching stony rubble, all this filtered into the world through the narrow opening of that eye dropper; and thus it reached him, lost among frivolous local news of every day, stuck away beneath an advertisement in some corner of *Il Corriere* or *Le Figaro* or *Le Monde*. To the embassies in near-by capitals, planted in countries where political exiles raised the dust of scandal, shouting their denunciations of crimes, the ministry sent a supplementary bulletin, argumentative at times, which palliated, corrected, or enlarged on what the news agencies had said. But in Rome, remote from that populated clot of prairie and mountains, nothing ever reached them, and except for the two of them, he and Leonor, no one ever seemed to stumble on the tiny little news item, rescue it from those torrents of print which crowded in on it and hid it. General Lafuente had suppressed another plot, ten lines of text with its elliptical deaths: that was the distant homeland.

He had met General Cándido Lafuente when he was barely a minor officer of the Obrajes regiment, the same day the mishap had occurred. And the friendship begun that evening, amid outbursts of desperation and vindictive cruelties, had outlasted the moment.

The distant homeland. He thought of himself and his wife, of what that piece of earth had cost them in happiness, of how much it had worn them with frustrations. Flags, mountain wind, a smooth sash shrieking so that the air would stir its sonorous tatters and carry them to distant snows, scissors to cut a ribbon and a ribbon to free a road. Road, school, and light, the mestizo teacher had demanded months before, yelling it hoarsely and supplicatingly to the authorities from an improbable position, grasping with one arm the iron grating of the church, gesticulating with the other, while his feet tried to get a hold in the uneven surface of the old crumbling plaster of the colonial wall. Road, school, and light; scissors for a ribbon, the ribbon for a road, and a bomb to carry it above face and memory. Dust on the leaves, an unreal recollection: boredom, mutilation, leftover time, life which they had spoiled irreparably.

He used to imagine himself in the presence of a psychoanalyst, telling him his own story so he might help him to find and reveal himself completely in some buried clue from childhood. But he thought he knew enough about psychoanalysis to study himself, without help, in dreams, impulses, disappointments. And if the imaginary psychoanalyst did not know the soul of America, perhaps he would likewise be unable to know his own. It was easy for him to discover the growing strangeness that had continued to alienate him from Leonor, that suspicious and elusive inner development of maturity that had gone on separating them, that had made them waken each morning on the same pillow more unfamiliar with each other. He might have been able to seek out the secret springs of resentment and responsibility which produced that distance, starting from the day when his wife's face was spoiled through her conscientiousness in always accompanying him, sharing his days and activities. ("The Arabico-Spanish zeal of our women, so often slighted and oppressed," he thought, transposing into sociological terms the story of their mutual competition.)

From that evening on, the lovely face had been converted into the unpardonable grimace, and it was the grimace more than the face which had grown old. She, the former Leonor, the woman before the bomb, would have had a less tense, less nervous, more noble old age. She would have had it if it had not died that night.

But America, too, an expanse of harsh storms, had something to do with the process of that unequal maturation, that incurable lack of understanding that had come to dwell between their two lives. America was the ideal theater for non-communication, for isolation, for the somber loneliness of man. With a certain incontrovertible melancholy, he reflected that their diverging adulthood could not have been so acute in Europe, a continent that surrounded the human being with other stimuli, without obliging him to subsist gloomily from his own resources, in that final hostile element that is at the bottom of every personality. He recalled now the scene in his father's study the day he informed him he was going to get married. The old professor smoothed his little French-style mustache, let his hand wander absently in his graying beard. He did not appear vexed but stricken, rather, in who could say what moment of his private past, that past children never get to know. Then one of his fingers began to tap the terraqueous globe, making it move with little bursts of speed, as if the world—with man and his store of happiness, the only thing an engaged man could think of—were spinning in spasms.

The accidents, the apprehensions, and the mystery of two people who, yoked together in youth, have to grow up together—that *is* marriage. He could not be sure that those were the words, but such was his father's idea, his prudent and aloof warning. He did not promise a violent and miserable future, the fleshly torment of Paolo and Francesca. He spoke from the serenity of his years, with neither grief nor trace of passion.

His father had died in America, at least, with the windows open to the hard frozen peace of the mountain, firm and silent as though the earth were taking back from him the moments of his life. The great doctor, the wise professor, the man of politics who disdained honors, had always thought of death with arrogant toughness and metaphors of a Masonic cast: "Until the earth reclaims our bones," "until we are only dust and darkness." God, the God of daily life and prayers, withdrew from the scene at such moments, as though the doctor experienced a visceral need to be alone and plumb his solitude.

For himself, primitive and courteous, perhaps that style of autochthonous death had been denied. Once or twice he had begun to jot down the lines of a poem in which he mourned over his indifference, his intractable alienation from things. But he

had left off writing in the middle with an insignificant image:
the plant with roots exposed to the sun. What point in finishing
a lament of this order if his very spiritual exile consisted in
alienating potential readers? He had turned back then to his
painstaking research, into which he was accustomed to let slip
(like mistakes in life, bottles cast in the sea) lines and cryptic
visions smacking hopelessly of prophecy. The work now progress-
ing at a leisurely pace was called *The Aborigines* and studied
the rise, the condition, and the destiny of those Indians and
mestizos whose faces had surrounded him from the days of his
childhood, those whom he sometimes dimly sensed pulsing in
his very blood. Some future critic might perhaps discover that
he had wanted to write a merciless essay in ethnic autobiography,
a form of dissolution of his own being in the being of the race.

In any event, this was an intention that could be redeemed on
the further side of death. The other things were trifles, like that
gay, clever, and irresponsible article that the little group had enjoyed in embassy circles. It had been published in the Sunday
supplement of the *Nación* of Buenos Aires and was called, lightly
mocking a title of Moravia, "Massimo, or Efficiency." In it the
master portrayed his servant, described the operations in which
he was so clever, the sly patience he had acquired from circulating
so much among South American diplomats, employers whose
obscure origins he scorned but whose unfailing eloquence in dollars he would serve to his dying breath. This account of modern
roguery sparkled with brief sketches, between the ubiquitous servant who disparaged him and the native ambassador who never
ceased to feel or know himself to be a foreigner. From the point
of view of the one who wrote it, it was a slight, imperceptible
exercise in confession of his peculiar and modest insecurity. From
the reader's point of view, it was Massimo who assumed a rich
prominence and whose caricature was an indictment of the
mercenary capability of an old and needy, flagrant and indecent
world. It was clear that Massimo did not read Spanish, nor perhaps any other language, beyond his glance every Monday at the
results of the soccer pools, that little sheet that for him was the
raison d'être of newspapers.

"Oh ancient Europe" was the predictable inner exclamation. But Massimo or efficiency had already discovered him and was approaching amid the ruins in the final glow of day.

II

He had hardly left the university, with his resounding title of Doctor of Law and Jurisprudence, when one night, at the gala dinner that the president of the Chalk Industries Company was giving in his house, he met Leonor. The company was always alert for "promising talents," the well-endowed young men, the first intimations that indicated in a person, with the leveling of the years, the intellectual or thinking elite of the country.

Furthermore, Primitivo was a member of what some university snobs were beginning to designate as the oligarchy, without knowing too well what sort of power they were referring to. The company president, Don Lucho Otero, boasted that he was more perceptive and that he guessed where "the talents of this country" were. He bit into an enormous cigar—on which he had left the little paper ring which showed off its high quality—and aimed his blows on the then sharp-cornered shoulders of Primitivo while he introduced him as the latest and most brilliant of his acquisitions.

"Don't make him conceited," Leonor said suddenly, and he at once adored that frankness, which in the country and at that time "one simply didn't allow." He must have looked at her with a mixture of aggression, gratitude, and perplexity, for she raised her head with even more boldness, knowing that the motto of "more courage" was the only one that could save her from an overwhelming delayed embarrassment, which always attacked her after a daring statement.

It was then that he asked her to dance, and he felt Don Lucho's hand withdraw its pressure; as a divine compensation, a second later Leonor's hand came to rest at the very same place.

It had been, in reality, a deceptive and unprofitable beginning, because she—better schooled, engaged in ideas and feelings with a frugality that insidiously threatened her, suggesting tacit indications of an unconscious masculine inclination in her—ended by showing herself as the woman who gave the superficial impression of a little girl in a moment of bitter-sweet, crushing indecision.

"Your parents must be planning to marry you to a gringo," he said to provoke her. And at once he described to her one of those insipid Anglo-Saxon mining engineers precociously aged by the bush country, work, whiskey, and homesickness—such was the horrible model of a colonial husband he placed before her.

"I'll marry whoever I feel like marrying, whatever my parents may say about it," Leonor answered, and he alone was aware of the favorable element in her attention, the propitious quality of her liberty. "Whoever I feel like marrying" could also be this swarthy local doctor, whose small stature and kangarooish flabbiness, terminating in an absurd fallen and roundish stomach, clearly anticipated the mature and chubby lawyer with "office, belly, and clerk," as he had written when a student in a satire aimed at one of his professors, hurling the boomerang which returns some day to face us with the mindless fatuity of our youth.

But that night everything had moved along in a swift and joyous mood, weightlessly brilliant and dreamy. The future had no mirrors to see itself in that salon, it was not a witness of the conversation.

. . . *Aux vagues senteurs de l'ambre.* Baudelaire's line, contradicted by the subtropical mist that came through the wide-open windows (for Don Lucho lived on the fertile, darkling plains, not in the vicinity of the mountain chain), floated above the recollection of that moment, undulated a perversely seductive current in the innocent improvisation of personal charm that he had had to impose on her, and which Leonor had absorbed, already half surrendering, with her watery black eyes as open as the balconies, but less surfeited and tranquil than all that was contained in the calm of the night.

When Don Lucho recommended him to the president and the latter named him governor of a district that included, among other regions, the Obrajes mine, one of the most important of the Chalk Industries Company, Primitivo and Leonor were able to marry. Perhaps he ought to have said it in a more romantic way, but this was the simple chain of events.

And thus it was that the strike raced to meet them with its cloud of dust that was to foul their limpid happiness; thus the first outbreaks occurred and the order to deploy the police.

The mouths of the tunnel opened on the height, toward which the riflemen climbed along a winding mule path. The stones were answered by shots and after a rock on the forehead and a bullet in the belly, the undifferentiated mestizos of the revolution and of the government wandered through the gullies and got themselves entangled, with the same glassy gaping faces, in thorns of the sort from which no human hand would come to free them.

With the whimsical and peremptory intransigence of a newly-wed—which produced the aphrodisiac effect of opium in Primitivo—Leonor insisted on accompanying him to the final inspection of the suppression of the riots in Obrajes. She insisted to the point of making a scene; and she went.

On the last part of the ride he had to leave the car for some spiritless mules, which were more humiliated by his mission than those other tired creatures, ragged and dirty, who surrounded them with a fence of rifles, with a mindless impassiveness which could have been either protective or menacing.

Beneath her scarlet silk parasol, which stood out like a printer's error among those gaunt and bearded faces, against that chalky, bony, ocher sky, Leonor followed—in another of her indefinable states, between amusement and alarm, the story to tell and the premonition of dying when it was only half over—she followed the slow and dull movements of the troops in the sun over the depths of a taut, clean sky propped up by the buttresses of the mountains. It was that fleeting hour without mist, the tentative beginning of evening.

They were already entering the town by the little road that twisted among the houses when they suddenly heard, not very intense, more commotion than noise, the explosion of the bomb. Primitivo had the scene vividly stamped on his mind, his eyes

had retained it with the clarity of a camera, he still seemed to
hear the near-by crackling, Leonor's scream, the muted trampling, the shots that rang out at once. The man who had thrown
it (a Jew, an anarchist, a mestizo? people had wondered afterward, as though anarchism was a race and excluded every other
affiliation) disappeared with his arm in the air in a cloud of dust.
He was killed right there by the firing of the guards, and no one
stirred to raise him up, or even to go near him. He stayed there,
in the early evening, touched by the hard, faint white reflection
of the sun on the mountain, by the fierce light that was refracted
by the snow. But the picture that Primitivo recorded was different: as in a wild-west film, in the foreground his wife putting
her hands to her bloodied face, in the background a ragged white
dog crossing the sunny street. The mules had been tethered in
the distance, and the fallen parasol with its handle sticking up
was a great mushroom of the same bloody florescence that was
spreading over Leonor's face.

As in so many other critical moments of his life, something
inside him held him back, a mounting paralysis prevented him
from approaching. He was standing—he could not say how he
had gotten there—on one of the slopes bordering the road, and
his dust-whitened suit revealed that the explosion had thrown
him far, knocking him on his back. From there, motionless,
stupefied, frozen in his tracks, he saw how the lieutenant rushed
up and took Leonor in his arms. Someone yelled, "To the hospital!" and it was then he felt, in a long comical undulation,
spiritless, despairing of everything, that his own body was col-
lapsing on the ground and his intense, upright paralytic tension
relaxed, and that to die and grow faint were, for the moment,
the same thing.

"Governor, governor!" he began to hear by his left ear with
ever-increasing distinctness. "*Señora* Cortés is being looked after
this very minute. I don't think it's serious, doctor. But let's not
go yet because you'd be upset seeing all the blood. The poor
little lady is being very brave, she's worried only about you.
Just a little effort now and we'll be on our feet!"

He sat on the ground, feeling his bruised and painful shoulder.

"I want to see her right now, Lieutenant. . . ."

"Cándido Lafuente, at your service," the other introduced himself, thinking that the pause was to ask his identity when it had been only consternation, irresolution, the strangeness of hearing himself say one thing and mean another. For he did not want to see her now but only when she had been healed.

"But it's not serious, Lieutenant Lafuente? If you can assure me of that, I can wait until they've attended to her. Oh yes, I want you to go to her and calm her, please."

Lafuente did not move, as though they spoke a different language. He turned around and someone handed him a glass.

"Doctor, please be good enough to drink this before anything else."

The long swallow of ill-smelling alcohol did not taste bad on that occasion; on the contrary, little by little it was restoring his strength, as though drawing it upward from the center of his chest. He got up then and began to walk, with a tenuous calm and composure, on the lieutenant's arm.

He was often to remember afterward that in that short walk he had allowed himself to feel an immeasurable and vague gratitude, as though the support that Lafuente offered him might blot out momentarily the accident that had occurred and drive it back into the past.

He had gone back to see him a couple of years later; and on resuming the friendship, he had felt once more that sensation of confidence that the brown face, the straight Indian mustache, and the slow manner of Cándido inspired in him. It had been at the house of Rogelio Murano, at one of those literary gatherings crawling with tropical poets, where one discussed (until they were satiated with intellectual chitchat and brandy) Arguedas' theory about the "sick nation" or some other such fashionable doctrine of the kind that seem at times to be more in evidence than the very surface of America.

The years had swollen that face with its taut slanted eyes, they had stamped the fold of the lips with a slightly disparaging grin. Like so many other mestizos, sad inside, Cándido Lafuente pursued drunkenness as an end in itself, as the way to go beyond a

limit and to get through not only that night but the silent Indian
existence that seemed to have had other avatars before this one.

With his military jacket unbuttoned and a ceremonious expression and on the point of breaking down—that exacerbated sub-
servience that later had recourse to violence, even to the point
of smashing glasses against the wall—Cándido would not allow
anyone to leave the reunion. "The night is still young," he said.

And when he was talking to someone whom he knew he could
get to like that night, as though friendship too had precursors
who might meet again, the sentence was different. Primitivo
associated it with the expression with which, that same early
morning in Murano's house, Cándido had detained him, placing
a hand on each shoulder.

"But brother, we're just now getting to the point of appreciating
one another."

A half hour later he was bullying him into drinking with him.
He rose abruptly, dipped a little spreader in sauce so hot that
it brought tears to the eyes, and passed it over Primitivo's lips.

"After the hot sauce you've got to drink. Let's have a drink!"

His intoxication was not always so enterprising. Primitivo recalled that moment at daybreak when, without their ever men-
tioning it afterward, he had been able to repay him his irrational
debt of gratitude.

It had been in the same house in which he had his lawyer's
office, through which during the day there filed a long line of
disturbed bankers and unhappy husbands, seeking his advice,
and within whose walls through the night he kept up, to re-
establish his equilibrium, an endless and aimless conversation on
the Destiny of the Nation or some other of those solemn excuses
that one's own lack of will power demands in order to drown it
in liquor.

Cándido had reached that point of extreme depression, of
abysmal alcoholic weakness, in which he could make sense of
only one idea, suicide.

"Brothers," he said, "there's no way out for this country, we're
all lost. I've made up my mind this very minute—I'm going to
kill myself."

He shoved, forcing a way through the guests with all the brute strength he had left, and managed to get hold of the wrought-iron railing of the balcony, lifting one leg to straddle it. While he struggled with two other drunken men (who unlike him were inspired by the occasion with a stubborn desire to live), Cándido Lafuente repeated his abuse against life and brutally proclaimed the senselessness of any solution except self-destruction.

Primitivo reached him and took his wild face in his hands, watching him anxiously. Suddenly the idea struck him that he could get through to the only accessible feeling of the drunk, revive the only saving response: the idea of a gentleman's obligations.

"But Cándido, you can't do this *to your friend*. You can't do it *here*."

They were on the edge of the cast-iron balcony above the barely visible abyss of the narrow alley, their eyes close to the façade of the Spanish house opposite through whose always open windows they could see the great philosopher and thinker, the only one they respected, reading, writing, walking, playing Indian tunes on the piano, invariably dressed in white linen, the powerful head meditative, fertile, oppressed, and the long bushy hair turning white, the man who seldom raised his mestizo Beethoven mask toward them (and in his absorption did not see them).

"But Cándido, you can't do this to your friend."

Such an image survived the passage of time. "Standing before those windows, which opened *en face de la montagne*," as he wrote in French one day, denying the naked South American carnality of that mountain-range landscape rising before those windows that never closed.

The years, fusing the clear images of remembrance, offered up a single scene. In the foreground, Cándido bending over the railing and himself taking the mortal, ashen face in his two hands; in the background the Indian philosopher, meditating with his white mane and dark face, like an American Buddha, his whole body vaguely draped in luminous floating garments that gave the impression of a serape rather than a European suit, although as

a matter of fact, with its poorly fitted tailoring, that is what it
was. This striking background figure was alone, on its face an
inscrutable expression. His enigma was not easily solved because
they had seen him read, write, and eat, surrounded by his children, always at the same time. Because of the elusive dignity of a
thinking man in an atmosphere that denied thought, because of
that depth that was beyond his eyes, rather than because of what
they had read of him (right now, mature and alone, he was
reading him with passionate admiration in the silence of the
embassy), the philosopher seemed to them all meaningfully affectionate and alive, unique and venerable above the wave of disbelief that left nothing standing. Like Cándido Lafuente on the
edge of the balcony, that apparition of a philosopher was also
the country, lost inside the country.

*With the National Revolution, a beggar sleeping on a golden
bed wakes up and starts to move.* The sentence was beautiful
and gave a name to a reality of blood and anonymous bodies,
the uprising, a whole people's agitation. Primitivo wondered at
times if that same beggar sleeping on a golden bed might not
be the one who had thrown the bomb years before, if that same
beggar had not been anesthetized for decades by the champions
of national conformity.

A beggar sleeping on a golden bed. . . . Cándido Lafuente
had confronted death with his breast exposed and once more
death had pardoned him.

The irrelevant detail that secretly contradicts us, a sardonic
accident may decide our fate. Lafuente was triumphant and
Cortés, undecided in the first hours of the outbreak, had gone
out to embrace him in the streets of the city, to mingle with the
earthy mob surrounding him. That countenance furrowed with
wrinkles and sown with sparse wisps of beard, that face bursting
with dust and fatigue, had received him with a broad, dazzling
smile. The ambassadorship was the consideration that followed
the surprise, the withdrawal after emotion, the honorable compromise. All things considered, the Revolution had accepted him
and, with the return of calm, had gently gotten rid of him, plan-

ning for him a mild, golden exile, like the bed from which the
hundred-year-old beggar of the slogan was rising.

He had found his first acquiescence losing its strength, and he
had tried with all his power to grasp a fierce reality that confused
him. Encarnación, his former mistress, was important then in the
first ranks of the revolutionary partisans; she was a providential
figure.

She, Goti, Primitivo, and Colonel Gaudencio, General Lafuente's brother-in-law, were sitting around the crude pine table,
a forest of empty beer bottles in their midst. He felt that they
were looking at him as "the doctor," as a man of different origin
and different class, that he was conforming to endure in a new
order, that he was giving up—who knew with how much repugnance—his reading and his refinements in order to keep on
good terms in that orgy of brotherhood with the masses who did
not bathe.

"Goti, little daughter, bring me a drink, will you?" Gaudencio
said, without asking for anything for Cortés, as a form of ominous
exclusion.

Seated almost on the edge of his chair, he smelled the odor
of damp cotton and felt the crafty eyes of the mestizo on him,
as though a heavy gelatin poured over him sickeningly. And Goti,
who was not his little daughter, brought a full glass. Gaudencio took it without enthusiasm and said, as though it were
the highest praise: "My swee-e-et little Goti."

. . . *wakes up and starts to move.*

He passed the back of his hand over his wet mustache and
sullenly turned to Primitivo.

"So, Doctor, as you've been a friend of Cándido's. . . ."

III

She had put her face in her hands because she felt the hot
lash of her wounds. The splinters had driven into her face, cutting
muscles and slashing the flesh. For a few days the horror had
disappeared under the bandages, which barely left a narrow peep-

hole for the eyes. When the doctor decided that it was healed and that the pinkish scars would form new tissue better when exposed to the air, he laid bare his work.

Leonor ran to the oval mirror on her bureau and found there an unrecognizable face, whose paleness contrasted with the purple furrows and the stretched features that formed a provocative, intolerable grimace.

Frightened, she threw herself violently on the bed and began to cry convulsively.

"My God, why didn't I die, why didn't I die?"

"She can hurt herself, the tissues are still very tender," the doctor said, contrite at the foot of the bed and wretched in the certainty that it was his own ineptness and not somebody's face that was so shocking.

Primitivo had been living in the next room, where the doctor had removed the bandages and taken out the stitches. The idea that with each movement the doctor's hand was uncovering a living, trembling, grimacing mummy was quite enough to draw him now to comfort that face, to approach it and confront it with a look which was meant to indicate love and kinship and only gave out a consoling energy, pity in the presence of her private desolation. *This is the face that is going to follow you from now on, forever.*

Then he had gone to the library, poured himself a long drink of cognac, and stayed staring through the panes at the chilly sunlit landscape of the mountains. "We'll have to invent a pretext to take down half of the mirrors," he thought, because at home they had them at the ends of the corridors, on the backs of the doors, on the sideboards in the dining room, on the bathroom cabinets.

A couple of days later they named him Minister of Public Works and Communications; life paid off in this irreconcilable way.

Not so much time had passed since the days of Baudelaire's *Invitation to the Voyage,* and everything had changed. He was living through one of those critical moments when the past overtakes the present, with a precipitate confusion of images, in quest of some final significance. To make a career of power, to dominate that mob of Indians and mestizos out of which had risen the hand that had changed to something worse than death, transformed the formerly tranquil presence of his young and beautiful wife into a nervous, disagreeable presence—did this have any meaning and could it be the goal of a life? Wasn't it a contradiction to live for those who filled him only with a mingled sense of fear, rancor, and vengeance?

In that same corner of the library, a week later, they came to an understanding. They appeared determined and expansive, calm and resolved to talk things through. But an odd uneasiness, an obscure awkwardness, something left over which they had not been able to discuss, hovered between the two of them.

"I want you to consider seriously my request for a separation," Leonor said. She had the virtuous and dulled look of one who attempts to cheat himself in the intention of freeing the listener from some obligation or other.

"I've already told you it isn't possible and that I don't see any reason for it," he said (*noblesse oblige*), turning toward the window so as not to look at her pinched and sorrowful mask, which could be *the* reason. "We've always loved one another and our feelings must undergo the test, adjust to different circumstances. That's all there is to it."

What different circumstances was he referring to? Perhaps those that drew them even closer together in their unavoidable confinement, drove them into each other's arms. What might be called, on the basis of its obligations, love without partiality was stronger than ever, or at least was more urgent and single. Isolation meant renouncing that idle and unrestricted social life (still redolent of the colonial era) that the ministers were forced to lead. Primitivo knew that his wife's misfortune had unburdened him of much of the foolish routine, and by chance might definitely help him to find himself, if there was anything that he had to try to seek within himself.

"I won't talk about divorce with you because of course I know it doesn't exist among us and because as Catholics we have to reject it." He was aware, from her tone of affirmation, that this rejection was not a circumstance she regretted. "I'm talking about something else—a peaceful separation with the hope that time will strengthen a resolve in each one of us. We can believe that there are reasons for us to be together only if we come together again after a separation. To go on now like this is 'conjugal inertia,' as you once said in speaking about your parents."

"You're very upset, even if you look calm," he replied, amazed, almost defenseless before the memory of his filial irreverence. "Nevertheless, I'll tell you something: there will be a separation, but for a different reason. I've already made all the arrangements to send you to New York to a plastic-surgery clinic. I can't go with you because the ministry is involved in all these difficulties."

"Send me to New York?" she said, really alarmed. "Primitivo, you know we don't have any money."

Now he made himself confront the rebellious face that presented a caricature of surprise.

"Next week they'll sign the contract for the Northern Railway ties," he said. "I'll have that money."

Leonor could not switch rapidly from one feeling to another with her hardened, almost swollen face. But her eyes took on a damp and ambiguous sparkle—gratitude, the fall from the paradise of half-innocence, the half-innocence of not asking, so as not to know, in which she had lived till then?

He did not say it. But he felt in turn that those eyes were discovering and perusing for the first time in him a different face, determined and covetous, taking on a look of boldness. He also had his after-the-bomb face. Good Lord! Face to face, it was possible now to enjoy a kind of relief in finding themselves lodged in the heart of certainty, of being able to look at one another without lying now that they were aware of the gross ugliness of life.

It was not a single operation, but neither was it a single contract. The surgeons slowly carved up Leonor's face and the commercial interests slowly carved up the face of the prairie toward the northern subtropics. And one thing equaled the other.

The cards and steely scientific photos documenting the facial process arrived, marked by the same cutting precision as if they applied to bridges or cordage or sent up a hymn to engineering in a flood of song. Far but secure, attended by the flattering retinue of diplomats and their wives, Leonor felt that she was returning to life and said so with tenacious perseverance and the conviction of a convert. Other snapshots showed her with her new friends swathed in fur coats in the snow of Central Park, visiting Famous Places and living Unforgettable Moments.

Now he felt the relaxation, the slack and indulgent will of abandonment that she had tried to inspire in him before the journey. Leonor was running, at last, in confusion (and he would say, by a strange transference of the psychological and the visual, with her hair undone) down a long vaulted gallery of mirrors —*Les riches plafonds! Les miroirs profonds!*—while he, driven by the engulfing compromises that financed that trip for her cure (and not for a vacation), was probing into the misery of the country and laboring in the torment of his naked nerves, goaded by the guilty sense of his corruption.

. . . *Aux vagues senteurs de l'ambre.* Now he could translate it by the simple phonetic resemblance, as they had done foolishly, with the *Fleurs du Mal* in their hands, when they were first married so as not to feel like outsiders in that land of irredeemable poverty: in the vague odors of *hambre,* hunger. He was walking through the vague odors of alien hunger, tireless and melancholy, with his stock of nighttime sophistries and the vexation of his unquiet conscience. "They did it to me and they've got to pay me for it," he used to think with artful rationalization to exonerate himself temporarily, as it was easier to do at noon than at nightfall. "They ruined her, let them pay me back for her." But it was hard to find the guilt in those tame, almost stony faces, in their muddy eyeballs, on those lips where the green trickle of the chewed leaf dried, at the corners of the mouths that jiggled two little drops of wet emerald up and down. And it was even harder to imagine that Leonor (she of the enthusiastic, saucy postcards full of sociological chitchat on "the American way of life" and so many other travelogue items, she of the diary with remarks about people, places, and stagnant spots of introspection offered up for the admiration of her peers and the disgust of her husband) could be "restored" to him some day and would again be the same as before.

"Primitivo, what would have become of me without the *vital* (she underlined the word) perspectives this trip has opened up for me? I think some day it's going to be Europe for the two of us. Meanwhile, I congratulate myself on having escaped from my native hole, that little terra-cotta rut where we've lived for so long as though it were the World."

On reading this, he felt a tender loss, deception, *vital* trickery (as she would say); and he too might have noted in his diary, if it had ever occurred to him to keep one, a peculiar psychic experience: that of the husband forced to accept, for appearances and at a level beneath appearances, the supplanting of his wife while he pretended to regard her as one and the same. "A theme of Pirandello," as Rogelio Murano used to say about one situation or other. But this time it was true. The smiling stereotype of a face the New York surgeons were sculpturing for him was, definitely, a lesser change. The profound thing was that sense of alienation, the delirium of identity into which her cards plunged him.

He ought to have called her, asked her to shorten her trip, to limit it to the needs of her treatment. But he did not. At this same time Encarnación had appeared out of the depths of the ripped-up land, from the bottom of the little terra-cotta rut. And while Leonor lectured, on Christmas cards where best wishes were printed in English, he felt that his desire for that other woman, whom he had known at a remote outpost when she was a railway telegrapher and whom he had soon after made his secretary, was making him retrace a dark road that seemed to have closed over the last years, the road that was leading him to a dim prairie city and the days of his youth. The image of Ilse in her house with its flagstone patio had returned with an almost aggressive vigor, refreshing and easing his existence, carrying him back to that time of innocence when he thought he was treading the primrose path if he nibbled on a bunch of grapes.

Encarnación was coppery and strong, devoid of any poetry, with powerful haunches. There was no area of the imagination that would permit her to be sublimated or idealized. But she was the love, the light, and the embrace of the country; she restored a lost depth of dryness to the throat, a dark savor of earth to the mouth.

"Don't flatter me," she said. "I can't hope for it to last."

It didn't last, naturally, but it managed to be something, in its brevity, without deceitful promises. It was the same Encarnación who one day brought him the cable from the main office in charge of the sappers' work. "Papito," she said calmly, with a serene resignation that appeared almost joyous, "it's all over. It says here that your wife is coming home on Saturday."

And indeed she came home, with a smooth, tense face wearing a perpetual smile. She came home with a clear skin and eager eyes, with a beautiful English tweed suit, leather purse, and shoes such as she had never used before. She came home, offering him her newly made-up cheek, her newly perfumed face that had seemed to blaze on the plane's stepladder. She came home speaking with a carefully chosen variety of subjects according to the international standard of elegance. Everything struck her as fabulous, everything amused her, life itself seemed "funny" to her.

With time, however, the newness wore off, routine living imposed its imperceptible adjustments. Leonor, with her naked countenance and brilliant toothy grimace, went back to the parties that the bomb had made her desert, and she allowed the others to enjoy their share of strident novelty in her face, experience, and manners.

But at the end of a few months she withdrew into seclusion, feeling perhaps that she could not communicate the possibilities of life she had glimpsed, that she lacked the persuasiveness for it to be anything but ostentatiousness inspired by a powerful fascination, and recounted to people who could not approach its source. Primitivo thought at times that the very experience she boasted of had been a fraud and that the happiness that might free her far away had been only a novel kind of epistolary sublimation, salvation through writing, an extravagant disguise of the loneliness that had begun to grip her.

Pride, misery, and grief. That is what time had brought, for that face that once the waters had calmed was growing old without the defense of a sincere expression.

One night, reading Victor Hugo, she had come across the two lines which were to follow her for the rest of her days.

Car je n'ai vu qu' orgueil, que misère et que peine
Sur ce miroir divin qu'on nomme face humaine.

Pride, misery, and grief. Could he have written them looking at a face different from her own? Pride, misery, and grief: her whole life was beginning to fit in these three words, and they were taken up, in an indiscernible blending, by the tenseness of the features, the bitter and expressive freedom of the eyes, which were made to say something beyond the slavish and intimidated expression, more than the implicit violence of the unharmonious nostril, cheekbones, and mouth.

This is what would not change with the passing of time and would grow old in its own way, without weakening its disturbing unfamiliarity.

Pride, misery, and grief. Slowly the years were beginning to insinuate a truth between them, an unuttered word, and to reveal the cards that could not remain forever face down. The protective awareness of what her hard and sculptured expression conveyed to others curtailed for her any possibility of infidelity, of seeking in other men what she did not find in her husband, the thing that was beginning to die without hope of restoration and could be covered by the tips of one's fingers.

Had she once really loved him? He thought so, and he did not want to wonder for how long. But then he had gone in for openly showing his compassion, and she had responded with her compulsive Catholicism. And both had been more apparent than love. The lack of children was in a way the commentary, the form of the sterility that had grown up between them. Conjugal inertia, as he had said.

Pride, misery, and grief.

IV

At nightfall, the gray salon of the embassy, in which Primitivo read or signed his correspondence, took on a light violet
tint, which spread to the walls and shelves full of alien books
belonging to the mansion he had rented with its furniture and
library, spread to the pictures that, on the other hand, the tenant
had wished to be his own in that private room. His own and
not belonging to the duke who owned the house and who had
handed over his *palazzo* crammed with academic medallions, the
amber faces of his ancestors, accompanying his final inspection
with the emphatic praise of those great artists, "today deplorably
forgotten."

They were his own, yes, but he could not say that he had
chosen them entirely himself. For he had been joined at that
very moment by Carlos Ventura, sent to Rome years before with
a scholarship in fine arts and absorbed into the embassy in an
unofficial capacity as the ambassador's private counselor, artistic arbiter, secretary for various secret arrangements, from the
category of "deliveries" (whiskey, caviar, Sèvres porcelain, auto-
mobiles) to the one including the mistresses that his predecessors
had had and Primitivo had not. Ventura knew all those duchesses,
countesses, and marchionesses who inevitably got around to
latching onto the Latin American ambassadors, whose excessive
exoticism creates the superstition of a great deal of money that
they sometimes do not possess; more or less apocryphal duchesses,
countesses, and marchionesses, reduced to a miserable level of
subsistence—incapable, however, of curbing their arrogance or
spoiling their fine manners, which make them circulate like birds
of paradise among the quiet, stolid, and grim South Americans
who are slightly intimidated by the unpleasant and wise traditions
of that international court of miracles which those ladies substitute
for their improbable European court, today no longer in existence.
Until alcohol or desire releases a hidden spring of violence in
those *stranieri* and the birds of paradise succumb in the least

pompous way, auctioning off even the souvenirs of their nobility.

When he had drunk a few glasses—and instead of Ambassador he called Dr. Cortés *"jefecito,"* boss, or, even better, *"hefecito,"* because like all his compatriots he aspired the *j* to the point of changing it into an *h* or the sucking hollow of an indefinable letter—Ventura used to describe his function as a pimp at the embassy, his inglorious go-between arrangements in which he displayed the innate tact of the mestizo, refined now with the self-taught tricks of the sponger.

"To survive in Rome, *hefe,* has obliged me to get wise. The things we have to do!"

And perhaps he was being "wise" in just this way when he ran to his ambassador with his version of the very latest gossip or a recent discovery.

"Excellency," he would declaim on these occasions, "you have no idea who this guy is! Now he looks like any other failure in his little dump of a studio on Via Marguta, but next year he'll sell everything he's done higher than Bernard Buffet. They'll be grabbing it out of his hands!"

Ventura himself was a mediocre painter, and his talent for living was far superior to his artistic inspiration. In such a situation—could you believe him? He swore you could, that night after night he rubbed shoulders with people who knew—critics, painters, connoisseurs—and thus he was in with people who would be famous tomorrow. Thanks to this, he was able to arrange some good deals for his ambassador.

The little gallery that went from the gray salon to the salon of mirrors was filling up with those elusively noteworthy works acquired precisely in the moment before the full revelation of the artists' genius, the certain awakening of interest, the attainment of fabulous value. Ventura's taste and inclinations ranged from social propaganda paintings to abstract art with such eclectic naïveté that Primitivo never knew if he was exhausting himself in buying for its own sake or honestly encouraging a promising future. There were the paintings, in any case, with the lighting, direct or indirect, that Ventura had planned to bring out their best qualities. This other court of miracles was rarely exhibited to visitors; for it was obvious that the guests would praise them, partly through their Philistinism, partly through awareness of gratitude for the hospitality they had received.

"I could have had a Chirico or a Pougny instead of all these young unknowns," the ambassador would say then to make excuses. "But Carlos thinks one ought to help those who are just beginning."

And Carlos would get a weak and indecisive approval from the visitor, more for his act of charity with somebody else's checks than because of the assurance that he was making an early harvest of famous works.

And he was also representing, among others, "the powerful and evocative Carlos Ventura, with the dramatic eye and cruel hand of a naked America," as some agreeable critic had said, whom Ventura pretended to consider of no importance.

As a matter of fact, he did not compensate for the acquisition of his oils with the canvases themselves but in supplying other needs: his artistry with meat pies in broth and hot sauce and the best *paellas* that could be eaten in Rome; and in this department he received enthusiastic eulogies from Americans and Europeans who had burned their mouths and praised him while they scratched their scalps between gulps of red wine.

"I came with the illusion everybody has," he would say cynically. "To be exhibited in the great capitals of the world. And it appears that I'm going to triumph some day not in the art of Picasso but in that of Brillat-Savarin."

"In that and in buying porcelains," Leonor used to correct him affectionately.

"And in playing the guitar," the most devoted guest added to occasion a request from the others.

When drinking had already awakened his native melancholy —that modest article we occasionally export—Ventura would make an almost imperceptible sign to Massimo, and a second later the guitar would be cradled in his arms, as though—stiff and turgid—it had been waiting for him behind the door of the dining room.

He would strum to arouse favorable anticipations of the treat
and force out his voice, always in the notes of the same melody,
monotonous, nostalgic, persistent.

> *I've asked to be buried*
> *Sitting up when I die,*
> *So people will say,*
> *He died but he's waiting for you.*

The weak little voice, poured out over a drone of alcoholic
hoarseness, in its trance of irresponsible judgment, coffee,
cigars, and liqueurs, possessed an evocative quality, a cloying
note of melancholy or a sudden outburst of extravagant boasting,
and—as the most insidiously persistent characteristic—an avowed
affection for poverty, which insinuated and threatened until one's
stomach was almost ready to do penance.

"If the *hefe* goes back some day and they kick me out of here,
I'll set up a little shop in the Termini and deal in meat pies and
Andean folklore," Ventura would say, his broad mulatto grin
stretching from ear to ear, so that his short even teeth came into
view. "One has to live. What things we have to do!"

But even at these moments Primitivo felt that he was—as he
had once written with youthful pedantry—*au carrefour des deux
chemins*. His very memories of America, native to that earth as
they might seem, alluded somehow to Europe and, even in the
instant when they had been actuality, had prophesied Europe
somehow as the life and appetite of their body.

While Ventura was singing those virile and dusty songs, re-
frains of the wilderness, fatality, and tragic events, he found himself returning to the time when he was seventeen and to the city
of the plains where he was born, grew up, and where his mother,
over eighty now, still lived.

He was small and thin, an insignificant—but demagogically
pure—virgin boy when he met Ilse. It had been at a Saturday
night party at the German Club, and after a eulogistic introduc-
tion to the assembled people he read a poem in which the sun
was served up in slices and the moon decapitated over the blue
pulverization of the rocks. Ilse approached him and without beat-

ing around the bush invited him to come to her house the next
night. She was twenty-four and seemed a hard person, enviably
secure, shockingly free and easy as she circled around the cautious and aloof young man, whose biological timidity was perhaps the only thing that stimulated her to passive seduction. In
this way he could think he had made a conquest of her; he
knew today, with a twilit enjoyment, both tender and distant,
that he had merely been her captive.

Ilse ushered him into a little drawing room full of snapshots,
with a bronze round table loaded with pipes and souvenirs of
Paris—*mein geliebtes Paris*—looking down at her from all the
corners of the little room. Heydel, Ilse's husband, was a mining
engineer, notoriously superior to her, notoriously bored, notoriously inclined to go off to sleep as soon as he finished his
tobacco.

They remained alone, and she overwhelmed him with dangerous and daring flirtation, which consisted of pretending he was
a child and putting candy in his mouth. The phonograph whined
out a French song while she felt his lips with the tips of her
fingers, which lingered provocatively in the act of feeding him.

When Heydel went back to the mine and Ilse persisted in feeling alone in the house and the city, both of them flat and vast
and colonial, Primitivo began to see her there almost every night.

Then she invited some melancholy foreigners, who were com-
pelled to be of few words and who arrived at the gathering with
their crude muddy shoes and sat on the floor of the little drawing room, propping themselves against gold-tasseled and gold-
bordered hassocks which Ilse scattered artistically around all the
corners.

Toward the end of that winter Ilse, almost without consulting them, introduced the ritual of the grape clusters. The crowd
was the largest, and she had moved them out on the patio with
its white and black flagstones, surrounded by a Roman arcade
soothingly decorated with tropical plants that stiffened in the
shapes of open fingers in the congealing drowsiness of the
night. There too the captious exiles would recline on cushions and

smoke, watching the distant night sky of that dry, merciless summer.

In sight of them all, Ilse filled a silver tray with enormous, beautiful muscatel grapes, slightly tarnished in the glow of the lanterns that lighted the corners of the patio.

Then she had the little smoking table brought out and placed the tray on it. Bending over it, with a syringe in her hand, she injected each grape with a little ether, just the right amount. It seemed a world of unknown refinements to a country boy who knew only those of literature.

When she had finished the injections, Ilse covered the grapes with finely cracked ice which Lutz, the most devoted of the wandering Germans, had been chopping during the ether operation, conscientiously hammering the bigger chunks wrapped up in a kitchen towel.

Naked and without sensuality, Ilse, Primitivo, and the foreigners would slowly concentrate on the grapes. They would pass their fingers over them to flake off the fine frost granulating over them. When they bit into them, the whiff of ether spread around the mouth. Seven, eight, or ten fleshy grapes were enough for Primitivo to begin to feel himself splendidly released from the body that bound him to the earth and from the proximity of the languid and silent revelers who were despondent even in the leisurely fulfillment of pleasure, desperately despondent because of something autumnal and Germanic that he would never be able to figure out.

Then he would feel Ilse's arm beside him, tracing out signs of her impudence and affection rather than a lustful invitation, and the frugal paradise of her presence.

Ilse and the grapes went on until that night, toward the end of March, when Primitivo introduced René Oteyza, his friend from the humanities class, into the group. René was a couple of years older than Primitivo, and that gave him an insolent right not to be surprised at anything, and to lie to the effect that, in those two years between them, he had tried everything. He claimed he was a sportsman, bragged excessively, and abounded in the weaknesses of a delayed and extroverted adolescence.

He pretended he was repeating something he knew, indulging for the second time what he had already tried. He took a cluster of grapes and shoved it greedily into his mouth, drinking in the ether with a burst of laughter that went against the convention.

But then, when he had chewed the grapes, he began to turn pale, fumbled for the cushions, slipped from the position he had taken, sprawling insecurely in a way that was meant to be striking, and ended up lying on the bare flagstones.

"It's a heart attack," Lutz pronounced with the hostility of disillusionment. "He can die."

"Yes," Ilse said, slightly titillated. "He's a stupid kid, a know-it-all. What ever made you bring us a creature like that?"

Primitivo was frightened, seeing René contorted and lifeless, beyond the anger he aroused. Then Primitivo dressed hastily—pants, jacket, shoes without socks—and ran to look for a doctor.

When he returned with him and crossed the darkened house at a run, accidentally kicking the cushions—that jungle full of cushions that seemed to come to life in the deserted rooms, dancing in disjointed and motley profusion like a chaos of enormous green rats—René already had a grin on his mouth and around his lips the ashen color of a man suffering cyanosis.

The doctor must have been shocked to see that woman and those men who had forgotten to dress to wait for him. And he must have told about it in the Cortés household.

A few nights afterward, when Primitivo returned, she received him alone, with a pale face, circles around her eyes, which were wet and red in her dry, tear-swollen countenance.

She took a fistful of bills—they were dollars—from her purse and showed them to him without displaying them.

"If you want," she said, "we'll go away from here."

"Where?" he asked, and he really wanted to ask: "Why?"

"Paris, anywhere. But right now, early tomorrow. Yes or no?"

He knew why he had not had the courage: his mother was still living, past eighty, in the provincial city, the old house, at the heart of the devastated plain. She would not have gone on living there—and perhaps in no other spot on earth—if he had run away.

He felt futile, cowardly, immature before that determined woman in her cold desperation who wanted to give up everything: Heydel, the house with the tropical patio, the world of relations who, for her, sprouted at the mouth of some obscure mine, not the one her husband managed. He felt empty, inconsistent, trivial; and he avoided seeing her for the rest of the time (a few months) that she went on staying there. Ilse, who received his silence as an irrevocable answer, also did nothing, made not the slightest gesture to seek him out, to insist, to tell him that she still waited for him. This studied inactivity was proper to her sense of dignity.

Where was she now, what had happened to her? Might he not pass her sometimes without recognizing her, in the Via Veneto at noon, on the Corso in the evening, would she not still feel that expansive southern love, at once ardent and hazy, which she had told him she felt for him and which—he had learned this in time—is the love Nordics feel for Italy, that adulterated sentiment full of climate, sun, chianti, a glow of oranges?

At that time he had the splendor of youth, the sap of animal beauty that redeems the adolescence of the ugly. Something had already begun to dry up inside him, but Ilse could not have been aware of it. He recalled her face, hardened at twenty-four, the clear eyes, the arms that took the initiative in love. The day she proposed that they run away an erosion of discouragement seemed to settle darkly on her features, gnawing and drowning and consuming them. Wouldn't the intervening years have completed the work of that moment of sudden aging?

Such memories always ended by bringing him back to his childhood. It might have been because in this way he could return to the child he had been before he met Leonor, return to a realm from which he could draw images, evocations, and recollections that belonged to him alone.

But they were always the same: his only sister dead at eight in Buenos Aires—he could never imagine her last painful day, which he had not seen and which they had told him about much later, linked to the word "nephritis," which sounded to him like something from the history of Egypt; his mother, who had gone on living in the ancestral house when his father had already gone off to the capitol to occupy his first legislative post; the grand aunt, who had read every book she could get hold of in that forsaken desert and who talked of the heroes of Balzac as though they were her next-door neighbors. She had died one day, at almost eighty, with all her sails spread. During the whole morning he had read pages to her from the Old Testament and Saint John of the Cross. And toward evening, when she already felt that she was dying, she called his mother, who was her favorite niece, and asked her to play Liszt's *Funérailles* on the piano. And so, surrounded by pillows, music, and nieces and nephews, she died, sitting up, delighted and smiling.

Today, at sixty-two, Primitivo knew very well he would never write that sort of family saga, that novel he had planned for some day on the material presented by the Cortés and Morillo clans. He had thought of making it go back as far as colonial days, pass through the time of independence and come up to its present days of weakness, the dilapidation of the estates, the expropriations for oil. In some drawer the note pads for the first three chapters were lying with the definitive title for that long story, which descended from epic to litany: *And then they rested*. It was he himself, in his little embassy office, who rested now for them.

The world of affections had gone on diminishing around him: time had brought him deaths, not lives. Forgetfulness blurred more and more the tintypes that surrounded him and to which he lifted his eyes less and less often. And the books he was doing research in—American archaeology, military histories of the Conquest and the revolutionary wars for independence—what did they have to do with the country in which he lived, with this Italy that he might prefer on the day when he knew it was time for him to close his eyes for good?

Therefore *The Aborigines* was the penance he had taken on himself toward the end. He had to return to his perplexed pages.

And he himself, what was he if God's work in him could be considered finished? The mestizo character that accentuated his features as the years passed, the body that surely contained, as others had said of Darío, "a few drops of the local red-skin or watered-down pickaninny," did they mean that he was a recessive, did he embody some mystery of crossbreeding that had been zealously buried since the days of colonial servitude, some biological accident that no one knew or that no one had wanted to tell him, nor he to ask about.

Leonor too had gone along half-nourished by alien lives, in a different style, which had made her lose sight of the human scale, the proportion of natural feelings. And that was how she had come to recount the illnesses of Louison with a prolixity that a father rarely employs to tell of the brief and alarming illnesses of his only son.

The visitor was sitting opposite Primitivo, one to the right, one to the left of Leonor, who sat at the head of the table. Two servants fluttered ceaselessly around them so unobtrusively that their presence was not annoying; with the scruple of never letting a glass be half-filled, they managed it so that only the long necks of the Rhine wine bottles or the dark throats of the burgundy observed the conversation.

"When Louison came down with the meningitis that left him with that tic, I thought I'd go mad," Leonor explained.

Louison was not a child but a lame sheepdog asleep beside the fire, who would suddenly shake his limp fur in flurries, as though to frighten away non-existent flies.

"Do you know what this woman did?" Primitivo said then, displaying his visible sympathy for her action with a comic flourish of his hands and a slight arching of his brows. "Well, she called a friend of ours, a pediatrician, and asked him to cure the dog."

"And he wasn't angry, absolutely not. Imagine, those were the days when we had to leave for New York, because they were sending Primitivo to the United Nations. We had to postpone the trip for a week and finally we made it by train and ship, because Louison couldn't have gone in a plane, weak and convalescing as he was."

At this point the visitor felt guilty for having provoked the kind of confidence that was now flooding him, only for having said —casually, without foreseeing or promising to share aberrant attachments—that he too loved dogs.

"While we were driving through the United States in the station wagon that the ambassador in Washington loaned us, we didn't have any problems. Because we stopped for the night at motels, and there we drove in with the car and made Louison jump out once we were in the garage."

"But in New York it was a different matter," Primitivo explained, always with the countersign of an expression to indicate his share of common sense in a story in which he too had played a role. "There we had to take a suite at the Waldorf, because it was the only place where they would let Louison lodge with us and have his meals on time."

"And when we had to go from there to Italy, according to the arrangement, the great tragedy took place," Leonor added, belying the size of her words as she had done before with her feelings. "None of the ships would allow Louison in a stateroom like everybody else, because they said they had a kennel in the hold. Louison, prostrate as he was, would have died of sadness in the bilge or the promiscuity of the other dogs. Just imagine!"

The verb had no imperative sense. The visitor absolutely couldn't imagine anything, because they were telling it as the most natural thing in the world.

"Finally," Primitivo abridged, "we met a Greek captain who was to take a one-class ship from New York to the south of Italy. He agreed to rent us two staterooms, for an extra charge. But, so as not to miss the ship, we had to take it before I was in possession of my diplomatic credentials. And we had to disembark at Naples though it's almost traditional for ambassadors to land at Genoa. How they must have hated us for these deviations from the Holy Routine!"

And Louison, from his place beside the fire, stretched out one of his hands, rubbed his nose against it, and affectionately directed a loving glance toward his masters—should one say "toward his parents"?—to show them that he was not unaware of the troubles he had caused them and to assure them that the knowledge of their trials strengthened the doggy passion of gratitude in his crippled body.

"That's why revolutions are fought in South America," Ventura used to say when he was among his Italian painter friends, and wine had stimulated what was most candid and heartless in him. "So a pair of nitwits can finance the voyage of a stupid dog in a de luxe stateroom."

The Revolution had not been fought for that, obviously. But the Revolution had not known what to do with Primitivo Cortés, that barnacle glued to his rock. He had gone on transmigrating (as from men to dogs) for years now, from his country to foreign parts, foreign parts that engulfed and tormented him, in his readings, thoughts, even his dreams, even while he was trying to make revolutionary speeches (which demanded all his oratorical skill) in the interregnum that had come between embracing Cándido Lafuente and the journey to New York, then Italy. He had often been tempted to write in his essays phrases like "the drama of the cultivated classes, the isolation and the lack of communication of the elite in this our Spanish America"; but it had seemed unpatriotic to affirm it just because his feelings proclaimed it. It was the reverse of that phrase popular with the generation of his youth: "The Culture bequeathed by France," which also had to be filed away because it had been mocked by the following generation, the one guided by the esthetes of nationalism.

He had wanted to deceive himself by accepting the illusion that it was his guilt of disbelief that had brought him to serve the new order. But it was not. It was his wish to expatriate himself, to let others expatriate him and give him (out of the misery of the impoverished country) the sinecure of an ambassadorship without any duties at all and send him forth to sail the seas with Leonor's face and Louison's meningitis. That was what it was.

And "that" had to end some day, end or have the bottom fall out of it some morning like any other, at the hour of breakfast and newspapers.

The secretary came in without any apparent emotion (he was a career diplomat), carrying in his hand the cable he had just decoded.

"Excellency," he said in the most neutral voice. "Serious news."

Without taking off the spectacles with which he was going over the *Messagero*, Primitivo read: "President Lafuente assassinated by aroused mob on the steps of Palace. Colonel Gaudencio has situation in hand and assumes power. Await instructions."

The four hours' difference suggested that it might have happened yesterday and that Cándido's blood might already be dry on the steps of the Palace in the morning sun.

He called Leonor and handed her the paper without warning her of the contents. She suffered a brief spasm of weeping and then regained control of herself. Primitivo thought he would have to telephone the Quirinale and inform the authorities in the Ministry. But a strange kind of weakness—the same as at Obrajes—held him back, tense and motionless, in the armchair where the news had paralyzed him.

"Lafuente assassinated by aroused mob." It was not very hard to imagine who had been arousing them. Nor was it very hard to believe that this was a farewell message from the chief minister, his between-the-lines accusation before resigning his post. "Await instructions." Surely it would be some new Minister of Foreign Affairs, a friend of Gaudencio, who would be giving them to him.

But now pity was winning out over self-interest. And he thought of Cándido, with his violent, spasmodic laugh, his friendly cruelty with all his teeth showing, his brutal outbursts of affection, the sudden silences into which he sometimes fell, his gruff sincerity that could insult professors, industrialists, the natty flunkies who served those industrialists; his heroic volubility in insulting them and then, in a half hour, eating and drinking unconcernedly with them, without the slightest care for appearances or for life.

"Well, old man," he remembered Lafuente saying when they parted, "you're going and I'm staying in this racket, and it's getting uglier all the time. You've really got the luck!"

The difference in luck was measured by the distance that existed between this armchair and the window looking out on the Roman noon and the blood people had walked in on the steps of the Palace, opposite the Plaza de Armas. It was measured by the difference between a life and a death, each equally useless.

He thought of the rivers of the country, which Cándido had sailed as a child, living in huts precariously erected over the frame of logs being hurled downstream. He thought of the jungle, where Cándido had so often scorned the possibility of sudden death and conquered it by ignoring it. He thought of the battles on the sandbanks, which had tattooed his body in his youth, the drunken carouses that had filled the idle hours of the battalion, the suicidal games with revolver and horse those carouses had led to, the study balcony where he had wanted to go forth to meet death. All that so that now, when he was almost sixty, they could assassinate him—the cable didn't say how—on the steps of the Palace, surely (according to the date) while he was walking out for the Te Deum, the patriotic mass in the cathedral, which was only twenty-five yards from the Palace, door to door, for the far ends of the steps and the cathedral porch almost touched.

The country was in that fury of knives, shots, deaths in the countryside, in those surprise attacks of death, like ritual celebrations of patriotism, the country was there more than in the lack of communication of the elite. In that easy possibility of stirring up the people with a calamity and driving them to seek justice in the name of the last speech that had inspired them, in that fluidity through which crime might come into the game even without being called for, there too was "this our Spanish America," more than in the studious solitude of those who demanded an enlightened Sorbonne all of a sudden in the gorge between two mountains.

He saw then that Leonor was drawing near the burned-out fireplace, carrying in her hand the candlestick of blest wood which Cándido had given her before they said good-by "as a token of esteem"; it was identical to two others, which he kept in the Palace and which now, perhaps, were serving tremulously at each side of the dark head.

She placed it on the mantel and, in the same sunglow which canceled it out, made it vanish, she lit it.

Primitivo saw her and held back; although he clearly understood, he made no comment on the pious sentiment of such homage, the absurdity of that glittering and indistinct candle beneath the glories of the Roman noontide.

Leonor remained staring at what she had just done, as though she had placed a crown at the foot of a grandee and had forgotten the rest of the ritual, the awkward and never codified epilogue to those ceremonies that end as soon as they begin.

Dully she turned around, as if unmindful of what she had done and without transition, faced Primitivo and said: "Now she'll have to choose between two roles."

Since there had grown up between them a silence that took no tacit communication for granted, Leonor was accustomed to conclude her inner reflections often with isolated sentences, uttered aloud and unintelligible to her husband. He had never been able to convince her that she should not come out of her own isolated silence with unrelated sentences of this sort, which remained floating in a region of childish mystery. This time, however, he thought he understood her. But to maintain principles he asked: "Who?"

"Clarita," she said with an ingenuousness that shed little light.

"Between what two roles?" he insisted, obviously now.

"A martyr's widow or an influential sister."

"But," Primitivo inquired, to figure out the ever-shaky basis for a woman's suppositions, especially his wife's, "do you think there's any reason to suppose that Gaudencio may in any way have been behind Cándido's assassination?"

This time it was she who did not want to understand.

"The two roles will be offered to her in any event," she said. "Either she withdraws to weep or she tries to govern."

"Gaudencio shouldn't be easy to manage," Primitivo ventured.

"He's unrefined and his wife's very coarse. Clarita is different, and she's his oldest sister."

While he imagined the two lignum vitae candlesticks shining on Cándido's oily temples, his dirty battered face, Primitivo thought again of the man's death and the excess of unconsumed life that had led to it. He remembered how innocently, without taking it as a joke, Cándido would listen to the theory of these who *die on,* which Rogelio Murano liked to repeat—and elaborate every time he repeated it.

"When there's a cataclysm, an accident, a catastrophe, everybody talks about those who live on," Rogelio would say. "As if they were the ones who violently usurped a destiny different from their true one. And the opposite happens. The survivors simply go on being what they were. So why not think of those who "die on," who were full of a life which should have gone on developing for them and which is suddenly cut off? These are the truly violent ones, violent without guilt and without a hell."

Cándido—Primitivo thought—was a typical *out-dier.* It was possible to imagine the half glass of wine he had left on the table, the half-smoked cigar; it was inevitable to think of the interrupted enjoyment that ought to have continued, because all of him was full of a capacity for pleasure that work and responsibilities alone could unsettle and defer but never destroy. He thought with affectionate envy of the strength of nature that had been cut off, the mestizo whom the world of physical possibilities for enjoyment seemed to have kept young, the comatose and prophetic drunkard who one night wanted to throw himself off a balcony because the country and its sons were locked in and had no way out.

Leonor had drawn the curtains of the room and now offered to Primitivo her profile, which was barely etched by the light of the candle, and the refraction from her arm, stretched out to touch the edge of the fireplace mantel.

He saw her, sensed his own immobility, felt the bones of his body lying on the chair. "Others die often for us. But that's occasionally the most deceptive form of our own death," he thought.

To dispel the silence, and as on some other days in his past when he had suffered an overwhelming deprivation, he tried to be mordant and impartial.

"My dear," he said, "I'm afraid we two, like the nation, are going to be involved *dans un gros déménagement.*"

But he found himself confronted by the grimace of so many years, more careworn, humble and human than he could have hoped. It was no longer the lovely face with wide-open eyes who imbibed verses of Baudelaire against the balustrade of Don Lucho Otero's horrible art-nouveau palace. Grayer, earthier, discouraged, and almost mummified, it was the face that had followed him during these last years, which summoned him now not to make his escape by means of trickery.

Then, without being aware of how it rose to his lips, his voice broke out in the throaty, slightly singsong Spanish that he had heard spoken from childhood and that had been buried under heavy layers of pilgrimage and culture:

"Well then, swee-et, what's going to become of us now?"

—Translated by DAVID RUBIN

NAUSICAA
by Alfonso Echeverría

ALFONSO ECHEVERRÍA, a thirty-nine-year-old Chilean author, belongs to a family of writers. During the last World War he spent two years in the United States working in dairy plants. In Chile he has at one time or another owned a small foundry, engaged in farming. and taught in a secondary school. At present he is a free-lance simultaneous interpreter. His first novel *La vacilación del tiempo* (The Hesitation of Time) was published in 1957. *El costo de la vida* (The Cost of Living), a book of poems, was published in 1959.

Because she was so tall, she wore sandals. In search of the letter that had gone astray, she had climbed up the stairway of the old Post Office building. And among rat-eaten mail sacks had talked to courteous postmen, who were unable to help her.

"Letters seldom get lost in the mails," they would tell her. "Unless they have the wrong address. . . ." And perhaps they were right. Had she written Monjitas or had she written Merced? After three months in Chile she would still mistake one street for the other.

They were both in her part of town, however. She rented a room on the top floor of a dark, drab building, looking out on the near-by hill. She could see the city's housetops from there. And she thought with longing of the days when that same hill was called Huelén, the days when the river spread out its arms to embrace it. But the good Chilean citizens had festooned it with walls and breastworks until it looked like a wedding cake; then they had renamed it Santa Lucía. It was the big urinal of the city of Santiago.

When would she begin to understand this country, to capture its elusive secret . . . so much more intriguing than that of the letter. But the others blamed her. She had broken the chain, that kind of game they liked so much. "Do you really think you may have written Mercy?" "Bet you Freud could explain that!" Truly at times her countrymen could become exasperating.

She would have liked to be left alone, unveiling the mystery of this country. But week by week she had to go with them on what the office called an orientation trip. They went in groups to various "typical places." A trip to El Teniente ("the largest underground copper mine in the world"). A trip to the coast. Another to Chillán. Another to Pomaire. A visit to Viña Undurraga. The female professors in their missionary shoes, the men with their optical gadgets and pornographic cameras, they all trooped onward, eager to learn and anxious to reform, but scarcely interested in simply *seeing*. That function was delegated to their cameras. Once captured, the scene could be shown later at home.

"Good place for a date," one professor said to another, on going through the winy corridors of an old cellar. And quietly she evoked the much more desolate and monstrous meaning she had seen attributed to that very wine . . . wine that was shouting like a dead animal, gushing out in the cellars like a bull's organ.[1] Would they ever understand this America's sullenness?

One part of the program consisted in exchanging impressions, and this was the chain she had broken. Each student was asked to write his comments on a special form and send it to the next during the day. This circular letter became a sort of group report that was used for future projects. "It's fun," they all said. And they tried to follow the rules of the games.

She would go then, that very evening, to recover the letter. But now she wanted to be quiet. Lying next to the chest where she kept her clothing, she gazed at a large Virgin by Cimabue, at something in her rather awkward that gave her comfort. And she thought of the old bootblack she had seen in the corner, sitting by his display of six or seven newspapers and eating a

---

[1] A reference to "Theogony and Cosmology of the Cookbook" by the contemporary Chilean poet Pablo de Rokha:

> . . . a stream of wine is shouting, is flowering under the
> subways, is shouting, shouting like a dead
> animal, shouting
> and showing Immortality its bull's organ.

bowl of "mote" his wife had brought him. There—or there-abouts—the secret lay. And maybe with compassion one could find it. The cat that climbed up to her window and the pigeons that kept drumming on the rooftop were a sort of confirmation. She was on the right course. She had sensed it in the old Post Office building. She had sensed it in the tomblike library, when seated on a narrow bench among poorly dressed students, in a room lacking light, lacking windows. The poetry she had come to study was still too harsh to her, and the Chilean style too dusty. But she was getting closer to its substance.

That evening there was a drizzle. She climbed up the narrow staircase of Merced 180. Steps led to an open door. Gently she knocked, peeping into the dark. Someone moved inside. She was blinded by a flashlight.

"I'm after a letter I sent here by mistake."

Drawing a curtain, the man let daylight in. But it was too faint to drown the flashlight.

"Yes," he said. "They slid a letter under the door." He began to search in a trunk. "I don't remember where I left it."

His shirt was peeled as if by sunburn. From boards and easels came a throb of color. And in a jar the brushes grew, like plants.

"Won't you sit. . . ." He gestured toward a couch. "Or help me find the letter." He looked at her from the floor, casting his light upon her silent figure.

The woman smiled. "Why don't you turn another light on?"

"The fuses burned out several days ago."

"Mean to say you're in the dark since then?"

The man was silent. "Since before that," he said. "But why did you send me that letter?"

"I didn't mean to. The address was Monjitas and I wrote Merced." She glanced at the glass panes, milky with dirt. "Never mind if you can't find it. We'll try to make another."

He was still crouching. Thick drops now drifted down the sloping window. "It's raining," she said. "I'm sorry to have both-ered you." She started to leave. But near the door she was stopped by an explosion. The flashlight was shining on brilliant violet mingled with green.

"Don't leave," he said, still aiming his flashlight at the painting. From his squatting posture he seemed to be directing a scene. He was ordering that rather crazy mime to speak on his behalf.

"Why not?" she asked.

"Because you're needed here." He stood up and stretched out his hand to her.

"If there were only more light," she said. In his voice she had noticed something broken, a mixture of command and supplication.

"Come and see these pigments. . . ." He shed the light on the stained chaos of a board, its round fat worms of paint.

"I'd rather see your paintings," she said.

"The life is here though. See that black, that clean bright red; that brown, like fresh dung."

"Have you been painting for long?"

He had sat on the divan and was covering the flashlight with his hand, illuminating his blood. "Just for one month. And my paintings are no good, really."

"Why do you paint then?" said the girl. There was a smile in her voice.

"What else can I do? That trunk is full of letters I used to write. Now I think that when writing I was actually painting."

"Aren't they different things?" She sat down beside him.

"I guess so, yes. Colors are aphonic. Sort of voiceless vowels. Yet there is some resemblance. And you . . . what brought you to Chile?"

"I came here to study," she said.

"And have you learned much?"

She looked at him suspiciously. "I know the city, but I don't . . . quite understand it. I don't know where to start."

"One must start with poverty. Understand the *pelusas*[2] and their dogs. Everything grows out of this great misery."

[2] *"Pelusas":* wretched, homeless children who live on the Mapocho riverbed.

"I suppose you're Chilean?"

"Yes, I guess so. Every time I get here I'm sunk in a black-out. That's a sign it's my homeland, no doubt."

"I see you've left the receiver off the phone. Do they bother you much?"

"I don't know anyone here. But they could call a wrong number."

"Or send letters to the wrong address. . . ."

"I'm happy you wrote Merced." He let the light drift over the floor. "And there's your letter, by the way. I can tell by the round handwriting."

She moved to pick it up, shuddering slightly at the sight of a sunburst of splinters she saw on the wall, in passing.

"Look how it's raining," he said, opening the window. "Rain is hopeless, hopeless. . . ." He had turned his back to her now, ignoring her presence completely.

"I have to leave now," she said.

"I'll see you home," he said absent-mindedly.

"Thanks, I live near-by." And once again they stood in silence.

"I'll see you home," he said after a while, wandering toward the staircase like a sleepwalker.

"You haven't asked me if I want you to," she said in the street, reaching out for the door handle he was opening.

"The other side is unlocked," he said gently. And the switch key turned a tiny light on. "Now we're leaving. The night's too damp for us to stay here."

Slowly the car plowed its way up the flooded avenue.

"You don't know where I live," she said. "It's in just the opposite direction."

He looked at her tenderly. The sad-eyed traffic lights did not seem to oppose their progress.

"Let's drive away from here," he said. And he went on driving at a lazy pace. The city seemed deserted.

"You're driving through the red lights! Good thing there are no policemen out tonight!"

But he was absent, unheeding.

"It's like sailing down a river, isn't it?"

She would have liked to resist, to withstand and direct him. But barefoot rain was like a humble lesson in passivity. And even the damp lights among the trees—round, red, tender—conspired in favor of tolerance.

"You must be very happy," she said softly, "disregarding the world the way you do." And to herself she added, with a shiver: "Maybe madness is just that. . . ."

"There are things I miss, though," he said, glancing at her. The car had stopped with almost tender caution.

"What kind of things, for instance?"

"Things like those the moon gives to vagabonds."

In the new-found quiet, their voices had taken a calm, more intimate tone. They were protected from heaven's downpour by this moving capsule. And all the night dissolving, melting, falling over and around them.

"What kind of things?" she pleaded.

"Things like these," he said. "Things on one's neck, one's throat, one's face." And there on the precarious verge of his raving he held her tender face, that had loomed larger and closer, and bent it softly backward, tilting the summit with its murmuring crater. "Things on one's mouth," he said, kissing her. "Things like this, like this"; and he tried to catch between his lips that breath made of berries, lust, tobacco.

"I'm afraid," she said, raising her incredibly long, cold fingers to touch his forehead. But cigarette smoke had left its trace in her lungs—the faint, persuasive fragrance of transgression—and her lips were warm and tender.

Rain glided down the windshield, and its motion was reflected on her face, sprinkling it with non-existent water. In phantom, smooth caresses the wiper washed the freckles off again.

He had grasped a mountain. He had climbed to its summit. Not so easily would he let her go. "I need to be rescued," he had told her. "I want you to help me save myself."

And stopping the car where she said she lived he saw her walk across the darkened sidewalk and saw her slip into a narrow, damp, somber alley.

"I'm engaged to be married," she had said on the way home. "I was engaged before I left for Chile. We'll be married in November, when my grant is up." But that—compared with her promise that she would come back to see him—was not important.

And so she did . . . come back. She showed up in blue, two or three days after the rainstorm.

"I came to say good-by," she said. He looked at her in silence. "I don't think we should go on seeing one another. It doesn't take us anywhere."

She was standing there without a pedestal, fortified by the cool serenity of intelligence. The neckline had been cut between her shoulders as by an arc of compass. It neatly freed her head from the woolen mesh that sheathed her body.

"So you came at last . . . I don't know what I would have done if this had lasted any longer." He let himself down on the couch beneath the window.

She looked at the silver stubble of his several-day beard. He was older than she had thought he was.

"I want to see your paintings again." She put her finger to a canvas. "They're so violent . . . yet controlled. For some odd reason they make me happy."

She saw him watching her through his dark eyes. It was getting hard to leave him. And looking out at the park. . . .

"How strange the trees in the park look!" she said. The trunks were almost naked, with only a few splotches of bark. "They look like burned arms. . . ."

He smiled faintly. "I had thought that too," he said.

"Really?"

Her face held such wonderment that he felt an urge to get up.

"I want you to stay," he said. "At least during this winter I want to be quite sure you're real."

"Do you . . . kind of doubt it?"

"Not right now, no. However, when I'm alone, what you leave behind is rather . . . intangible."

"You know, you frighten me," she said, stroking his eyebrow with her fingertips.

"You frighten me too, thank God. What would one do without a little awe?"

"Trouble is it isn't just a little. It's a lot."

"Yes, thank God, a lot. That's what makes it hard to quit."

"You make me think you're crazy. I find you so . . . strange. But . . . you know? I trust you. That's what counts, of course."

He kissed her hand. "Why don't you fix us some tea?" he said. "You'll find everything you need out back. Tea will help us think more calmly."

She hesitated. "That's almost a housewife's chore. . . ."

"All the better then."

The hum and smell of kerosene gave the room an air of refuge.

"Do you like your tea with sugar?"

"I'd like a slice of lemon; makes it look clearer. But I don't think there's any left."

"We'll use an orange then. There's one on that desk."

She squeezed a few drops into the brass-colored brew.

"I'm happy you're back," he said. "I've got so much I want to say to you."

"You've never even asked me who I am. Not even my name or my nationality or my mother tongue."

"Those are mere accidents of fate. They wouldn't change the truth I know about you. As for your mother tongue, all I can say for sure is that it can't be more lovely than your Spanish. You seem to be *discovering* the words you utter. You pronounce them so clearly, with a kind of childlike wonder, as if you were still outside, still on the brink of our language. You give to it the grace and innocence it has lost in use."

"Now about the name. . . ." He stood up and walked to the window. The empty cup he thrust onto his finger by the handle, and with this ring on the back of his hand he made a gesture of uncertainty. "There are lots of names I could give you. . . . But none of them so pure, so elemental and so true as Nausicaa."

"Homer's?"

"No, Ulysses'. She found him when he had lost his ship and crew, found him sleeping in the dead leaves 'like an ember in the ashes.' Ulysses had been shipwrecked—she saved his life. And do you know how she happened to find him?"

"She was playing with her friends and. . . ."

". . . and the ball got lost. Like your letter."

"How strange," she said, smiling.

"It would be only a coincidence if that was all there was to it. There are so many things in common . . . you'd shudder at the power of myth if only you knew them. I just want to tell you that Nausicaa was blue, like you this evening. And that despite her youth (she was the youngest of Ulysses' lovers) he told his story to her only."

"And what did he do with the others?" she asked gently.

"That belongs to the myth. Some day I'll tell you if I remember. Meanwhile you should know that you're Nausicaa and that you found him in the shrubs, not long ago, when playing."

That evening they decided to postpone their final parting, so putting an end to the anxiety of a precarious friendship. But the frequency of their meetings did not abate the feeling of unbelief which for reasons to them unknown she had the power to stir in him. "Truth is incredible; only the commonplace is always obvious," he would say to himself; but that did not dispel his wonder. When, talking over the phone, he could hear her breathing, he marveled at the wire's ability to deliver a smile that was only breath. . . .

And at the appointed hour he would see her come, almost barefoot, from afar. Because even at a distance she looked tall, she swept away visual habits, she seemed to shatter size-space relationships. And this catastrophe she could unleash in optics came over him like a great relief.

Often she would come from the Mapocho River, her eyes the ambiguous color of its moss-lined stones. Her tender look would speak to him of poverty, of children that live beneath the bridges, and of that viscous density of its chocolate waters, flowing past small islands inhabited by cats.

Could he be sure that never, never before he had seen her?

She would enter quietly, and often would sit on the carpet,

bringing her ankles to her thighs. This placid bending of the knees seemed to express her completely. Her name might have been "Genuflection."

From the painting's clamor he would glance at her. Her size was like a challenge to the twentieth century. How could she be so big and soft? Hands made to clasp a waist, lap made to be stepped on by a child, she seemed to emerge from another era. And nonetheless she was deserted: a Madonna without an Age in which to shelter.

Despite her alien, nomadic nature, she seemed to have the power of homeland. He felt her near, like a surface, yet deep, oceanic, out of sounding.

And she would watch him in his clumsy skill, dogged in his decision to shake off the shadows that seemed to trap him. She felt grateful to be there, on the floor, a silent witness of his toil, his persistence and ignorance, his utter want of plan. He would press a red against a yellow, flatten the prominence with a spatula, and hands still stained with the zeal of his venture he would fall upon her with such delight that when their lips met there was a clash of teeth.

Chaotic and planless it all was. A blend of work and lust. But involving such patience that it came near to heroism. She saw him humble yet unyielding, bent on saying what say he must, even though it took him a lifetime to find the words. Shipwrecked and storm-tossed, her fallen hero. But how firmly set on clambering out of his chaos.

She would become a shore to sustain him.

When they walked into the garden of that reddish inn, the very water dripping from the faucet gave them the impression that time had not yet crossed the gateway. A stiff and sullen dog came out to bar their way, but she bent down to whisper in its ear, as to an old friend, and carrying her greeting further she lifted the dog by the armpits, flattening its ear against her cheek and soothing its suspicion with her courage and confidence. The dog stayed in the garden, bewildered, while they crossed the narrow threshold of a patio of harness and trappings and passed on to the stillness of a counter.

They climbed up a curving stairway, drawing creaks from the boards they stepped on, and entered the upper story of the tavern, with its dark lights, its beams set askew by the weight of time. There, once seated, she let the shawl slip off her shoulders, slowly uncovering the white soft bones of neck and shoulder, so that their profile flowed there, against the wall, like a mountain range. There was a moment's hesitation, while he wondered if he could endure eternity.

"I'll put it back on if you like," she said, smiling.

But a waiter had brought a card. And they ordered a grape liqueur that was sweet and sour, and over that flavor of alcoholic sun they talked.

Why did she bend her heavy head, why slightly forward, this wise, ignorant, slavelike child? Her clumsy, thick, submissive lips were parted, as though all her will were doomed. Only to place his palm under her chin he would have wished time to stop, to halt right there the process of its nights and days, waiting for another chance to carry on.

But a piano, in the meantime, was summoning the notes out of their sleep, beckoning them forth from silence, calling them to live and die. And they came forth—melancholy, compliant, trembling—they gathered near the moment in which they would be uttered, there to enjoy a life's brief spell—and perish. This obedience to such a fleeting destiny was almost painful. It seemed to stress the cruel evanescence of that very night. What could one do with the singularity of each and every note, how could one save it from its loss?

If there was still some hope of arresting or retarding that unceasing flight, it lay in the profile of the tender slave, in the knot of hair behind her head, in the large, sloping, sanctifying neck. It lay in this place of thick adobe walls and tiles, with slivers of light across the floor, and green, ineloquent, red, somber lanterns in the corners. It lay mainly in the woman, her passivity and serfdom. Her slow-moving look, her slow-spoken words.

And that delay with which she breathed, while listening, as though emotion could retard the sea swell of her breathing.

Meanwhile the waiters had been setting quietly the horizontal altar where they would officiate. Discreetly they placed the cups, and forks, and knives, discreetly they poured the wine from a white napkin. Guileless priest, she cut a toast in two, flattened a piece of butter on the bread. And the wine's warm level she raised to her lips, sipping it as if it were human. The density of her cheekbones[3] gave her the appearance of a giant cat, and in her eyes there was something mossy and earth-green.

From what catacomb had she emerged? Why did she remind him of wooden benches? Of large walls in churches? She seemed to belong to the Catholic faith, not to the arid, masculine, puritan world, that rations children and minces sacrifice.

He had ordered a pack of cigarettes and torn its red paper to split it open. "I like the way you tear the pack," she said. "Most people first pull off that little strip of cellophane. You don't seem to understand these things." So, with a few words and a single gesture, she wiped away the moment they had been living, erasing the past as a wave would the sand.

"To be tactful one must be awkward," he said. "And we're the proof of it. We and everything we do."

"What we do is awkward?"

"Yes, and good. I don't think we're inventing. We did all this three hundred years ago."

"Are we that old?"

"Much older, no doubt. But we stopped *being* three hundred years ago, or more. Now we've come back . . . forgetful, young. We're beginning to remember the things we did. Every moment brings back a fragment. Even when our clumsy car stumps off the curb, first one wheel and then the other."

"But there were no cars then."

"It wasn't a car . . . and it wasn't this language; but the plot is just the same. We're acting a play that has been long rehearsed."

[3] In English in the original text.

"How many myths are there?" she asked with a smile.

"I don't know. . . . But none of them have faded. It wouldn't be love, otherwise."

She looked at him, believing.

"When you walk out of that somber alley where you live, and wait on the sidewalk for the flat-nosed boat that comes to save you, don't you feel that it's a scene we know by heart, a scene we've *lived* before? There's something known in the dampness of your building and in the way you slip into the car. It reminds me of a half-naked woman I saw in a Venetian painting, waiting by a castle for the man in tight black breeches that was coming in a boat to her rescue. We *are* that woman and that boatman. I don't carry the long pole I used to push on, but we've taken up the story where it was broken off."

"That's why it's so inevitable," she said softly.

"Don't you remember the taste of this wine? And the growling dog you took in your arms? And the huge jar overturned in the patio? I would like you to remember, I would like you to help me remember."

"So when we meet again, in another three centuries, we'll be a little further ahead in the tale. . . ."

"No, that's sad," he said reproachfully. "The end must happen now. We can't go on gambling with the future."

In small cups of liquor they sipped the taste of the orange trees that peeped in from the patio. And breathing slowly she raised her eyes toward a cobweb on the ceiling.

That night they drove away from the city, under a railroad pass and by the lights of an outsized drum. They drove to where everything flattens and the city dies and turns into landscape. And by the shadows of dusty bushes they stopped.

They were not far from the airport and not far from the huts and fences. He had uncovered her soft breast and she was giving it to him, as to a child, surrounded by the drone of airplanes and the infinite barking of dogs. Suddenly something rose, a giant plane managed to hoist itself from the ground, it passed roaring over them, leaving them alone in the country. A car that might look like a toy car from above and a motherly girl of naïve breasts, in the masculine era of air transportation.

She was the source. She could make the air more tender and urge on the flight of the largest airplane. She could shelter the poorest hut and she knew about dogs and anguish and poverty. She was the Virgin of lighthouses, gas tanks, suburbs, and bridges.

And a slanting aircraft rose in him, striving to pierce that vast air space. But no, not yet, there was no clearance for the flight tonight. "Leave it in its hangar, where I can feel it against me, pressing its nose against my legs." And "Look, a plane!" she said suddenly, and he saw in her eyes the wonder of a plane that comes down at night, upon a city, bringing passengers and distance. He did not see the enormous shadow, nor the intermittence of its red and green, but in the gleam of her pupils he could feel the miracle and marvel.

What was the meaning of this aircraft murmur? Not a menace, not a warning. But something to do with power, space, the faraway. Something like irretrievable loss. And he was kissing her devoutly, brandishing his fist against her lips, turning his menace into caresses that cleared her temples smoothly—while he told her to her face that he wanted to kill her. And she lifted her absolute, enduring head, and consented to die, to die right there, but not tonight, not now, not yet. He had slipped down to her feet and was clasping her legs, still looking up at her with hunger and anguish, till from the corner of his open eyes he felt a warm liquid flowing, as if an orgasm of rare relief had come to his eyes.

Now she was beginning to understand him. And to understand the strip of chasm where she would live until November.

The verses she had felt remote and alien now seemed to express her as though she herself had brought them into being at some forgotten moment, despite the worn-out, yellowed volumes in which they were printed. "I feel ashamed of my sad mouth, / my broken voice and my rough-skinned knees." Another woman, just as big and lonely and vulnerable was speaking in her name. A teacher rather lost, rather unique, had felt the shame she knew so well, she to whom her size had always seemed a God-inflicted punishment. (But in love just a little could bring about a change: "Under your gaze I can turn lovely / like weeds which the dew has watered." And in another valley of this same land, another had decided, like her, to be silent: ". . . I shall keep silent, lest they find out my happiness."[4]

She understood now how passion here could grow in man both strong and gloomy, overthrowing reason through chaos and wonder, and flowing from source to outlet "in unrelenting movement".[5] And the more serene and distant voices she had studied at home, the classic voices of the Spanish language, now came clad in a grace and meaning she had not found in them before. She understood the Soul's distress in her search for the Spouse, and what "the meal that brings love and gaiety" must have meant for both. And having known herself how time-present "in an instant is gone / and emptied," she would now be careful to follow the advice of mourning Manrique: "Let no one, no one dream / that what he expects / will last / more than lasted what he saw. . . ." She had had to travel to this shadowland of the American continent, where time is sober and destitute, truly to understand the rending melancholy of the Coplas.

Because she was the humble, gentle guest, she made him prone to hospitality. Though never before had homeland ways appealed to him, now he wanted to grasp their features, convey them, see them rekindled in her being. He wanted to bestow, surrender his native bourne to her. To define the local traits, so sharply in contrast with Spain's emphatic style. (". . . And this canvas shows the eldest of the Carreras, when the country was still stern, and virility had an appropriate sadness"). And how rigor had yielded to bad taste. The larger families had built expensive vaults in the cemetery—the Pereiras a Persian, the Cousiños an Arabic mausoleum—and honor vanished hand in

[4] Quotations in this paragraph are from *Shame* by the contemporary Chilean poet Gabriela Mistral.

[5] From *Ars Poetica* by the contemporary Chilean poet Pablo Neruda.

hand with austerity. A bland, contented middle-class took over, and all the nation began to wear away.

But she didn't have to be told. She knew all this by instinct. She had strolled through the enormous park that served the dead as a dwelling, she had looked at the huge lime and stone cleft slashed by the river through Santiago, that dry and open bed where garbage is dumped from the market; she knew the plazas, the churches, the railroad stations, and she loved the country in its misery and beauty. Without needing to be told, she felt moved as she captured here and there the distant echo of the national style, when finding it in things so hidden as the docility of the native horse, so responsive to the rein. And no longer did she feel bounded by the ever-present *cordillera*.

That nineteenth of September they had attended the grand festivities held each year by the country to commemorate its birth. They drove back along the wide avenue that flows into the Alameda, cleared, on that occasion, for the awaited troops. The ample width of Avenida Ejército made their car seem even smaller as it moved along that paved, deserted bed, sidewalks lined by thousands of waiting citizens. Children, mainly children, thousands of children sitting on the curb awaited the troops' return. (With patience they awaited also their own far looming growth.)

And now they were back in his studio. He, perched on his drawing table, she, as always, on the floor, leaning an arm on the table and her head pillowed on the arm. The lamp shade's yellow warmth blurred the outline of her figure.

Her arms and shoulders in soft lemon wool, she seemed imprisoned by her own slow breathing. She was his self, she was his soul. Here he was in his soul's company. Who she was he could now tell, he could now spell her name, at last. The day's parade had heralded this very encounter.

"Something quite unheard of, this celebration the people held for you. The army, the navy, the air force, and the cavalry and the tanks and the people, they all came out in your honor. Remember the flags, if you don't believe me, their red and

white so clean . . . and all those bayonets shining, and how the
stiff cadets in their battalions lifted their white starched pants as
they went by, lifted them high to strike them down again, tossing
their heads toward you. All this for what, for whom?" he looked
at her and asked. "For us alone," he added.

For true it was that things had been released, that evening;
poverty set free; and wine, that reddens faces; and people clambering on the trees, and the air itself, released. And what dark
warning in the drums—insistent, violent, curt—a beat bespeak-
ing death or destiny. All this feast and splendor to blazon forth
the fact that now at last Ulysses had found his soul.

But did she know it? Did she know that always she had been
his self, even before, long before she met him?

"Yes, maybe yes, when I stayed alone at school, some evenings, and the children had left, and I gazed through the windows into nowhere."

"Yes, and also when you were stooping down, and also when
you were eating, say, a bowl of soup, and also always, when you
didn't even notice you were someone or somewhere."

Sifting her in silence through the ages, what soft patience had
time used to shape her. Millions of mothers and fathers coupled
at random before they vanished. And from this pointless family
she had emerged at last, free from traces of time's handling,
washed clean of recollections.

"How come you were ever *born,* I wonder. Who was it said
you were to happen, at the very moment when you were needed
most?"

She breathed almost without motion, astonished by her very
existence. The studio he had to quit, that very evening, and this
made his words more grave and final; but did not rob the air
of its stillness.

A moment comes when intimacy can be put off no longer.
They could have found it at Merced, but there she had denied
herself. Now he didn't have the studio. "Somewhere else then,
but it has to happen, has to be." They agreed that they would
have lunch together on Wednesday.

And already the city's look had changed. New buildings had arisen, pierced by looming galleries on broad rectangular columns. Leaning against a column he waited for her, at the time of day when streets are crowded. So many small and ugly citizens. Where was his milky, blue, ingenuous girl? At last he saw her coming from afar. Her hair was loose and she was walking toward him, in that month of October of year fifty-seven of our twentieth century. But she looked sad. She said only, "I'm here," when he asked how she was. And as they stepped into the elevator she told him she had received a cable that her fiancé's father was ill. "I'm sorry. . . . Is it serious?" "I don't know the details." And they walked quietly out at the top floor, amidst tables, courteous waiters, plants. And next to the city they sat.

Soberness diminishes, discriminates, divides: it says no. Alcohol increases, incorporates, inclines: it says yes. While slowly they lunched, a soft and heavy plane passed by. "Strange how they follow us, the planes." And her hair fell downward as she looked at her plate. "Let's forget it if you're so sad. I had bought you some flowers. I saw them in a basket at the corner of Huérfanos and the man's little son carried them to the hotel for me rather grudgingly. When he took the tip I gave him he looked away, ashamed of having done this errand. But let's forget it if you feel that way." "I guess you know me too well," she said. "You know I'm going." And as the waiter had left the wine on another table she poured him some from her own glass. "They should put the wine on the table," he said. "I don't like to be rationed." But now they were content—and calm. "I took an apartment where they won't see us on leaving the elevator. But it's at the end of a long corridor. You'll have to forgive me about that corridor."

"It doesn't matter. I've made up my mind. We'll go anyway."

And they entered a room done in brown dignified tones. "Order something like rum," she said in his ear. "I could drink a whole bottle."

And rum produced an eclipse. They awoke at night in the dark bedroom, remembering only that they had entered there at another time of their lives. In the half-open bathroom there was a broken glass and garments scattered on the floor.

"What have we done all this time?"

"So many things," she said, kissing him. "Although I don't quite remember."

"To think that we've been here nine hours."

"I have to leave," she said, getting off the bed. And he saw her walk, desolate, soft.

"Take some flowers," he said. And he saw her lean over the buttercups, carefully choosing two or three. He thought of the moon. "So many things have happened and there's so little we know. It can't all end like this."

"We'll come back," she said. "Some other day."

But they didn't.

Instead, they drove down to the coast, at night, under the orbit of the first satellite launched by man: a tiny dot in the sky, which travelers on the road were trying in vain to pick out.

They had sandwiches and drinks with them and had to stop at a hut to ask for the bottles to be opened. And to the little girl who came out of the kitchen with an opener: "We'd like to buy it. How much is it?" "How much did you pay for it, grandma? For the opener you bought yesterday?" "Sixty pesos, child." "Sixty pesos, sir." The countryside was not out for a profit. The humble countryside accepted them.

And coming to the mouth of the Aconcagua River, near the end of their three-hour trip, they went by a festival of vertical cylinders and aerial ladders and black and silver towers—and flames—all the nocturnal harmony and extravagance of a large oil refinery proclaiming the innocence of our Age.

And an empty hotel registered their name that night.

It was dark when they entered and they hadn't turned the lights on. She had stretched out like a seashore; she could not tell how far her body reached. Only the sea could be heard below, only that slow multiplication. Hundreds and hundreds of fluid fingers fondling the shore. Her lover was a forest, her lover was speechless, her lover was absent. He wasn't . . . he was there! But not his hands, not his limbs, only his lips skimming her surface. Who was this ghost lying in ambush?

I haven't even looked at this room we're in. . . . Though I know there's a balcony and we're near the ocean. . . . What's this dark beast doing beside me . . . ? How calm the sea, tonight. . . . Only the touch of its fingertips. . . . My male measures me, lightly. . . . Yet this smell of forest. . . . Must I grope until I find him . . . ? We'll be cruel, if he wants. . . . My fingers, too, can be light. . . . But this wild smell of beast, from where . . . ? How slow the sea, how slow and monstrous. . . .

So, with caution, with wonder, with awe, with uncertainty, hardly skimming each other's border, they felt their way through darkness. Maybe the waves, their weight, their endless falling and folding down below, or maybe the gentle tickle of night's air, or maybe just their long-felt want of one another extended their love till late, slowing down their movement till every second lasted longer.

"You're a good lover," she said at length. "I've learned a lot tonight." "All brides should take this course," he said. And this fake cynicism created the *distance* that bound them.

When she turned on the light, some while afterward, she was surprised not to find him at her side. Almost immediately she *saw* him, sleeping crosswise at the corner of the bed, sleeping at her feet like a half-dead survivor, with the frightening expression of one who is away, maybe not even real, maybe not even born yet.

She had seen a lion in the zoo, sleeping on his back with his hind legs spread apart . . . so human, she thought at the time, so human. . . . The lion, too, has velvet knees, and legs perhaps softer than human legs, and a belly that rises gently with its breathing . . . and when a beast opens its legs that way it takes on an attitude of passive scandal. . . . Only this time there was a wooden flooring and paper-covered walls (not the cage's cold cement); there was an open wardrobe stained with the dye of a bathing suit, and this was a room, a room. . . .

She moved to her motionless lover and dragging him toward the pillow she placed him in a human and parallel position, rescuing him from the jungle, if nothing else. . . .

But sleep changes the scene. What is the magic instant in which it makes us appear in some *other* part of the story?

She gets up gently and tiptoes to the light, suddenly breathing a waft of sea, of fresh paint. She smiles at the beach.

Her night is over. His is still around him. She goes over to see him. A few ribs show under his open pajamas. And dark vegetation coats his breast. If only he were sick . . . what a chance to offer her sacrifice, to heal him like a wounded stag. But unfortunately no, that is not so. Though he sleeps there so tamely. . . .

She sat on the floor. She wanted to release him from his sash and buttons, to leave him open, as in the night. But she didn't dare. "To get into his pajamas he must have woken up. At what time of night, if I was sleeping by him?" She examined him from close up. Was this child her lover? How near to her and how remote. . . . Such fine ankles, such white feet. There was really no reason for fear. Yet she feared more than ever.

What special mastery did he exert over her? If only he had been a man, like others. But all his earnestness was set on being Nobody. He created a kind of vacuum. There was his hand, dangling and white. The girl bent to touch it. He answered with his throat. The hand was seeking, feeling her mouth. It had emerged from its vacuum.

"What are these," she said, pointing to a row of riblike irons sticking out of the sand.

"They're ships . . . that got stranded."

"They look like carcasses. And look at those birds!"

All alike, spattering the beach, they looked somewhat like ducks, somewhat like pelicans.

"They're not even scared," she said, opening the door and making them fly with a gesture. She was happy, she was out on the adventure of open space. But the car was nearing a village.

The fishermen had hung their nets across the beach, together with large white rays, the kind that come up unwanted in the catch. And there were lime-painted houses, with red or green windows and doors.

The road narrowed as it skirted a hill. It was a mere path now, over flimsy bridges and lined with grottoes. The hill bulged out to squeeze it against the sea.

And at the end of an unexpected opening resembling an amphitheater rose a gigantic rock, shutting off the beach. It had an oval window, looking out on still more sky, more sea.

They got out of the car and jumped a gorge of water, climbing up the rock so as to pass through its eye. And there the immense variety of marine life made them stop. A black violet colony of little shells coated the stone. Soft seaweeds slipped their arms between the rocky islands, appeasing the gulf's sea swell with their weight.

"What a thick mixture. It's like a soup!"

But he had squatted down and was listening to the boiling of the tiny black mussels. "Hear them shout!" he said, bringing his ear closer. The whole throng of bivalves seemed to be gargling on the rock.

He pulled out a shell and examined it closely. Its owner peeped an eye and a hand out, scanned the universe through its crevice, and shrunk back again. And while—his back to the ocean—he was holding in his fingers this precarious being, all of a sudden he felt the menace, the great impending threat concealed in time, and an obstinate desire to protect, to rescue that which is weak (and strong), saving it from the loss that haunts it. He kissed the little shell he had picked up.

Perhaps on other shores the sea was exploding its violent gunpowder. Here its aim was more like breeding. It kept a sort of nursery. And the girlish, female feet standing near-by helped give each tiniest mollusk an almost cosmic meaning. She had discovered a little pond carved in the rock, filled with water so clear it was hard to see. But on touching its surface she scared away a future fish hiding at the edge, and afraid of the well's furtive dwellers she had to submit to just looking at the clean pebbles on the bottom.

"Come and see what's here!" he said suddenly. Between the mighty suctions of the water he had discovered two starfishes sticking to the rock, real sovereigns without a kingdom: he black and gold, she yellow and red. It was good to know that in spite of all this oscillation and danger there was a place for calm and majesty.

But they left that boiling broth (cold to the feet that tasted it) and jumped over into a cemetery of calcareous shells. On that beach they sat, searching among the hard remains some that might be queerer. He offered her what he had found: little combs, spirals, tiny oval dishes with the Virgin of Lourdes. But she refused to take them. "I don't like to keep things," she said. And in her swimming suit she walked toward the shore, showing her feminine being against the sea.

Once again they passed next to the huts stuck in the granite, next to dirty children with clean smiles, and grottoes with candles, and puddles of oil, and once again they saw the useless rays dangling from the cords.

And in a poor tavern with red and white tablecloths they ate; a moist-eyed woman served them a soup of abalone and a wine that was weightless like a breeze. And always there was that vastness of the beach.

The shore was eating with its empty vessel, homeland was eating with its vagabond. She was the bread and he was the wine she was drinking. All of which is odd, false, unlikely. And nonetheless it was true. However absurd, however superfluous it might be deemed by history, it was the universe they had engendered.

"There's no point in drifting any further," he said on the way back. Again they were driving across the dunes, by the skeletons of the shipwrecked vessels. "No point in stepping on this silly accelerator. I want to be duned, drowned, stranded. I want you to *die* me, take my life, wipe it out completely . . . shape it back again."

Now the road veered away from the shore. They were passing near the tanks of an air base.

"I also want to die," she said at length. "When we reach the hotel. . . ." she added, pensive.

"And suppose we crash, suppose we're smashed, suppose we lose the track and never get there. Shape me now, but now, in one of those pine woods."

She looked at him softly.

"There's a wood right next to us," she said.

So they left the pavement and stopped the car by a ditch. And they had to step into this dry canal to get across, and from it he saw her climb up to the fence. And perhaps because in English the lower leg's hind part is called the calf he felt there was an animal tenderness in that part of her body.

But they were entering the penumbra of the pines, stepping on the brown filaments that time had stored. The barks were covered with thick drops of resin. There was something testamentary in the grove, as if it had been there awaiting them for centuries. What old inheritance had they come to demand?

"Wait," he said, "I want to give the wood some of that wine we had." And opening his pants he cast an arc of pale urine on the rug of rusty needles. Proud of its own insolence, the trunk grew larger in the girl's sight, casting the thin gush further and further.

It was a vegetal—hence indifferent—wood. Impregnated in piety, however. Humbly she crushed the rusty flooring, for something like a legend had taken hold of them. She was the first, the only woman, the God-created female. All the history of mankind had suddenly vanished. They were alone, they were beginning. They had found the kingdom that once was theirs.

Submissive to the holy fable, as if repeating the scriptures backward, she was now untying her useless garments. And yes, the old parchment setting of wrinkled barks and cracking needles made human flesh all the more naked. For there were marks of age in the conifers. A biological weariness. While they—of humankind—were still in childhood.

She plucked a pine thread from the air, showing her armpit of scant soft hairs. What a smooth, what a white and perfect

arm she had raised. The tender mass of her body awoke his
gratitude for the gift that God had made him.

Expelled though she had been from the first garden, paradise
was still her property. And this time she would give it to the
partner she alone had chosen.

Yet this gentle preface led abruptly to a chasm. Down fell
her limbs and her big hips sunk in the silky bed of prickly
threads, and like a vessel he laid her back on the enormous
dry neglected carpet, resting her head on the sloping surface.
He had come to take his boundless virgin, too large and tame
and timeless, who lifted her knees like the letter *A* of our human
alphabet.

And once his chaos had been exhausted, he sunk his head
next to her waist, sunk it deep into the earth itself, and leaning
on his nape he rose like a topmast, falling backward on the
green and the old. And there he rose again on his shoulders,
rose into the air with all his body, and fell once more into nowhere, breaking the branches that scratched his flesh and sinking
all the more into the void, tearing everything in the act of sinking.
And she who beheld this outburst, this agony, these final fish
leaps in the inverted belly of a boat, she who was a witness to
this mad and hopeless mutiny achieved in turn her own sweet
fit of freedom.

Now their awe had been accomplished. They were taken over
by wonder. Accidentally he had fallen near to her, and there,
in opposite directions they lay, their faces close, their bodies
apart, abated and bewildered by their reckless revelry.

"My love, what happened? What was it you did so fierce and
lovely?"

"I don't know myself. What was it?"

"Are you so dark you don't remember the things you do?"

But now he was kissing the tender cushion through which she
spoke. And panting softly from their recent love, they looked at
the branches against the sky. They were inside a cloister. They
could leave, be born, start afresh. Everything on earth was theirs
to take. She sat up and he knelt behind her, looking at the long

white arm that flowed toward the earth. And his still grown, ebbing sex he pressed against the softness of her back, which bore in all humility the print of pine threads. A sea sand hush came to them from afar.

This green and brownish chamber, this birth-giving cavity they left at last. They were out into a world already peopled by the human species. But nonetheless they were the first.

In the end, love wrecks reality. Shapes begin to lose their shape, features slowly founder. Nothing is left beyond a seamless evening.

Where does she come from when walking down the stairway? She comes from within—the soul of vastness. Now that things have ceased their warfare, all the world is in, all the world is soul, all the world is single in its vastness. There is no sign of battle.

Once again the Earth has tilted, turning its back to the Star. Those darkened light their lamps up, to see at least a little. Others prefer to sleep, sheltered by the shadow of the enormous planet. The lovers drive across the narrow strip that separates the Ocean from the Andes.

In order of stature the phantom posts paraded against them, growing larger as one by one they neared the car and missed their blow. The narrow bridge became broader, became imminent, became past. And as they plowed through the night, staining the windshield with insects and blinding the timid hares, as they made this journey of intercourse with mystery, they held a slow, grave conversation. The road was long, the night so wide, they were so lonely and so near the ground, only one foot above the pavement, with all the landscape flowing beneath them. . . . Their voices gained in poise and confidence. They seemed to soothe the distance.

More than ever did he appreciate the beauty of the Spanish language. Spoken slowly by the girl, as if each syllable were new, moving, tender, it acquired a chiaroscuro of dignity and grace.

Of her previous lovers she spoke, of a Spaniard named Rodolfo, "a love very much like ours, though not so . . . deep." And this last word was spoken with candor: she had hesitated in saying it.

She was to leave, however. She was to leave during the week. She was to leave within an air of the color they give to sea on maps: a blue grown pale from so much washing.

Well he knew that she would leave no traces. Not of her lips, nor of her long, untrammeled fingers, nor of the metallic flavor he had found on her ear (left—he thought later—by the earring she had taken off). Like an eraser that wears away on rubbing out, she wore away on loving. Now she had banished, with all her traits erased forever.

"Like sea needs water to be the sea at all, I need you,"[6] he had once said, quoting the Wizard. For they fitted in the same shore line, coincided in the same depth, without a lack or a surplus. But now came *parting,* and with parting the big question: What, what does one do with the past?

When looking at that milky, shapeless pathway on the sky, from her hemisphere she would see it overturned. And on the year's first snow, when her students would race up the stairs to see her, breaking into the room where she'd be ironing the damp shirts, smuggling snowballs in their chilly hands, another season would be heating the South. And all her trip would leave in her remembrance would be a taste of the abyss. A faint, forgotten notion that she had learned to blend the wild Chicago windswept streets she brought inside her with that which she had found in this other, more somber America.

Yet the stones would not remember the gentle dialogue that gradually bound them. Nor was there memory in the dog for the

[6] From *Last Poems* by the contemporary Chilean poet Vicente Huidobro:
  "I love you woman of big journey
  as the sea loves water
  that gives it being
  and a right to call itself the sea. . . ."

few words she spoke in its ear. And the tender glue that stuck her body to the lover's had been washed away forever.

What could be done, then, with the past? Leave it to the fetch of accidental memory?

The sea has its archives. Animals and plants there living produce on dying a vast rainfall that is stored in its depths. Where do *we* have our archives?

Nowhere. No such things exist.

—Translated by the Author

THE HARP
by Tomás Mojarro

TOMÁS MOJARRO was born twenty-eight years ago in Jalpa, Zacatecas, Mexico. He majored in comparative literature in Guadalajara, Jalisco. In addition to his short stories, which have appeared in a wide range of magazines and literary supplements, he had published one full-length book: *Cañón de Juchipila* (*Guns of Juchipila*). He spent two years as a Fellow of the *Centro Mexicano de Escritores*. His most recent novel, *Bramadero* (*The Rutting Place*), will soon be published in Mexico. Sr. Mojarro is working in the editorial offices of the *Fondo de Cutura Económica* in Mexico.

The hands of the large, silent clock on the front of the building pointed to nine thirty-five, but it was only a little past daybreak.

"Let's go," the man said. He walked out of the railroad station, followed by his wife and children, and began to cross the small plaza out in front. The children, all helping to carry the suitcases and paper bags, looked up in wonder at the city's tall, dim smokestacks and buildings, now faintly washed with gold by the light of dawn.

"Look, Mother. . . ."

"The poor old man. Out begging so early in the morning."

In the middle of the plaza, a dark figure was scratching a few bars of music on the strings of his harp; it was as if he had begun his day's work while still half asleep. He was leaning against the base of a flagpole that soared up out of the shadows, its tip lighted by the beams that pierced through the scattering cloudbank in the east.

"Let's give him a coin, Mother. . . ." When he spoke, his breath became a light mist in the chill morning air.

They came to the spot where the old man was plucking his harp. His absent-minded gaze was turned toward the northern part of the city.

The woman stopped. "Here you are, *señor.*" And she reached out a coin.

The old man started violently, as if threatened by a wild animal. He retreated a few steps, with an angry look on his face. "No, I'm not what you think. I'm not a beggar!"

"No? Excuse me then. . . ." Embarrassed, she withdrew her offering and hurried to catch up with the little group that was going toward the center of the city.

The old man sat down again, his face still twisted into a scowl, and huddled up close to his instrument, as if trying to draw a little warmth from it. Then his old, numb fingers played over the strings again, while the children all turned their heads, looking back at him in silence. Their breath turned to puffs of mist in the chill of early morning.

"Wait a minute, Father. I'll help you." I helped him lift up the harp, and my father climbed onto the adobe wall and jumped down among the mounds of earth in the graveyard.

"It wasn't such a good idea to bring your instrument with you."

"My harp goes where I go, or we don't go."

"All right, Father."

We crouched down in the hollow of a grave, behind a clump of tall weeds, and waited for the Rurales to arrive with my god-father Joaquín. They would be guarding him with the rifles that would take his life. And all this because he stabbed the mayor of the village between the ribs.

(We're not from these parts; we're from Santa Cruz de Valparaíso, a long way to the south of here. My father and my godfather were born in Santa Cruz de Valparaíso, and so was I and the rest of us. We lived by growing corn during the rainy season and then eating the harvest during the dry season. But in the last few years the droughts were so bad that Santa Cruz de Valparaíso was starving to death. . . . And where could we turn for help, except to the Almighty? . . .

Then one day we learned some news: "They're hiring farm-hands in Jalpa to go to the north!"

I slung my carrying-bag over one shoulder and my sarape over
the other, and my father slung his instrument on his back. He
took off his sombrero and made a solemn oath: "I promise in
the name of the Blessed Savior that I won't come back until
I've at least gone as far as Texas. I promise to bring back something to eat for my family or die in the attempt. I promise this
in the name of Our Crucified Lord.")

"I think my godfather's crying."

"Get down a little lower. Say the Litany of Christ Adored."

The moonlight flickered on my godfather's mop of hair as he
entered the graveyard ahead of the pointing rifles.

"Most adored and blessed Christ, whose glorious passion and
death redeemed the world. . . ."

(Who could believe that this was the same man who was so
happy just two weeks before, striding along the trail in back of
my father and in front of me? He kept chattering about this
and that, and laughing every little while, and sometimes singing
a few verses:

> *"When my brother, the one who died,*
> *Used to tell his beads. . . ."*

And then my father played his harp, and the fields and slopes
were flooded with the music.

> *"He was a true saint*
> *And not a rascal like me!"*

And meanwhile, all the trails that led to the village of Jalpa
were changed into trails of sombreros, going to Texas or California. . . .)

"I wasn't in my right mind. The liquor, you know. . . . That
was the cause of everything that happened."

We saw the Rurales shining their flashlights all around, as if
they were looking for a good place to do what they'd come there
to do.

"The others must be up in gringo country by now. And my
compadre[1] and my godson and myself have missed our chance.

[1] Term by which the godfather and godmother address and refer to the
father of their godchild, and by which the parents of the godchild address
and refer to the godfather.Tr.

But what's lost is lost. If you'll just let me go free, everything'll work out all right. Don't you hear me, *señores?* Aren't you listening to me?" None of the Rurales said a word. And when he couldn't hear even the slightest suggestion that there was any hope left for him, we could see the despair on his face.

"Are you praying, son?"

"Yes, Father."

(I thought about how we arrived in that village, not so long before. I remembered how we wiped the sweat off our faces as we went in to speak to the mayor. My father had his harp over his shoulder, and he looked like a small angel, an old one, with only one featherless wing. "Leave that here," my mother had told him. "It'll just be a nuisance on your trip." But he shook his head and loaded the instrument on his back. "It's as if I were taking you all with me. Your voices are all here inside it." He walked ahead of us the whole way with his harp on his back, and it was still there when we went in to see the mayor. "Have you got any money? Give it to me and wait till I call you," the mayor said. But the truck was already overcrowded, and we could only stand there watching it head for the north. That was when my godfather started getting drunk.)

"Listen, Father. My godfather's crying."

"Be quiet. Say the Litany."

One of the Rurales said, "Stand with your back to the trunk of that mezquite. And commend your soul to God, if you want to."

"But my wife, *señores.* The children that God gave me. Who'll look out for them?"

And then my godfather, only a few steps away from where we were hidden, sank down, sank down until he was on his knees, while the tears poured over his cheeks.

"In the name of God, *señores!* In the name of the Blessed Virgin I beg you not to kill me!"

The dogs were barking in the village, and the coyotes were howling on the mountain over the cemetery.

"Don't bawl. I always thought the men from Santa Cruz de Valparaíso were famous for their guts."

My godfather's tears were streaming down his face in the moon-

light. I could feel a kind of howling in my chest, like the howling
of wolves and coyotes, and it made a lump of pain swell up in
my throat.

"In the name of the Holy Virgin, let me go! I'm begging you
on my knees!"

My godfather, a man from my own village, weeping and
weeping. . . . And suddenly I realized that my father had got
up. I turned my head to look at him, and he was sitting on a low
tombstone, with his harp between his legs.

"What are you doing, Father?"

But now the whole graveyard was filled with music, with the
very song that would reach to my godfather's soul.

"They've been smoking marihuana. We'll have to search them
to find out where they hide it."

("Ah, godfather, you can't turn coward, not at a time like
this. Look at him, *señores*, look how he's grinning. He's standing
up straight now, and look how the music has squared his shoulders.
Look at him, look at him, *señores*."

> *"When my brother, the one who died,*
> *Used to tell his beads. . . ."*

"And look how his eyes are gleaming, and his teeth, and look
how his guaraches are planted on the ground, as if they're taking
root." And all the while, my father's harsh voice was cutting
through the shadows of the graveyard.)

"Viva Santa Cruz de Valparaíso!"

"I tell you they're all hopped up on marihuana. Help me search
the three of them."

(And the music my father played was like a human voice,
like the voice of a woman, a suffering woman half choked with
angry sobs. That's the kind of music my father played as he sat
on that tomb with his harp. It also had something of the blessing
my mother gave us when her two men—her son and her husband—started out on the way to Jalpa. And it was also like the
songs of the mockingbirds, and the sounds that animals make.
. . . "That's what your music's like, Father: humble, prayerful,

angry, pleading. Listen to it, godfather! Listen to it, it's from where you were born! It's as if the women were covering their faces with their braids. As if the tears were running down their faces. As if Santa Cruz de Valparaíso had come to say good-by to you, godfather. To watch you die and then close your eyes.")

"They're drunk. They've been smoking marihuana."

"Viva Santa Cruz de Valparaíso, *compadre!*"

"Viva, *compadre,* and God help you!"

"They're all drunk, all three of them."

Suddenly my godfather's wild happiness came to an end. The rifles exploded like the rockets they shoot off during fiestas. My godfather was only a little lump of shadow on the dark earth of the graveyard, and the wind was poisoned by the smell of gunpowder and the howling of the dogs.

"Arrest those other two!"

But the rifles were still firing at that huddle of dead emotions, to be certain it was dead, and my father and I jumped over the graveyard wall.

"Don't let them get away! The bastards are all hopped up!"

We ran as fast as we could through the weeds and brambles. My father had his harp over his shoulder.

"I think they're shooting at us, Father!"

"Don't be afraid. Keep running. Say the Litany, but keep running."

"But where? It's so dark. Where are we going?"

"To the north. To the north, until we're stopped by God's own hand."

The policeman approached him slowly, his night stick dangling from his hand. When he was close to him he stood watching for a moment. The old man was eating a slice of melon, with his eyes still turned toward the north.

"What are you waiting for?" The policeman was looking at him suspiciously. "You're a stranger here, aren't you?"

Not far off, there was a ragged old man with large, bright

eyes, leaning against the wall of a storehouse. He was busily rubbing his hands on his khaki trousers.

"Have you got any work? Is that harp your own?"

The old man calmly brought the instrument up closer to his legs. It was so decrepit that it seemed to be the same age as its owner.

The policeman walked on for a few steps, looking at him from the corner of his eye. He reached the wall where the ragged old man was rubbing his hands on his trousers.

A sign on the wall, written with tar, said: *Workers! strike for minnymum wage and garrinteas!*

The policeman tapped his night stick against his hand and went back to the old man with the harp.

The clock on the station wall still said nine thirty-five, but it was the middle of the day and the workers were opening their lunch boxes.

"Are you a beggar?"

The old man shook his head.

"How do you make a living then? What are you doing here? Have you got a home?"

"I just came out of the hospital. I broke my leg."

"Where are you from?"

Out in the street, the cars and trucks rushed at each other like beasts of prey, all roaring and snarling.

"And how do you expect to earn your living here?"

In the station, a train shot out a spurt of sound and then began moving away toward the distant north. Its puffs of steam dissolved in the sharp noonday light.

My eyes are fixed on the sky, on the clouds in the sky, on the moon wrapped up in clouds in the middle of the sky. And I'm here in the middle of the world, in a field I've never seen before, and my body's lying here among the stones and dry weeds like one more stone or weed.

If I lower my eyes a little, I can see my father looking down at me.

"How do you feel?"

"Not too bad. Where are we, Father?"

When I try to sit up, I can feel terrible pains in my sides, in my head, in all parts of my broken body.

"Don't move. Just lie still. We're waiting for a bus to come by."

"But, Father, I'd like to know where we are."

"We're in the hands of God. Stop fretting."

The sound of the river is crawling over the sandy field. I'd like to know whether the river is going north or south. Whether it's going to California or Santa Cruz de Valparaíso. But the only sure thing is that it's going somewhere, murmuring as it goes. When I raise my head a little, I can see the railroad tracks and the bridge, and farther off the black shadows of the mezquites.

Everything is silent. It's as if I'm giving up my soul to the Creator in some world that's different from the world that I was born in.

"You don't have to believe me, Father, but I think I'm getting a little afraid. . . ."

"I'm here. Just be quiet. A bus ought to come along in a little while. The road's right over there, next to the tracks. Sleep a bit, if you can."

"I feel as if I'm breaking apart inside. . . ."

"You're imagining things. Have faith in God. He'll save us. Ask Him to forgive your sins. Are you listening to me?"

I'm listening to the sounds that are coming toward us out of the distance, with a rhythm like the rythm of the harp when my father plays it. They're growing louder, they're coming toward us like a dust storm, like a whirlwind, like a tempest . . . like a landslide crashing down on my ruined body.

"The train, Father. . . ."

"The train won't stop. Just wait, we'll catch a bus any minute now. A few have gone by already. Can you hear me? But they were all going south. Are you listening? Pray to God, and before you know it we'll be heading north."

The train has passed us, howling with its fiery tongues. The rhythm is dying away, little by little . . . the rhythm of an old harp played by a quiet, prayerful old man. . . .

"I think I'm dying, Father. . . ."

"Go to sleep."

But when I close my eyes, the river of the night swirls me away, and the darkness is full of huge, senseless images that I can't control. And then I see that nightmare for the second time, that nightmare of clubs and flashlights that overtook us in the middle of the night.

"Run, Father, run, the men with the clubs have discovered us! Run, run! If they beat you with their clubs, I'll feel every blow in my own flesh. Run, Father, run! Now jump! Jump with me! Jump away from those lanterns! From those clubs that are beating your arms, your legs, your shoulders, your arms and legs again!"

My father was a little slow in jumping, because of his instrument. He and the harp landed on the soft sand near the riverbank. I was already sprawled out on the rocks, trying not to lose consciousness. And that's what's happened to us tonight.

"How are you, Father? Are you hurt very much?"

"No. I'm all right. But wait, I can hear something. It sounds like a motor. Wait, son, don't go to sleep."

But I'm sinking into a hot, deep well, and there's no way to stop myself. My father's a long way away from my sleepy eyes. But I can see that one leg of his dungarees is stuck to his skin.

I tell myself that my father's leg is hurt, but the effort of thinking all these things is too much for me and I close my eyes. I can see dozens and dozens of spots. They're all black and burning red.

"Just wait a little, son!"

I hear him telling me, or shouting at me, or begging me, with his voice full of anguish and despair.

"Open your eyes! The bus is coming! Let me go ask for help. But don't die, don't die here all alone. I said, open your eyes! Open them! Can't you hear me? Open your eyes, Florencio!"

The owls are hooting at each other from the mezquites. The vague, hoarse murmur of the river keeps on going . . . to the north or the south, I don't know which. And I'm sinking into the mud, and every breath is harder than the last one. I can see my father outlined against the clouds and the moon. I can see his eyes, and his long mustache, and his trembling lips. His eyes are two pools of grief. They were dry for such a long time, but now they're overflowing with tears.

"I'm going to lift you up. Put your arm around my neck. Help me lift you up, Florencio. Help me a little, won't you?"

"It hurts too much. If I try to move I'll just die all the quicker. Leave me alone, Father."

"Listen, son. Listen! Can you hear it? It's a bus coming toward us. And it's going toward the north. Can't you hear it, Florencio?"

As I lie here dreaming I can hear it bellow like a river in flood, like a wild torrent ripping at its banks, and then go past us and go on into the distance. For a moment, the only sound is the vanishing sound of the bus and the thin chirp of the crickets in the weeds.

"It's God's will, Father. It's God's will."

"Yes, it's God's will, son. . . ."

And as I'm lying here in the middle of the world, in the middle of this field, in the middle of this night when God is taking back my soul, I can hardly make out the shape of my poor father with his injured leg and his worn-out harp and his cold, swollen fingers.

"Listen to it, God. Listen to my father's harp. Listen to it, and tell me if Your angels play any better. Your angels and archangels and seraphs. Any of Your heavenly musicians. Listen to my father, God. Tell Your musicians to come down and hear him, to come learn the music of an old harp and a sorrowful old man. And see his tears, God. See them trickling down the creases in his cheeks. Please look at my father, God, please look at him. . . ."

I can hear the music of the harp, so sad and gay, so lively and plaintive and despairing. . . . And I'm leaving this field now, slowly, slowly, with one of my guaraches already inside the gates of Heaven. . . .

"Hurry up, the train's going to leave!"

The three men started running, with their sombreros on their heads and their sarapes over their shoulders.

"Let's go! Let's go get contracts for the north!"

They ran toward the brightly lighted building with the clock on its front. The clock still said it was nine thirty-five. To the east, against the dark, dim mass of buildings, the many-colored tubes of the neon signs flashed on and off, convulsively, like dying snakes.

"Here we come, Ciudad Juárez! Here we come, the three of us!"

At the base of the flagpole a drop of weak yellow light hung down from a wire. Under it, the old man with the harp looked at the shadows looming in the north. He seemed to be trying to stare through them, or to divine their forms and preserve them in his memory.

The wind brought a few scraps of song out of a near-by cantina. It was as if it had brought out some drunken whores to amuse itself with their shouts.

A locomotive complained to itself as it moved a line of cars. Then it left them and went off in another direction, grumbling like a peevish old woman cleaning up the kitchen.

"To Oregon! We're going to Oregon!"

Not far off, a man and a woman were embracing in the shadows, forming a single dark shape, while a baby girl, just able to walk, toddled around near-by them, looking at everything as if for the first time.

As the three men passed the old man with the harp, one of them said, "Come on, we're going to Texas!" and laughed. Then, after a few more steps, he turned back, smiling, and tossed a coin on the pavement. "Ask God to take care of us, won't you?"

The old man was still gazing at the shadows. He stood up and turned his head, a look of anger on his face. But then he saw that gentle, happy smile, as full as an October moon.

"We're going to the north. Ask God to let us get back to Mexico again. . . ."

The old man's anger faded away. Something like the sketch

of a smile appeared on his lips. He took off his sombrero. "May God go with you and protect you."

His eyes never left the three men until they entered one of the tall doorways of the station.

He placed his sombrero upside down on the pavement, but slowly and timidly, glancing from side to side. Then he began to pluck the strings of his instrument, hoping that the music would bring him a few coins.

"Will you let me listen to your music from up close?"

The new beggar looked around suspiciously. His fingers hesitated, as if they had barely learned how to play.

"I like your music. And you look like my papá Juan. You're big like my papá Juan."

The woman in the shadows said, "Martita! Come back here!"

"You're big like my papá Juan. And you know how to play music. And look, you've got money, like my papá Juan."

"Martita! Marta!"

"But you've got your music and my papá Juan hasn't got anything. Just a big yellow dog. . . . What's your name?"

"Do you really think I'm what you said?"

"Yes. What's your name?"

"Here, take it. It's a coin. Take it as a souvenir. It's yours."

He put on his sombrero, then looked up over the windows and roofs to the clouded sky. A long freight train was sleepily dragging itself toward the north.

"Ask God to help me. . . ."

"Are you going away? Where?"

"To see what happens. Ask God to let me see you again."

The freight train began to move faster, as if it were gradually waking up.

"Good-by, darling."

The old man started walking toward the tracks, looking back at the circle of light where the little girl stood watching him, silent and motionless.

"Good-by, darling. But we'll see each other again if that's God's will. . . ."

He began to run, as if hurried along by that one old wing on

his shoulders. Then he disappeared among the shadows of the
freight train, which was moving faster and faster toward the north.

The freight train departed almost silently, almost stealthily. A
little later, the muted whistle of a locomotive reached the plaza.
The girl was still gazing into the shadows. And for a moment the
station and the plaza were silent, as if trying to hear how many
echoes would come faintly and more faintly out of the north.

—translated by LYSANDER KEMP

A PLUM FOR COCO
by Laura del Castillo

LAURA DEL CASTILLO was born thirty-four years ago in the province of Buenos Aires. She studied philosophy and literature at the University of Buenos Aires. At present she is working for the newspaper, *La Prensa*, in the Argentine capital. She is the mother of six children. Her novel, *Mirar el limonero y morir* (*Look at the Lemon Tree and Die*), was the first work by an Argentine author published by the *Casa de Cultura* of Ecuador.

When he woke up, it was raining. The rooftops got bigger under the rain, and his helplessness grew and grew inside him. A gray light fell from the window. The boy sat up and saw Nana over by the curtains, her old hands resting on her skirt.

"Nana," he said, "I don't like holidays."

She didn't answer him. A tear fell from her eyes, a tear as old as her hands "because Nana's been old for a long, long time." That was what his father said and he believed everything his father told him.

"Where's Mama?" he asked.

Nana started really crying and took a little folded hanky from her pocket. Coco got up and looked through the window at the garden fountain, which was splashing in the rain. And he remembered that his mother said to him one day:

"You must have been born from a spore that fell in the garden, over there by the fountain: and a nightingale beside the spore, to guard you."

"No," he cried, *"I want to have a mother."*

And Nana had gotten angry:

"Why must you say things like that to the child?"

"You don't understand," his mother had answered. *"And you don't know what's happening either."*

"I know plenty," Nana had said, *"but you don't have the right to make the child suffer."*

Then his mother had cried, and Nana too.

Coco finished remembering and went back to bed. He suddenly felt that they were all crying. And he asked:

"Where's Papa?"

"In the big room, with Aunt Celia."

"I want to see him because he may be crying."

"Men don't cry," Nana said. "And little men neither."

"Someday I'll cry: I'll cry today."

Nana got up:

"Stay in your room. I'll be back in a minute."

And she left.

But Coco got dressed quickly and ambled into the hall. He noticed that his mother's room was locked. "That's so I won't go in," he thought while starting down the steps. From the vestibule he could make out a corner of the living room and the big screen that stood against the fireplace. He remembered his mother's voice the day the screen arrived:

"It has a painted ibis."

"No," he told her, "it's a heron."

And from then on, everyone in the house called it a heron. One of its feathers swooped up from the gray silk and across the front of a lotus.

Coco scurried behind the screen. His father and his father's sister were talking next to the heron. With them was the idiot girl whom Celia had raised like a daughter. Coco could never get the girl to play, and he felt scared too when he saw her chewing her doll.

His aunt was saying:

"We've talked too much, Max. Now you have to calm yourself and trust in God."

"There's no more God," his father said. "There's only someone who's playing a game with us."

The little girl's mouth made a funny noise. It sounded like *da-da*.

"That's blasphemous," his aunt said with conviction.

She always said things with conviction.

"I want to know where I come from!" his father cried.

And he filled up his glass from the blue bottle.

"You'd even deny your parents," Celia said.

"And where did my parents come from? Tell me that!"

And he drew near her, his eyes brooding.

"From your grandparents," Celia answered.

His father laughed. Then he laughed again, this time louder, and threw his handkerchief down on the floor.

"And them? And the others? And everyone else?"

And his hand drew a horrible parabola in the air.

"We come from God," his aunt said.

The little girl's lips made the same sound as before.

His father tilted his head back and opened his mouth. Coco watched him laugh, his tongue twisting in the red hole.

"You make it so simple," he cried.

And he walked up and down on the carpet. The tip of his shoe was shining and the boy followed the dot of light with his eyes.

"I'm a castaway," his father cried. "And those who came before me were castaways too."

And he stared desperately at his sister.

"You've cut yourself off from God, Max," Celia said.

She straightened her hair in the mirror. A violet feather hung down from her hat; a second one, more of a sunflower color, circled the brim. But his father stared out of the window, which was filling with rain.

"I want to know where I come from," he repeated.

The little girl was still mumbling.

He fell back on the sofa.

"I've even considered the ocean," he said, half to himself. "But I've gotten so far from that first drop, that I wouldn't know where my gills were, or my scales."

He got up and studied the bottle.

"I'm lost beyond all the oceans in the world," he cried.

"You've forgotten your traditions," Celia said. "You've stopped thinking about your home and your parents and your roots."

Her brother stared at her with contempt.

"I don't have any roots!"

"Yes, you do!" Celia said.

"If that's so," he exclaimed, "I demand mine back!"

And he drank some more.

"You're talking nonsense."

His aunt scolded his father in her old woman's voice. But she was old in a different way from Nana. For her it was like something burning in back of her eyes, like a dark, ancient grape pulp that was starting to wither.

All at once, his father was crying. The boy cried too, from in back of the screen, and stared at the heron through his tears.

"You've had too much to drink," Celia said. "That's what comes of these holidays. And that's why Zulema left too."

Then the boy remembered his mother's absence from the house, and he wished that she was there so he could say to her: "You're right, Mama: it *is* an ibis."

His father glared at Celia:

"You're wrong: she went because of Clara."

"Ah! that's something that I will not speak about. That's something that's indecent."

And she took her bag.

The little girl made the same "da-da" sound.

When his father and his aunt had left, taking the little girl with them, Coco came out of hiding and ran up the staircase to his room.

Nana was waiting for him.

"Where are you coming from?"

"From the ibis," he answered.

Nana was taking his clothes out of the bureau.

"Where are we going?" the boy asked.

"To your granny's house. Where your mama is."

Then Coco gave a little laugh.

"Soon?" he asked.

"Yes, right now."

The boy laughed again.

"Are you happy?"

"Yes!"

And he looked out of the window. A leaf had fallen on the statue's long hair, and now it was sliding down its shoulder and into the water.

"Nana," the boy said, "the leaves are sailing like boats."

Nana hugged him. She had soft, wide breasts, like pillows.

"Will you come with me, Nana?"

"Of course I will. I'll never leave you or your mother. I brought you up and you're mine, even if I'm just a servant."

"But Mama and I both have mothers," the boy said.

"That doesn't matter: sometimes you can have two."

They picked up the valises and left the room; but Nana went back to look for her silver clasp.

His father was waiting for them at the foot of the stairs. He watched his son coming down, hand in Nana's, and took him around as if they were saying good-by forever. Coco grew sad, but with a happy sadness that was different from other sadnesses.

"Let's go, Nana."

And they went into the garden.

There the sun had just broken out and was coming very close to the pebbled walk, its golden shadow striking the acacias. He saw it moving around and tracing the shapes of the fruits as it slid down the tree trunks; and it lit up the veins in the leaves, as though it were playing a game. And Coco shouted for joy, because it had been raining for a week.

They took an auto, and then a train. And at the river bank, where the delta begins, a launch was waiting for them. He sat down next to Nana. All those channels emptied into the sea. "Everything empties into the sea," the boy thought. "Everything goes out and returns." That was what his father told him. "It's an endless circle that all of us are part of."

"Over there's where it empties out," he said and pointed toward the south. "I came from a drop of water there."

"Who told you such foolishness? God made us, and that's where we come from."

"You're wrong," Coco insisted. "Papa says that we come from the ocean."

"It's a sin to talk like that. Now, be quiet!"

The launch skimmed the water, and the child felt his women coming closer and was happy. His grandmother was waiting for him, and his mother too, and Nana was right there beside him. All three of them with their big laps and breasts.

They drove past islands, sea moss, giant river trees. But the river always went back to the sea.

Nana handed up their valises. Coco ran up the steps from the landing and spotted his mother in the cane field. He stopped short, lifted his head, and called to her; it was a strong cry, full of life, as if he were just being born. His mother turned and ran toward the trees, and Coco followed her red hair coming closer. She reached him at the first line of plum trees. When they ran back across the meadow, his mother put her cheek against his and laughed up close against his mouth.

The days ran also.

During the morning Coco chased a little brown bird. Then he explored the islands. But before starting out, he climbed up on the roof to get a view of the river. Two herons plunged their beaks in the stream and a bird shouted, *Benteveo, benteveo*.

He still remembered Clara. She lived on the delta all year and had a house on the next island. He crossed the wooden bridge. Along the way he picked up a branch for whipping the willows. He heard a noise in back of the rushes and climbed up a plum tree. From there he saw her: she was sitting on a stump and smoking.

All of a sudden, he saw his father running up the beach. The man who'd brought him was rowing away. Coco climbed up another branch and ate a plum. His father put his arms around Clara while she buried her head in his white knitted shirt. The boy liked that shirt because his mother had knitted it in the winter. And winter things had his mother's smell, and the smell of fires and baked apples.

The wind from the river carried their words to him. Clara had broken away and was now over on the sand.

"You're dead!" she was crying. "You're all dead! I don't want to be forced to live with dead people!"

And she wiped away an angry tear.

"What should we do, Clara?" his father asked, as he did so often. And his eyes twisted and questioned the willows, the herons.

The boy saw it all through the leaves of the plum tree, but the sun came out and the fruit gleamed, and so did the toad eggs. The world was indifferent and red. And he heard the leaves crack from inside as they grew. And his bones too, and the grass and the seeds. And he thought: "Life cracks like that on account of the dead." Because one day in the cemetery his father told him that the dead fertilized the earth, and that the seeds and the carob trees and the horses and the ants were all filled with the dead. But if the dead made things live, what was life and who were the dead people? Why did people always say that somebody "died"?

And the boy felt like crying in the plum tree that was filled with the dead; but the sun and the fruit turned red, and he remembered the red blood when he cut his finger the day before and how Nana had stopped it. And he remembered what she sang in the kitchen:

"Heal, little cut, heal: if you don't today, by tomorrow you will."

And Coco laughed. "Nothing's really bad," he thought. "Everything's good to either laugh or cry." Because everyone laughed or cried all the time, and on holidays too. His father didn't understand things; his mother didn't understand things; his grandmother didn't understand things; and because nobody understood anything, the only thing left in life was to cry or to laugh like an idiot.

Or else you could fish or bake apples in the oven or watch the boats going by or duck-walk across the rug or have babies. You could do all those things without understanding them, and

you could also pet the gold-eyed cat or maybe get drowned in
the water.

While Coco was thinking, his father was sitting sadly on the
grass and looking all around him.

"I don't know what to do," he mumbled.

"Live," Clara said.

"Live," the boy thought, and he listened to the black cow low-
ing.

"Live!" Clara cried.

For a while his father didn't answer; then he said:

"I'm like a doll made out of ashes. I'm one of those corpses
that looks so perfect with its boots and the laces on its boots and
a vest and stockings, but on the slightest contact with the air it
turns to dust. Everything that happens destroys us or puts us together again, and we go back and forth without being able to end
it."

"I want to be alive," Clara cried.

"I want to be done with it," his father said.

The cow bellowed behind the willows and the black calf took
hold of her udder.

Clara fled across the sand but he didn't chase her. He stood
there watching the wind churn the river. Coco climbed down
from the tree and ran toward him.

"Coco!"

The boy buried his head in the white knitted shirt and breathed
up the smell of the winter. Then he burst into tears.

When he came back he looked for his women. He found them
on the sun porch, knitting and gazing at the river. The boy could
read their silent thoughts: they were either watching for the boats
or for the women with the baskets. And he saw in them too a
deep-seated, burning hatred for some unseen enemy. And even
though they didn't know what form that enemy would take, who
someday was to violate their house, they kept this vigil all the
same. And their hearts, because of it, had changed to pincushions.

The boy was careful not to tell them about his father. And
his grandmother, to make him happy, said:

"Tomorrow will be bad out, and I'll make some apple tarts for the child."

Coco ignored her wheedling and ran after his cat. But he did want to make his mother like him, with her nice red hair, so he said:

"You're right, Mama: the heron *is* an ibis."

He would have been happy if she had answered: "I'm glad you've come around to it." But his mother was busy with her own thoughts and all she did was cut a hole in some white silk. So Coco decided to upset her.

"I saw her today," he said.

Then his grandmother raised her head. So did his mother. And so did Nana.

"Who did you see?" asked his grandmother.

"Who did you see?" asked his mother.

"Who did you see?" asked Nana.

"Her," the boy said.

And he took the scissors out of the sewing box.

"Where did you see her?" asked his grandmother.

"Where did you see her?" asked his mother.

"Where did you see her?" asked Nana.

And all three fixed Coco with their knitting-needle eyes. He knew those eyes and their knitting-needle hearts and thighs too and how they always spied on doors. He knew them and he thought: "When I grow up, Papa won't be the only one."

"I was walking on the island," Coco said. "And I heard her shouting: I don't want to live with dead people."

"With whom was she talking?" asked his grandmother.

"With whom was she talking?" asked his mother.

"With whom was she talking?" asked Nana.

Coco cut out a purple tulip from a magazine.

"Put down those scissors," said his mother.

Coco put them down.

"She was by herself," the boy said, lying.

And he picked up the scissors.

The three women stared at him. They formed a triangle of stares with Coco in the center, squirming around on the floor as he looked for some fishes he'd been wanting to cut out for a long time.

"Put down my scissors," said his grandmother.

Coco put them down.

"What else did Clara say?" asked his grandmother.

"What else did Clara say?" asked his mother.

"What else did Clara say?" asked Nana.

"Just a word," the boy answered.

"What word?" asked his grandmother.

"What word?" asked his mother.

"What word?" asked Nana.

Coco took advantage of what was happening to do something the woman never let him do: he put his feet over the back of a wicker chair and let his head dangle a little above the floor. Then his grandmother's eyes were where her mouth should be, and so were his mother's and Nana's.

"Answer!" ordered his grandmother.

"Answer!" ordered his mother.

"Answer!" ordered Nana.

But Coco got on his hands and knees and crawled across the tiles and sat down on the other side where the sun's rays came together in a green-colored shadow. From there he eyed his women closely. The three of them were glaring back at him, and their heads were shining and their eyes and the rings that they wore on their fingers.

"Someday Clara will come here," the boy said.

And he picked up the scissors.

"Put down the scissors!" screamed his grandmother.

"Put down the scissors!" screamed his mother.

"Put down the scissors!" screamed Nana.

And Coco put the scissors back in the box.

"She won't come to this house," muttered his mother, threading a needle.

"Why not, Zulema?" asked his grandmother. "Clara's unhappy. She's suffered enough."

"She has no right to take my husband."

His grandmother grew silent, as if she had been thinking for a thousand years.

Then Coco said:

"Is it true, Granny, that they left Clara on the doorstep, in a basket?"

"Who told you that?" asked his grandmother.

"Who told you that?" asked his mother.

"Nana did," said Coco.

Nana sank into her seat. Coco took the scissors out of the box and went through the pages of the magazine, looking for a river to cut out, with a fish and a heron.

"Put down the scissors!" shouted his mother.

His grandmother went over to Nana:

"Why did you say things like that to the child?"

"He had to know," she answered.

"Nana, I don't understand you," his grandmother said.

And she looked at her sternly.

Crying, Nana got to her feet, and Coco cut out a sheep with a bell around its neck.

"Put down the scissors!" shouted his mother.

"Nana," his grandmother called, "come back here!"

Nana came out of the kitchen and dried her hands on her apron.

"Now listen to me, Nana. Clara is my daughter and I will protect her."

"It isn't fair," Nana said.

"Why isn't it fair?"

"I don't know, it just isn't. She doesn't keep to her proper place here."

"Explain yourself!" his grandmother said.

"That's all," Nana said.

"Watch out," his grandmother said. "It'll cost you dear, hounding Clara. And before you try it, commend yourself to God's mercy. That God of yours, who has a big stick and punishes everyone and coughs and wears a beard."

Nana fled down the hall.

The next morning, his mother's brother, Federico, called in from the doorway:

"Hi there!"

When the boy heard him, he came running from the pantry. He saw him outlined against the light coming up from the road. His uncle Federico took him in his arms and threw him joyfully up in the air.

"I've come to snatch you away."

Nana came out of the shadows with her wet hands.

"Who'll take care of him at your place?"

"I will," his uncle said.

"I'll go with him," Nana said quickly.

"We don't want any women," Federico explained.

"No women," Coco said, backing him up.

"We just got here a few days ago," Nana said. "Why does he have to go away?"

"Because I've taken a liking to him," Federico answered.

"It isn't fair," Nana insisted.

His mother appeared and Federico kissed her on the cheek.

Later on, the boy and his uncle took the launch and then the train, and went back to the city.

Coco went around Federico's house, opening all the closets and going through all the drawers.

"What should we do now?" he asked.

"Let's invent a day."

"What kind of a day?"

"A happy day," his uncle said. "A pure day, with nothing false in it."

He leaned back on the sofa and continued to ramble:

"I'd like a day that isn't patched together. A good clean day with nothing to think about, with love and hate floating past us like two rivers."

"Is that all?" the boy asked.

Federico stretched his legs and looked at his nephew.

"Well, to be smart by instinct, without having to learn."

"You *are* smart," Coco said.

"No; I feel patched together like an old piece of cloth. I don't want people sewing me up!"

He got to his feet.

"I want to be a compact sort of beast, powerful and wise. And then I want to feel as beautiful and peaceful as a god."

He walked around the piano without speaking. That was when Nini came in.

"Who's that?" Coco asked.

"That's Nini," Federico said, introducing them. "And she admires me," he added.

"I admire you too," Coco said.

Federico stretched out on the sofa again.

Nini was looking for a vase for the violets that she'd brought. Federico followed her with his eyes: she was quite brown.

The cat looked in from the door, then jumped up on the chair.

"Lucky that we brought the cat," Coco said.

"You're right," Federico said. "I like his eyes."

"Me too," the boy said.

Federico lit his pipe and yawned. After a while, he looked around him and said:

"We have everything we need to be happy: a sprig of violets, a child, a cat, and a girl. But they bore me!" he cried.

Nini, in front of him, looked up. Federico leaned over her:

"How do I stand you?" he asked.

Nini avoided his hands and moved around the room with her yellow skirt whirling.

Clara came in and watched them from the doorway: she was surprised to find Federico with the child and the girl.

"Come on in," he said.

"I want to talk with you, Federico."

And she noticed that Nini was looking at her with disgust.

"Go to my room," Federico ordered the girl.

She left. Federico and Clara ignored Coco and the cat.

All at once Federico said:

"I've got to be good today."

And he banged the table with his clenched fist.

"What is it?"

"Nothing; I'm bored stiff already. . . ."

"I don't know what's wrong with you," she said.

The boy put the cat on his knees; it raised its head and looked into his eyes.

"I needed to talk with someone," Clara said. "I didn't have anywhere to go."

"What do you want from me?"

"Let's be nice to each other."

"There's the cure," Federico said. "Start by stroking my head."

Clara didn't answer. He laughed softly, with his laughter trailing off. Clara's eyes grew wet.

Federico got up and kicked the chair.

"I don't want to be tender," he cried. "I should have beaten the kid and the cat!"

Coco heard him and started to cry, because now he missed his mother and Nana. Federico took him in his arms and rocked him, putting his cheek against the boy's.

"I love you, Coco honey, I love you."

He kissed him again and again, before setting him down on the rug.

"How do I stand them?" he asked. "Why do I bother with these little animals? I don't want them tying me down! It's like wanting to go on a trip and not being able to, because there's no one to feed the canary."

"Why don't you want us to help each other?" Clara asked. "Why do you try so hard not to love me? Aren't we brother and sister?"

Federico looked at her and took a new pipe out of the box. He stuffed it with tobacco from a brown pouch and lit a match. Coco grew used to the peacefulness and got himself a scissors to cut out pictures with on the rug.

"We were brought up together," she went on. "It's natural for you still to love me."

"What's that got to do. . . ."

"Your sister hates me."

"Zulema's your sister too."

"She hates me because of Max; he's her husband."

Federico stretched his legs. His powerful, golden legs.

"At least I've got these legs," he said out loud.

Clara seemed not to have heard him.

"Stay here with me," he said and took her hand.

She smiled:

"I love Max."

"Love's a bloody pain."

He got up from the sofa.

"But I'm a man," he said. "I'm young, and it might as well be me as the next guy. Why complicate things?"

"Is it all the same?" she asked.

"No; but there are just so many possibilities. We all know who's possible for love or an affair."

"Are you possible for me?"

"Me or someone else. Why must it be Max? Love's infinite and it regenerates itself. There's a wheel in there"—he pointed to his golden skin. "Make the wheel spin, Clara."

She looked at him.

"I'm sick already, Federico."

He was pacing on the rug.

"I always imagine myself in a bright landscape," he said, "with young girls and vineyards, where love is something different."

And he looked at Clara through the smoke.

"But it would bore me, because I'm sick already too. And sometimes I feel that God and sin and literature were really good inventions."

"Yes; we force ourselves to keep suffering. . . ."

Federico turned and stared at her. Clara got up and seemed to be looking for something. She stopped at the window and looked out at the rain. Then she came back to him.

"I'd like to give you something, Federico, but I don't have anything."

"I don't have anything for you either."

Clara came closer:

"I could be yours today."

"You'd think about Max."

"Would it matter?"

"Sure it would matter: I'm sick too."

She turned from him and took her coat. Federico helped her on with it and handed her her bag.

"It's cold," Clara said.

And she opened the door.

Coco cut out a tire and rolled it over the floor.

The trees made the shadows. He woke up and listened to the rain; then he remembered that they were in Federico's house.

"Puss, puss," he called softly.

The cat sprang onto the bed.

"Are you sleeping, Coco?" Nini asked from the door.

And she came in, with the same yellow skirt on.

"What did you come for?" the boy asked.

"I came to take care of you."

And Nini rolled up the blinds and looked at the rooftops. The boy got up to watch the tiles, because the water running down them was carrying the leaves along.

"Where will the leaves go?" Nini asked.

"To the ocean. Everything goes to the ocean, the same way that rivers do."

"But there's too many leaves. The ocean will get full of leaves, because every spring there are new leaves."

"Oh sure; it's full of leaves already, and cats and buttons and hairpins and dead children."

"If that's so, why doesn't it overflow?"

"Because things get made from other things. My father says that we all go around in a circle."

"You make me sad," Nini told him.

"I was here before," Coco said, repeating his father's words. "Thousands of years ago: and then I went all the way around again."

Federico entered the room.

"You here?" he asked Nini.

"Yes," she said and showed him the violets.

"Get out," he ordered. "Your father might turn up and he wouldn't like to find you in the house here."

"Fathers don't turn up. They peek from behind windows if they want to see where their daughters have gone to."

"Why are you such an idiot?"

Nini bent down and picked up some fallen flowers.

"Someday I'll kiss you," Federico said. And he clenched his teeth, as if he hated her.

Coco said:

"I'm cold."

He went back to his bed and climbed in next to the cat.

"Get some more sleep."

And Federico pulled Nini out of the room.

In his bedroom, he sat down on the sofa and lit his pipe.

"Get undressed," he said. "I'm tired of playing the fool with you."

"Someday," she answered, while she looked for a vase for the violets.

"No, right now."

Nini looked upset and put the flowers down on the bed.

"Go over by the fireplace," he said. "I don't want you to be cold."

And he threw on an enormous log.

She unbuttoned her blouse and started crying. A branch striking against the glass seemed to startle her.

"It's only a branch; don't be afraid."

Nini stood on the carpet, naked. She covered her chest with her open fingers and a high flame lit up her belly.

"Take your hands away. I said I wanted to look at you."

Nini obeyed him, gazing off at the fire, while the water kept beating outside. But soon she began to smile. The smile moved over her whole body, slowly coming to rest on her teeth, where it faced him in triumph.

"It had to happen sooner or later," Federico said. "Everything comes to market. It's inexorable, like the seasons; the stars revolve and cycles are closed."

His open hand drew a parabola in the form of the universe.

Suddenly Nini fell to her knees and bent her head over her joined legs. Her laughter was lost in her hair, so that no one could tell that she wasn't really crying.

"The same thing happened to Eve for eating the apple," he said.

And he smiled. The smoke from his pipe hung in the air.

"Get dressed. One of these days I'll finish the job."

Nini obeyed him with a tender look. But a little later she approached him with her yellow skirt still off. Federico seated her on his lap.

"Sometimes I bore myself," he said.

And he threw her onto the big cushions:

"My whole being would have to throb with a magnificent precision. That's what I've always looked for: that perfect kind of throbbing. But suddenly something insane happens, and whatever it is inside me goes wrong. My nerve fails, and I don't want any more."

He tapped his pipe against the fireplace.

"Making love, lighting the fire, cutting a log, writing a letter, petting the cat, everything has to be done with precision. That's all I want: to enjoy things or to suffer from them, but in an ordered way, that perfect kind of throbbing."

"I'm sad," said Nini.

"I'm sad too."

The child stood in the doorway, sobbing.

"Were you there, Coco?" Federico asked, and took him in his arms.

He brought him over to the fire.

"Go along now, Nini."

She put on her shoes.

"It's still raining."

And she opened her umbrella in the doorway.

"I'll put you to sleep," Federico said to the boy. "It's still early."

Coco looked at the violets and closed his eyes. The cat jumped up on the bed.

"Tomorrow I'll take you to the island."

Clara started the motor. The launch bobbed on the surface of the river. It was the only time of day when she had the sense of having overcome something. And she laughed out loud, even while the branches struck her face. She headed for the small island and the house that Max had built there in the first days of their love, when they were happy. She thought of the hill full of plum trees and the river with its willows that came right up to the house, "those damn willow trees that always grow up crying." She crossed the dark rivulet, with its smell of slime and decay, and remembered the *benteveo* bird and the herons. She circled the large island toward the south; it had taken root in the tide and grown as powerful as a continent. They were almost the same age; Clara had witnessed its birth: a sand shoal, smooth as a loaf of bread, that floated with the current inside its parent river. And she remembered Federico shouting from the canoe:

"The sand bank's got rushes already!"

She fought against the memories: from the time she first saw Max she felt that she was standing naked on a beach. *Benteveo, benteveo,* cried the bird, and the *chajas* buried their beaks in the sand.

She found Max waiting in the entry. And she stood in front of him but didn't kiss him. She couldn't get past her own body; he looked so dazzling to her, like a figure drawn in blood on the floor. She ran into the house. Max followed her:

"What can I do for you, Clara?"

She didn't answer at first, and when she did, it was almost to herself:

"Nothing. Your body ends there—" and she pointed at him— "that's you and this is me. I'm *here*."

And she dug her nails into her arm.

"But it couldn't just have vanished," Max exclaimed.

Clara looked at him sadly:

"You never knew what to do for me; I didn't either, for you. I've never known how to help you."

As he listened, Max paced around the room.

"Clara, we're defenseless; love takes away our weapons."

And he looked at the bed, the fire, the chairs, the drops of water that were running down the wall.

"Yes; you're a wound inside me that I'm tired of."

"I don't want you to suffer," he pleaded.

And he held out his hand to her. Clara moved back to the window.

"What's happening to us?" she asked.

"I don't know," he said.

"We're like prisoners. We've all been trapped."

But Max looked at her, as if he were recalling something:

"It has to be like this. I believe in God, Clara. I believe in God!"

"You're lying!"

"I believe in God!" Max shouted. "I have him here, inside me."

"Fine then: all of us drag around some invalid, some dead man."

"I want to help you," he said again.

He came closer.

"Not with your god. Your god makes life unbearable. Your god is weak, limited, worthless."

And she wiped away an angry tear.

"Protect our love. Bury it somewhere, Clara." His voice was pleading with her.

"Love isn't enough to bring us together. . . ."

"We aren't free, Clara."

"I am. I'm free. I'm free from inside! I can use my kisses and my blood and my thoughts any way I want to!"

Then Max bit her on the mouth.

Federico dropped Coco at the landing and went back to the city. The boy strolled over to the house. Before going in, he caught the smell of apple tarts. Only the day before, his grandmother had said: *Tomorrow will be bad out.* And now it was tomorrow and the weather was still nice. He felt happy that she had made a mistake, because he liked his women to be mistaken. He found them in the kitchen, seated by the fire like three house cats.

Nana took the tarts out of the oven.

"Look, Coco, see how crunchy the sides are."

And she showed him a place where the crust was bulging.

"Press into this and hear how it crunches."

"No," his mother said. "The child has filthy fingers."

Then Coco tried to upset her:

"I know something too," he said.

"What do you know?" asked his mother.

"Don't start up with him," said his grandmother. "He's angry with you because you didn't let him touch the cake."

"What do you know?" repeated his mother.

"What do you know?" asked Nana.

"I want to try a tart," the boy said.

"They're still hot," Nana answered. "I'll put them on the window to cool."

And she brought them over to the window. She put the pan on the ledge and looked up the road.

"There she comes," Nana said, as if she didn't want to say it.

"There who comes?" asked his mother.

"There who comes?" asked his grandmother.

The boy didn't say a thing, because he had seen her earlier, before the women had. He had seen her pushing back the willows and the branches, and avoiding the rushes that grew near the shore.

"It's Clara all right," said his grandmother.

"It's Clara all right," said his mother.

And she passed her hand through her hair.

"Do you want me to speak to her?" his grandmother asked Zulema.

"No, there's no reason for you to meddle."

The boy was glad that his mother had said that. His mother who had red hair and red cheeks and a red mouth. His mother who was red all over like a womb or an open wound.

"I'll wait for her outside."

And she went into the hall.

Nana and his grandmother stayed in hiding like two caged cats. The boy knew them all, and he knew their fiery eyes when they were fighting over something. "The four mainstays of this house," his grandmother had once said. They would fight the same way over a man as over a bed or a pot or a hammer. They would fight over a whole thing or over a part of it. And they were always on the watch. They knew just where to tap the walls and they could hear the finest grains of plaster coming loose. They moved over everything around them like a tremendous glob of gelatin that takes the shape of what it touches. His father was different: his father drifted over everything, because he wanted to touch bottom; and he remained on the surface because the things were only things, little bits of clay that had no value. Because the women knew it, they could take control. They could sit around and tend the fire and track up the rugs and take bread out of the oven. They could also go to bed if they had to and spread their legs to have children. What else was there? Here or anywhere? And what was this "bottom of things"? You didn't have to know it to go on living.

His grandmother put the apple tarts on a pink porcelain plate. And Coco felt how much he loved his women, though deep down, like all other men, he hated them for just such things. He took the opportunity to slip out behind his mother.

And so he saw them face to face: they planted their feet in the mud, like two lovely mares about to bite each other. Their eyes gleamed. Their leg muscles were tense and stood out against the fabric of their slacks. They had breasts of iron; and their teeth and fingers were like iron spears.

The boy was sorry that his father wasn't with him, to enjoy them there like this, so violent and lovely.

"Why did you come?" his mother asked.

"I'll tell you inside."

And Clara motioned toward the house.

"I don't want you going in," his mother said.

"I'll go in just the same, because it's my house too."

"It isn't any more."

But Clara forced her way into the hall and his mother followed.

Coco stood by the door and watched them intently.

His mother turned toward her sister. She stood on the carpet and a ray of sunlight danced along her shoulder.

"What do you have against me?" Clara asked.

"Taking Max from me."

"You don't own him."

"Yes; I own everything."

And she took in the universe with a sweep of her hand.

"We aren't anybody's masters."

"Max is mine!" his mother shouted.

"Only on a temporary basis. Everything is on a temporary basis."

"Then what would you want me to do?"

And she advanced on Clara.

"Face up to it and be quiet, the way other women do."

"Is that what you do?"

"Me? I look after the cripple, I support him. What else am I supposed to do?"

"Find someone besides Max."

"Max is free; he'll come to me if he wants to."

"I don't want you sleeping with him!" his mother shouted.

And she stood on the edge of the carpet, with her breasts heaving and her eyes staring right into Clara's. The boy saw her as something magnificent, and he remembered how her arms felt around him.

"That's the only thing you care about," Clara said.

"Is there something else? Can I possibly have what Max thinks or what he feels?"

"I *do* have that because he loves me."

"I'll be satisfied with just the other."

"You make me sick."

His mother kept advancing with her red mane:

"What can I ask for besides pleasure or money or children? What else is there?"

"Love, you idiot!" Clara said.

"You make me laugh," his mother said. "You talk just like a man. One's either a woman or one's a man. We women are good for having children or for sex. And for enjoying what we have, like animals."

"And what if Max was an invalid, like my husband?"

"I would have killed him long ago," his mother said.

Clara took out a cigarette and lit it with a piece of burning wood. His mother did the same. They blew out smoke, and the boy admired the gray threads.

"I've thought about it often," Clara said, "but I haven't done it because of Max."

"You're satisfied with so little," his mother said. "You're satisfied with only Max's thoughts."

And she looked at Clara with contempt.

"You're obscene," she said.

"No," Clara said. "It's only that one can't have everything."

Clara sat down on the edge of the sofa and crossed her legs, as if nothing had happened.

Nana came in with a tray and put it down on the coffee table.

"Get out, Nana," his mother said.

Nana obeyed in disgust.

His mother passed the sugar and stirred her coffee. To the boy they looked like two old friends who were having coffee together. His mother took a sip and said:

"In the beginning we're the same as the men: we analyze love and want all of it. Afterward not; we can't mix matters up once we're married. There's a house to keep up"—she motioned toward the living room—"because an illusion isn't any help here. We have to be realists, and that takes something out of us. It's painful being realistic."

Clara had been listening and sipping her coffee.

"Is one happy like that?" she asked.

"Good God," his mother answered, "haven't I told you already? I'm satisfied with the house and the child. And enjoying a man in bed. I like that," she added.

"And love is so simple?" Clara asked, but almost to herself.

"Who's talking about love?" his mother said irritably.

And she stood up.

"It's those damned concepts that enslave us from childhood," she shouted. "Why that figment? That horrid figment that we spend our whole lives tracking down?"

She looked at the flower stand and the pictures and the rain that was just letting up.

"You're kidding yourself," Clara said. "That's how you keep up your realism, by kidding yourself, because any other way you couldn't stand it. . . ."

Zulema stared at Clara for a moment. Then she took her cup and flung it at the fireplace. A piece of porcelain flew into the flames and a large ash fell onto the floor.

"Let's smash everything," Clara said. "Let's smash everything and everyone and kill ourselves!"

"If a wind would come!" exclaimed his mother.

And she pushed back her red hair with both hands.

Clara poured fresh coffee in her cup and passed it to her sister.

"Let's have some coffee," she said. "Let's do anything but what we're doing."

"And what are we doing?"

"I'd imagine we were suffering," Clara said.

"No," his mother said, "we're living!"

Coco went out to the garden and ate a plum.

The following afternoon, Coco saw Clara when she tapped on the window. His grandmother raised her head from her knitting.

"Can I come in?" Clara asked through the glass.

"Come on," his grandmother said.

She came in and dropped her raincoat on a chair near the fire.

Then she lit a cigarette.

"Is anyone else in the house?" she asked.

"Do you mean Zulema?" his grandmother asked and put her knitting aside to look at her.

"Yes. . . ."

And she sat down in Coco's little chair. She looked young and frightened. The boy liked her because he was young and frightened too.

"Did you get wet from the rain?"

Clara shrugged her shoulders:

"What does the rain matter?"

"At least take your shoes off."

And the boy ran to put them down by the fire.

Clara looked around at the walls and the ceiling:

"I like your house," she told his grandmother.

"It's your house too, child."

Clara glared at her:

"I'm not your child."

His grandmother didn't even blink:

"Who told you that?" she asked.

"Nana," Clara answered. "Someone had to tell me."

"A long time ago?"

"Long enough."

"When?"

"The day I ran off to the island, over the vacation . . . when they found me at night."

"Ah!" his grandmother exclaimed.

And she took up her knitting again.

"That wasn't what you thought, was it?"

"No, I thought something else. . . ."

"I know what you thought, but that didn't happen until I was married. . . ."

And she smiled happily, perhaps remembering.

His grandmother looked up from her knitting and seemed to be thanking her for what hadn't happened.

"It makes me happy," she said.

"Why?"

"I suffered a lot with that thought. . . ."

Clara laughed and pushed her chair back.

"What importance could it have?"

"For me it did," his grandmother said. "It was humiliating."

"Oh God," Clara said. "It's wonderful to know that there's

someone left who thinks that it's humiliating. There's something ancient in that, something proud. . . ."

"And isn't it humiliating?"

"No," Clara said. "Only natural, like in animals."

And she threw the cigarette butt in the fireplace. Coco kissed the cat's head.

"What do you think about Max?" Clara suddenly asked.

His grandmother had gotten up and was getting the green box of cookies down from the cupboard. On hearing the question, she turned her head and answered over her shoulder:

"Why should I worry about him?"

She came forward, holding the box in her hand.

"He's your daughter's husband. . . ."

"What about it? I didn't bring him up. Besides, I only worry about the women."

Her hair gleamed under the lamp and her old cheeks were glowing.

"And why the women?" Clara asked, laughing.

"Because it's from us, from our bodies, that new people come forth, not from them. . . ."

And she motioned toward her legs with the box.

"And the men are nothing?" Clara asked.

"The men? Oh God, they do what they do, but we're the ones who have the children. And that's the important thing."

She tore open the box, as if she were angry.

"But I'm not your daughter," Clara said.

"It's all the same thing: I raised you and I love you just the same."

"No," Clara said, "because I would have wanted to be born from your blood, to have come from your womb."

"I tell you that it's all the same!"

And she gave Clara a cookie, and one to the child.

"No, it's different," Clara insisted, "because the features are missing. You have a face and a heart and a mouth, which keep your mother's features. And you know what they were like in her: her smell, and her color, and how it felt to touch her."

His grandmother stiffened in her chair, as if about to object, but Clara went on:

"But I can't touch my roots. I come from the air, like some parasite!"

Then his grandmother put down the box and shouted:

"Why don't we be frank?"

"All right: let's be frank. . . ."

"Yes; what do we have to lose?" his grandmother asked.

"What should I do?"

"Not feel the way you do, Clara. You'll never be a woman if you don't feel the earth in you. Send out roots! Let tentacles grow from your body, like an octopus, and grab hold of whatever you can! Take possession of a man. Really and truly take possession."

"It's impossible . . . I don't have any children. My lineage begins and ends with me. I know my limits: put yourself in my place."

His grandmother shook her by the shoulders:

"Why do you feel like that, Clara? Why?"

"Because I'm trapped. I'm cut off from the past because I have no mother, I'm cut off from the future because I have no children. I'm hanging suspended in time, and I can't go backward or forward."

She sat down in the armchair and the two of them stared at the rain. The cat moved softly across the rug and put its head against Coco's.

"Puss, puss," the boy called gently.

And he kissed its ears.

Clara snapped out of it first.

"It's funny," she said. "After all those years I finally get to tell you what happened. . . ."

"And what did you do on the hill?" his grandmother asked.

"I walked until I got thirsty. Then I met a girl with a goat, and out in the middle of the river, but very far off, I saw a canoe with a fisherman."

"Was that all?"

"I fell asleep. I slept just a little and then the ants bit me. . . ."

Coco got up to hear the story of the ants and the girl with the goat.

"It's time that you told me, because I raised you . . . and I still don't know you."

"Is it enough that I love you?"

"Yes, it's enough," his grandmother said.

And she counted the stitches. She got to sixteen and changed to the other needle.

"What're you knitting?"

"It's for Coco's new brother."

The boy had nearly fallen asleep beside the cat, but now his eyes filled with wonder.

"Oh God!"

"Are you all right, Clara?"

"Yes."

And she threw a log on the fire.

His grandmother mused over her knitting:

"There are times," she said, "when I feel nostalgic about my little children: I feel as if all my children had died. . . ."

"They *have* died," Clara said.

"No, they've only changed. They've gotten older and sadder."

"Yes, these are different children. Yours are dead. All women see their children die."

Clara got up.

"Are you going already?"

"Yes."

"I don't want you getting wet."

Clara kissed her and smiled at her from the doorway before going out.

"Has Clara gone?" the boy asked.

"Yes, she's gone and . . . damn this anguish!"

Once more his grandmother counted the stitches. She reached eighteen and changed to the other needle.

The next morning he crossed the bridge and came to Clara's. He stepped through the doorway. In the hall, he heard someone call him:

"Coco!"

Then the boy saw the invalid seated in the room, with butterflies covering the walls. He loved that room, because there was one blue butterfly there that was sprinkled with green and whose wings dripped silver, as if a spider's web had covered it forever. "Once it was a bird," Coco thought. "And then a spider must have eaten it, a spider with a silver web, and it must have woken up again and been a butterfly forever. Because there must be things that live forever."

"Come here," the invalid said.

"I was looking at the butterfly," Coco said.

"Do you like it?"

"A whole lot."

"I'll give it to you."

"When?"

"When I die."

"Will that be soon?"

Guillermo laughed at Coco's hurry.

"Maybe. . . ."

Coco left the butterfly and looked at the shotgun over the fireplace.

The invalid followed his look.

"Would you like to play with it?"

"Gee, yes."

"Then take it down."

"Papa wouldn't let me. . . ."

"I'm letting you, so we can play together."

Coco went over to the fireplace and stretched up his arm: "I don't reach," he said.

"Pull over a chair."

Coco climbed up and got it.

"Bring it here."

Coco ran up to him happily, clutching the shotgun.

"Will we kill Indians?" he asked.

"Sure."

Coco stepped up to the blue stripe that ran down the middle of the rug.

"I mustn't be able to get away," he said. "I must have gotten as far as the seashore. The blue stripe is the ocean," he explained.

"Jump into the water."

Coco pretended to dive.

"Swell," the invalid said. "That was a beautiful dive. Now come forward and . . . aim."

"Where do I aim?"

"Here, at my chest."

Guillermo's eyes gleamed in the half-light.

"Are you the Indian?" Coco asked.

"That's right: but get up closer: put the barrel against my chest."

Coco laughed from excitement.

"Is this right?" he asked.

"Swell: now squeeze the trigger."

Coco lowered the gun:

"Is it loaded?"

"No, it's only a game."

Then Coco raised the shotgun again and aimed it at the invalid's chest.

"Do I squeeze the trigger?" he said and turned his eyes away, without meaning to, toward the butterfly.

The invalid didn't answer.

"Now?" Coco asked again.

"No," Guillermo said. "We're through playing."

The boy lowered the gun, a little disappointed.

"Hang the gun back where it was."

Coco obeyed.

"And take the butterfly."

Trembling, Coco removed it from the glass case.

"Is it mine?" he asked.

"Yes, Coco, it's yours."

Before he left, the boy gave another short laugh. Outside, he put the butterfly down in the field, underneath the sun, and stepped back a few steps to observe it.

Coco saw his father arriving and loved him. He sank into his arms as in a cloud.

"I've come home," Max said and held his son tight.

"It's great that you're back, Papa!" and Coco smiled with his one loose tooth.

The day was simple, just like the cows and the yellow wheat. Max could feel it as he walked toward the house with the boy on his shoulders. Zulema was waiting in the hall.

The bees sipped the honeysuckle flowers. That was because they were bees. And men, because they were men, came home and made up with their wives. All our feelings had their counterparts in nature or in country life, which made them familiar and easy to bear. Max held his wife close: he would have liked to make love to her at some comfortable place near the fire, to know his head was resting in the house and not rolling in the gutter like some useless garbage. Because Max realized that all evil was in the mind. The head went its own way apart from the rest, colliding with tree trunks and stones and other heads. And the body was something the head had sloughed off. And the body should have been able to make love and have a decent and rewarding sex life, but the head wouldn't let it because it liked to roll around like a senseless stone. And it fell on the highway where the hogs nosed it and the horses kicked it and the moss sometimes grew in its ears. There was only one class of privileged heads: those nice tranquil heads that didn't know anything but could pretend to know everything, because they were the ones that remained serenely at home.

Zulema tried to push his arms away, but Max wouldn't let her; he wanted to feel her body and not Clara's. Federico emerged from the shadows:

"Let her go, Max!"

They looked at him.

"Let her go, Max!" he ordered again. "You don't love her any more."

Zulema went up to her bedroom, crying. Max sat down on the wicker chair, rested his head on the back, and looked up at the ceiling.

"I want to love her," he said almost to himself.

Federico sat in the doorway that looked out on the road and lit up his pipe.

"You can't any more, Max. There are two kinds of people: the sort that travel and the sort that stay put. You're a traveler. The stay-at-homes, like Zulema, are only points of reference for our lives. Zulema doesn't move: she's rooted, like one of those buoys they anchor in the ocean to warn against danger."

"I want to go back to her," Max said.

"You're acting childish; you want to hang onto the order she represents, and it makes you sad to think you've kicked it over. Let her go, Max; men have no business going home and settling into a lie. And you wouldn't make a very impressive liar: you'd come up with the ghost of a lie that's worm-eaten and covered all over with mold."

"I want to believe that nothing's happened," Max pleaded.

"But it *has* happened, Max. Clara's happened."

"Clara's only a girl. . . ."

"It isn't that simple. No one's only a girl or an old woman or a man, but everything that we're looking for at that particular moment. Go and look for your fulfillment, and this time it'll be Clara. You have to live each phase of life completely, right to the end; then when you've had enough of her, throw her over. That goes for Clara too."

"I'm tired, Federico. . . ."

"And because you're tired, you beg your wife to take you back, like some poor, sick kid. What does Zulema care? She'll take you back because you're the one piece she's missing to make her world complete. She wants everything to be just perfect and everyone to sit around the fire together, the way they do in paintings."

"Men always go back," Max insisted.

"You make me sick," Federico said. "I'd like to spit on your marriage."

He stood up in the doorway and knocked his pipe against the wood.

"Federico," Max said, "I feel the ground giving way. Help me, Federico."

"You're on your own, Max. Get out of it by yourself."

Max rose from the chair. The bees buzzed around the honeysuckle. The island was at peace and the cows were suckling their calves.

"It's hard for me, Federico. I'm a man who's mixed up. Who can't go back home because he's so awfully mixed up."

"You want to live without paying for it, the way a child does: to have them forgive you when it's all over."

Max sat on the lawn outside the house and breathed the fresh air.

"Let life be a little more easy, and let me sleep in the fields. You expect too much, Federico. If there are any charitable institutions left, let's escape to them. They know how to forgive, and they're right too, not to expect so bloody much from a man. And if I don't live to the fullest, what about it? Am I so important or something? As long as there's a house and a bed and a woman and a good fire in the winter. Why make me go out when the weather's lousy? I'm tired, Federico. . . ."

"That's right: go cuddle up in Zulema's lap or in God's. . . ."

"You make everything so complicated. God and Zulema aren't complicated. They're very, very simple, and they don't make speeches. You wear me out with your speeches. You're a little punk, Federico, and on your deathbed you'll end up calling for God."

Federico came at him:

"I ought to break your head," he said.

Max got up slowly.

"I'll go see her," he said.

Federico's gaze followed him through the gate. Coco ran after him with short little steps, his legs numb from having crouched so long in the eaves.

"Wait for me!" he cried.

Max turned around and took him in his arms.

"I'm tired, Coco."

He stopped and rested his head against the boy's chest. Coco threw his arms around him.

"That's why they're born," Max said. "Because we need someone to love us."

Clara saw them approaching and came out to meet them. Max put his son on the grass and rested his head against the willow trunk. He looked at her intently.

"What's wrong, Max?"

For a while Max didn't answer, but stared at the things around him as if taking leave of them.

"Why are you looking like that?"

"Because I'm saying good-by," he said. "And let's not make any speeches about God."

Clara scrutinized him:

"You look like an insect that's fallen over on its back."

"Good-by then."

"Good-by, Max."

He took the boy's hand and squeezed it.

Clara ran toward her house.

Summer awakened. Everything filled up with summer. A summer wet from the river, like those in the jungle. Coco went down to the beach, where Federico and Nini were. Clara ran after him, trying to catch him. Federico saw her in the sunlight and nearly naked: he had never seen her so sharply. When she got close, he murmured:

"Let's go off together. Forget all these dead men."

But Clara kissed him on the cheek and ran on the sand without stopping. The spaces between her toes filled with water.

Benteveo, benteveo, screamed the bird.

Federico watched her move off.

"Summer at last," he said.

He raised an arm toward the sun.

"We're all brown," Coco said. "Just like the birds in the river."

"Do you mean the herons?" Nini asked.

And she stretched out on the sand in her blue bathing suit.

"The herons are pink."

"No, red," Coco said.

"No, they're white," Federico corrected him. He reached out his hand and stroked Nini's neck.

"Can I go fishing?" Coco asked.

"If you've got legs and a pole. . . ."

And Coco ran into the cane fields.

"Surubi, surubi!" They heard him calling the fish's name in the distance.

"Will the fish come for him?" Nini asked.

"Everything will come and everything will go away."

"I want to get drunk," Nini said, stretching her legs.

Federico found the thermos and held it against Nini's mouth. Then he rested his head on the sand.

"You have a virgin mouth," he said. "There's never been a first time."

"I want to bite the sand," she said, "and scream and scratch and get drunk. I want to go crazy!" she added. "And have breasts like Clara's."

"Someday yours'll grow," Federico said.

"No, they won't. I'm twenty now and they haven't grown yet."

"It's good to be young and have little breasts."

"Sure," Nini said. "Clara's are lovely and what good are they? Her husband doesn't have hands."

She laughed loudly.

"He never had hands!" she cried.

And she went on laughing.

"Other men have. . . ."

"Do you mean Max?" she said. "He's got hands in his brain."

"Shut up!"

"She loves Max but he won't ever go to bed with her."

"Shut up!"

Benteveo, benteveo, screamed the bird.

Nini crawled along the sand and put her feet in the water.

"I hate her!" she shouted.

"Shut up!"

"You won't sleep with her either. Never!"

And she started to cry, burying her head in her knees.

"What's wrong with you?" he asked.

"Nothing."

"You make things too complicated," Federico said. "Can't you just be natural? If you want me to make love to you, don't try so hard to look crazy. Just say it."

"I *am* natural. That's why I cry and get drunk and scratch the ground and feel so miserable."

"You make me tired."

"Then why do you put up with me?"

And she cried even harder.

"Come here, Nini."

Nini obeyed him.

"You look helpless," he said. "And I hate helpless people. They cling to you like little bits of lint."

"You have no pity," Nini said, still crying.

"I like my freedom," he said. "The helpless ones get under my feet."

Nini watched a canoe turning around.

Benteveo, benteveo, screamed the bird.

"That's the *benteveo* calling. I like to hear it, because it reminds me of when I was a little girl. . . ."

"They remind me of when I was a kid too: when we'd go out to the island and fish with Clara."

"What did you fish for?"

"Patís, surubís, el dorados. . . ."

And Federico shut his eyes.

"Your eyelashes are just like gold, and you've got gold hairs on your chest."

Nini caressed him.

Then Federico kissed her on the mouth. And she melted for

him and half-opened her eyes and saw a branch and a cloud passing over.

He tried to push her off but she fell on his mouth.

"I want to be like this always," she said. "Just like a poor girl. . . ."

"The afternoon's almost over," he said and pushed her away.

"But we won't go back now. We won't ever go back," Nini said. "I want to forget."

"What do you want to forget?"

"Everything, except that we're alive."

"And am I alive too?"

"Yes, you too."

"Get undressed then. I want to see what it's like to be alive."

Nini dropped her bathing suit on the sand.

"Get away from the beach, the boats are coming."

"Should I go by the trees?"

And she ran naked over the sand. Federico followed her into the willow grove.

Coco came back along the beach.

"Nini!" he shouted.

"Are you alone, Coco?" Clara asked. She was coming back also.

She knelt and picked Nini's bathing suit up from the sand.

"Sure I'm alone: let's go find them."

"No, let's wait here. Meanwhile we'll build a sand castle."

Coco filled his pail with water from the river.

"But it's night already," he insisted. "They'll never come now."

"Forget about them," Clara said. "It's such a lovely night."

Clara made the towers for the castle.

"Now let's make the moat," the boy said.

"No, let's not do any more: it's getting too dark to see."

"Why are you crying?" Coco asked.

"Because the bird's calling, and I remember when we were children. . . ."

"Let's go then!"

"Yes, but first kiss me, Coco."

Clara seated him on her bare knees.

"I love you, Coco my dearest, I love you."

And she kissed him again.

"Hello there!" Federico said and picked up the blue bathing suit.

"Where's Nini?" Coco asked.

"She'll be along," Federico answered.

"Let's go," Clara said and took the boy's hand.

"Nini's bad," Coco said as they walked along the sand.

"Why is she bad?" Clara asked.

"Because she went away."

"She isn't bad. She's just a girl."

Federico and Nini followed them across the wooden bridge.

"Go to your mother's," Federico said. "Your father should be there and you can go back with him. I'll be sleeping on the island tonight."

"I want to go back with you."

"No, Nini; do what I say."

"I'll go, but I love you."

Federico patted her head.

"Are you happy?" she asked before going.

"Sure," he lied and ran to catch up with Clara and the boy.

"Clara?" Federico called from behind them.

"What?"

"Give me your hand and I'll guide you; it's too dark to see now."

She put her hand into his, as Coco kneeled down to break off a shoot.

"Will this be good for fishing?"

"Yes."

"Clara?"

"What?"

"Nothing," Federico said and went on walking.

"It was a great day," the boy said.

They didn't answer him.

"I said it was a great day," he repeated.

"We heard you," Clara said.

Federico stopped and made her stop.

"Why aren't you walking?" Coco asked.

"Clara," Federico said, "I suppose you guessed everything?"

"Yes."

"What did she guess?" the boy asked.

She started walking again.

"Clara, wait a minute."

Federico stopped her again.

"What do you want?" she asked.

"To hold you. I want to give you something. . . ."

And he took her around under the plum tree.

"Rest your head on my chest," he said.

"Yes."

"Now relax."

"Yes."

"Press up against me."

"Federico. . . ."

"Yes?"

"Nothing."

"You were going to tell me something?"

"Not now," she said and stepped away from him.

"What're you doing?" Coco shouted. "Why aren't you walking?"

"Yes, let's walk."

They began to walk.

"Where are you going now?"

"Home," she said. "Where did you think I was going."

"I don't know. I don't know why I asked."

"Let us walk you to your house," Coco said.

"No, we'll say good-by here."

"I want to go with her!" Coco cried.

"No, my dearest, I'll go by myself."

And she kissed them both.

"I want to go with you! I want to go with you!"

And the boy flung himself on the ground and started crying.

Federico took him in his arms, and by the time they got to the big plum tree, he had fallen asleep.

The next morning, when he woke up, he heard the rooster crowing.

"He's up in the eaves," Nana said while she polished Coco's shoes.

"We'll have to clip his wings," Coco said.

"I'll do it today," Nana said and went on polishing.

The smell of bread drifted up from the kitchen.

"Did you make bread, Nana?"

"Yes; I'll bring you some in a minute."

"No; Papa doesn't let me eat in the bedroom."

"What does your papa know?"

"He knows more than anybody," the boy answered. "Papa and Uncle Federico."

"What good's what they know if they don't give the orders?"

"Who gives them then?" the boy asked.

"The women," Nana said firmly.

And she put the shoes down next to his bed.

"And what's more important, giving orders or knowing things?"

"Giving orders, of course."

Coco pulled up the blinds and looked at the sky. A great white cloud was moving across it, with lots of smaller clouds trailing behind as if it were their leader.

"There go the clouds," the boy said.

Wild ducks flew by toward the west.

"And the ducks too," he added.

"Yes," Nana said. "Everything flies past that window, except for the dead."

"The dead do too; they fly up into the clouds and the ducks."

"Why are you so silly?" Nana asked.

"You're the one that's silly, because you don't know that things are full of dead people."

Nana got angry.

"You explain that foolish talk."

And she handed him his clothes to dress himself.

Coco didn't answer but kept looking at the wild ducks.

"There's a south wind blowing up," Nana said, "and that means a storm."

Coco saw the two men coming through the *ceiba* trees; he watched them stooping to avoid the branches. Federico stumbled on the giant anthill.

"Can I go with them?" he asked Nana.

"Yes, but put on your jacket. It's turning cold again."

Nana followed their movements from the window.

"Where are they going?" she asked herself.

But the next minute she had started to straighten the bed.

Coco ran out and followed the men through the trees. He didn't like the delta willows. They were thin and sad and their leaves were always crying.

They crossed the last bridge and stopped in front of the house. *Clara isn't there,* the boy thought. And the southwester blew stronger and bent the poplars forward.

Before going in, Federico wiped off the soles of his boots and Max did the same. Then they stepped into the darkness. The boy ran as far as the hall and stopped there, not daring to move any further but waiting outside the door like a watchful but dwarfish sentry.

Through the half-open door he saw the wheelchair and the invalid's empty sleeves.

Federico and his father had gone as far as the rug, but paused at the yellow stripe, where the dog's collar had also fallen.

"There's a storm blowing up," the invalid said.

And his voice tore through the boy like a horrible corkscrew.

The others didn't answer. Some leaves brushed against the window.

"There's a storm blowing up," he said again.

"We heard you the first time," Federico said.

The dog barked.

"I'll light the fire."

"There may still be a spark left."

The boy saw him cross the stripe and rake the ashes with the poker.

"It's out," Federico said.

Max took a bottle from the cabinet and filled some glasses. He pushed the table forward.

Federico, on his knees, arranged the logs and put his lighter to the papers. The flames shot up the flue.

Max helped Clara's husband drink, then dried his lips with a handkerchief.

Federico stood up and asked:

"How long has she been missing?"

And he hung up his jacket.

"Since she went to the river with you."

The water beat down with greater force.

"How did you know she wasn't here?"

"At night when she didn't put me to bed."

"And what did you do?"

"Waited in the chair until it was light." Then he added, "She won't be coming back."

And he raised his dark, tormented eyes to them.

His father's hands were trembling:

"What makes you say that?" he asked.

Federico pulled out his pipe and began to stuff it with tobacco from the pouch he'd removed from his jacket. The boy stared into the green flames that lit up his uncle's red mustache, and he laughed in the darkness, through the opening in the door.

"I just know it: she won't be coming back," the invalid repeated.

The dog barked again and Max watched the flashes of lightning and the smoke curling up toward the ceiling. He managed to move, but very slowly, one step and then another. Coco noticed the way his boots were dragging across the rug. A willow leaf clung to his heel and slid behind him like a little green snake. He stopped in front of the invalid.

"She's got to come," Max said. "She'll be here any minute."

Coco saw them staring at each other through the cold. The

invalid jerked forward in his chair. Suddenly his father bent down and kissed him on the head.

Guillermo looked up.

"I'm glad you've come back, Max."

"It's so hard to be decent," his father said.

"It isn't your fault," the invalid answered. "It's this series of wounds we inflict on each other."

"Yes," Federico said and reached for his jacket.

"It was such a long time since I'd last been in her room," the invalid said.

No one answered.

"And this morning I got there with the chair," he continued. "Her bed's narrow, like a little girl's. . . ."

Max walked over to the door; he was ready to head out. Federico too.

"What should we do?" they asked.

"Look for her," Federico said.

"We'll come back later," Max said.

And they left. Coco followed them into the storm. His uncle's jacket was puffing up in the back. They walked past rivers of leaves.

"It's hard to be a man," Federico said.

"Yes," his father said.

Coco stopped at the wooden bridge, and with his dirty fingers took hold of the tooth that had just fallen out; all that morning he had jabbed it with his tongue.

In the kitchen, Nana was drying the last cup.

"Do you know what happened?" Coco shouted from the door.

"I know," she answered. "And don't you dare repeat it."

"What would be bad about that?"

Nana turned around angrily and threw the towel down on the table.

"Is it good to always be talking about death?"

"What do you mean?" Coco asked, looking surprised.

"I mean Clara. . . ."

"Silly," he said. "I was asking if you knew that my tooth fell out."

"Ahh," Nana murmured, and she wept with the spoon still clutched in her hand.

"I'll put it under the pillow, so the rats'll leave me some money."

And he laughed and thrust out his hand for Nana to see it.

"Why are you crying? Aren't you happy that the tooth's out?"

"Yes," Nana said. "Let me have it."

And she put it for safekeeping in her apron pocket.

"Don't go running off!" his grandmother shouted from the doorway.

But the boy had disappeared in the willow grove and was watching the canoes bobbing in the fog. The branches bobbed too and the rushes and the mud in the inlets.

The people gathered in small groups along the beach.

They brought her in, naked, with a yellow something thrown across her breast.

An old woman set her baskets down on the sand:

"They should've thrown her back in the river!" she shouted.

"That kind of fish won't do anyone much good," someone else said.

Zulema fell to her knees.

Benteveo, benteveo, screamed the bird, and the *chajas* buried their red beaks. All at once the willows started turning purple and the color spread out like a wall of fire.

Nana brought the sheets and they covered her quickly, her breasts still bulging underneath the cloth.

After they carried her off, the sand where she'd been remained moist; and though the spot grew a little bigger, it still kept her shape.

Nana followed the procession with cold, lifeless eyes. His mother's eyes were like glass. His father kept behind the others: one, two, three. We all have to go, but no one knows by what road. The boy ran ahead of them without understanding these things. But his mother didn't understand them either; nor his father, nor his grandmother, nor Nana.

They put her on the table in the guest room, then the strangers went away. The last of them came back to ask for his umbrella.

"Pardon me," he said and closed the door.

When they were finally alone, they stared at each other, because they didn't know what they would do with the drowned body. Then Federico took two steps forward:

"I feel like laughing," he said.

And he laughed. He went off into gales of laughter. He stood next to the lamp and he rocked with a laughter that was really tremendous. And Coco's father leaped at him and seized him by the throat.

"You're an animal," he said and clenched his teeth.

Federico tore himself loose:

"Don't you dare touch me!"

After a while, he said:

"She was a good-looking woman. Why didn't you take off with her?"

Coco's mother gave a stifled cry:

"I come before. . . ."

"And why should I worry about you?" Federico asked. "Don't you have your two breasts and your two eyes and two legs? You don't give a damn who the man is: all that interests you is your womb and your house. You want the whole works, everything: you want to run it all."

Nana brought a fresh log for the fire, and his father looked around him for a place to sit.

"Why didn't you just take off with her?" Federico repeated.

"I couldn't desert them. . . . "

"You're lying. You didn't go because you were afraid to. You couldn't upset things. No one's got the courage to upset things. To kick them over and make a new start!"

"Celia's coming," his grandmother said, looking out toward the landing.

"You have no pity," Max said to Federico; then he buried his head in his hands.

Federico laughed again.

"Pity?" he asked. "What should I have pity for? For your fear? Or for that drowned girl in there, that green, slime-covered body?"

And he motioned toward the guest room.

Celia, Max's sister, opened the door:

"Good evening."

And she set her valise down near the stairs.

"Good evening," the others said.

"Sit down, Gamalita," Celia told the little girl who had come in with her.

The idiot sat down.

Coco noticed the polish on her shoes gleaming and the sapphire stone on her finger.

They were seated all around the living room, making two main groups on the rug. Something tapped on the window and his father looked out:

"It's a branch," he said.

And went back to his place.

"They'll all go back to their places," Federico said.

The fire sent up sparks and the rain fell more strongly.

"There *is* an order," Max said. "It's like throwing a pebble in the river."

The idiot's doll fell down and her lips made the sound "da-da."

"Great," Federico said. "Now order's re-established. She throws herself into the brook and, *splash!* peace reigneth over all."

"That's right," Celia said, picking the doll up. "She died because she wanted to destroy the order."

"But dying also preserves it," Federico cried.

His father circled the room.

"I don't know what to do," he said. "Death brings so much disruption with it, because it severs the strings we've artificially established with life. We're all kidding ourselves!" he exclaimed.

The idiot's lips made the sound.

"If that's the case," Federico said, "if neither life nor death is any good, why did you let your son be born?"

"Because it's all part of the scheme to kid ourselves further, to keep us pulling the wagon. Like pruning trees or writing letters or fishing or getting married. Where's the difference from collecting stamps?"

The boy cried and felt cold, but the cat slid onto his knees and began purring softly and looking at him with its gold-colored eyes. Grapes were gold-colored too, and fish, and the hair of newborn babies. The world was full of newborn things and they circled the world like an endless river.

"Who's playing games with us?" his father asked.

"Da-da," answered the idiot.

"Yes," they said. "We have to keep on and on and on. One, two, three: obey, obey, obey."

Then his mother stood up and broke her needles in two. The boy could feel her red hair bristling.

"We'll go fishing," Max said. "We have to go fishing. It's our duty either to fish or drive the launch or run the mill. Or else we can prune the fruit trees in the morning."

Federico lit his pipe.

"All of us are filthy," he said. "Only the boy and the cat are worth a damn."

And he went out, slamming the door.

"Life killed her," his mother said. "It was life that did it."

The boy saw his father staring at her red hair, which was shining like a lamp.

"What else could it have been, if not life?"

"I or you or Mama or Nana. All of us killed her!"

"Yes," they said, "because for a while we were life."

"How will I ever understand?" his mother lamented. "What must I do to be good? To understand infinitely?"

And she wept over her knitting and her broken needles.

"Come to bed, Coco," Nana said.

While they were climbing the stairs, the boy asked:

"Nana, is Mama good or bad?"

"Neither," Nana said angrily. "She's human; that's all, just human."

As Nana was taking his shoes off, the boy heard his grand-mother saying:

"Why don't we try to live without so many reflections? You've got to be old and have one foot in the grave to realize how much time you've wasted thinking. Where does it get you? You've got to be old to realize that it's senseless tending rosebushes or exterminating ants; you have to let them feed on their own. None of you can possibly start a plant! What *are* you good for? Where have you gotten with all this talk? In the meantime the house is leaking: it's falling in ruins, and the garden and everything else is falling in ruins!"

"Your grandmother's right," Nana said. "They're all a bunch of fools."

"Nana," the boy asked, "why are you and Granny so angry?"

Nana took a second blanket from the closet and placed a pan under the leak in the ceiling.

"Why are you angry?" the boy asked again.

"Likely because we're both old," Nana said.

And she left. Coco heard her moaning at the door of the guest room.

He watched the old women through a break in the vines. The cat rubbed against Nana's feet and stopped on the sky-blue part of the tiles. Nana was sitting next to his grandmother, as she always did when they were alone, when he and his cat were kept out. All at once Nana laughed. Coco watched her with amazement.

His grandmother looked up from her knitting:

"What are you laughing about, old woman?"

"I don't know."

"Tell me what. I'm asking you."

"I think that everyone. . . ."

"And who's *everyone?*"

"Max, Zulema, Federico. . . ."

"I don't see the joke," his grandmother said and put the knitting down to get a better look at her.

"I do, ma'am, if you'll forgive me."

"Well, tell me then. . . ."

"You see, they all fit so well into this house. . . ."

"Myself too?"

"Oh yes . . . even better than the others."

Nana stared at her a moment with her old eyes. She took out her handkerchief and began to laugh again. Coco watched her, feeling happier each minute. His grandmother waited.

"Remember," Nana added, "you raised them."

"And what's that got to do with anything?"

"It's got a whole lot to do with it. Zulema, Clara, and Federico: not one of them really worked at being happy. They were so confused, ma'am. . . ."

"We don't decide these things, Nana. They happen by themselves."

Her bony hand straightened her bun.

"Everyone talks about things," Nana went on, "and no one knows what to do about them. They're just like puppets. Puppets that aren't good for anything. But people have to do some good in life. They have to be good for something. I'm sorry, but that's the way I see them; they give me lots to laugh at . . . and to feel bad about too."

Coco called "puss, puss," but the cat ran into the rushes. There was a lot of sun, a real sun, golden and full of spots. The island up front kept growing.

Nana looked all around her, as though she were afraid that someone might hear her:

"Listen to what I'm saying, ma'am: Clara shouldn't have died."

His grandmother trembled:

"Why do you say that, Nana?"

"If only I'd raised her!" Nana answered with a sigh.

"But you did; you raised her too."

"No, ma'am. You still don't see what I'm saying: if I had raised her by myself."

And Nana folded her hands on her skirt. Now his grandmother

took off her glasses and stared at her: the look in her eyes had grown dark and intense.

"I don't know what you mean," she said.

"Then let me explain: if my sister, the night she brought the girl from the country, hadn't given her to you. . . ."

His grandmother tried to fit the parts together. She struggled to be calm, to see the earlier arrangement before events threw everything askew. She wanted to understand and be strong, but it was like a frayed and dirty photo. She grew motionless and probed within her; she probed herself; she probed the others. Until she succeeded in getting to her thought:

"Nana," she said at last. "During those months . . . you were away in the country. . . ."

"That's right, ma'am. And that was my mistake. . . ."

His grandmother waited: she waited with her legs and hands and skin. Coco waited too, but then a bird down at the river caught his eye.

His grandmother got up. She wanted to find someplace to go: to break into the house, to tear open all the kitchen shelves, to uncork the bottles, to check the temperature, to water the plants. But she came back to her chair:

"Now tell me everything."

"You raised her in this house, where everyone laughed and made me cry. . . ."

She shook her head and went on:

"Max was crazy about her . . . Federico the same."

"And what does that have to do with it? Clara was beautiful. . . ."

"Ma'am, she was the daughter of a servant."

His grandmother stood up and moved closer to Nana; closer to her heart, to her wide, soft breasts, to her belly and her bush.

"Who was the mother?"

"I was."

Coco brought them the dark little bird, which flapped its wings against his face. His grandmother busied herself with him in her confusion:

"Tomorrow will be bad out and I'll make the child some tarts."

"Yes; we'll go on living as if nothing had happened."

"Has something happened?" Coco asked.

"No; nothing's happened."

Max lay meditating on the grass, his eyes fixed on a single willow tree. And Coco climbed the farthest plum tree in the grove. Winter was over. The boy's heart longed for the warm breezes that would blow up from the river in the evenings. Federico appeared with his shotgun and fired at the herons and the *benteveos*.

"Leave my birds alone," Coco shouted from his branch.

And Federico, not being able to spot the boy, walked up to Max and stretched out at his side. He reached out a hand toward the same willow.

Max brushed a mosquito from his cheek. The sky looked empty to him, like the eye of a needle.

"Well, she's gone," he said.

"No, she's not," Federico answered.

"Where is she then?" Max exclaimed, sitting up.

"Here," Federico said and touched his forehead.

"Love's insane," Max said. "The black wind, the fury, the hatred. And death too. . . . "

"Go and chew on the earth!" Federico said. "Claw at the grass! Be an animal!"

Max moved closer to him:

"So you loved her too?"

Federico stroked the grass with his fingers:

"Since we were kids. . . ."

"And did you ever sleep with her?"

"What does it matter? That only quiets you down for a moment. Love doesn't reach into another person's body."

"There must be something else. . . ." Max thought out loud. "Something to get deeper in!"

"The body has its walls; it's senseless."

"I'd like to make an incision through my back," Max said.

"And empty myself out through a hole in my eyes. And watch the blood running out like a fountain."

"Vomit your heart out, you idiot!" Federico said.

"I'm jealous," Max said very suddenly.

"She's dead!"

"I said I'm jealous!"

"She's dead!"

"I'm jealous, you animal!"

And Max leaned forward and broke off a branch that was hanging from the willow.

"She's dead!" Federico shouted.

"I'm jealous! I'm jealous!"

"I hate you," Federico said.

Max hit him in the face with his fist. They rolled over on the ground like rotten fruits fallen from some tree. And they went on like that, hitting and biting each other. When they were quiet again, Max looked with disgust at the tuft of red hair he held in his fingers, and threw it away. For a time they remained motionless, with their mouths against the earth.

The ants dug a deep hole. The willow shook its branches as always, and Coco, on the highest branch in the grove, hunted for the year's last plum.

"Bite the earth!" Federico said. "Everything makes me sick."

"Cry!" Max shouted and raised his head.

Federico obeyed him, his eyes smeared with grass.

Max let his head drop to the ground when he saw Federico crying; then he cried too, his hands covered with dead mosquitoes. Suddenly he saw a spot of blood near his eyes.

"It's all this miserable blood," he said.

"We're the ones who are miserable. . . ."

"Like beggars."

"She had something," Federico said. "Beauty and life. And no one took her, not you or me or the cripple. A bunch of imbeciles! No one was capable of immortalizing himself in her belly. Only the river, the filthy slime of the river, and death."

"So many longings! And what do we get out of life? Tell me that!"

"A glass of wine, some candy, a kiss, a ring on our fingers, a plum."

Federico raised his eyes toward the far tree, and he saw Coco reaching his hand out happily to snare a small bloody planet.

"That's it," he said. "A plum. A plum for Coco."

—*Translated by* JEROME ROTHENBERG

THE YOKE
by Faustino González-Aller

FAUSTINO GONZÁLEZ-ALLER was born in Spain but gives Cuba
as his permanent residence, having lived in that country for
many years. He has worked as a newspaper correspondent in
several countries and is presently with the radio and television
section of the United Nations. He is a playwright as well as
a movie script-writer. In 1950 he received the Lope de Vega
Prize for one of his plays.

I will never understand why shootings traditionally take place
at cockcrow. The men of the execution squad are usually half
asleep at that hour or so drunk with *chicha* that they don't even
know where they are aiming. On previous mornings we watched
the shooting of our predecessors through the window of the shed
in which we were crammed. They all writhed like snakes cut
through the middle until they were given the *coup de grâce.* They
could have started with it: a bullet behind the ear and all over;
but they had to carry out the order given them by phone from
La Paz by General Ichazo: "I don't want even one of them left
to tell the story; but I want it all done quite legally." In the
first three days over five hundred mine workers, men and women,
died like dogs, in the cockpit or at the foot of the crushing mills.
And yet it had all started with a peaceful strike. We merely
wanted to show, by downing our tools without dropping them,
that we opposed our exploitation by the tin-mine bosses, backed
by the Peñaranda government. But the soldiers arrived by the
Oruro train and went into action against us more furiously than
if we had been Paraguayans defending a position in the Chaco.
The sacks of half-refined ore were left empty and full of holes;
still, their contents could be picked up and used again. But the
corpses of the *palliris,* the women mine workers, many of whom
carried their *guaguas,* their babies, tied to their back, were of no
use except for the cemetery. The shaft miners, who started de-

fending themselves with sticks of dynamite, were bayoneted. The procession of the dead, carried the next day through the main street of Catavi on their way to the cemetery, was like an *aysu,* a landslide of ponchos, *chulu* caps, and sandals, rolling in dry blood and tears. The laments of the living exasperated the soldiers, who used their rifle butts to stop children crying for their mothers.

Those of us who were not carried stiffly in that procession to the tomb were hunted later over the flatlands of the Plateau, as if we were rats, *vizcachas.* Oh God, it would be better to have been killed in the hunt than to suffer the slow agony of men condemned to death. The eight of us still alive in the shed of the muleteers' inn, which juts out a little from the immense plain, where the wind gets tired of blowing, were the last survivors among those taken by the *kkepis,* the policemen, on their rat-hunting expedition. Next morning would be our turn. The bodies of those shot three hours earlier were stretched out three yards from the adobe wall of the inn. Two roosters, which had come from the chicken run to scavenge in the dead men's clothes, had blood on their beaks when they lifted them. Whatever their damned purpose was, I shouted at them to scare them away:

"Risp! . . . risp!"

They moved away, proud and unaware of my revulsion.

"Tomorrow they'll do the same thing to us, and there won't be anybody left to scare them off," Juan Fernández said behind my back. He was rubbing his eyes to speed his awakening. Then he took some coca leaves out of his pocket and put them in his mouth, while looking with indifference at a countryside filled with sun and wild straw. The calamine roofs of Catavi were shining in the far distance.

"Do you think the soldiers' truck will come today to pick up the dead or will they wait till tomorrow? I'm asking because, if they take them all at once, the government will save itself a trip," Juan Fernández made a low-voiced comment, still speaking in Quechua.

I could never make out when this *cliceño* Indian was speaking

seriously and when he was joking. He always wore a broad-
brimmed hat over his many-colored *chulu* cap. He was quite
short and had eyes like a toad. His lean body was almost hidden
by a filthy vicuña wool poncho. He had taken off his sandals in
our prison because he liked to step on the guano that covered
the floor of the shed.

"Ay, *tatito!*" he exclaimed. "These dead *chotos* are sure in
luck! With that meal of lead pap they received today instead
of their usual corn *api* they no longer feel or suffer."

He always called me *tatito,* little father, a title of honor, because he thought I was the leader of the strike, which wasn't
true. Any one of those sleeping men could have been the leader,
or any one of those who died.

And this is what really mattered. The real leader was the
new consciousness that had been born in the trenches of the
Chaco; a consciousness engendered among the Bolivian youth
that had uselessly fought for the right to live a bad life that
drained Bolivia's heart's blood. And right after the end of the
war, the voices of those who escaped from the disaster penetrated
deeply into the meekness of the Indians, snatched from their homes
in the arid *punas* to work in the mines. The leader? That's what
President Peñaranda and the despoilers of Bolivia would have
liked to find: a leader. Then they would cut off his head and
it would all be over. But the leader was a sentiment, and they
knew they couldn't finish it off that easily. Though the attempted
revolution had failed in 1943, it would be followed by another
. . . and another . . . and another. . . .

The infinite Plateau with its bands of colors, shifting like the
clouds, was there to confirm it.

"How many hours have we left?" Juan Fernández asked suddenly.

"Don't think about it," I replied. But how could one not think
about "it" when death was our only way? Outside were the dead;
inside, those who were going to be killed. We all knew that there
was nothing in this world to stop Garlic Teeth from shouting
tomorrow: "Take aim! . . . Fire!" They had given him a chance
to acquire merits, and he would exploit it to the last. Would I

ever stop knowing him as I knew him? Three years ago he was
foreman at the *La Deseada* mine, until they cut his face in a
fight, near the cliffs. From then on he was afraid and never
showed himself again at the mine; but he had a strange love
for tin, as if he belonged to the owner's family, and he kept
close to the management. It was whispered that they advanced
him money to start the grocery he owned on the slope of El
Orden hill, as a reward for his denunciations of this person and
that.

When his business started to prosper, he married Aurora, the
little *chota* who had come with her parents from Cochambamba
and was as sweet as the *pancae*. Our jaws dropped with surprise
the day we learned he had taken her to the room behind the
store. All the girls dreamed about that room because it contained
a gasoline stove, a bed for two, and a wardrobe with a mirror,
filled with linen sheets, vicuña blankets, and colored towels.

On his wedding night Garlic Teeth closed his store before ten,
but not before showing off a proud appearance to the curious
gathering on the street outside. He had put on a new suit, and
a Panama hat with a broad brim that partly covered up his
scar.

He consulted his pocket watch, with its thick chain, and went
in to become a husband.

That night I had to pour the contents of several *tutuma* gourds
down my throat to relieve a pain that was gnawing at my insides.
They say she wept between the new sheets. Who knows? No one
can prove these things. The fact remains that Garlic Teeth was
the first man to enjoy the privilege of lifting Aurora's petticoats
and, within a short time, she became legitimately pregnant. That's
life for you. That bastard of a *cholo!* And he is, a real *cholo,* that
one, one of those who deny their own mother. And because he
was a renegade and a traitor, there he was at the inn, jailor
and executioner, acquiring merits so as to become a junior
lieutenant of the *kkepis.* I know he coveted an officer's stripes
to show off before his wife. One day, in a fit of jealousy, he
said:

"You think I am a dirty *chichi* fit only to sell carbide, cod, and coca? . . . That's what you think. But one day you will see me in uniform, wearing a sword. Anselmo Ramírez is not just anybody, believe me. . . . My patience with you is wearing thin. . . . I have the blood of a colonel! Do you hear me?" And everybody in the store heard him shouting like a madman. And afterward, he would fall at the *chotita's* feet and beg her pardon. That was his weakness: to love her as he did and never to feel sure of her. To be brief: when the strike broke out, he and seven other traitors volunteered to search the Plateau for us and to lock us up in that inn a mile and a half away from Catavi. They put him in charge because he had the reputation, from his prospecting days, of knowing the terrain like nobody else. They say that the chief of the expeditionary force gave him these orders: "If you catch them, you'll get your reward. But don't bring them to me here at Catavi. I don't want any more trouble. Lock them up anywhere, far from here, interrogate them till they sign a confession of guilt, and then shoot them in three morning shifts. I'll send you a truck every day to pick up the bodies that'll pile up. . . . I want the people of Catavi warned by seeing the leaders stuffed with lead . . . while a spokesman reads them the statements of these two-for-a-penny revolutionaries. . . . forward march!"

The inn was abandoned when Garlic Teeth reached it three days ago, with a file of thirty prisoners fastened to the tail of a mule. He and the others were armed to the teeth, and they amused themselves by walking beside the prisoners and dealing out lashings. When the oldest of us—like the doctor, the engineer, or the teacher—fell on their faces because the mule jumped unexpectedly after being goaded, these monsters roared with laughter that reverberated in the silence of the plain. The sun was setting when they shoved us into the inn. A bitter north wind furiously whipped the earth and our bodies.

Our keepers were shivering, too, and Garlic Teeth ordered them to light a fire on the hearth of the ample kitchen. What he pompously called a "court-martial" started an hour later. Not to be born would be a better fate than to suffer the treatment they gave us that night. After we signed what they wanted, they kicked us into the shed. We fell upon the guano floor, bruised and with our skin torn in many places. I remember that the doctor revived me by emptying a pot of water on me.

"Courage, *niñituy*, my boy! . . . breathe deeply! . . . Can you do it? . . . Look! They didn't break a single rib! And now, piss, and if you don't piss blood all will be well. . . ."

And he started to laugh. The doctor wanted to turn the incident into a joke because, after all, what the devil did it matter if one's kidneys were crushed or one's ribs broken just before one was buried? I said as much to Juan Fernández when they threw him next to me two hours later.

"Courage, *niñituy*, breathe deeply. . . ."

When the *cliceño* with the toad's eyes recovered his breath, he muttered between his teeth:

"I know that someone, someday, will kill that herd of yellow *pongos*. . . ."

He began to weep convulsively, consumed by rage. His face was swollen, and so was mine, and so were the faces of the others. For a long while we all kept quiet and bore our pain and disgrace in silence. It was Juan Fernández who broke it in a muffled voice:

"I don't mind if they put a ramrod through my belly but it hurts me really deep that these sons of bitches dared to hit me across the face. . . ."

The next morning they shot twelve. They put them before the shed window and Garlic Teeth gave the orders in a voice that pretended to be apocalyptic:

"Take aim! . . . Fire!"

Hours later I saw Aurora arrive, riding a mountain mule. Two donkeys followed her, their backs loaded with supplies. She didn't look at the window, and I didn't want to call her. Oh God, how beautiful she was! Almost more beautiful than when I courted her on the walk around the plaza. But those days were gone, as if a breeze had swept them out of time. Pity, because her complexion was still the color of ripe peaches and her eyes changed their hue like the endless plain of the *papel-pampa* in mid-afternoon.

Seated on the mule, she didn't look pregnant. She wore a hooped skirt of green and red plush. Between the folds of the poncho she wore to protect herself from the merciless lashings of the cold wind, I could see her ripe bosom rising from the opening of her *tocuyo* cloth shirt, made even fuller by the black velvet bodice. When she was only fourteen and still called the Uncle Generoso's *imilla,* his little girl, Aurora's heart was free to be given to the man of her choice. At that time she liked to hear me sing to her the *huayño* of lovers. But so much has happened since those days and, in any case, what's the use of remembering?

During the night, her presence made itself felt. A jailer brought us for dinner a lamb hash she had cooked. We didn't know which of us was due to be shot a few hours later; but the food was good and we enjoyed eating it.

None of us in the shed slept that night or the night before, because Garlic Teeth selected the next victims by pointing at them with his finger. We waited, with the vomit of disgust in our hearts, for the moment when that loathsome creature made his appearance. We could hear the laughter of the others who were enjoying themselves drinking *chicha* and singing to the accompaniment of guitars and *charangos:*

> *Almost, almost have I loved you*
> *Almost, almost have you loved me*
> *But for that damned almost, almost*
> *I almost would have married you.*

"You, you . . . and the roadworker . . . and you . . . and the father of the pug-nosed *ñato.* . . ." He selected the twelve at his own caprice, and they went out silently. They faced the execution squad without any noticeable trembling. Afterward, as I already mentioned, things were different because their aim was so bad. A very lively *chasquiri,* a pieceworker, whom we called "Bark of the *Molle* Tree" insulted them till the last moment, and they could stop his jeering references to their mothers only by finally hitting his spine.

The next morning they killed the ten whom I used to see, with Juan Fernández, straddling the road. And on the following

day the eight of us still left would also go to push up mallows
from our adobe graves. And on Thursday, Garlic Teeth would
be a junior lieutenant of the police and would have his stripes
and his sword to parade before his wife.

On the previous day, the truck, sent by the head of the expeditionary force from Catavi to pick up the dead, had also
brought a priest in case any of us wanted to confess. When he
told "Bark of the *Molle* Tree" that he would be, within a few
hours, in the presence of God, the mestizo asked him with an
air of astonishment:

"But what is there for me to confess, *tata? . . .* that I have
always been a slave?"

And he added, philosophically:

"If God lets me live the other half of my life with a free soul
and a free body, then I'll render accounts to him. But as it is
I don't know who owes an accounting to whom. . . ."

The priest left with the bodies and promised to return the next
day. And though Juan Fernández said nothing to me, I believe
he had his eyes glued to the Catavi road for the truck with the
priest.

He moved away from me for a moment to wash his face in
the chipped washstand that stood in a corner for everybody's use.
That was the only piece of furniture the shed had: the rest was
dampness, cold, guano, and cobwebs. The other six men who
shared the improvised common cell with Juan Fernández and
myself were asleep by the wall. The shed had only one heavy
door, which opened to the passage leading to the kitchen. By
day, its only light came from a narrow glassless window with a
thick bar in the middle. And at night they let us have a carbide
lamp, hung from one of the beams that supported the straw and
calamine roof.

At seven in the morning, the jailer on duty came in with a
kettle of coca tea and a loaf of rye bread under his arm. The
noise he made in entering, or the smell of the tea, woke the
sleeping men. To tell the truth, I don't know whether they were
asleep or numbed by the dawn executions.

The man who brought the kettle was of the chubby type; one

of his hips had been broken by an ore cart. He had adapted himself to his lameness and walked lightly. He didn't seem very proud to be a jailer; but then he could have been a cuckold without being proud of it either. He was one of those characters. He left us the kettle and the bread and went away limping.

We poured tea into the mugs they had given us. The bread was lukewarm and soft.

"It's our turn next morning," the doctor said, just to say something.

He was tall and skinny. He was then on the verge of fifty though he looked ten years younger. After fighting in the Chaco, he came to the village to cure the incurable: the mine sickness. It was he who shocked public opinion in Latin America by revealing in an Argentine newspaper that the average life span of the Bolivian miner was thirty-eight years. This cost him a beating and a year in jail. Later, at a Congress of Industrial Medicine, he said that, from the Spanish discovery of the first mines at Potosi till today, eight million Indians had died of cave-in accidents or of silicosis. They crushed him a lung at the next beating and exiled him for two years.

A man whom we nicknamed Viracocha[1] because of his refined manners started to sing the "Farewell to Life" while he pissed against the wall. I must confess that, though he was a revolutionary like the rest of us, I didn't like the guy. He spoke in a petulant tone that provoked our immediate anger. Sócrates García, the schoolmaster of Catavi, reproached him sulkily:

"This is hardly the moment for jokes."

"Can you think of a better one? . . . I want you to know that I am satisfied. After three days, I have just found out that my heart is free of fear."

And he went on singing. Viracocha came from another part of the country. He appeared one day at Catavi, nobody knows from where. All we know is that, no one can quite tell when, he pushed in the swinging doors of Roque's *acallantu,* where some

---

[1] Viracocha: the Inca sun god; also name of an Inca ruler. Tr.

of us miners went to drink Punata *chicha*. He greeted us as if he
had been one of our group all his life:

"Well, what's new, friends? . . ."

He wore a blue cashmere suit and a white piqué waistcoat.
But he wore no hat because he had beautiful blond hair, which
he displayed proudly. His face was pale, with little blue veins in
the temples. His eyes looked green, but nobody could say that
they weren't gray or brown. They certainly sparkled, on occasion,
with roguery or understanding. This may seem strange, but that's
what we all noticed about him, one by one, as time went on.

He asked for a seat at the table where we were conspiring and
said, as if he knew our innermost secrets:

"I agree with you."

We looked at each other and thought he was a joker or a madman; but, as the months went on, we realized that he was neither.
One day he confided to us:

"I was born to be a revolutionary, just as Michelangelo was born
to carve his Moses. It would be absurd for me to resist my
destiny."

And it was true that he carried a rebel between his breast and
back.

When the miners protested, he marched at their head and
shouted, and they had to listen to him because God had given
him a "beak of gold." When the *palliris* complained because one
of them had conked out while removing the ore and the mine
owners refused to pay any indemnity to her children, Viracocha
bearded the manager in person, made some terrible threats, and
always got something. He spoke at the meetings allowed by the
authorities, wrote for the newspapers. . . . He was an essential
part of our revolutionary machine; but, though we made use of
him, none of us really liked him. Why? Maybe it was because
while we all, or almost all, had some kind of a job connected with
the mine, Viracocha was just a professional gambler. He would
challenge anyone to a game of dice and had a rare ability to rob
a poor sucker of his last shirt. Saturday was, above all, his big
day, the day when he, as he put it, "sharpened his nails to shuffle
the cards." The contractors and the engineers lost heaps of pesos

to him on the green baize tables of Madame Lavinia's brothel. Did he cheat? Nobody ever knew or would have dared to prove it to him. He had the reputation of being a good shot. One night when, as was his habit, he was carrying food and medicines to the Collada cabins, they attacked him by surprise. The next day, the *kkepis* found a contractor from the Saturday gambling parties lying on the roadside with a little hole between the eyebrows. They would not accuse him, but everybody suspected that Viracocha had done it.

Viracocha was an extremely careful man. So when he told us, as a joke, we supposed, that he had woken up, for the first time, without fear, we all burst out laughing. Who would believe him, after seeing him fight against the men from Oruro? And afterward . . . I myself saw him in action when Garlic Teeth hunted us over the Plateau, because we were hiding near him.

Garlic Teeth ordered his men to advance toward the stones of the *sayaña* that was Viracocha's parapet; but only after making sure that he had no more bullets left for his rifle. And they stepped cautiously because they were afraid of the pantings, like those of a trapped beast, which issued from the diceplayer's chest. And here in the shed he was calmly drinking his tea and looking at Sócrates García with a compassionate smile crossing his strange eyes:

"But if you don't like it, Sócrates, I won't sing. . . ."

Sócrates García was a poor man burdened with many children. He officiated mornings in the notary's office of Doctor Enciso as his bush lawyer or *kelkeri,* to use the Indian word; in the evenings he taught adults to read, in a granary that the mine owners had turned into a school. I believe that Sócrates, after three days in the shed, still didn't quite realize that he was to die at dawn the next day. Nonetheless, he was consumed with anguish. He was a white man, but his skin was ashen and his lips livid, as if an angina were brewing in his aorta. I'm sure we all regretted that he was here with us, because he had really nothing to do with what had happened at Catavi five days earlier. True, he had the reputation of being a revolutionary; but of a romantic, hackneyed, and historical variety. He was a son, grandson, and

great-grandson of men of his kind. He came into this world burdened with the name of Sócrates and he, in turn, crowned the
uncertain destiny of his children with the names of Liberty, Garibaldi, Robespierre, and Fraternity.

The fifth man due to die next dawn was an engineer from
the La Graciosa mine. I felt him joining me at the window to
take a look at the bodies. He lit a cigarette and said to himself,
with an immense sadness:

"There they lie, silenced forever; they can't tell us anything
about those beyond."

His round face was made to look even rounder by the merciless
beating they had given him. He was a native of La Paz, of
German descent. He had delivered telegrams as a boy and studied in his spare time. He won a scholarship to study mining in
Germany; when he returned with his diploma, they gave him an
important post at Catavi. But he didn't want to play the bosses'
game. He lived modestly on the outskirts of the village, bred
pigeons, and wrote a book which, I believe, they never allowed
him to publish. When a miner knocked at his door and asked for
help, he helped him. When the strike began, he was there by the
ore-crushing machines, with a placard inscribed: WE WANT ECO-
NOMIC FREEDOM FOR BOLIVIA AND A NEW DEAL FOR THE MINERS.
With his eyes fixed upon the dead, he mused:

"It's horrible . . . horrible. . . . Oh, our poor country! . . . So
much useless hate and so little love!"

Juan Fernández came up to the window again. His face was
wet. It was as if his earthen mask had been flooded. When he saw
that the eyes of the engineer did not leave the lifeless bodies, he
asked him:

"Do you think we'll see them tomorrow?"

"Tomorrow? . . . Where?"

"Up there," replied the *cliceño,* innocently pointing his finger
at the sky.

There was a noisy burst of laughter. It came from the doctor,
who liked to boast of his atheism. Juan Fernández was abashed.

Viracocha's eyes lit up with sudden fury, unusual for him, and
he said:

"You may be an unbeliever, which is fine since you are a rationalist—something that, incidentally, won't be much use to you within a few hours—but to sneer at a religious sentiment makes you look smaller in my eyes. . . ."

I have already mentioned that Viracocha spoke petulantly. The doctor stopped laughing and spat out some blood. This happened to him after any exertion because of his wounded lung.

One man in the shed never moved. We didn't actually know, all those three days, when he was asleep and when he was awake. He was a young man consumed with idealism. He came from a rich Sucre family and, one day, broke with it completely to share the destiny of the downtrodden people of his country. And he came to Catavi "walking the roads," as he put it. He was the son of Spanish immigrants, but he talked about the Incas as if they were his true ancestors. He worked in the mines and married a *chola*. A son, born with a dusky skin and straight hair, was his greatest pride. He bestowed upon him the Inca name of Huascar, not by having him baptized but in a ceremony that he improvised, facing the sun on Haliama Mountain.

At that moment our attention was drawn to our companion number eight, who was painfully trying to get up from the floor. That one had, indeed, pissed blood after the beating. His skin had become livid, and his eyes were burning with fever. He was a giant of a man, but he seemed to have lost ten or twelve inches of his height between night and morning. He walked slowly toward the window, his body deeply bent. We all looked at him silently. The doctor wanted to take his pulse, but only got a rough refusal:

"It's too late now to do me any good. . . . Friends, I want to ask you a favor. I am in horrible pain, and I'm sure I won't be able to bear it till dawn. In the name of that which unites us, I beg you to kill me. . . ."

In spite of his feverish look, we knew that he spoke with complete self-possession.

"Why don't you decide by lot who will put me out of my pains? . . . If those cowards hadn't robbed us of everything we had, I would have committed suicide. But, as it is, I have nothing to do it with. Please friends. . . ."

His name was Almenar, and he was the leader of some kind of union that the *chasquiris,* the pieceworkers, had formed. But he didn't live from this; he went down into the mine tunnels and worked harder than anyone with his pick. Garlic Teeth hated him because he suspected that Almenar had had something to do with the scar that disfigured his face. But his hate was quite unjustified because, though the giant was feared for his outbursts of fury, he fought on such occasions like a bull with sand thrown in his eyes. One might expect him to crush one's bones with his gorilla arms, but not to cut one's face deliberately. But Garlic Teeth expected from everybody what he would have done himself.

Almenar spoke again, anxiously:

"Will you just let me writhe with pain, friends?"

The doctor gave us a sign to indicate that the man spoke the truth.

"Do you have your dice with you, Viracocha?" he asked.

Viracocha took out of a waistcoat pocket an ivory box he always carried with him and held it in his palm to show it to us. He did it with a cunning smile, a signal to us that he didn't intend to be Almenar's executioner.

The dice rolled on the guano, and the lowest number was cast by the engineer.

"I can't do such a thing," the poor man said, horrified, in a tremulous voice. "This is, in any case, a job for the doctor. He'll know how to do it. . . ."

"Agreed," said the doctor.

He asked Almenar to take the laces out of his boots. He tied them with a strong knot and asked the giant:

"Are you ready?"

Almenar crossed himself and knelt down. It all happened very quickly. I didn't want to look.

"Get a hold on yourself and don't move or the laces might tear," the doctor advised Almenar in a voice hoarsened by the effort.

I first heard a rattling in Almenar's throat and then the noise that his giant human mass made when it fell heavily on the guano.

We were seized by an indefinable malaise, something like nausea.

The doctor and Juan Fernández dragged Almenar's body into a corner so that the guards, when they came in, would think that he was asleep. The doctor mopped the perspiration running down his forehead and spat out some more blood. Viracocha had filled his mug with tea and was offering it to him. The professional gambler's expression was mocking.

He said, hoping to mortify the doctor:

"By practicing euthanasia you have behaved like a true rationalist!"

The doctor cursed him, and Viracocha burst out laughing. It was true, of course, that Almenar had delivered himself from twenty hours of agony; but he also left behind him an atmosphere of irritating affliction, of insupportable guilt feeling, even though we could justifiably hold that we were not guilty of anything.

For two hours nobody said a word. We could only hear, every now and then, the rattling of the dice which Viracocha mechanically shook in the hollow of his hands. There were only seven of us now left to wait for the next cockcrow.

At about ten in the morning, Viracocha made an impudent announcement.

"Gentlemen, I propose a couple of things to raise our spirits: we can either play poker or sing the Marseillaise together. Or else, if you insist on meditation and silence, I will recite you some passages from the Holy Bible. Though you may not believe me, I know that book by heart."

We all looked at him reproachfully. I do think, however, that something laughed inside me when I listened to that cynic with his delicate manners and suggestive voice. Nobody answered him and he went on, imperturbably:

"No? I'm sorry. Engross yourselves in the study of death and, within two more hours, you will be yelling like hysterical women. You have just seen that death is only an attitude. I beg you to forgive me."

And he started to play solitaire with a pack of cards he carried in another pocket, taking every now and then a drink of tea.

At eleven we heard the noise of the truck rolling across the plain. Juan Fernández glued his face to the window. He was anxious to know whether the *tata* had come as he had promised.

"I see him," he observed, happy.

The truck stopped next to the dead. The priest looked at them for a moment and blessed them. He then walked toward the part of the inn where Garlic Teeth in person was waiting for him. Our executioner wanted to kiss the *tata's* hand but the latter evaded him with a discreet movement. The two men disappeared from the window's angle of vision. Juan Fernández, impatient, had gone to wait at the door of our reception room.

The driver and two *kkepis* began to load the bodies into the truck. The spectacle was repugnant to me and I turned my back on it, but the noise of the bodies falling into the truck penetrated our cell and ate into the small supply of our remaining courage. We all covered our ears, except Viracocha, for whom noises and silence were equally unimportant.

"Fear, fear, fear," he repeated to the tune of a *tonadilla*.

"This is horrible! . . . And tomorrow they'll do the same thing to us!" shouted the engineer, close to madness.

"But it will be better tomorrow, because we won't hear it," Viracocha answered him, switching to the tune of another *tonadilla*.

The shed door opened and Garlic Teeth appeared, followed by the priest.

Don Gerónimo was about sixty years old at the time. He had been parish priest of the church of San Juan at Catavi ever since he had left the seminary. He was a mestizo, in whom the traits of the white man were more marked. He was wearing a woolen cassock over which he had put a rainproof poncho only twenty years younger than himself. His hair, absolutely white, was always combed in the style of the late Kaiser. Poor *tata* Gerónimo! It hurt him so much to see us that his transparent eyes were trembling on the verge of tears.

"Let's see if you have better luck today with the rest of these renegades!" Garlic Teeth exclaimed contemptuously. The cracks of his lips were dirty from the dried *charqui* meat he was always chewing.

His hands were placed defiantly on the two pistols that dangled from his waist. The two cartridge belts hanging diagonally from his shoulders made him look like a guerrilla fighter. The high boots he had put on for the manhunt were now clean, the work of Aurora's hands. He gave us all a mean and nasty look, to which we replied with hatred.

"When you're through, father, please come to the kitchen for a drink of *pisco* and some roast lamb *chalonas* my wife is preparing for those damned *kkaras'* lunch. . . . So that they afterward complain to the Heavenly Father that I ill-treated them! . . ."

And he burst out laughing as he closed the door.

Juan Fernández confessed in a corner. We could hear the mutter of his Quechua words. Then he went to another corner to recite the prayer of penitence.

Tata Gerónimo observed that Sócrates was looking at the ceiling; that I was staring through the window at the distant hillsides; that Viracocha was absorbed in his cards; that the young man with Galician blood and an Inca heart had his eyes fixed on his knees; that the dead man's eyes were out of orbit and gazing into nothingness; that the doctor was looking at the engineer and the engineer at the doctor. He finally said:

"What words can a poor country priest find to melt your indifference! I can only assure you that injustice is not of the Kingdom of God. . . . And for the benefit of those of you who believe in true justice and want to participate in it, I trace over your most intimate wishes the Sign that opens the gates of bliss. . . ."

Tata Gerónimo made a sign of the cross in the air, and I believe we all looked at him. He then offered to take messages to our families, but nobody gave him one. Only Sócrates asked him:

"*Tata:* tonight I'll write a letter to my children. I'll put it in the back pocket of my trousers. The bullets won't hit it there, because I don't intend to run. When my body is taken to Catavi, look for the letter where I told you to and deliver it to Robespierre. . . ."

The priest clasped our hands and went away weeping. I'm sure he didn't drink the *pisco* because, within two minutes of leaving the shed, he was sitting with the driver and the *kkepis:*

"We can start whenever you're ready," we heard him say.

And the truck, with its cargo of corpses, vanished into the plain, raising clouds of dust.

The engineer kept on muttering, in a voice suffocated by anguish:

"It's absurd . . . it's absurd. . . ."

Around midday another guard entered the shed, carrying the mutton ribs promised by Garlic Teeth. They arrived in a pile, smoking, on an earthenware dish; cooked *tunca* came in a separate casserole. The chubby cripple who stood guard at the door, with his rifle pointed at us, passed his comrade a demijohn of water they had left in the passage.

We didn't help ourselves to the food until they had gone. Our lunch passed in silence. The engineer and the young man who wanted to be an Inca refused to eat. Viracocha gnawed his rib bone clean and went to sleep.

The hours passed slowly. One could feel, in this silence, the slow pulsations of an hysterical agony. Our palms were exuding lukewarm moisture. We all breathed rapidly, and breathing oppressed us like a physical burden. Suddenly the engineer broke into a shout:

"Why? . . . Why? . . . I have the right to know: in the name of what law can they take a man's life?"

And he banged desperately on the door. When the doctor finally managed to calm him, he saw that the engineer's hands were bleeding. Juan Fernández hadn't even moved. Chewing coca, he was gazing at the horizon, where the sun was already doing its evening rounds. Viracocha changed his position on the guano and slept on. When the young idealist heard the engineer's shouts, he merely pressed his chin harder against his knees.

"Come, come, friend, all that you will get out of this is that Garlic Teeth will laugh at you. We are all afraid, but dignity must come first. . . ."

The doctor put the engineer into a corner. The latter's body was like a rag.

Sócrates had started writing in a copybook his letter to his children. I am sure that from that moment he was no longer with us. His letter began, more or less, like this:

"My beloved children, Robespierre, Fraternity, Garibaldi, and Liberty: When the sun shines upon the age of free men, you will be able to say proudly that the humble holocaust of the one who brought you into this world was not in vain. . . ."

At nightfall it started to rain. The drops that splashed on the embrasure of the window sprinkled my face, relieving the tension that overwhelmed me. A guard came in to light the gasoline lamp and the shed was transformed into a ghostly contrast of shadows lying in ambush.

Viracocha bestirred himself with an enormous yawn:

"If those bastards had at least brought us a bottle of *pisco*, the remaining hours wouldn't pass so slowly."

"What time have you got? . . ." asked the engineer, who wanted to check his watch.

"Twenty after seven," the doctor answered him. "But what the devil does it matter what time it is?"

I noticed, for the first time, a touch of irritation in the doctor's usually placid voice. I thought that the engineer, overcome by his insurmountable fear, would end up by making us all lose our self-control.

One has enough troubles of one's own on such occasions without anybody else giving us his share!

"It's absurd . . . absurd. . . ."

This time it was Viracocha who made the angry retort:

"If you say that crap once more I'll push that lamp into your face, you heap of pigeon shit! . . . It's absurd . . . it's absurd. . . . And you're telling us? . . . Well, of course it's absurd. . . . But shut up unless you can come out with something more brilliant. . . ."

The engineer, ashamed, covered his face with his hands.

About nine a jailer came in with our supper and the packages of cigarettes they gave us every night. I really don't remember what he brought us to eat. Whatever it was, Viracocha, the doctor, Juan Fernández, and I ate it. The idealist, as usual, didn't even raise his eyes when we offered him the dish.

The engineer refused the food with a sign of his hand.

And Sócrates kept on writing.

This prison guard tried to be a little bit more human than the others and asked us whether we wanted anything special.

"*Pisco,*" Viracocha requested immediately.

"I don't know if I can get it for you, but I'll talk to the chief."

That particular guard had the characteristic cough of the mine sickness. He was a weak type, with a flaccid mustache covering his mouth. I knew him because we had worked together at one time. I thought then that he was a good man; but, when he lost his job, Garlic Teeth saved him from some trouble and there was apparently nothing left for him to do but to sell his conscience to his benefactor.

All our other executioners-to-be were more or less the same kind of people: mercenaries bought for a gourdful of *chicha* or a dish of hot *api*. May God forgive them!

He returned with a bottle of *pisco* and said:

"I am not a bad man . . . I was hungry and my lungs were gone. . . ."

And he left us, hating himself a little less.

Viracocha took charge of allotting the drinks to himself, Juan Fernández, and me, the only ones who craved alcohol. I'm sure he served himself more *pisco* and more often, but neither I nor the *cliceño* let him see we knew it.

After ten o'clock an icy wind started to blow around the inn; it came through the window in gusts that shook the lamp. If the floor of the shed hadn't been covered with guano, I think we would have died before we were shot. But the fumes of the guano protected us.

The doctor, Viracocha, and I sat in a group under the lamp, with the bottle in the center. I can't figure out even now how the devil Sócrates managed to write his interminable letter, seated as he was in a place where the light barely penetrated. Every now and then we heard the engineer sigh. If this silence continued it

wouldn't be long before we were all screaming like frightened
women, as the diceplayer had predicted. So I proposed:

"Let's play cards or sing the Marseillaise."

Viracocha smiled as he shuffled the cards.

"It won't get us anywhere to torment ourselves by thinking,"
he said.

One of the guards, in the kitchen, began to sing in a low voice.
Soon another one joined him and, one by one, they turned into a
choir that converted the sweet melody of the Marseillaise into a
graceless braying, accompanied by handclapping to enliven their
drinking bout. Our card game continued, but it didn't stimulate
us. It was useless for Viracocha to pretend to challenge us, because anything that we could win or lose was completely value-
less. Suddenly, the professional gambler stopped playing. For the
first time I saw him look really worried.

"It's useless, my friends: the cards feel as cold and stiff as
corpses. It doesn't matter to those who play for beans; but this is,
for me, the beginning of the end. . . ."

He had a drink.

"Maybe you'll think I am crazy but, as long as I felt the
warm breasts of the queen tremble under the caress of my fingers,
I could think that death wasn't close to me. Think it a gambler's
trick if you will, but I know what I'm talking about. I was once
in São Paulo, and an Englishman, who could play cards in his
sleep, got up from the table and said: 'Gentlemen, I'll see you in
hell. My queen has just died.' And, within half an hour, he died
in his room of coronary thrombosis."

Viracocha got up and moved into a corner. We all looked at
him with astonishment. He had knelt down with his face turned
toward the wall and arms forming a cross. The engineer burst out
laughing and, pointing his finger at the gambler, let out a stream
of insults:

"So you're scared, too, you braggart! . . . Well, why don't
you push the lamp in my face now? . . . Vermin! . . . Tad-
pole! . . ."

Viracocha's arms trembled while he was saying in a low, tremulous voice:

"Don't try my patience, engineer, because I want to have my peace before they put me out of my misery! . . . Don't rub me the wrong way, engineer, by your mother! . . ."

I got up to cool down the engineer, who kept up his torrent of insults. I had just grabbed him by the shoulders when the door opened. It was Garlic Teeth. His expression was quite different this time. With all our shouting, we hadn't realized that the guards had stopped singing. The entire inn was now silent from end to end. And behind Garlic Teeth stood all his men. They were all bleary-eyed with *chicha* but they tried to hide it from us. Garlic Teeth started to speak in a weak voice. It was the doctor to whom he addressed himself:

"I have no authority to spare your life but I could intercede for you with the commander at Catavi if you take care of my Aurora. Hm! . . . it really hurts me to ask you for help but who the devil can help her to give birth in this empty *páramo?* . . ."

The doctor had a coughing fit. He made an effort to retain his equanimity and kept his eyes shut for a few moments so as not to betray his emotion. The storekeeper's voice was now like a roar:

"And don't think you can take your revenge on me with my *chola* . . . you son of a bitch! . . . because I swear that if you don't help her, I'll kill you by tearing off your skin strip by strip. . . ."

The doctor rose painfully to his feet.

"Take me to her. . . ."

And he left with them. It was fifteen minutes before midnight. In just over four hours the first rays of daylight would hit the horizon.

The rain kept falling into our cell, carried through the window by the gusts of wind. Sócrates went on writing his letter, indifferent to everything around him. Viracocha, who hadn't even turned around when he heard Garlic Teeth, was now beating his chest with tremendous power, saying:

"Mea culpa . . . mea culpa, Domine. . . ."

The engineer joined me and Juan Fernández under the lamp.

"I have a feeling that I'll die with some dignity," he said.

He seemed more calm.

Even though there were still some livid marks under his eyes, he looked as if he had picked up some unexpected energy.

"I hope you'll understand that my previous hysteria is accounted for by the simple fact that I am not made to be a hero. . . . You'll permit me to take a drink? We human beings are contradictory creatures. . . . Why shouldn't we think that it is better to die by shooting than from pneumonia? . . . I have just recalled my father's horrible agony, and the memory has restored my serenity. After all, I'll be spared all the agonies my poor father suffered under those spotless linen sheets. Just think of it! . . . My father was fifty-two when he left this world, and I am now fifty-three. . . . I'm old enough to catch any kind of disease tomorrow, eh? And then the priest would come to see me the following week and say: 'My son, you have to prepare your soul etc., etc.' Well, these things can't be avoided in the end. And then I'd hear somebody whisper in the next room: 'Don't make so much noise, the poor man's breathing is already stertorous!' And my feet would grow cold first, and then my hands; the end would come with the knot that strangles the heart. . . . I definitely believe this is better. . . ." He was speaking gently, taking every now and then a drink of *pisco*. The *cliceño* was listening to him attentively, his toad's eyes fixed upon the engineer's round face. I have never seen a man so obviously at peace as Juan Fernández was becoming now. If it hadn't been for his occasional chewing motions with his ball of coca leaves, he would have seemed a bronze statue.

"What do you think of my point of view?" the engineer asked me.

"Looks all right to me."

What else could I have answered him, knowing that he was clinging to his speech as a last hope against complete despair?

"And you, my boy?" he asked the Indian.

"I believe, engineer, that they are doing me a great favor by taking my life. I don't remember a night as beautiful as this since I was born. After all, when we go to the market we all tell a different tale about it, according to how our sales went. . . . For you, judging by the hard way you are taking death, this world was a reward; for me it was a punishment. That's why I am not afraid to leave this world soon. . . . Within a few hours now, no one will profit any more from my misfortune. . . . Where I go, tin and silver are of no use, you understand? . . . And everybody gets the same portion of *chancaca* and *quinua*. . . . I am not trembling, as you, because this is the most beautiful night of my life."

The engineer, incredulous, touched the Indian's hands.

"Yes, it's true, you're not trembling."

The shed door opened once more, and the fat limping guard made me a sign. Seeing that I didn't follow him, he shouted at me from the doorway:

"Hey, you! . . . come!"

I went out into the passage, still not understanding why he had called me. Halfway to the kitchen, he gave me a push:

"Get up those stairs!"

What he called stairs were only some stone slabs, arranged like steps. They led to a kind of attic that must have been located, approximately, above the kitchen. Shoved by the rifle butt, I went down a passage, much narrower than the one downstairs, which led to a damp and miserable room. Its only light came from a grease candle placed in the belly of a gourd. Several asymmetric doors led from it to the different rooms of the inn. The lame guard knocked on one of them with his knuckles, and it was Garlic Teeth himself who opened it to him.

"Is it true what the doctor says?" he spat out at me point-blank.

"What?"

"That you are a good hand at helping in childbirth?"

The doctor, who was standing behind Garlic Teeth, gave me a signal.

"Yes."

"If you help him, I won't shoot you tonight."

My legs flagged. I believe that, for a moment, I lost all notion of where I was. I must have looked altogether puerile or feminine at that point.

"The doctor says that, with that cough of his, he will hardly have the strength to pull when it's needed."

"And since this is her first. . . ." the doctor corroborated with another wink.

I heard the weak moans of the girl who had more or less been my fiancée when her breasts were first beginning to swell. Just as well that Garlic Teeth didn't know it. If he did, I wouldn't be where I was now but buried alive with my tongue cut and my eyes gouged out.

"Go in," he ordered me.

I went in and turned my back on the place where I believed Aurora to be. It would have been dangerous for her to catch sight of me suddenly. The room was small and rectangular, with adobe walls. Garlic Teeth bent over the field bed on which his wife was lying. I think he wanted to kiss her, and he was murmuring to her tender words that made me feel like laughing. An iron washstand, a rickety chair, and a gasoline lamp completed the furnishings. When Garlic Teeth drew himself up, he had already forgotten the honeyed tone of voice with which he had addressed his wife. He said to us, resuming his imperious manner:

"I've already told you what this is all about. . . . She is sacred! . . . God help you if anything happens to my *chotita!* . . . And I want my son to come out without a single scratch! . . . You understand? . . . I'll leave you alone because I believe that a husband shouldn't see certain things, but there'll be a guard at the door and another one under the window . . . so none of your tricks! . . . When you need hot water, give us a few knocks on the floor. . . . This room is exactly on top of where I'll sit down to wait." He left the room, clicking his heels. When he reached the lame guard, he warned him:

"Shut the door and don't look through any holes. You are not a technical expert so there's no reason for you to see what my wife has under her petticoats."

We heard him walk away, and the lame man barred the door. The doctor was smiling and I asked him:

"But why did you choose me? . . . I've never seen an umbilical cord in my life. And, besides, the engineer is more afraid than I am."

"We're all afraid. The only difference is that the poor devil can't hide what he feels."

"There's one exception among us: Juan Fernández."

"True."

"And Sócrates?"

"No, not while he's writing the letter. The silent young man has been, I think, theoretically dead for the last three days. Almenar asked us to kill him because he knew he would make himself a laughing stock facing the execution squad and not because his kidneys hurt."

"Viracocha?"

"I couldn't tell you for sure where that man's courage ends and where his fear begins. He's a mystery to me."

I was visibly irritated. It annoyed me that this country doctor should have performed such a merciless vivisection of our respective states of mind. After all, except for the engineer, we had all tried to keep our dignity in so painful a situation. I turned toward Aurora who was looking at me with stupefied eyes as if seeing me in this inn had been a great surprise to her.

"You won't think, hearing the doctor talk, that all of us who are your husband's 'guests' are just scared hens. . . ."

"Here, hold on my friend!" the doctor exclaimed. "I never said such a thing. You asked me and I gave you my opinion. A man may behave like a hero on the battlefield and like a fainting schoolgirl in the dentist's chair. What's one thing got to do with the other? Whether they hurt you in cold blood or whether they tell you they'll execute you at a given hour, vertigo is still the natural reaction . . . and now you'd better turn your back because I want to examine the girl."

I did as he told me and lit a cigarette.

"How old are you?" the doctor asked Aurora.

"*He* knows," she replied in the tender tone of voice I remember her using in bygone days, when she told me: "I shall have to obey my father; but whoever the man may be, you'll always be the one between my blankets."

"And why should he know?"

"Ask him."

Aurora wanted to give herself the pleasure of finding out if I hadn't forgotten what had happened between us. Although I was standing with my back to her, I could feel her moist eyes staring at me, just as she used to stare at me from the grocery for hours, surrendering her soul to me because she couldn't give me anything else. Lucky for us that Garlic Teeth, who fancied himself a detective, didn't notice anything.

"How old is she, damn it?"

"Seventeen," I replied.

"Does it hurt here?"

"Yes, doctor."

"Did you fall or hurt yourself recently?"

"Not that I remember."

"I can't feel the baby!" said the doctor with marked anguish. I knew quite well what the tone of his voice implied. He wanted to appear more optimistic and added: "Of course, I have no stethoscope, but. . . ."

I am sure that Aurora was as fully aware as we of the gravity of the situation. Her pupils, like burning irons, were pinned on me. She followed my movements without batting an eyelid, like a dog watching a family drama from his corner. I moved to the window and noticed, through the dirty moisture of its panes, the silhouette of the guard that Garlic Teeth had posted a few yards from the house. He must have been cowering under his poncho because his figure barely stood out above the rachitic plants that sprinkle the Plateau. Every now and then, the light of his cigar made an appearance in the slit between his broad-brimmed hat and the raised fold of his poncho. There he was, indifferent to wind and rain, his eyes glued on our window. It would have been useless to attempt escape on that side. And the limping guard stood by the door, with his itching trigger finger.

Aurora began to moan again.

"You have pains every half an hour," the doctor observed, "and you have already opened a way as wide as a *tostón*. . . . When the pains return, try and push from the inside out and make it as wide as a Bolivian peso. . . . Then the thing will go better . . . and we'll see how we can all get out of this mess!"

"How long now, doctor?" the girl asked without any anxiety.

"Who knows . . . ? Maybe three or four hours. . . . And now take a rest and gather your strength for the time when you have to push."

I did not want to turn around, so that Aurora couldn't notice that I was desperately holding on to the few grains of courage I had left. I believe that, out there in the shed, once I had got used to the idea that they were going to shoot me, I managed to get my nerves under control; but standing in that room I felt that my morale was about to crumble. I'd rather have kept on sitting under the lamp at the side of the *cliceño*, counting the minutes, than to be given a new hope of survival based on something as problematical as the first cry of a newborn child.

The doctor moved to the window, lit a cigarette, and said to me in a low voice:

"We must have no illusions, my friend. It's possible that the fetus is holding his hands against the mother's belly. While he's in this position and I have no stethoscope, I cannot hear his heartbeat; but it may well be another reason altogether. . . . I don't know. . . . All I can say is that I don't feel too happy about the way things are going."

"Well, if the baby is stillborn or Aurora gets into some unexpected trouble, there won't be a God in heaven who could persuade Garlic Teeth that it wasn't our revenge. Then why don't we warn him?"

"Him? . . . Have you gone crazy? . . . Drop it! . . . Who knows how things will yet turn out?"

We smoked one cigarette after another and silently scrutinized the darkness of the night, as if some salvation were hidden behind its veil. It was absurd; but we kept looking.

"Doctor, he has moved."

The doctor, hearing Aurora, rushed to her side. So did I and looked, too. Why not? She didn't object, because shame and desire were of secondary importance in those circumstances. The doctor put his ears to the girl's naked belly. I saw him smile.

"Yes, there he is, the *llocalla*. . . . Bless his little heart! . . .

In five more minutes your pains will start again, and then you'll push with all your strength, promise?"

She promised. The doctor was patting her hips to lift her spirits. I bent my head over Aurora's and whispered into her ear:

"Save him! . . . You must save him! . . . You mustn't let his heart stop beating. . . ."

She smiled and strongly grasped my hand. Suddenly, her features contracted in a grimace of pain. Her nails were clawing at my skin, but it didn't bother me. The doctor was pressing her groin. Sweat was running down the face of that sick and ill-treated man. His cough rudely interrupted his words as he spoke:

"Harder! . . . harder! . . . harder! . . . Why should this child come into this world except to do us a favor? Perhaps to die, as we, one night? . . . Who can understand these mysteries? Ah, that's better. . . . The placenta is broken. . . ."

Suddenly he gave me an order:

"Tell that lame swine to bring some towels or cloth or anything to dry this. . . ."

I shouted the order and the lame guard, without opening the door, seemed to understand what I wanted because, immediately afterward, I heard his unequal steps receding in the passage. Aurora was silent again after her spasms of pain. The doctor breathed deeply, anxiously sucking in the air his lungs craved. He was wiping his forehead with the sleeve of his shirt and there was a touch of hope in his smile.

"Who knows?" he repeated.

He went to wash his hands in the iron washstand. Suddenly the door opened and a changed-looking Garlic Teeth appeared in it.

"Boy or girl?" he asked.

"Neither boy nor girl yet," the doctor informed him. "His membrane broke and I need something for drying."

"But is *she* all right?"

"Yes, I'm all right," Aurora replied with disdain.

"Gimpy said something about you needing rags for drying and I brought you this. . . ."

It was a bag, empty and dirty. When she saw what her husband had found for her, she rebuked him indignantly:

"There are towels down there, you devil of an idiot! I brought them here myself from Catavi. . . ." Garlic Teeth was perplexed.

"Yes, my dear, but I was in such a hurry that I just took the first thing I could lay my hands on. . . ."

The scarfaced man stood like a fool before the *chotita* from Cochabamba. It was obvious that she had taken the measure of his brains and had less respect for him than for the "dumb boy of the llamas."

"They are in the green basket," Aurora explained in a cutting tone.

"Yes, my dear, I'll send Gimpy for them right away. . . ."

These words fell weakly from his mouth. And he left. When he passed his subordinate, he roared at him with fury:

"I told you before not to look at what is no business of yours, you clumsy idiot! Follow me, that's all! You get everything wrong! . . . And not one drop more of *pisco!* . . . We must keep all our wits so that the full punishment of the law falls upon these men! . . . And I represent the law!"

Aurora shut her eyes with rage. I am sure she didn't want to look at me then so as not to read any reproach in my eyes. Poor Aurora! And what could I reproach her with? My own position was hardly brilliant, to put it mildly, at the time she married that grocer. I was on all the foremen's black lists because I had the reputation of being a rebel. She, the child of starving parents, could not very well go the same way and link her fate with mine, which had only hunger to offer her. So it wasn't surprising that she went with another. She was regretting it that night; but I did not feel the satisfaction of reproaching her. The lame guard brought in the towels and barred the door again. The doctor carried out his duties while advising Aurora:

"And now try to doze until the next pains."

Aurora calmed down, and we walked toward the window to smoke. It was about half past two in the morning. The first rays of the morning sun would hit the crests of Oruro at about five. In little more than two hours our companions would face the execution squad. The doctor and I had a slight chance of saving our lives, but how could they escape their death?

We tried to speak two or three times about our brothers in misfortune, but the subject always fizzled out in monosyllables. The truth was that their problem was no longer our problem. Three hours earlier they had been identical, but not at half past two in the morning, and even less so half an hour later, when Aurora's uterus acquired the width of a Bolivian peso.

At half past three, the fetus's heart was still beating and, at four, the doctor touched its head. From that time onward, the spasms became more frequent and all we could do was to wait for the decision about our deliverance to be made on the one and a half square meter of field bed on which Aurora was lying. There was the beginning and the end. At twenty to five, the lame guard asked through the door whether everything was going well and the doctor answered him, "Yes." And it was true. My shirt was wet through with sweat. The doctor coughed constantly, from sheer nerves. Suddenly, between the ever-stronger spasms of Aurora, the doctor said to me, pointing to the horizon:

"The first rays of daylight."

Some whitish fringes preceded the daybreak. A rooster crowed, then another. We became aware that for our companions, the hour had struck. We heard voices under our window. It was Garlic Teeth who marked the time of the execution squad in a martial voice:

"One, two, one, two, one, two, one . . . two!"

We put out the lamp and opened the window.

"One, two, one, two . . . !"

A few meters below us, flanked by the platoon of *pongos,* walked Juan Fernández, the young idealist, Sócrates García, the engineer, and Viracocha. Garlic Teeth, with his pistols, marched at the head of the group.

"Halt!" he ordered.

They made them stand in a row, in the same place where they had shot the others. The guard who was watching our window remained crouched under his poncho and didn't even turn around to look. The lame guard had joined the execution squad, very pleased to let his trigger finger have some fun.

All our companions, without exception, seemed calm. The rain had stopped, but the wind lashed out even more violently than at midnight. The ends of Juan Fernández's poncho looked like the wings of a condor; gray hair flowed on the head of Sócrates like a cascade of foam; Viracocha's hands were folded in prayer and his head was bent low; the engineer stared defiantly at the execution squad, his arms crossed on his chest; the young idealist, tall and thin, looked like a bush in the plain.

"Have you anything to say?" Garlic Teeth asked magnanimously.

I heard, for the first time, the voice of the young idealist:

"I would like to turn around. It's not that I am afraid, but the sun is my god and I want to die facing it."

Viracocha raised his head. He seemed like a different man, one whom we had never known. And when he spoke, his voice had a strange tone:

"Although I am a renegade priest, I haven't lost the power of absolving the sins of others. . . ."

And he made the sign of the cross over the row of his companions.

The others said nothing.

"Take aim! . . . Fire!" Garlic Teeth shouted the orders with deliberation.

The volley shot down the five men and frightened the wild pigeons that had begun to play in the wind.

Aurora screamed. I closed the window and the doctor ran to attend the girl. Garlic Teeth, who hadn't heard his wife's scream, possibly because the shots had deafened him, entertained himself by giving the *coup de grâce* to every one of our friends. Fortunately, the execution squad had aimed better this time, since none of the bodies were twisting convulsively.

"Come here!" the doctor ordered me with fear in his voice.

When I approached the bed, I saw him struggling nervously to remove from the newborn child the umbilical cord wound around his neck. I helped him as well as I could. When we had set the baby free, the doctor grabbed him by the feet, put him head down, and slapped him. But it was all useless: Garlic Teeth had a stillborn son.

Aurora began to recover her consciousness which she had lost some time ago.

"Light that lamp," the doctor ordered me while his hands moved between the girl's blood-covered legs. I lit the wick and brought the lamp to the bed. The doctor bit through the umbilical cord at some point and tied it into a knot. Aurora was now detached from her son.

"Is he alive?" she asked weakly.

"No," I answered her.

She grabbed my clothes and, drawing herself up, screamed: "Run! For God's sake, run quickly! . . . He'll kill you! I know it!" There was terror in her eyes, as if she saw that something worse than death was in store for us. The doctor and I looked at each other for a moment. I went to the window and saw that Garlic Teeth and his men were already walking toward the house.

"If we could break this door," I said while already throwing my body against it.

The two boards of the door broke, leaving an opening in the middle.

"Quick!" I shouted to the doctor.

And I squeezed through, I don't know how. The doctor, who was thin, had it easier. The candle that had illuminated the big room had gone out in the belly of the gourd, and we could barely see beyond our hands; but we groped our way through to the narrow passage.

"Follow me! . . . Quickly!"

I heard the doctor's panting breath behind me and, every now and then, his cough . . . that damned cough of his! I wanted to reach the kitchen before Garlic Teeth. He must have left some arms there; with them we could at least die fighting and wouldn't have to make him a free gift of our skins which he had promised to tear off strip by strip.

I stepped on the first slab and pulled the doctor down by his hand so as to stop him from cracking his head against the ceiling.

We reached the lower floor. I couldn't yet hear the voices of the guards in the kitchen, our objective, some twenty yards away.

"Run after me even if you die!" I ordered him.

And we launched ourselves toward the arch of light at the end of the lower passage. The floor was earthen; it had been inlaid with some wood since rotted. Hit by our running steps, it made some ratlike noises. I got there first because even the doctor's instinct of self-preservation couldn't stop his cough. I hid behind a load of wood in the kitchen, almost at the corner of the passage. I wanted to find out from there where the arms were. I took a quick look around the room where they had beaten us three days earlier. A fire burned on the hearth, and a pot, probably containing *api,* was hanging over it.

The doctor managed to reach my side and I yelled at him: "Why don't you swallow that cough of yours . . . dammit!"

Some of the guards' clothes were hanging from the walls; dishes with remains of food were on the large table, with some empty *chicha* and *pisco* bottles. But I couldn't see any arms anywhere.

"Look!" said the doctor, pointing to a spot on the floor. Almenar was stretched out there. They must have come to pick him up with the others; then they saw that he was dead and dragged him to the kitchen and left him there because he was too heavy for them.

"But where were the arms? Can't you see any?"

There were none in sight, which meant that we would fall once more into the hands of Garlic Teeth, this time in the simplest possible manner.

And yet I knew that there was, somewhere, the famous machine gun that the leader of the expedition from Oruro had given to Aurora's husband to hunt us with on the Plateau. That machine gun was my hope and I couldn't see it. If I could only get its mount against my hip, its whole barrel would get to work like a mechanical reaper in a field of rye on the bodies of the *pongos* who opened the kitchen door.

I left my hiding place behind the wood to explore the various corners of the kitchen, but I had to get back immediately because I heard the voices of the execution squad in the yard. I grabbed, in passing, two knives from the table and gave one to the doctor.

"What can we do?" he asked me.

I saw from his eyes that his spirits were faltering and that he was about ready to give in. I didn't think of such a thing—not because I had more guts than he but because my lungs were healthy and I was twenty-five years younger. A man of my age had still so much to live for, so much to do! And at that particular moment something in me revolted against the idea of giving up what by rights belonged to me to that *chichi* with the rotten soul.

The engineer had been right when he said: "In the name of what law can they take a man's life?"

The doctor could give up his life if he wished; but I would lose mine only at the point of a knife. I crouched down so as to be able to leap forward at the suitable moment toward this door which was about to open. It opened and Garlic Teeth and his men came in. The lame one said:

"Who would have thought he was a priest?"

"But wasn't it a sin to kill him?" fearfully asked one of the guards whom we knew in Catavi by his hump and his blind eye.

Garlic Teeth burst out laughing.

"If Viracocha is a priest, I am the Archbishop of Lima. What a thing to say! Don't pester me with your squeamishness, 'humpy'!"

That was what he called the deformed dwarf, who could, nobody knew how, ride a mule bareback for two days and split a ram's horns with his bare hands. He gave Garlic Teeth a most unfriendly look, which made the latter realize that he shouldn't fool with him.

"What's happened upstairs?" he asked, looking at the ceiling, and ordered:

"Come with me, Gimpy. I think the *chota* must be about ready to give birth."

I signaled the doctor. The two men had to pass by our side and we could take them by surprise, jump on them, and put knives to their throats. Using them as shields, we could go out to the yard and lock up the others in the kitchen. The doctor grasped my intention and prepared himself to attack. He was pale and trembling, but ready for anything.

The guards sat down by the fire because they had brought in the outdoor cold in their clothes. Garlic Teeth and the lame one walked slowly toward the passage. I counted their approaching steps and estimated the distance. My muscles were tense. I felt the handle of the knife in my hand, bathed in sweat.

"Where the devil are the bread knives?" one of the men asked.

My heart was strangled for an instant. I believe that the doctor, too, was about to collapse.

"I stuck them in the crust when we left," another one answered him.

"Hell, they're not here."

Garlic Teeth and the other stopped in their tracks. It was then that the doctor coughed. Ah, if it had been Juan Fernández or Viracocha! But that man's lungs ruined everything. They grabbed him behind the woodpile and me halfway through the passage.

"Don't shoot!" Garlic Teeth ordered.

I defended myself with my knife, my teeth, and my feet. I was blind with rage and despair. It was the hunchback who subdued me by twisting my arm, almost wrenching it out of its socket. To finish me off, he stopped my breath with a well-aimed kick in my belly. They dragged me into the kitchen half-conscious and put me next to the doctor, who kept on coughing, as if he had been pierced by a thorn. I recovered my senses completely when I heard Garlic Teeth shout. What did he want? It sounded like a woman's moan but it doubtlessly came from a man. Garlic Teeth came into the kitchen, carrying his dead son in his arms, crying and howling.

"They killed him! They killed my little angel! . . . Look how pretty he was and they killed him!"

The child, livid and covered with grease from the placenta, looked disgusting, but Garlic Teeth kissed him again and again and covered him with tears.

I can't say whether the spectacle was pathetic or ridiculous— I was trembling with rage—but the guards wept with their master.

"We didn't kill him!" I shouted. "But even if we did, what are you people crying about? . . . Why do you obey this bastard?"

Garlic Teeth controlled his grief for a few moments to say:

"The full weight of the law will fall upon the murderers of my little boy. . . . Give them a couple of picks! . . . They will dig their own graves and we'll bury them alive in them. . . ."

And he again gave free rein to his grief, embracing and kissing the little body of his son.

The guards pushed us out of the kitchen. We crossed the yard, and the hunchback showed us the place to start digging our graves, not far from the corpses. All the guards came to witness the punishment decreed by Garlic Teeth—there was nobody left in the inn for them to watch. Garlic Teeth sat on a stone with his child clutched to his breast, as if to protect him from the cold that he could no longer feel.

The hunchback and the lame one were put in charge of the punishment. I stuck the pick into the ground. I was burning with inward rage; but nothing mattered to me any more, except to suffer as little as possible. I simply had to have a quick death, buried alive or any other way. I thought of flight, but what good would it have done me? They would just catch me after a few yards and return me to my grave-digging, kicking me and hitting me with their rifle butts to speed me on my way.

Again and again the tip of my pick cut the soil. Near-by, the doctor was trying to do the same, but with constant interruptions as he was overcome by fits of coughing. Once his legs gave way, but the hunchback straightened him up again by hitting him with his butt. Oh, my poor companion! The first rays of the rising sun marked his thin and bluish face with all the anguished suffering that is the symbol of our people. There he was, trying to keep on his feet to dig his grave. The yoke that held him down would not let go of him till the end: until it snatched his last breath.

"That's deep enough. . . . In with them!" ordered Garlic Teeth.

They pushed us in and we fell into the deathbeds we had ourselves prepared. I closed my eyes. I felt no fear; I just felt cold. A heap of earth fell on my chest and another one on my face. . . . But, suddenly, what happened? I heard machine-gun shots and some shouts. Something fell heavily upon me. It was much heavier than a heap of earth. I wiped the dust from my eyes and saw the sinister Quasimodo straddling my legs, his eyes open and three bloody holes in his shirt. He was dead. I looked up and saw the lame one's head hanging over the edge of the grave, with a bullet hole in the right side of his nose. I drew myself up, bewildered and uncomprehending. When I climbed out of the grave, I saw all the guards lying in grotesque positions. Garlic Teeth, too, was dead.

He was lying at the foot of the stone on which he had sat with his son. Even in death he was still clutching his son between his arms. There was an absolute silence that even the wind didn't bother to disturb.

Aurora stood in the front doorway of the inn. She could barely stand on her feet but did not let go of the machine gun that she had used so effectively. I ran toward her. When she saw me near, she dropped the machine gun and stretched out her arms to me, trembling:

"Take me away from here! . . . Oh God, take me far away!"

I held her fast and pressed her to my breast, I don't know whether from love or gratitude. Thanks to her, everything had changed in a moment.

"Take me far away from here," she begged me again and again, crying.

I remembered the mountain mule that had brought her to the inn and went to look for it. I think I must have saddled it in less than five minutes. When I returned to the doorway, Aurora was coming back, carrying the corpse of her child. She had taken it from Garlic Teeth.

"I want to bury him far from here. . . ."

I seated her on the rump of the mule and it was then that I remembered the doctor.

"One moment, Aurora."

I ran toward the grave and saw my companion stretched out on the ground.

"Let's go!" I shouted to him. "Grab my hand so that we can escape."

He smiled at me sadly.

"I can imagine what happened. . . . I am glad for you and for

Aurora. . . . But I have only a little time left and I want to die
in peace. . . . Good-by, my friend . . . and good luck!"

"But why don't you want to come with us?"

"Leave me; it's better this way. . . . What do you expect to do
in the future?" he asked me in a voice reduced to a trickle.

"The Revolution . . . as long as Bolivia needs it, I shall live
for nothing else. . . ."

He smiled at me again with his eyes already closed by exhaustion or death.

Aurora had ridden the mule to the edge of the grave. She
looked at the doctor and crossed herself.

I mounted the mule and we rode away at a quick trot. When
I turned back to look an hour later, the inn was only a flaw on
the plain.

—Translated by Izaak A. Langnas

GLOSSARY

Chicha: alcoholic beverage made of fermented maize.

Palliri: woman worker in the mines who selects the ore.

Guagua: suckling baby.

Chulu: woolen cap worn by Indians.

Cliceño: native of the Bolivian district of Clizon.

Kkepi: policeman.

Api: corn pap.

Tata: father, master, priest.

Choto: man of a class between the *chola* (see below) and the *criolla,* or
native white. *Chota:* woman of the same class. Its diminutive form,
chotita, is generally used as a term of endearment.

Puna: arid and cold Andean highlands.

Tutuma: vessel made of a small gourd. *Tutumazo:* a drink from a *tutuma.*

Cholo: a mestizo. The word is sometimes used contemptuously. The feminine form, *chola,* is also used with the additional meanings of "mistress" and "concubine."

Chichi: dirty, despicable. Also noun.

Niñituy: diminutive of "boy."

Pongo: indigenous serf.

Papel-pampa: Andean steppes.

Tocuyo: rough cotton cloth.

Imilla: little Indian girl.

Huayño: sad and plaintive folk music.

Charango: musical instrument similar to the banjo, usually made of armadillo shell.

Chasquiri: laborer paid by the job, pieceworker.

Molle: tree typical of Bolivia.

Acallantu: red handkerchief hanging from a pole, sign of a *chicha* inn. Loosely, the inn itself.

Sayaña: piece of ground enclosed by standing stones.

Charqui: dried meat, similar to *tasajo* or jerked beef.

Pisco: brandy.

Chalona: rib of mutton.

Kkara: man of the people, used contemptuously.

Tunca: potatoes preserved by freezing.

Páramo: cold, bleak upland of the Andes.

Chancaca: condensed sugar-cane juice, sold as candy.

Quinua: cereal of the Bolivian Plateau, similar to millet.

Tostón: Spanish colonial coin, no longer current.

Llocalla: baby about to be born.

THE BLACK SHIP
by Carlos Rozas Larraín

CARLOS ROZAS LARRAÍN, of Chile, has been at various times a farmer, a congressman, and an importer. But his great passions remain mountain hunting in the Andes, and lake and deep-sea fishing. His first book, *Isla Negra* (*Black Island*), which appeared in 1959, was a great success and quickly sold out its first printing. *Campo Viejo* (*Old Field*), his most recently published work, has received unanimous praise from the Santiago press. In production at present is a volume of short stories called *Senderos de agua y piedra* (Paths of Water and Stone).

Juanito Maulén had never known who his father was, and until that day he had hardly given the problem a thought.

His old mother—not so much old as worn-out—lived with her children in a slovenly cluster of little huts, this sort and that, all hidden among the great rocks of Point Molle, some fifty yards from the sea.

He had eleven brothers and sisters. They were of all ages and sizes and even colors. One of the smallest girls was blonde and blue-eyed, but the rest were very dark, like the fishermen of the region.

Juanito was a dark, serious boy, tall for his age and rather reserved. He was the third oldest of the children, with a whole swarm of younger sisters and brothers who ran or toddled or crawled here and there—usually half-naked—among the huts and the rocks. The rocks were black and enormous; they served as a natural breakwater against the crashing of the surf. Without them, the huts would have been swept into the sea.

The cold winds from the south rarely troubled the area. They stayed up above in the saw-toothed mountains, humming or howling, and only occasionally descended to the coast with their icy daggers. The north winds were milder but filled with rain, which had to be controlled by a series of wide drains. The men who built and repaired the drains, over the course of a good many years, all slept for a while like husbands with Esperanza.

Esperanza was Juanito's mother. Her first three children were the result of her first love affair. A lusty young fisherman named Juan Belmar had taken her off to his hut. It was the first hut at Point Molle, and he had built it himself.

He was a fisherman because that was the family trade; she was a farm girl—from the coast, it is true, but still a farm girl. The difference is important. A fisherman might eventually become a farmer, but he would always feel discontented and out of place. The country people along the coast, however, could turn from farming to fishing with relative ease. (Perhaps it was a regression toward the sea of our earliest ages.)

The fact is, then, that Esperanza went off with Juan Belmar, and the farm girl was soon at home there among the rocks that the high tides of February splashed with foam. She lived very happily, after her fashion, because her man treated her well. He drank, of course, but he also taught her to drink, and they always got drunk together, either by themselves or in the company of their fishermen friends, whenever there was money. And Juan Belmar earned plenty of money: the fishing was good and he was a good fisherman.

When the sea was calm he set out his nets and lines. When the swordfish arrived, and above all the tuna, he went far out to sea in his little boat. That is how he earned such good money. Esperanza learned to drink as well as Juan Belmar did or even better.

Her first two children were born in that hut among the rocks. They were both husky boys.

One day while she was pregnant with her third child, Juan Belmar went out in his boat and did not return to the cove.

But Esperanza was more than twenty years old now, and she had lots of friends, the friends who used to come to the hut to drink with them.

Her life was not difficult, because everybody helped her. A little while after Juanito was born—the last reminder of Juan Belmar—another fisherman came to live with her.

They built an extra room for the sons of Juan Belmar, and Esperanza lived for a year and a half sleeping with Angelito and getting drunk with him. He was the father of her next child, a lovable little girl, very dark and vivacious.

Later there were other men, and they all planted their seeds. And thus the huts and the children went on increasing, there among the surf-beaten rocks.

The older children learned to gather shellfish, and also to catch the small fishes that swam among the tangled seaweed in the holes in the rocks. They sold their catches in the near-by village.

Then one of them learned how to swim underwater. He brought up sea urchins and giant scallops, which sold for good prices. The sons of Juan Belmar earned their own living, and even helped Esperanza when she had been drunk for several days or when she was pregnant and her man had left her.

By the time he was six, Juanito could pry crabs out of the fissures in the rocks, and also locate the hiding scallops. At ten, he went out fishing for conger eels with the man who was living with his mother at the time.

They went out before sundown and rowed for several hours, until it was completely dark. El Llayo had a knack for catching eels. He made sure that no other boats were following him. He knew the secret places where the fishing was best. They fished without any light, so that no one would be able to find them. In the morning they returned with a whole boatload of eels.

One night they were fishing at about fifty fathoms, in the midst of a heavy fog. They already had a dozen eels in the boat when they were startled by the hoarse foghorn of a steamship bellowing in the darkness.

El Llayo had eyes like an owl's, but he could not make out anything through the dense wet curtain that surrounded him. And the eels went on biting.

The foghorn uttered its plaintive roar once again.

"It's out beyond us," El Llayo said. "Don't worry about it, sonny."

He yanked at the long line to set the hooks and then pulled it in as fast as he could. There were two enormous eels on it.

Juanito's eyesight was accustomed to the fog and the darkness, and when the eels were in the boat and he was helping unhook them, he could see how big they really were: the biggest they had ever caught.

Suddenly the foghorn sounded again, but this time it was so close that they could almost feel its vibrations in their bones. They could see lights approaching in the fog, and then the shapeless black mass of a large ship. It roared like a bull as it charged through the dark waters.

El Llayo jumped for the oars and rowed frantically, desperately. The oarlocks shrieked and *El Piquero* bounded away like a horse raked by the spurs.

The great ship, as black as the Demon, passed them no more than five fathoms away, and only a miracle saved their boat from capsizing in the steep waves that surged from its bows. All its lights were on, and every few moments it sounded its deafening horn. It left a broad white wake, in which the little fishing boat danced a perilous, drunken dance. Then, like something glimpsed in a nightmare, it vanished in the swirls of fog.

Except for the horn, Juanito would have thought it was a dream. He could hear it roaring for long minutes after it had disappeared, each time more faintly. His heart was bobbing in his chest as crazily as *El Piquero* had bobbed in the wake.

El Llayo drew a deep breath and muttered, "What a bastard!" Then he lit a cigarette and tossed his fish lines into the water. Juanito also threw out his lines, but remained as silent as usual.

The eels had stopped biting. Perhaps an hour passed without a single bite. El Llayo pulled in his lines and took up the oars.

Finally he said, "Well, the bastard scared them away, all right. God knows how many days before they'll come back." And he spat over the side.

They rowed to another fishing place, which El Llayo located in the fog and darkness by virtue of some mysterious instinct. They caught five more eels—but the small black variety—at about thirty fathoms.

At dawn they returned to the cove. It was a cloudy morning, and a cold, threatening wind had begun to blow from the north.

Other boats also arrived. The fishermen helped each other pull the heavier boats and launches up onto the beach. They dragged them up on sliders made from bundles of wet seaweed, which they placed at intervals under the oaken keels.

Among the boats Juanito saw one that was unfamiliar to him, and El Llayo greeted a fisherman Juanito had never seen in the cove.

The stranger was tall and very strong, with black hair streaked with gray. His face and powerful neck had been burned almost black by the sun, and a whitish scar stood out on one side of his face, running from his left eye to behind his ear. He was dressed almost in rags: both his trousers and his heavy jersey had been torn, mended, and torn again.

Juanito felt nothing, either in his heart or his waking mind, when El Toyo—a coarse fellow of about fifteen—slapped him on the shoulder and pointed to the newcomer. "That's Juan Belmar, your father," he said, his thick lips spreading in a grin.

Juanito could not understand at first, but then, in his ignorant precocity, he had a confused impression of something animal. That was his father? That ragged, ugly old man? How could he be, if he had never even seen him before? "The hell with El Toyo," he muttered, and spat like El Llayo. Then he took another look at Juan Belmar. There was something about the man that pleased him. He could not tell what. He was certainly very manly, very big and strong and serious. But . . . he could not be his father, not if he had never seen him before!

He decided to forget about the question, and began helping El Llayo clean the eels. The other fishermen gathered around to watch them unload the boat. As always, none of the others had caught so many eels as El Llayo, nor such big ones.

Juanito admired him and was fond of him: he was his sea-going friend and companion. True, he might be smaller and slighter than that Juan Belmar, the man El Toyo pointed out. But, as a fisherman, there was no one like El Llayo.

They brought the eels to the pickup truck from the port. It arrived every morning to buy the catches the fishermen had brought back. El Llayo saved out one of the best eels to take home. Then the two of them started walking toward the huts among the rocks.

Juanito remembered the tall, dark-skinned man he had seen and asked, "Llayo, who was that big man you spoke to at the cove?"

"Which one? The one that arrived today in the yellow boat?"

"Yes, that one."

El Llayo gazed at him a moment and answered slowly, "Ah, now, that bully-boy's named Juan Belmar. He's from here, but he's been away for a long time . . . in the north, they say. Must be about ten years by now."

Juanito was silent, thinking. He himself was about ten years old; he had heard his mother say so a few days earlier. Then he asked, "Llayo, is it true he's my father?"

El Llayo was walking ahead of him, taking great strides along the rocky path. The eel that dangled from his shoulder swayed back and forth. "That's right, kid, they say he's your father."

The boy followed him, half trotting. He was thinking about what he had been told, and his head was crowded with a jumble of ideas that had never entered it before.

They reached the huts and went into the dark shack that served as a kitchen. The pots and pans that hung on the walls were gleaming in the shadows.

It was August, and nine in the morning, but Esperanza was still in bed in another room, sleeping off the wine or brandy she had drunk in the night . . . had drunk while Juanito and El Llayo were almost being killed by that great black steamship. The boy was hungry and wanted some bread and some hot coffee. For a moment he hated his mother.

El Llayo stirred up the fire, put a kettle of water on it, and began to make some toast. There were still enough live coals to heat the water quickly. "God knows how late the old lady stayed up drinking," Juanito said to himself. "While El Llayo and I were out in the fog. That big black ship, it damn near ran right into us!"

As he drank his coffee and ate a slice of toast, he decided that Juan Belmar might be his father but El Llayo meant a lot more to him . . . more than his father and mother and all his brothers and sisters. "We were out fishing last night, the two of us," he thought, "and the old lady was here getting drunk, God knows who with." Now he was drinking coffee with El Llayo . . . and El Llayo had made it.

"The hell with the old lady," he said to himself, spitting. "And with that Juan Belmar too."

Outside, his younger brothers and sisters cried or fought with each other or raced here and there. His two older brothers were still sleeping because they had both gotten drunk with Esperanza.

The baby, El Llayo's son, was asleep in a basket in one corner of the kitchen. His only blanket was an old rag, but he slept very calmly, with a scrap of dry bread still clutched in one grimy hand.

A huge silhouette appeared in the doorway, blocking the light. El Llayo and Juanito looked up. It was Juan Belmar.

He walked in as if he were at home. He sat down by the fire, poured himself a cup of the coffee El Llayo had made, and then helped himself to a piece of toast, which he ate in gluttonous mouthfuls.

El Llayo got up and hunted for more bread in the drawers of the ramshackle cabinet. No one—neither the two men nor the boy—spoke a word.

Then they could hear the hoarse shouting of Esperanza. She was in one of the little yards between the huts, putting a stop to a fight between two of the children. A few moments later she entered the kitchen. Without speaking, she advanced like a sleep-walker toward the shelf where she kept the brandy, and from there, turning her head, she saw the hulking form of Juan Belmar outlined against the light from the doorway. She was so startled that she left the bottle in its place. El Llayo watched the changes of expression that passed over her face. It was the face of an old woman, but it still had a sort of coarse beauty.

She went over to peer at Juan Belmar, at his graying hair, his mouth, his glowing eyes. She seemed almost to be smelling him, because her sight was still dulled by the brandy. She touched his face with her hand, trying to turn it toward the faint light from the doorway. Then, still dazed, she ran her index finger along the scar on his cheek.

He smiled for an instant, showing his white teeth, and then roughly pushed her hand away. She stood looking at him for a long while. Finally she sat down by the fire and began to weep in silence.

The minutes passed. El Llayo and Juanito merely stared at Juan Belmar and Esperanza, and no one spoke. Then Esperanza dried her tears on the hem of her skirt and said, "You've come back, Juan Belmar!" It was as if she were speaking to herself.

Instead of replying, he got up and went over to the shelf where she kept the brandy. He took a long swig, straight from the bottle, and smacked his lips. Then he jutted his chin toward Juanito. "And this one?" he asked. His voice was hoarse and cracked.

"Yours," she said. "His name's Juan. He was born after you left."

"But there's a lot more of them," he said with a trace of a smile.

Esperanza was silent. El Llayo got up from his seat by the fire. He walked over to the shelf and filled two shot glasses with brandy. He gave one of them to Esperanza and tossed off the other himself. The silence continued. The north wind blew harder and harder.

"And there's a lot more huts now, too!" It was the broken voice of Juan Belmar again. "All those kids and those huts . . . are they all Llayo's?" There was a strange note of mockery and provocation in his words.

El Llayo pushed Juanito toward the doorway. The boy backed up, frightened. His young mind was a wasp's nest of ideas that told him nothing. Nothing, at least, that he could find words for. He went out backward, still chewing on a piece of toast.

When he reached the threshold, he stopped and looked at El Llayo and his mother. El Llayo gestured impatiently and said, "Go down to the cove and bring me back my knife." His voice was calm and natural. The boy turned and ran off. He wanted to bring the knife back as quickly as possible, because El Llayo must have a good reason for wanting it.

Juan Belmar looked at El Llayo and broke out into a loud laugh. He grew silent, and then laughed again. Finally he said in a heavy, serious voice, "Look, boy, I'm not asking for a fight."

"Neither am I," El Llayo said placidly. "I just need my knife to skin this eel."

Juan Belmar took out his own, which was thrust between his red wool sash and his tattered shirt. El Llayo did not even blink. Belmar felt its sharp edge with his thumb and then reached it out to El Llayo. "Here, try this one, Llayito."

He was treating him with a sort of grave contempt. Esperanza seemed to be weeping with her face in her hands, but she watched both men from between the cracks of her fingers.

By noon, it was clear that no one could go fishing that night. The north wind was stronger than ever, and the sea was growing rougher by the hour.

Esperanza made a stew with the eel El Llayo had brought home. Instead of drinking, she took great pains to cook a good meal for Juan Belmar.

Later, she demanded the money El Llayo was paid for his catch, and sent the two oldest boys to buy wine and brandy. Then she sent Juanito and two of his sisters to the scattered huts of her friends, inviting them to come there that night to celebrate Juan Belmar's return.

The boy was disgusted. He also had a vague notion of disobeying her. Why should she celebrate Belmar's return? He had not even greeted his own children, or her either, after leaving them on their own for ten whole years. And the money was El Llayo's and his! Because he—Juanito Maulén—had also fished for eels, both before and after that great black ship went by. That great black ship that charged them, bellowing, in the fog. And El Llayo saved them from being killed! If he had not rowed *El Piquero* so well, making it leap and bound, where would she get the money for the wine and brandy? From Juan Belmar? And why was his own name Juan Maulén? All right, his mother's name was Esperanza Maulén, and everyone called them the Maulén chil-

dren, even though they had various fathers: Juanito knew this,
and it was all right . . . but . . . the other men would come back
now and then, with money and presents for Esperanza and the
children. They would get drunk with Esperanza and then go away
again. But El Llayo never went away. How many years had he
stayed there? Four, at the very least. But this big, black-faced
stranger had not brought them anything at all. . . . And the
money was El Llayo's and his, Juanito Maulén's! He ought to
have expected it. That Belmar was big and black like the steamship last night, and just as dangerous . . . but ah! that Llayito!
He was no giant, like Belmar, but he was a real man. He could
take care of himself the way he took care of *El Piquero*.

The boy was still smiling at the thought when he met Angelito.
He blurted out his mother's invitation, and Angelito said he would
be very glad to have a few drinks with Juan Belmar.

Juanito walked on, thinking, "That stupid Llayito! Wasting his
money on a fiesta for that Juan Belmar! And my mother looking
at Belmar as if he were St. Peter!" The figure of St. Peter that
stood on a tall rock at the cove was fastened there with cement,
and was made of bronze, and was green instead of black; also,
it was a lot smaller than Belmar . . . was even smaller than
Juanito himself, because one day he had climbed up on the rock
to measure himself against it. And besides all this, St. Peter had a
beard, and wore a long robe that even covered his feet, and held
a bunch of keys in one of his hands. Sometimes a sea gull would
perch on top of his head, and St. Peter would just stand there, as
calm as you please, blessing the boats with two fingers of his right
hand and holding those keys in the other. No, Juan Belmar was
not St. Peter, so why should she look at him like that? . . .

What would Juan Belmar do if a sea gull perched on his head?

Juanito was still grinning when he delivered Esperanza's message at the next hut.

That night, as the tide rose, the waves pounded the rocks more
savagely than Juanito had ever seen them do. As he left the hut,
one wave sprang so high that the foam drenched the roofs and

yards. His younger brothers and sisters were crying pitifully in two of the smaller huts. But in the main hut, in the kitchen, the men and women did not hear the thunder of the surf, much less the wails of the children. All of them were getting drunk by now. Celinda, the oldest of the Maulén girls, had fed the youngsters and then put them to bed.

The two oldest sons had been allowed to stay in the kitchen, but El Llayo—his friend Llayito!—had ordered him to get out. "Damn it, that was unfair!"

Another wave crashed. It sounded louder than the explosions the road builders set off when they were opening that tunnel up there in the mountains.

Juanito was restless, and could not have slept if he had wanted to. The people in the kitchen were shouting so loudly that at times they made more noise than the surf.

The boy knew that on the landward side of the hut there was a crack that let you peer in. He went around to that side and put his eyes close to the crack. The smoke coming out of it made him wince and blink. At first he could hardly make out the dark figures in all that smoke from their cigarettes and the fire, but little by little his eyes became accustomed to it.

His mother was sitting at Juan Belmar's feet, now and then looking up at him. She seemed to be just slightly drunk. Belmar had taken the only chair in the hut, while the others sat on straw mats, on boxes, on stones, or on the dirt floor, leaning their backs against the walls. There were about fifteen men and only four or five women.

He could see three demijohns of wine and countless bottles of brandy.

But where was El Llayo? The boy looked for him, puzzled, in that crowd of noisy drunkards, but could not see him anywhere.

One of the women poured several liters of wine and three bottles of brandy into a large pot; she added some sprigs of marihuana and set it on the fire. Directly in front of him there were two men singing in raucous voices, with their arms around each other's shoulders. They stopped for a moment to drink out of the same glass, and then burst out singing again. One of them

was Angelito . . . but the other one? Ah, yes! The other one was
El Lobo. Juanito had heard that El Lobo's father knew more
about the sea than any other fisherman at the cove. But El Lobo
had certain ways about him that always caused Juanito to feel a
deep revulsion.

El Lobo often tried to talk with him, but Juanito merely walked
away. Of course, El Lobo was a skillful fisherman like his father.

"The hell with El Lobo and his ways! That Llayito, where is
he, where is he sitting?" Juanito strained his eyes to look into
every corner of the hut.

Another wave broke, and even from the landward side the
boy could see the foam shooting up above the huts. How white it
was, against the black sky! "Damn, but the sea's getting rougher
all the time!"

But Angelito and El Lobo! . . . What was going on? Angelito
had lived with Esperanza for a while . . . and they even said
that he was Celinda's father. . . . Yet there he was, with El
Lobo, and they were hugging and fondling each other. As El
Llayo said, a real man never behaves that way. "Where the hell
is El Llayo?"

Suddenly the crack in the wall grew dark. Someone sitting on
the floor just under it had stood up. Then the shadow moved away
and he could see again. It was El Llayo. He was walking un-
steadily toward the big, dark-skinned man, toward Juan Belmar . . . toward his, Juanito's, father.

Esperanza was watching them as intently as the boy. El Llayo
was also manly enough. He was almost as tall as Belmar, but a
lot lighter. But he was a lot younger, too. Still, his father looked
terribly strong, with those shoulders of his, and that neck. Like
the bulls Juanito had seen one day when he went inland. Yes,
just like the bulls!

El Llayo was carrying a glass and a bottle of liquor as he
stumbled over toward Juan Belmar, the bull. Esperanza was still
sitting on the floor in front of Belmar, looking from one to the
other. There was something strange in her expression, something
Juanito had never seen before.

Belmar was silent until El Llayo was in front of him. When

he finally spoke, he used the same tone of voice that had annoyed Juanito earlier. "Well, boy, what do you want?"

El Llayo teetered back and forth, clutching the glass and the bottle. Despite all the shouting and laughter, the boy could make out every word they said. All his attention was concentrated on them. El Llayo asked bluntly, "Have you come to stay, Negro?"

Belmar grinned at him. "You know this is my hut, don't you? Are you going to run me out if I decide I'd like to stay?"

El Llayo stood looking at him in silence, as if confused. He swayed again, first on his heels, then on his toes, and drank another shot of brandy at a single gulp. His expression changed and he started laughing.

"If you want to stay here, Negro . . . stay. . . . What do I care what you do? . . ." He could hardly form the words. Juan Belmar stood up with a shot of brandy and tossed it off in the same manner. Then he wrapped his arm around El Llayo's shoulders.

The boy watched them from his vantage place, and Esperanza watched them from the floor. The others were not paying any attention to them: they were all too busy drinking, talking, and singing. A few of the men had begun to molest the women, and this led to all kinds of noisy arguments.

El Llayo put his arm around Belmar's waist and asked Esperanza to fill their glasses again. She refused at first, but obeyed him when he shouted at her in a harsh bellow.

Juanito watched the two men as they talked and drank their brandy. They were embracing each other, and their heads were close together. Were they like Angelito and El Lobo? No. The boy could understand the difference, though he could not have explained it in words. Belmar left El Llayo for a moment and came back with a bottle for the two of them. They drank again, with their arms around each other, rocking and swaying like *El Piquero* in rough waters.

Then El Llayo invited Belmar to go outside. The boy could not hear the reason he gave, but both of them went out. His mother got up from the floor and tried to stop them, but she too was reeling drunk. She grabbed Juan Belmar, grabbed his torn jersey, and he slapped her square in the face with the back of his hand. Juanito saw his mother collapse in front of the threshold. A trickle of blood began to run from her mouth.

The men left the hut, stepping over her sprawled body, and someone closed the door behind them. The boy trailed them in the darkness. He knew the paths among the rocks better than anyone else.

Juanito told time by the sea, not by a clock. The tide was full now and very high. It would be about midnight, then. The north wind had died down, and the sky was clearing a little in the south. The moon was no longer full, but it was still large, and it struggled to break out of the gray clouds that imprisoned it. The sea was still very rough, pounding and pounding at the shore. The exploding foam seemed to light up the black summits of the rocks. Belmar and El Llayo, supporting and embracing each other, went staggering down the path that led to a deep hole among the rocks at the sea's edge.

Suddenly the moon came out. A wave broke with a deep, hollow roar, like a cannon fired off in a cavern, and the spray leaped high in the air.

The two men had thrown their glasses away and were drinking straight from the bottle. They sat down—they almost fell down—on a clump of seaweed, and Juanito hid himself near-by. His father was talking hoarsely and indistinctly. "You shouldn't be scared of the sea, Llayito. You're a coward, boy. If you're scared of women and the sea, you're nobody. They're the same, boy. Women and the sea. If you're scared of them, they start ordering you around. And then you haven't got a chance, boy."

Two waves, one after another, broke on the rocks, and the white spray fell over them like a caress.

"If you leave them, they hunt for you. See? Get up, boy, I'm going to show you something."

They stumbled on toward that hole among the rocks. Juanito could not tell who was leading the other, but he knew where they were going. The path was only a few fathoms long, but they kept stopping every few steps to raise the bottle.

Juanito followed the two silhouettes along the path. They were

equals: Belmar was older and stronger, El Llayo was smaller
and quicker. Juanito felt a premonition that made him tremble
with fear, and he tried to drive it from his mind.

. . . El Llayito could win, despite the older man's bull-like
neck and shoulders. But El Llayito seemed to be the drunker of
the two. The damn fool! Why did he have to drink so much today?
El Llayo was his friend . . . and the other one was his father. And
what did he know about him until this morning? It was Llayito
who taught him how to fish for conger eels, how to prepare the
lines, how to weave nets and cast them and draw them in. And
this year they were going out in *El Piquero* to fish for tuna. But
his father? Nothing. Not even a good-morning. Just Esperanza
wasting money on him, money that he and El Llayo earned by
catching eels in the fog, when that great ship almost killed them.
Wasting money on him, on El Negro, and looking up at him as if
he were St. Peter. And how did he thank her? By knocking her
down when he left the hut with El Llayo. The blood ran out of her
mouth. . . . His mother, Esperanza, was nothing but a worn-out
old wh . . . well, all right, he knew that; he had heard many men
shout the ugly word at her. Still, Esperanza had raised all of them,
all of the Maulén children. Esperanza Maulén. He himself was
Juan Maulén, not Juan Belmar. And for the last two years or more
El Llayo had supported Esperanza and her whole gang of children, and had built two extra huts for them with his own hands.
Also, he owned his own boat, and even had an outboard motor . . . an old one, but in good condition. When the time came,
they were going out fishing for tuna. But the other one, his
father . . . what had he ever done for them? Juanito spat.

The two men drained the bottle. Then Belmar threw it away
and it shattered on the rocks.

The sea was quiet for a moment, as if it were gathering its
strength for another assault. Juanito heard El Llayo saying: "I'm
not scared of the sea, Negro. You're the one that's scared of it.
You're scared of everything. Come on, we'll find out."

His voice was harsh and cracked. Juan Belmar seemed to be the one who was obeying orders now.

A huge wave broke on the rocks. Another. And another.

"If they go to that hole in the rocks," Juanito thought, "they're both going to get soaked by the waves. And they're so drunk that a big one could knock them down and carry them out to sea."

But they kept on going, their arms around each other, discussing something in lowered voices. Juanito moved up closer, only a few paces behind them, without their knowing he was following them. El Llayo was whispering something in El Negro's ear.

A wave drenched the three of them from head to foot. Then another broke and drenched them again. Juanito tasted the cold clean brine on his lips.

Belmar realized, vaguely, that something was wrong, and he stopped out of sheer instinct. But El Llayo was not as drunk as he appeared. He grabbed him by the arm and said, "What? Are you scared of the sea?"

There was no answer, but Belmar tried to pull himself loose. They were on the very brink of that deep hole among the rocks. The sea was calmer for a moment. El Llayo punched him in the ribs and asked hoarsely, "Now what, Negro? What's the matter? Which one of us is the coward?" And he punched him in the face.

Juanito saw Belmar draw out his long knife. Its blade glittered in the moonlight and flashed downward like a stroke of lightning. El Llayo crumpled to the ground, and Belmar fell on top of him. A wave drenched them once more, almost sweeping them away.

Juanito was agile as a cat. He picked up a large stone, ran over to Belmar, and crashed it down on the bull's head.

When the next wave broke, El Llayo was already on his feet. With the help of the boy and the water, he pushed Belmar toward the hole. El Negro fell like a huge boulder. They saw another wave rising toward them, and hung on to the rocks with straining fingers. It was enormous, like a house with a white roof. Then its heavy, foaming mass poured over them. Juanito held his breath, clinging to the rocks like a limpet. Then he looked around. He saw El Llayo squeezing the water from his eyes. And Juan Belmar, his father? He was not there. Juanito looked down into the hole. He

was not there either. There was nothing in the hole but the swirl-
ing foam and the seaweed twisting like serpents.

El Llayo and the boy ran along the path that led to the huts.
When they were beyond the reach of the waves they both stopped.
The sky had cleared and the moon was very bright. They looked
back and all around them. No one, no one at all.

The sea continued to explode in that great hole in the rocks.

They looked at each other. El Llayo smiled wearily, but the boy
was very solemn. "Did he cut you, Llayito?"

El Llayo was still drunk but he remembered everything that
had happened. He felt his side and then held up his hand in the
moonlight. It was red with blood. "It looks like he got me here.
But it can't be too bad. It doesn't hurt." His speech was thick and
blurred. "No, it can't be too bad. Doesn't hurt at all."

He raised his heavy jersey. It had a long slash in it, and was
still sopping wet. There was also a slash in his shirt, with a dark
blood stain along it. He raised his shirt too. He had a long cut on
his side, but so shallow that it was little more than a graze. He
almost fell over as he bent and twisted to look at it. "Damn if I
wasn't lucky!"

Juanito touched it with his finger. It was not even bleeding any
longer. The cold salt water had stopped the bleeding very quickly.
He could hear the drunkards still shouting and singing in the
kitchen. How long had all that been going on? He could not tell,
but it seemed a whole year. By now they were making even more
noise than the sea was.

El Llayo wrapped his sash around the cut. Then he pulled
down his shirt, and over it his jersey.

They heard a rasping moan. Another wave exploded and
drowned it out. They looked back. They saw the thing. Crawling
toward them. Dragging itself along the stony path. A thing out of
a nightmare, crawling toward them, moaning.

It was Juan Belmar. It could only be Juan Belmar. El Negro.
The bull.

But his face . . . his whole head. . . . They could see it clearly
in the moonlight. It was battered to a shapeless, bleeding lump.
The waves had smashed it against the rocks again and again. They

saw the gleaming whites of his terrible eyes, but the rest of his face was nothing but a bloody pulp. And he still came toward them, hitching himself along on one arm and one leg. His other leg had been broken in so many places that it looked like some strange reptile following him along the path; his shattered left arm was dangling and flopping at his side.

He crawled forward for another yard and then collapsed, face first, on the stones.

El Llayo and Juanito were paralyzed. They watched him come toward them again, little by little, moaning like a wounded dog as he struggled to reach the hut.

El Llayo, still drunk, looked at him with the staring eyes of a madman. At last he made a sign with his thumb and forefinger. A cold shiver ran down Juanito's spine.

"The cross, Devil!" El Llayo shouted. He grasped the boy's hand and lurched away, pulling him along.

They ran, ran without stopping, until they reached the cove. Somehow, between them, they found the extra strength to drag *El Piquero* down to the water. A wave broke in front of its bow, moved smoothly up the beach, and set it afloat. They leaped aboard and El Llayo began to row.

The moon was still shining and the sea was growing calm.

At daybreak they were far out from the land, asleep, rocked by the waves. When he woke up, El Llayo took the oars and rowed toward the south, where he had come from when he was a boy. The winter sun arose, but Juanito went on sleeping, his face to the sky.

Far off, a great black ship was cutting through the waves, trailing its long plume of somber smoke.

Translated by LYSANDER KEMP

THE CAUSE
by Haroldo Pedro Conti

HAROLDO PEDRO CONTI was born in Chacabuco, Argentina, in 1925. He is a graduate of the Faculty of Philosophy and Letters of the University of Buenos Aires. A two-time Fellow of the *"Gente de Cine"* Club, Conti received an award from the Organization Lacino Americana de Teatro (Latin American Theater Organization) for his play, *Examinado (Examined)*. A novel, *El Paseo de Aleluya (The Hallelujah Walk)*, will be published shortly.

I

Pedro Romita entered Rinconcito toward nightfall.

He was coming from the south.

About five miles back, or a little past Absi the Turk's warehouse, he had first caught sight of the tower of the Rinconcito church rising above the flat, empty plain toward the northwest.

He had fallen asleep to the jogging of the wagon. Two hours had passed since his last stop. At the start he'd been thinking of one thing or another. But after the first hour he dropped off to sleep: the wagon rocked him like a hammock.

Now he was simply watching the tower, which shot up over the horizon like the turret of some giant castle, thrusting upward with such force that it seemed to pierce the sky. The horse hadn't seen it yet, because the horse was much lower down than he was, with its head bent to the ground. And the wagon seat was so high and far back that from where he was he could see a good deal farther.

He felt good when he saw the tower.

Soon after, the four silos of the Victoria Mill appeared, and a little later, the dome of the ancient town hall.

That's all there was of Rinconcito, that and a few more houses. Still, if you stood in the center of town, especially on a Sunday

afternoon, it was hard to imagine how insignificant the whole
thing was. You had to come at it from the south, moving slowly
over that immense silence, to really get the picture.

To the right of the tower, or just between the tower and the
silos, was his house.

Right there, stuck in the middle of all that solitude, was a
house, and a fire going in the stove, and a little group of people
as insignificant as Rinconcito itself, who were waiting for him.

He felt really good when he saw that tower.

Sometimes he asked himself how anyone could feel important
in a nothing town like that, lost from the world in the middle of
that valley. And yet, Rinconcito was a world of its own.

It had two daily papers, *The Voice of Rinconcito* and *The
Plaindealer;* a train station; a monument to the War of Independence that was supposed to be the second largest in the country (18×20 feet, counting the base and pedestal); a Social Club;
a *Circolo Italiano;* A Sports Club; running water; and the venerable tower that could be seen from so far off. In 1934 it
had its last epidemic and in 1945 its first congressman. In 1948
it installed a network of loudspeakers. In 1951 it nearly got a
branch of the National Bank. And now there was talk that the
annual bike race was putting Rinconcito on its itinerary.

Quite a town.

Sometimes he would curse the hell out of it. In 1932 he decided
to pull up stakes and go live in the capital; he packed a valise
and took a sulky as far as Piedrabuena, twenty-five miles away,
because that was before the train stopped at Rinconcito.

But when the train covered those twenty-five miles again and
he saw the tower in the distance, his heart sank. He waited till
they were going past and jumped. The valise went first; then he
closed his eyes, held his breath, and bailed out. *The Voice* gave
it a mention under "Travel."

From then on, even though he still cursed the town, it wasn't
very serious.

In 1936 he married Juana Ardolino. That was the same year
she was elected Carnival Queen, which made her a celebrity. If

she hadn't once been queen, maybe she wouldn't have nagged him so much about his rotten luck. But, with all her nagging, he had his own nostalgic memories of that '36 Carnival and of little Juana in her dazzling crown of cardboard and tinfoil. The dance in the Town Hall was, in fact, memorable. Time can make many things fade, but never that dance. An orchestra came up from the capital, and the Arts Club built a real stage in the garden and put on a group of *tableaux vivants* that were clearly inspired. The town priest lent them his harmonium, and Professor Venturi, a young man then, sat behind a screen and played something to fit each *tableau* in what *The Voice* called "an elegant and meticulous style."

How many times, jogging along on his wagon, with no one to talk to but that knock-kneed horse, he remembered back to that night!

At the time of his marriage he was working as a clerk in Mercurio's, which was the store on the main square.

Afterward he started a store of his own.

At first, things went well. But during the '43 elections, he lost his shirt.

Rinconcito was split between Whites and Yellows. The Whites were the ruling party there, just as they were in the rest of the country. They had been the ruling party as far back as anyone could remember, and it didn't occur to them that they could be anything else. The Yellows, on the other hand, had been waiting a half century to take control. Neither party had any real ideology: one was simply the ruling party, while the other wasn't.

Romita was a Yellow, i.e., awkward and resentful and quite poor.

The Whites were good for one thing only: to rule. The Yellows, on the other hand, had a wide range of activities, from constructive criticism to wild-haired conspiracy, with whatever came in between.

The Whites had given the country all its rulers. Some good, others bad. The Yellows had given it its orators, its martyrs, its subversives, its schoolteachers, its bad examples, and those count-

less numbers who had died of hunger. In 1931, the party split.
In 1935, the splinters split. In 1943, when the splinters could
barely recognize one another, they banded together in a United
Front. It was an exciting alliance. "Yellows of the world, unite!"

The excitement even got to Rinconcito. The good fight was
about to be fought. The Yellows' campaign slogan: The People!
The Whites' campaign slogan: The People!

The Yellows whipped together a monster rally for the last day
of the campaign. The Whites offered what they always did: two
pounds of steak, a quart of wine, ten pesos.

The Yellows had a speaker's stand and an enormous campaign
sign and a sound truck. That and a great deal of hope.

That was when the strangers from Piedrabuena dropped by.

Romita was up on the speaker's stand (almost as high off the
ground as the seat on his wagon) and was telling them all the
things that a poor man likes to hear. Earlier, when he'd tried
them out on Juana, they hadn't sounded so good. But here, with
their faces staring up at him, he was a changed man.

He was getting to the top of his form, when the platform took
off like a shot, as if it were a wagon or something. The strangers
from Piedrabuena had fastened one end of a rope to the stand,
then started up a truck that held the other end, dragging off
Romita, platform, and all.

Well, it was pretty funny all right. . . .

That was when Romita got to see one thing clearly. You were
either on the top or on the bottom. He was on the bottom. What
did it matter, White or Yellow? He was fated to be on the bottom.
That's how things went in Rinconcito; that's how they went in the
country; and, though he couldn't swear to it, that's how they
probably went throughout the world.

The campaign cost him his store.

Juana had told him:

"Don't play around with politics."

He played and lost.

But what she didn't understand was that it didn't make any
difference; whatever he did, he could only lose.

It was a perfect time for her to bring up that '36 Carnival.

He didn't have much money left, but it was enough to buy the wagon and take up the lonely life of a pitchman.

Every day he went somewhere new: north one day, south another, east a third day, west a fourth.

It left him lots of time for thinking.

A Ford or Chevrolet, now, would have been a different thing. But if he could afford something like that, he wouldn't have been doing what he was.

Romita didn't hold any grudges against the Whites. He had those reserved for the Yellows.

And when he came back to Rinconcito from all those places, when he pushed his way through that silence, he got to understand something else. Rinconcito wasn't the entire world. It was only a part of the world. And all its valued possessions were no more than a seed scattered and lost in that vastness.

But there was something buried in its people that was greater than the Whites and Yellows. Something in those poor and silent people who were themselves scattered across the land.

That was what they'd set thing right with.

He was waiting for "the day."

He entered Rinconcito at nightfall. Lights were going on all over town. High up in the tower the church's massive clock was shining like an ancient yellow moon. The Town Hall dome, the *Circolo Italiano,* the Nuns' School, the Social Club, the windows of Mercurio's, and, farther back, the monument to the War of Independence, as oversized as ever. . . .

Juana opened the gate.

He unsaddled the horse and slapped it on the butt. Its enormous, beaten shadow glided toward the empty lot in back.

It was a cold night late in autumn; the sky was cloudless and his footsteps clattered on the frozen earth.

He rubbed his hands together, moving toward the house.

The warm light, the voices around the fire: what further greeting did he need?

His mail was waiting on the kitchen table: a letter from the representative of the Society for Economic Development; a bound copy of "The Basic Principles"; a memo from the Second Re-

gional Conference of the Y.S.L.; and a pamphlet from the Latin
American Printing House for Basic Education.

The world remembered him. Now, wasn't that something?

II

This was Pablo's little world:

First and foremost, Pablo himself.

Graduate of the Faculty of Humanities, Class of '46. Left it
feeling that he owned the world.

> *I, Pablo Grieben. . . .*
> *A kosmos. Behold me!*

Then his world got noticeably reduced.

Four years after graduation, he was a brilliant failure. He
wasn't like all the others, of course, just lived like them.

At first his dreams nourished his hopes. Later they nourished
his anger.

By 1950 he was on the verge of taking a job with the Department of Education. In 1951 he not only took it, he married Ana
and had a daughter. From then on, he kept asking himself how
all this had happened to him.

His mannerisms and attitudes were those of 1946. But what
did they come to now that he was domesticated and breaking his
back? Sure, he could still shoot his mouth off, talk big. Who has
to stop talking? But inside he was wracked up over a debt at the
Savings and Loan Association and the installments that were due
on their nine-foot refrigerator.

Marcelo: chronic student and chairman of the F.S.U. Supported the Reform.

Had fought with the cops at a Y.S.L. meeting. That gave him a
special aura. The Y.S.L. could meet every year, but his survival
was assured. When the Reform finally triumphed, he'd have to
scrounge around for something else.

Ciro: director of a workshop group, the Intimate Theater

(I.T.), a charming little playhouse in the basement of an elegant confectioner's.

On one of its walls (dull white) they had a reproduction (glossy black) of Paul Klee's "Mechanics of an Urban Sector." On another wall, an enormous photo of the group's permanent company, which was about as permanent as Ciro's line of thought.

His stand-by was Giraudoux's *Ondine*. Ciro made the name as French as he could, running the words together into a single title: *Ondinedegiraudoux.*

It was a time of press conferences, of intrigues, of "launchings." Linda Parker (b. Julia Rochstein) started on the road to stardom when he "launched" her. She was the Ondine for 1953.

Ciro was marvelous and probably queer. And the Intimate Theater, in turn, was the final retreat, the asylum so to speak, of those disenchanted souls that flocked to it.

Pablo lived there for a while, before he got married. He slept on the stage, in a big Turkish bed from Act Two, Scene Two of *The Confederates*. Before sacking out, he would ring down the curtain, because he felt he was being watched from the orchestra.

They used to meet there sometime after six in the evening. They would discuss things and scheme. . . .

Ciro would say something unbelievable. Then Hernán would say something unbelievable. Then Nita would guess there was "no way of getting away from it." She was always saying or doing something she couldn't get away from. As a rule, Pablo said nothing.

At nine they would go across the street to the Gambrinus, a bar with Munich atmosphere. Half of them would ask for *"pesceto al horno"* while the other half got *"busseca a la lombarda."* And they would go on discussing and scheming. . . .

Hernán: had been a "bright young man" since 1949. In two years from now, maybe three, he would have to be something else.

That same year he'd published a 150-page novel, with half a dozen illustrations, a foreword, a dedication, and extra-wide margins. A pretty solid achievement, all things considered. And in a country like this, where nobody published, where the last thing that could happen to a person was to be found writing something, where being a writer meant wanting to be it somewhere else. . . .

That year too he'd won a first prize from the League of Writers and was runner-up in the city-sponsored contest (he was a Yellow). He had the good fortune to start imitating Faulkner just when Kafka was on the wane.

Nevertheless he had talent; that is to say, he was doomed to a life of despair.

Nita: who owned a sports car and a Russian wolfhound named *Dasein*. Once a month she smashed the car up and, aside from that, did almost nothing.

Her grandfather had once been Secretary of State and her father Ambassador to France.

I.T. was the latest of a long line of crazes. Nita got a real kick out of being a part of their minor desperations. Helping them hanging posters, eating *"busseca a la lombarda,"* reciting Neruda, sitting in the last row of the Opera, invoking Heidegger (or, at the very least, Sartre), even playing poor miserable Flo in *Waiting for Lefty* . . . how deeply moving to give voice to her cry: "Don't you see that I want something else out of life. Sure, I want romance, love, babies. I want everything in life I can get."

Nita was one of Marcelo's conquests. They played the Queen and the Commoner from the next to the last meeting of the Y.S.L. Sooner or later the great renunciation would take place and Nita would return to her own kind of world. The spirit of class. . . .

Someday she would say: "There's no getting away from it."

And in fact there would be no getting away from it.

Fernando: editor of a literary review. Promoter of minuscule talents.

Ana: started as Pablo's mistress. Later his wife. After that, Pablo had a certain respect for her, at least a certain apprehension.

When Pablo met her, she was working for a fashion designer. Later she let him support her.

Generally a rather ingenuous person. Maybe she didn't consider the same things important that Pablo did. That riled him. But there were other times, when he stupidly felt the ground giving way beneath him, that she showed a cool and profound sense of life.

Pablo was convinced that he should never have gotten married. But having gone this far, he was also convinced that he loved her. At least he couldn't get along without her. That riled him too. But in a different way. It turned his anger against himself.

A man is "master of his fate" up to a certain point. Circumstances account for half of what he is. Things turn up to confuse him, in spite of all he does.

In his own case, he was the victim of a lengthy "softening-up" process. Look at all the things he accepted already. Tomorrow there would be even more. Where did Ana figure in all this?

She was a victim of circumstances as much as he was and had the same right to rebel that he did. With the very important difference that if it ever came to it she could go on without him. Certainly their daughter was enough to keep her living in spite of it all.

The I.T. people felt a little uneasy with Ana around. She was there because Pablo was one of them.

Even so, Ana understood them and even excused them a little. In spite of the vast distance between them and her secure grip on the world.

And there were others, of course. An exiled student, a poet of the new imagination, a movie actress, an editor, a liberal, a nonobjective painter, a communist, a man who ran a jazz combo, a p.r. man. . . .

I.T. was an island of the lost, an island in the middle of that sad, interminable city. And the city was an island too, a lost island in that sad, interminable country.

From that world of theirs, running blindly after trifles, they were hardly aware of a city or a country. Still, from time to time, they had a presentiment of some bitter and prolonged loneliness, and then a dark fear swept through them.

III

The old man stood at the door of his cabin and stared into the distance.

The sun in a straight line was setting over the immense plain. The wheat hid the far borders of the field, so that all of it, as far as the eye could see, seemed to be his.

Things had gone well that year. Maybe it was time now to buy the Ferguson tractor.

He had been at it since '32, maybe longer. More than twenty years now. He'd worked like a mule in his time, that one hope spurring him on, but whenever he thought he'd got there, his money wouldn't stretch far enough. Yesterday's money wouldn't stretch into today. Today's wouldn't stretch into tomorrow. And that's how things went, year after year.

This time he thought he had it licked.

IV

The colonel stared at himself in the mirror.

He was getting old.

Getting old and still a colonel!

Bad luck, that was it: worse luck than most. A man should start to get old from brigadier on.

He rubbed his jaw and pulled the flesh tight on his right cheek.

Back in '32, with his boots shining and six feet tall, he had shown great promise. But then his hemorrhoids started acting up, and now he was still a colonel.

He wrinkled his forehead, arching the eyebrows.

Or take that imbecile Palomeque, who couldn't even get on a horse right: he had not only made major general, but was in line for Secretary of War. What had he done worth remembering, except to fall from his horse during an Independence Day parade? And now he was way ahead of him! Giving him orders as if he were his father!

He pressed his teeth together and examined some stains on the incisors that reminded him of an old bitch his mother used to own.

What had his brilliant service record come to? His performance in the General Maneuvers of 1938; his report on Communist infiltration of the Explosives Section; the improvements in the cooling system of the X-23 machine gun; the reorganization of the Department of Statistics and, a year later, of the Army Tailor's Office; his tactical strategy in '41 when he'd led his "red" group in a decisive thrust against the "blues," who were better positioned. . . .

Medals! Nothing to show for it but medals! Medals for valor, for merit, for initiative. Nonsensical medals that his bloody wife was saving in an old cigar box. Well, wasn't there a medal for failure? They ought to make one and pin it on him.

He hadn't gotten as much as a military attaché's post in a foreign embassy somewhere.

He tried to bend over and got stuck halfway in what looked like the first movement of a *contretemps*.

How then could you explain his failure? There should at least be a reason for it.

Possibly that he lacked a sense of timing.

He got into the '35 revolution too late. In '37 too early. The '35 one succeeded, the '37 one failed. The one in '42 caught him by surprise—he was on leave then—and in '46 he was at the mountain hideaway with Rosita.

Call it Fate. What can you do against fate? If he'd broken with Rosita three days sooner, he'd be a brigadier by now. Maybe a major general.

Look how far that lucky Palomeque had gotten. Not only was he bucking for Secretary of War but he also controlled the major shares in the Amerinda Trading Company: import, export, rights, of succession.

The asshole! You ought to hear him talking about duty, self-denial, sacrifice.

He snapped to attention in front of the mirror.

Straighten those shoulders, pull in that gut!

Maybe he should just retire. A retired colonel is like a character out of a novel. All right then: he was going to think it over until the next promotion list.

The phone rang.

Damn! It was Rosita! . . . Another revolution?

V

The officer left his platoon and walked across the deserted street.

They saw him coming toward the gate, his movements slow and steady. He stopped in front of it and checked his watch.

He had a hard, pale face, an emptiness behind the eyes. The heavy trench coat made him look broader than he really was.

"You've got twenty minutes to clear out." He spoke in a calm voice.

There was no trace of violence in it, only a kind of peaceful resignation.

Salamanca—the one the men called Blackie—shrugged his shoulders from behind the grating. The officer stared at him a moment before he turned to go. The two men stared at each other in silence, divided by a wall of death.

The officer made a smart turn and crossed the deserted street again. With the same slow, steady movements.

The twenty minutes passed without a single sound.

On one side stood the soldiers, gloomy and immaculate, flanking a 35-ton Sherman tank.

On the other, spread out behind the wall, that black gate in the middle, stood the workers.

The sky was cloudless and very far away.

Twenty minutes passed.

The officer looked behind him and said something. The 35-ton Sherman gave a lurch, then they heard the dark treads crunch against the pavement.

The tank had reached the middle of the street, when something whistled above their heads; something rebounded on the
tiles of the patio, something like a piece of iron pipe.

Salamanca managed to get a look at it; it seemed so harmless
lying there.

Then it burst in two, and a thick cloud of smoke poured out
of it.

The smoke smelled sour, sickening; those who were nearest
felt their skin start to burn. They couldn't see any longer. How
could they, they couldn't even open their eyes. They howled and
covered their faces, bending their heads to the ground like animals.

The tank kept coming.

The first row of soldiers started moving up behind it. They
were clutching short, black submachine guns.

The tank wasn't a person, but the men were men like themselves.

Those who were peering over the wall started shouting and
raising their fists at the soldiers. Some waved a flag. Others held
up a large sign. Salamanca remained where he was, motionless
behind the gate, his hands tightening around the bars.

More grenades landed, thrown by the advancing soldiers.
Then someone up there, some group or another, decided to fire
back.

A soldier was shot.

Now things started happening.

The soldiers calmly raised their guns and fired two volleys
against the top of the wall.

Some bullets ripped into the plastering. Then there were more
shouts and a few of the heads disappeared.

Salamanca kept clutching the bars.

He looked peaceful.

The tank put on quite a show. It moved right up to the gate,
where it stopped for a moment, as though it were still undecided.

If he stretched his arm through the bars, he would just manage
to touch it. It was a dark, warm mass that smelled strongly of oil.

It seemed to be weighing its moves.

Finally it decided and, with a slow, heavy movement, threw itself against the gate.

The battle lasted ten minutes. Plus the twenty minutes waiting made thirty.

The officer glanced up from his watch and studied the sky. It hadn't changed.

The Sherman was in the center of the patio, while some soldiers mopped up the rest of the factory. A group of workers, with their hands in their pockets and a rolled-up flag, stood quietly against a wall. Two soldiers walked past them, looking bored. A shot rang out and then another gas grenade exploded.

The stretcher bearers removed a body that had been lying in the middle of the patio.

A tiny cloud of smoke drifted slowly out from a second-story window.

It was cold.

The officer stamped his feet against the ground and straightened his trench coat with a shrug of his shoulders.

The cold snap would last as long as the clear weather.

The Sherman had torn the gate off its hinges. Half of Salamanca's body stuck out underneath it.

The officer approached it slowly. He kept his hands behind his back and nudged it with the tip of his boot.

Salamanca seemed to be sleeping. But, in fact, he was dead.

Two times they circled the block. Three would have been too much. The second time past the gates it looked like one of the men had turned around and watched them.

They parked the car a little down the road and waited in silence.

It rained from time to time.

They had stopped the car in back of a flower stand, which partly hid it.

Vega passed the pack around. They smoked in silence.

There were three men in the gateway. Even if they weren't in uniform, something about them told you they were cops.

Carlitos Salamanca sat beside the driver. He was wearing his only suit and a black tie. Every so often he wiped the windshield, which kept misting over.

Finally the hearse came, and another auto.

They took the coffin out.

The old woman and Clara were both there. He didn't recognize the men with the coffin. They must have been cops.

He got out of the car and removed his hat.

So, those strangers were going to bury his brother. They seemed to be showing the proper respect and maybe they were even sincere about it, now that he was dead. But they wouldn't have thought twice about arresting him, if he tried to go up there.

The three guards removed their hats when the coffin went past them at the gate.

For a long while he stood near the idling car, his hat in his hand.

Vega tapped him on the arm and he climbed back in.

One of the guards was crossing the road.

They drove off.

VI

"Tomorrow I'll be going into town," the old man said.

Pedro looked at him in silence.

"Requena was over yesterday . . . said they were giving credit."

"What kind?"

"Agrarian loan, they call it."

"Never heard of that one."

"You pay down on delivery and the rest in installments . . . the machine's the bank's till you can cover what you owe."

"How much down?"

"Thirty, I believe."

For a while, then, they didn't speak.

"I was just calculating," the old man said at last. "I reckon this time she's going to be ours."

VII

Things went off as follows.

Tuesday: the phone rings. The colonel thinks: Rosita! And he automatically brushes off his jacket.

But it wasn't Rosita.

Instead he heard the slightly petulant voice of General K. He snapped stiffly to attention, which was likewise automatic.

By the time he hung up the receiver, his prospects for the next twenty-four hours had altered radically.

Wednesday: the first group of men passed through the north gate of the Campo de Marte at four in the morning.

The colonel followed behind in an open jeep. He was in full battle dress, a pair of field glasses slung around his neck.

As they went out the gate of the Campo and veered toward El Dorado, he devoted a nostalgic, passing thought to Rosita.

Thursday: R.P., the Government Party leader, accused the Army of breaking its pledge to the people. "What else," he declared angrily, "are we to make of these inopportune maneuvers, which are taking place precisely when the government is enduring the most savage onslaughts from its enemies?"

Friday (A.M.): this time circumstances favored the "Blues."

The colonel gritted his teeth and adjusted his field glasses.

No doubt about it: the position was indefensible. . . .

His beard itched and he wondered what he would do if this were real.

"Die covered with glory, what else?"

The idea made him feel a little better. If only Rosita could have seen him. Dirty, hungry, and exhausted: he felt a strange new sense of dignity.

Friday (P.M.): one hope remained. Command Post "Vermil-

ion," with which he'd lost contact a couple of hours earlier, was
showing signs of life.

He saw them reappear over a hill to the northwest, as if risen
from the earth in the dying light of evening. . . .

(An hour later): been trying to reach "Vermilion" for an
hour: can't get through. . . .

(Another hour): the phone rings. At last!

"Hello . . . hello . . . this is 'Golden Grove.' " . . .

Damn it! It wasn't "Vermilion" at all. It was his wife.

He heard her loud and clear, her nasal voice cutting through
his fatigue and uncertainty and caution, asking if they could count
on him that weekend for their game of bridge.

"By tomorrow," he answered, "I will be technically dead."
And he said it with a bitter irony.

Then he hung up.

Friday (late at night): a war correspondent succeeds in infil-
trating through the enemy's lines.

The colonel receives him with great emotion. This man has
theoretically risked his life that public opinion be kept informed.

And with the enemy artillery sounding in their ears, the colonel
embraces the war correspondent and reaffirms his undying devotion to the cause of a free press.

The correspondent mumbles some clumsy words of thanks and,
reaching into his mud-encrusted jacket, removes from it a mud-
encrusted copy of *The Progressive*.

And the colonel reads, by the light of bursting shells, the statement by Congressman R.P.

For a moment he is lost in thought.

"Well," he thinks, "I should have guessed as much when Rosita
showed up again."

Then he howls:

"This one's all mine!"

And he rushes for the phone.

Saturday (2 A.M.): impossible to get through to General K.
The attack's been halted for the time being, pending new instructions.

What are they pulling off in the capital?

(5 A.M.): the first group of men starts marching.

The correspondent asks where they're going.

"To the defense of the Constitution!" cries the colonel. And his jeep takes off with a roar, into the ambiguous brightness of dawn.

The colonel never got to El Dorado.

It wasn't in the books.

He never even made it halfway.

Command Post "Bison" ("Blue") had fouled things up.

That damn fool Lieutenant J., who thought he was a real take-charge man, saw "Golden Grove" moving up toward the highway and thought: "Aha! the asshole's simulating a retreat."

And he gave orders to cut them off.

Command Posts "Bison" and "Red Devil" then executed a classic pincers movement, while a strongly reinforced "Margareta" (all of them "Blues") smashed straight through the center.

At first the colonel didn't know what the hell was going on.

When he finally re-established phone contact, he heard, at one and the same time, that the Revolution had triumphed throughout Amerinda and that "Vermilion," having recovered from its initial shock, was ready to attack.

The colonel, who by then was in a blue funk, hit on one of his master strokes.

While "Golden Grove" fell back rapidly, "Vermilion" took "Margareta" from the rear. "Bison" and "Red Devil" then smashed into each other. By the time they realized their error, "Golden Grove" turned in its tracks and crushed them.

Stupendous!

A week later, the colonel—still a colonel and always a colonel —received the Medal for Strategic Merit.

VIII

The old man got back from town in the early evening.

They ate in silence, the kerosene lamp flickering between them.

When they finished, the old man lit up an Avanti with deliberate slowness and leaned back against the wall.

"That credit's nothing but a fake," he said.

"I figured as much."

They were silent some more.

"The only thing I deduced for sure is that if you want to get something, you got to start off by being rich . . . even if it's only credit."

"That what they told you?"

"Well, maybe it's what they was meaning to tell me."

Silence.

"To begin with, the tractor costs a sight more than what I thought."

"A man always comes out behind."

"That's it all right."

The lamp sputtered and seemed about to go out.

"I'm going to try me another plan," the old man said.

"What kind?"

"Don't know . . . most any kind . . . First we're going to bring in this here crop and then I'm going to try me another plan."

"I reckon that's that."

"That's that all right."

IX

North, south, east, and west: they came from all over.

They brought their old resentments and their stupid hopes.

They kept arriving, more and more each moment, but they

hadn't started out today or even yesterday: they had been on the go since time began.

The majority had dropped along the wayside, without the slightest trace remaining of their pain, their humiliation, and their failure. And the ones who came today were coming for a fresh deception.

They burst on the plaza like an enormous wave, a wave of dark faces, of men without names, a wave that trembled with a secret power.

Now, once again, someone would say to them: You are the people!

                                    x

General K. appeared on the balcony and said:

"You are the people! . . ."

The wave stirred, it grew choppy and burst into a roar that swelled and surrounded and flooded the general.

"We have crushed a government of shame! . . ."

Roar.

"corruption! . . ."

Roar.

"surrender! . . ."

Roar.

"For the hour of the people has arrived! . . ."

Shattering roar.

"We have come to restore order, to restore legality and respect. . . ."

Murmur.

"and social justice. . . ."

Crescendo.

"because we are of the people. . . ."

Roar.

"by the p. . . ."

RRoar.

"and for the p . . . !"

RRRoar: frenzied, insane, and thunderous.

XI

The wave reached Rinconcito. . . .

The multitudes started marching from the Sports Club.

There were unfamiliar faces with them, faces that had been bent to the ground for all those years.

They carried a banner and a bugle and a double-barreled shotgun.

The bugle, the same one that was used for Sunday auctions, sounded the call to step off.

Twice they sang the National Anthem and once "The Heavens and the Earth Declare His Glory," because those were the only songs they knew.

Flowers fell on them from the balconies of the *Circolo Italiano*. But in the Social Club, the blinds were drawn, an act of silent, stifled indignation.

Leading the marchers were Romita and the local druggist and the editor of *The Plain Dealer* and Domingo Parisi of the Socialist Libertarian League. They were the "new men."

They had set up the old parish harmonium on top of Romita's wagon, and Venturi the schoolmaster, who was now an old man, played the *Marseillaise* and part of the overture to *Die Meistersinger* and a section of the First ("Spring") Symphony by Schumann.

When they arrived at the Town Hall, Romita climbed up on the wagon and addressed the people of Rinconcito.

They only caught half of what he said, but his voice was strong and he spoke for them.

At the conclusion of the speech, or what he figured was the conclusion, Lalo Speciale set off a noise bomb of the kind used at the Festival of San Isidro Labrador, Rinconcito's patron saint, and the horse took off like a bolt out of hell, dragging the wagon with it, and Romita, one hand still in the air, and Venturi, pale as a ghost, who was taking a second crack at the *Marseillaise*.

It was an unforgettable day, in every sense of the word.

XII

K. said:

"Our politics are the politics of the soil."

Shouts.

"We are going to drive the money-changers out of the temple."

Crescendo.

"We are going to root out the gangs of traitors who take orders from abroad."

Howl.

"Amerinda for the Amerindians."

H O W L.

XIII

Great news!

F.A.D. (Foundation for Agrarian Development), in line with the latest government policy in agrarian matters, has just put into operation a new plan of tremendous scope designed to improve the annual national yield. Among other things, this plan envisages the establishment of liberal credits for the acquisition of agricultural machinery, including such items as tractors and tractor supplies of domestic manufacture.

Domestic manufacture?

That's right, domestic manufacture. New up-to-date K. tractors, as good as any anywhere, defying comparison with all foreign makes whatsoever, which will no longer be admitted.

That, more or less, was what they heard from the man in the dark glasses, who arrived in a souped-up car and waved a stack of papers in their faces.

"Just fill out this and this and this. K.'s thinking about you, buddy. We're here to help you!"

It almost made you cry. All these years, he'd been struggling by himself and now, suddenly, here was this archangel in dark glasses, slapping his back and shaking his hand and rushing off amid whoops and hollers to some other person whom he didn't know but for whom he also felt a deep concern.

He had been set on a Ferguson, but maybe they weren't so hot after all.

He would have liked to talk it over a little, especially about the motor, because that was what he knew best even though he'd never had a Ferguson, but then he thought of how busy the man was. He wasn't a dumb, isolated farmer, only concerned with his own little problems, but an archangel who had to think of everyone.

The car pulled out with a tremendous roar. And the old man was alone again, with a stack of papers in his hand and not knowing what to expect.

XIV

Labiche ate his spaghetti. He wasn't one of those hungry stiffs, like Salamanca, who couldn't even talk right.

They should have seen him at the delegates' meeting. After that it was clear that what was needed was more men like Labiche. New Men. That was it.

When he jumped to his feet, they all clammed up. What a guy!

"The boys are 100 per cent for the Cause!" he said.

And the boys responded like a single man.

Labiche!

"Because this is the Cause for the People! . . ."

LABICHE!

Sure thing he wouldn't stop till he made the Central Council.

"There's a small, sniveling bunch that don't agree with us . . . but we're gonna fix them! . . ."

Toss them out!

He meant Salamanca's men, of course. They wouldn't have anything to do with Labiche.

"It's time they found out who's in the majority. . . . All they
care about is stirring up one lousy strike a year so you boys can
get your skulls cracked. . . . Well, we're fed up to here with
it! . . . THEY AREN'T WORKERS! . . . they're a bunch of
lousy troublemakers! . . ."

Fact was he had a lot in common with K. Where had he been
all this time?

Well, the "fat cats" had stood in his way. That was it! And
it took K. to come along so that guys like him could move to
the top.

"I'd just like to ask these people what they've done for you up
till now. . . ."

And the truth was that they'd done nothing.

Even Salamanca had to admit it. They'd done nothing. They
weren't able to do anything. They were nothing themselves. So
much so, that now they weren't even workers.

XV

The wave kept growing.

K. the Worker said. . . . K. the Teacher said. . . . K. the
Soldier said. . . . K. the Man of God said. . . . K. the Liberal
said. . . . K. the Statesman. . . . K. the Journalist. . . . K. the
Athlete. . . . K. the Father. . . . K. the Son. . . . K. this. . . .
K. that. . . .

It didn't matter what he said. Anything went. He was the Man.
And a great multitude responded to his voice, an enthusiastic
multitude, an uncontainable multitude, an ecstatic, a delirious
multitude. . . .

The wave grew until it flooded Amerinda.

If K. had said: "I am an asshole, I am the country's number-
one asshole," they would have cheered that too.

XVI

They hadn't done anything to change themselves. But that didn't matter, because things had changed them. They couldn't keep living on the fringes forever.

Ciro was preparing the tenth, possibly the eleventh, version of *Ondinedegiraudoux.*

Hernán was writing his second novel, *Eddie,* in a corner booth at the Gambrinus. He had 350 pages in final shape. The plot was *Oedipus Rex* brought up to date, with the action taking place in a small Central American town outside an oil refinery. Eddie was the leader of a jazz combo touring the interior. . . .

Fernando had led a revolt of young writers against the old guard in the W.D.C. He was now tied up with that.

Marcelo had suffered a real triumph at the final Y.S.L. meeting. Not only had the cops beaten them up, they had forced them to chew their handbills and rub the slogans off the walls with their fingers. Someone even got killed. A student as usual. So that between the funeral, the silent protest march, the demonstrations, and the memorial masses, Marcelo collected a really impressive set of bruises. Especially the scar over his left eyebrow, which looked so good on him.

Nita had given up sports cars after her last one, a Porsche Super-1500, ran over a stray mutt. She turned to hermetic poetry, including a young hermetic poet, who took over from Marcelo.

Pablo: Pablo Grieben, thirty-four years old. Loving husband, model father. . . . What could he look forward to now? Nothing. Better keep playing the game.

So he dreamed. He dreamed in the balcony of a crummy movie house, he dreamed standing in front of a travel agent's window, he dreamed and fingered the compass his old man had left him. . . . Maybe it was true, maybe the world was as big and terrific as it was cracked up to be. But not for him it wasn't. . . . The plan now was to finish his thesis. A scholarly study of

Pierre de la Ramée. "The Influences of Ramée's Thought on the Philosophy of New England." Pretty crazy sounding. . . . But who was this Pierre de la Ramée? What did he care who he was?

The wave hit them finally. Even them.

The P.C.M. (Popular Cultural Movement), itself an offshoot of the Y.P.K. (Young People for K.), had joined with N.A.G. (National Action Group), a subsidiary of the W.D.C., to found a new organization called F.I.T. (Federation of Independent Theaters).

Soon after, I.T. received a formal membership application. Ciro didn't understand a thing about politics; in another age he would have been the favorite of some enlightened monarch. He replied that I.T.'s choice in such matters was N.O. (NO).

On the day of the opening (*Ondinedegiraudoux*), the C.M. (Civil Militia), the shock troops of the Y.P.K., broke into the hall during the second act, beat up the audience, destroyed I.T.'s 146 orchestra seats, and set fire to the props. Meanwhile the "boys" sang the "Youth for K." song in their rich bass voices.

After they left, a platoon from A.N.A.R.S. (Anti-National Activities Repression Squadron) showed up and shoved everyone into a police van, with the exception of a certain Hans von Wittenstein zu Wittenstein, who managed to escape through a skylight in the ladies' room.

A.N.A.R.S. was Lieutenant Colonel J.'s private baby. He explained to them personally, a few hours later, that he was damn well not going to tolerate any more troublemaking.

The next day *Opinion* printed a photo of what they said was I.T.'s permanent company under the headline: DEGENERATES TOUCH OFF THEATER RIOT.

A month later, I.T. was displaced by C.U.T. No. 6 (The Civic Unity Theater).

Pablo received a questionnaire from the National Loyalty Review Board, which included the following:

"10. Details of your co-operation with the present government: (*a*) activities in which you are presently participating; (*b*) activities in which you are not presently participating; (c) propaganda carried out on behalf of the present government; (d) what special tasks of a political character have you performed this year? (e) do you regularly participate in song fests for the patriotic holidays? in politico-cultural events? in meetings? in agrarian magazines? in the sessions and sub-sessions of the K.-ist Party? (f) have you engaged in conversations with persons who are enemies of, opposed to, or indifferent toward, the present government? (g) what steps have you taken to attract such people into the ranks of the Party? . . ."

Pablo gave rather generalized answers: "No, no one, nothing." A week later he was fired, "owing to a reorganization of administrative personnel."

J. decided to stop playing games with the Y.S.L. His approach was pragmatic. He detested the purely spectacular methods of the C.M. Someday, given the opportunity, he would do away with the C.M. itself.

Three days before Independence Day, Marcelo and six other Y.S.L. members were arrested. During the holiday parade, as the C.M. goose-stepped past the Altar to the Fatherland, a grandstand with twenty-three dignitaries of questionable loyalty suddenly blew up.

The next day A.N.A.R.S. announced the arrest of seven terrorists, "all militant members of the Y.S.L." and all directly implicated in the bombing.

Eight days later, and one before the Mass Protest sponsored by the women's branch of the P.K. and the Committee for a Nobel Peace Prize, soldiers at Fort Providence shot down the seven prisoners, who were trying to escape during a change of guards.

In point of fact, the "break" took place on the A.N.A.R.S. firing range, for reasons of convenience.

Hernán found it impossible to go on working. The truth was that he'd lost all interest in *Eddie*. Things were moving too quickly.

He told people that he'd gotten fed up with the business of the Sphinx. He'd started by making Eddie the kind of person who couldn't figure out the time of day, and now the Sphinx was screwing it all up. He had to begin from scratch.

Hernán fixed the main reason for his failure on the sterility of the form. Faulkner had it made because he lived in the Deep South. Hemingway had been all over the world and, just as a starter, could draw freely from two world wars, the civil war in Spain, and countless bull fights. But what could anyone do in a dull, washed-out country like this? Pablo once asked him if he couldn't do something with what was happening around him?

But what was really happening? People behaving like fools. Who could write about *that*? You'd have to be a fool yourself.

Pablo had been on that kick for a while, ever since it hit him where he ate. Being a lousy little insurance salesman made him committed. He even shot his mouth off on street corners. In a word, he was hooked.

"I think it would be plain dishonest to write about something I don't understand or really feel . . . and anyway, I don't see what you can write about your own stupid lousy luck. . . ."

That would really be far out. What Hernán longed for were the big themes. . . .

But circumstances took a hand, in spite of him. . . .

It began with Marcelo's death.

After inflammatory speeches by the Y.S.L., which was trying to make as big a noise as possible (and literally succeeded when the Y.P.K., being neither dull nor lazy, blew up a near-by mausoleum as a show of strength), Hernán delivered a eulogy to the deceased on behalf of all his friends.

Hernán's sense of life was largely literary. All the howling by the Y.S.L. or the F.S.U. or the L.D.Y. (League for Democratic Youth) was so much crap to him. He saw Marcelo's death as a stunning triumph for the Dionysian principle. Socialism, itself the manifestation of a decadent concept of good and evil, had merely been the pretext for a "life of peril." The tragic spirit, the abandonment of reason. . . .

But, in saying this, his voice was muffled, stuck inside his throat, like reading poems to a literary group in someone's house.

The Y.S.L. members were slow in reacting. A few may even have thought he was flattering them. But after a while, they all sensed some kind of insult.

Whatever the case was, Hernán didn't get to finish his oration. The slow, fragmentary reaction by the Y.S.L. came at exactly the same time as the bombing of the mausoleum, and while the rubble was still smoking, A.N.A.R.S. staged a spectacular raid.

The uproar was tremendous.

But above all the shrieks and curses, Hernán's remote and spiritual voice kept droning from the loudspeaker:

"An ultimate, a primordial adherence to life, a youthful recusation of the decadent axinomancy. . . ."

Finally, a single, stupid, brooding face emerged from that rough ocean churning at his feet; and suddenly he felt them beating him and dragging him with such precision, such thoroughness and speed, that for the moment he was helpless to react.

Slowly and without once looking up, Colonel J. read the six-page, double-spaced copy of Hernán's unfinished speech.

"This isn't a speech," he said finally, "it's a monograph." And he leaned back in his chair.

Then he reached for his humidor—a music box that played some measures from *The Student Prince*—and offered Hernán a cigar.

"Let's see now, with what are you affiliated?"

"With life," Hernán answered, for the sake of conversation.

"Yes, of course. But aside from that, are you affiliated with the Y.S.L.? the F.S.U.? the L.D.Y.? the Y.P.K.?"

"None of those three."

"Four. . . ."

"None of those four."

For a moment Colonel J. studied the smoke ring rising from his lips.

"Let's say, then, that the Y.P.K. represents life."

Hernán looked at him steadily.

"I don't see it that way."

"Then think about it."

"I don't have to think about it."

"No, really, think about it. I'm going to give you every chance to think about it."

The "chance to think about it" was part of the "method." The "method" was a special plan for intellectuals.

Hernán was transferred to a clean, roomy cell. He was treated with special consideration. They let him read and write. He had good food, a decent bed.

But suddenly, when he was least likely to expect it, a bunch of wild-looking men would break into his cell and beat him senseless. The experience was brief but intense. They would come in and go out.

The rest of the day, the others would ignore what had happened. The guards would always act surprised. The inspecting officer (not always the same one) would come rushing in, make some excuses, shout a few orders. A mistake of some sort . . . it's really too bad . . . we'll have to investigate . . . accept my apologies. . . .

And suddenly, it would happen again.

He left Fort Providence a month later. Maybe two. He had lost track of time.

"And? Did you think about it?" J. asked him in a pleasant voice.

"No, I didn't really have the time."

"But maybe you'll be able to now?"

"Yes . . . I think I will . . . now. . . ."

There were times when he asked himself: why should I bother about these people, with all their silly problems and coffee-shop ideologies? They look happy getting beaten up. Great, let them get killed if they want to. . . .

They weren't genuine. Hernán's specialty was genuineness. The others didn't have it. The things they talked about were idiotic.

But when it came to a showdown, they died like dogs. They

died for botched ideals, for faces that they didn't know; they died so some idiot could write a dissertation on Pierre de la Ramée or on "The Will to Power," or a third-rate novel if he felt like it. They were ungenuine and they died genuinely, so some asshole would have the pleasure of being 100 per cent genuine.

Who were they? . . . I don't know, I don't remember. . . . Not even the law student? Don't you remember the law student they killed in the park? . . . Which one, which student? . . . And that moth-eaten logic professor, how they shoved a hose up his ass? . . . Don't you remember the refrigerator repairman whose prick they cut off? . . . Don't you remember the electrician who shot himself, because he couldn't take any more and turned in his friends? . . . And that pale little girl from the high school, don't you remember anything about her? . . .

I'm sorry, I don't know. I only remember some winning general or another. They took over Amerinda, right? I don't know those other people. . . .

There were ten of them. There were a hundred. A thousand. A thousand times a thousand. No history's big enough to hold them. . . .

Why don't you tell me about a clean, respectable battle? Don't come at me with a police ledger. Read the *Outline of Amerindian History,* two-volume set, 21st printing. Can you think of something more detailed? . . . Now, where does it say about that?

It doesn't. It can't. It's the toilet of history.

The sewers of the city. . . .

So, when all was said and done, it didn't matter if he believed in all those things or not, or if he even thought about them. Because it wasn't important . . . it wasn't important for you to be absolutely genuine to die for a kind of dignity you didn't know existed until now.

The new printing law took care of Fernando. The C.D.D.I. (Committee for the Defense of Democratic Institutions) had gotten up a list of publications "of foreign origin incompatible with national sentiment." That "national sentiment," if it existed at all, was a pretty spurious business. Even the Amerindian National Anthem, with its lofty operatic style, was strictly import.

Fernando's real crime was his failure to endorse the Annual Literary Prize for the Outstanding Contribution to Arts and Letters. K. had written an artillery manual when he was a major. That year a second printing came out—really a first, since the earlier version consisted of 200 mimeographed copies.

The C.D.D.I. handed its list to A.N.A.R.S.

General J. decided that Fernando would like a massive dose of "the method." He was the type.

On the same day they nabbed Fernando, there was a raid on the Independent Union of Kitchen Workers. Some "infiltrators" were trying to drag the boys out on strike. A.N.A.R.S. had its work cut out for it.

J. decided to apply the "law of flight." It was the heroic way out.

Fernando was removed from his cell the next morning. There were five of them in all. They were taken to the gate and told to move. When they reached the middle of the street, the guards mowed them down with machine-gun fire.

J. heard of the mix-up a month later, when he asked how "that egghead was doing."

Marcelo's death inspired Nita to write her "Song in the Manner of an Epilogue":

> *The absolute earthworms*
> *frequent your pupils*
> *and coin on your face side*
> *bifocal enigmas, etc.*

And many years later, many deaths later, when others would have fattened on the blood of others, her words would appear in an authoritative "Anthology of Resistance Poets."

XVII

Well, what had been happening with F.A.D.?

One day, when he was at the bank, he asked about the credit. The clerk pulled out a batch of papers as thick as a fence post and explained to him very carefully that F.A.D. had been absorbed into I.R.R. (Institute for Rural Reactivation) for the sake of greater efficiency, and that the new I.R.R. plan was point by point better than the older and more limited F.A.D. plan.

The old man was deeply moved by the plan. There were a pile of things in it that he wouldn't have thought of if he'd spent his whole life trying. And even though there wasn't a special section on tractors, the one on farm implements was full of facts and figures.

At least he now had a pretty thorough notion of how to set about getting that tractor. Maybe what he was lacking before was just that, a plan. He'd have to start right here. . . .

XVIII

Delicately did the colonel run his fingers across his abdomen. It was the same as ever, maybe worse.

A few days back, he had felt new hope on reading Gayelord Hauser's *Look Younger, Live Longer*. After Chapter IX, with its horrible statistics, he began to follow the Ritual of Living: 10,000 units of Vitamin A and 1000 units of Vitamin D after breakfast. But nothing happened. He stood there now, stuffed full of yoghurt and brewers' yeast and more desperate than ever. Every time he saw himself in a mirror, it threw him into a rage. What a miserable sight! His massive belly hung in great swollen folds over two white and timid legs that seemed unable to support their wretched burden. Farther up, two flabby teats that looked obscene in profile. And capping everything, a pouting face distended by a double chin.

But, damn it all, what good were proteins against his over-all bad luck? His misery had deeper roots. No primary or secondary proteins could change his fate. How else would you explain the precipitous series of misfortunes that had culminated in the latest, and most likely final, betrayal by Rosita? And when you realized that she'd done it for a lousy naval captain!

Last year's disastrous maneuvers (and hadn't Fate had a gay hand in that one!) won him the undying hatred of that suspicious and hair-triggered general. And then an inoffensive article of his in *The Army Journal,* a discussion of certain problems relating to the placement of artillery with relation to the line of fire, field of fire, and combat zone, was interpreted, fantastic as this may seem, as a maliciously subtle attack on the Institute for Military Cartography, supposedly aimed at getting him promoted.

Still, he clung to one final hope.

And, while clinging to it, he marshaled his emaciated forces (the adjective hardly applied!) and with a spectacular convulsion of his 250 pounds, accompanied by the spasmodic flapping of his arms, executed an apoplectic respiratory exercise of the "superior thoracic" type (listed by the Wronski and Vitone manual under *"voce, mimico e truccatura"*).

That "one final hope" was an extensive and ambitious project for the renovation of war materials which, in accordance with the modernization program announced by Secretary Palomeque, had turned over to him by the Army Quartermaster, "for the purpose of putting in operation all measures necessary for the security and defense of the Nation."

XIX

He had to fight for the Cause. Here was the land, circling Rinconcito like a sea, and on it the men of the land, tough and cut off. He had to go to them, to preach the good news.

Romita traded the old wagon for a six-cylinder Chevrolet pickup, then mounted a loudspeaker on the roof of the cab. Rinconcito's Civic Unity chapter had arranged for the loan at the

Piedrabuena office of the Agrarian Bank. It was the only way he could work it.

Romita traveled through the land, selling and preaching.

A great cloud of dust announced his arrival from far off, and by the time he cut off his motor, a crowd had had time to assemble. Romita leaped from the cab, stack of papers in hand, the sweat pouring down his face, which now seemed sunken from fatigue. Then he delivered his tidings:

"The land's been managed like it was some kind of merchandise . . . but now we're going to replace the commercially based farm system with a new one, a system that holds as sacred a socialized concept of land."

Or, again:

"It's high time that we guaranteed to the farmer the stability of his soil. . . . We're going to give the land to the men that work it, without any strings, and we're going to take it from the men who debauch it, who keep you from fulfilling your purpose. . . ."

They looked at him in silence, sometimes bending forward to hear better or agreeing with a circumspect nod of the head.

But the land stayed the same as ever.

Sometimes he spent whole days away from Rinconcito, sacking out wherever the night caught up with him, dead on his feet from weariness and hunger, but filled to bursting with the Cause, which lighted his way from within.

He had read a lot (almost everything, from Saint-Simon up), had conjectured a lot, had suffered a lot, and now, grown ripe in wisdom, would plant first seeds in that thirsting soil.

> *From my throat issue voices a long time silent,*
> *voices of long generations of slaves and prisoners,*
> *voices of cycles of preparation and growth. . . .*

North, south, east, and west.

There was so much to do. Things weren't happening as fast as he would have wanted, and, aside from the Civic Unity group, you couldn't notice any changes at a first glance. But, with things like this, it was a question of patiently waiting. The farmers knew that better than the others. You plant your seed today, and the land stays the same for a long time, and the sun and the rain beat down on it, and you wait in silence, and then, all of a sudden, the fruit's there, after all that time.

There were men a long ways off who were looking out for their interests. Things were being set in motion there, and Romita and the Civic Unity folks, well, they were like messengers that were preparing the country for what was about to come. That's what the Cause was. First the Revolution; next the planning; after that, the laws; and from one day to the next, the work of men.

Meanwhile, he had to fertilize the soil.

XX

Pablo had told him Fifth Street, across from a grocery, between a newsstand and an empty lot. This had to be it.

He walked into the repair shop and asked for Di Salvo.

Di Salvo came out in a couple of minutes, wiping his hands with a rag. He was a little man in blue overalls smeared all over with oil.

"You Di Salvo?"

"That's right."

"I've come about a two-door Mercury, '57."

"Blue?"

"No. Red. Black top and hood."

The man looked directly at him.

"Come on."

As they walked through the shop, he thought that it was really pretty funny.

Di Salvo opened a door in the back.

They turned around and eyed him with some interest. Hernán knew most of them by description.

Pablo left the others and approached him.

"This is Hernán," he said, and led him gently into the center of the group.

He acknowledged them with several nods of his head.

He had come out of the dim light in the doorway and was standing under an overhead light in the middle of the room. That way they got a better look at him. The room had the same strong smell of motor oil. It must have been Di Salvo's office. The table was littered with cigarette packs and a cylinder that they used for an ashtray. On one wall a Goodyear poster: "3-T Nylon Tires!" A Mobiloil sign underneath it. . . . Everything outside that rim of light seemed to be floating in air.

A young man in a leather jacket had stood up and was offering his hand.

Allende.

He'd heard a lot about him.

"Good to have you, man."

He smiled and nodded back.

Allende had a hard, intense face, which the lamplight made more striking.

He had been a law student, but gave it up in his second year to go partners on a truck. It looked like a good deal at the time. Not that he meant to quit school, but, as almost always happens, he never went back.

Four years he was on the road, eating in crummy diners and sleeping in the cab of the Mack trailer that became like a part of his body.

Then two years ago, they elected him secretary of the Teamsters' Union, but the Labor Federation challenged the election and had the union's books seized. Allende got out alive through an A.N.A.R.S. error. They got his Mack mixed up with a White truck that covered the same route. The White crashed and burned on Route 9, killing the two drivers. That was the Official Version.

Allende was the prototype. The perfect Cause Man. A solitary star who knew his course and took it with precision. If the need arose, he wouldn't have thought twice about killing Hernán with the same hand that he held out to him now.

The others followed suit. A thin, wasted-looking math professor, showing obvious signs of stomach ulcers; a student; a dental mechanic; a publicity agent; another student; a reporter; a build-

ing contractor; a railwayman; a high school girl; another student.
. . . There they were with that ideal of theirs. They had all read
Ingenieros, Rómulo Gallegos, Icaza, Miguel Angel Asturias. . . .
They were swamped by that elevated style, simple and grandil-
oquent by turns.

Di Salvo had opened the door on their shadowy world. Maybe
he should thank Di Salvo. Here was something to write on that
was worth the bother. . . . Here was the dark blood of America.
Candidates for martyrdom in the yellow Saints Book of a police
ledger; twisted heroes destined for a common grave; mutilated
corpses waiting for identification in the County Morgue. . . .

Okay; the main thing, after all, was that he wasn't in it alone.
At times like this, it was so easy to feel alone, to think that you
were the only one who jammed his hands in his pockets and
swallowed his anger. But here were others who had it just as bad.
Who sang dirty versions of the Y.P.K. Song and scribbled on the
walls of public toilets and felt their guts crawl every time they
heard Chief What's-His-Name.

And if he knew now that there were others like himself, what
counted even more was that there were others better than he'd
ever be.

XXI

After two months he went back to the bank and asked them
how the plan was going.

"Which plan?"

"The I.R.R. one."

"The I.R.R. takes in a lot of plans."

"Well, I can't rightly describe it. I thought there was just one."

"How far would we get with just one plan? The over-all Program
comes first."

And after the over-all Program, a series of general plans, and
within each general plan, a number of specific plans.

The old man scratched his head.

"It's a bitch to keep straight."

Now, let's have none of that. You make the trouble for your-self when you don't have a plan to start with.

"What I don't have's a tractor."

"What's that?"

"I was just saying that that's what I mean to have, plan or no plan."

"A tractor. . . ."

"A tractor."

"I think you may be referring to Section 24 of Plan No. 6."

"Maybe so."

"The section on farm implements."

"That'd be it."

"Good, that's extremely important."

"I know that to start with."

"Something we can't pull out of a hat."

"I reckon it's not."

The clerk was leafing through a stack of papers about the thickness of two fence posts and, after consulting Section 24 of Plan No. 6, declared:

"It's under discussion."

The old man scratched his head.

"Another plan?"

"Yes. And this one is thoroughly specific."

XXII

The renovation business got so hopelessly involved that it ended in a front-page scandal. The first public notice grew out of a report prepared by the Subcommittee on Inter-American Affairs of the United States House of Representatives and distributed to all members of the Foreign Affairs Committee. The report recommended a series of revisions in the Military Assistance Program and the gradual suspension of arms shipments to Latin America "in view of the use of materials supplied by the United States to maintain governments in conflict with basic democratic practices."

A week later, the Ways and Means Committee announced that since the inception of the Inter-American Mutual Security Program, the nations of South and Central America had acquired and paid for armaments valued at $37,897,216, excluding those supplied under the terms of the Foreign Aid Program which, in the majority of cases, remained unpaid at the time of the report. The document then listed the total expenditures per country, noting in the case of Amerinda, "a recent project for the renovation of war materials" that indicated an additional outlay seven times greater than that in the memorandum.

To top it all, Senator George Forwood, chairman of the Senate's Committee on Interstate and International Commerce, announced to a reporter from *Visión* that several Latin American countries— Amerinda among them—had been spending forty per cent of their budgets on military projects while the United States, since the end of World War II, had appropriated $250,000,000 in military aid funds for Latin America.

A typical case of bad luck.

K.'s anger, transmitted through the figure of J., passed rapidly and scorchingly down the chain of command, landing like a thunderbolt on the puzzled colonel, who retreated as decorously as he could into a state of retirement.

XXIII

Juana had said:

"A White is a White and, more than that, a Yellow is always a Yellow, no matter what names he goes under."

But he knew that Juana was full of resentment.

Still, old Parisi was starting to say the same thing.

Romita's stock answer was that nothing got done without faith. More often he didn't bother answering. He was sick of trying to show people who didn't want to be shown.

"The Cause starts with us," he would say, but there was no enthusiasm now, only stubbornness. The noise of the motor still throbbed in his ears, and he felt separated from them by the awful silence of the road. "What can we expect from the others, if we lack the faith we call on them to have?"

"You're talking like a preacher," Juana would say.

"Maybe I am one, after my fashion," he would answer.

And he would sit down to a dish of warmed-over dinner, spreading the newspaper out in front of him.

Sometimes he managed to add, in a conciliatory voice or, maybe, as if he were begging:

"You don't have to take it so badly."

And he would slap her on the thigh, as he used to slap his horse, when he had the wagon and had just unhitched her. And, whatever he meant by it, in a minute he was lost in his reading.

But one fine day he began to feel really alone. It wasn't the same loneliness as before, with a house and a fire to look forward to. No; this loneliness was bitter from beginning to end, no matter where he was at. What had become of all those people who marched with him from the Sports Club to the Town Hall? And especially the "new men," the men who were waiting for the big day the same as he was? . . . You could find them hanging around the old clubhouse of the Socialist Libertarian League, sounding off about crazy schemes that they'd read somewhere, quoting all kinds of people from Proudhon and Marx to Kropotkin and Sorel, when all their *élan révolutionnaire"* really came to was a little window dressing and the hangdog dignity of the "intellectual elite" of any provincial town, with no prospect before it but to languish and die.

> *We will knock down the old nag of history*
> *with a*
> *left!*
> *left!*
> *left!*

Once a year they paid homage to Guernica or the Spanish Civil War or the *"Conspiration des Egaux,"* while the rest of the town regarded them as visitors from another planet, a little put out by their puny and incomprehensible indignation.

As for the Unity people, they were a petty little bunch who

spent their time cooking up popular demonstrations to catch the
eye of the higher-ups. Right now, for instance, they were organ-
izing a monster rally for the anniversary of the Revolution. There
was going to be a parade of farm workers, led by 20 K.-tractors
courtesy of the I.R.R., and the laying of a cornerstone for a
small memorial obelisk to be set up at one end of town.

The men of the soil, those silent men who only shook their
heads from time to time, listened to him with their old impene-
trable air, narrowing their eyes at his face, as if to let him know
they saw a stain there, or staring doggedly at the soil, which
looked the same as ever.

And those other men, the leaders of the Cause, the only ones
who maybe, maybe could have understood him, seemed farther
off with every passing day.

XXIV

Pablo decided it was better not to go home.

He decided also that from here on out, it was better to act on
impulse, not to think too much about the thing.

He went back to the café, asked for some change, and dialed
the number.

"Ana? . . ."

"Where're you calling from?"

"In the bar here. . . . How's the baby?"

"I was just putting her to bed."

It was the last time he'd hear her voice. The voice he
loved. . . . His face stared back at him, dead earnest, from the
mirror with the Cinzano sticker.

(Ana, dearest. . . .)

A man with a briefcase walked up behind him and started
thumbing through a small address book.

"Ana. . . ."

(Had he ever once called her dearest . . . only that, dearest? . . . so she couldn't doubt him? . . .)

A noisy crowd of workers came into the place; they pushed some chairs around and ordered cokes in loud voices.

"Ana! . . ."

"Yes . . . what's wrong?"

"I don't know . . . I can't hear too well."

"Where are you?"

"In the bar; didn't I tell you in the bar?"

The man in back of him started looking for a coin.

"I was expecting you," her voice said, far out in the distance like a solitary light.

Someone was expecting him, at that hour, in that city of corpses. He wasn't alone. Because if he was, he wouldn't have died so many deaths in anticipation.

The man found his coin.

Here, at this moment, in a corner of the night somewhere, a light was shining for him, a table was set for him, a voice was saying "hello" to him, a smile that he loved. . . . And he was going to lose it all, whatever he had. That was his country. That tiny apartment with its two ways of life, with its first-class mortgage, its nine-foot refrigerator that they hadn't paid off, with the pictures that they'd bought at auction, his books (those wise books that he loved), the phonograph with the automatic changer, the voices of his friends around the table, Saturday night, the preparations for a trip, the morning paper, the noisy presence of Susana in every corner (now I stand above your crib, I bend to feel your warmth, your fragrance, to kiss your forehead, to compare my large hand with your tiny one), the fights with Ana and the making-up, the pain, the sudden rub of love (oh God, you're something . . . now, come on, right now . . . no, you're crazy . . . there, it's good like that), their quiet, silent presence in a single room, the subtle current flowing between their bodies (and you look at me, your soft eyes stare with wonder as I look at yours) . . . and all his hopes and all his desperation expanding and contracting between four walls. . . . Because beyond that door there was a face, a shadow, a flowing together, just one among so many, dragging their insignificant lives behind them. . . . His life no different, really, than the others. But for him it was tremendous. Ana, do you remember, Ana? Oh Ana, oh my dearest. . . .

They first met at Mingo's Bar. He was all promise then, what else? Full of talk, hours' worth of talk on anything. And she would listen and would say how good he was. Because for her he was always something special. In spite of everything. How could he thank her? He was such a big man in her eyes. . . . He had taken her to a concert by the National Orchestra: Brahms' First Symphony. . . . My God, the way it starts off! You almost stop breathing: have you ever stopped breathing like that? . . . or crossing the plaza outside, fumbling and nervous, when he kissed her for the first time . . . he'd tried it in his mind a thousand times before and now it didn't matter, it was good. . . . He remembered also how she smelled, her hair, her hands, the funny way her eyes looked, soft and moist . . . and then that desperate evening on the coast (can you walk? . . . please don't cry, love) . . . his final year, the last exam: metaphysics, dread . . . coffee, sandwiches, Benzedrine . . . she put up with his poverty, his rotten temper . . . disappointment (forgive me, please forgive me . . . you who can give so much love, who know how to give it, forgive me) . . . their favorite record: "Deep Purple," their favorite actor: Gérard Philippe . . . date of marriage, April 9th: would she know he remembered? . . . in sickness and in health . . . their apartment, stacks of papers . . . also furniture, dishware, the painters (make the bedroom pink, the foyer brown . . . I'm tired . . . something always left to do . . . I'm tired) . . . Susana . . . He would have made them all put down their cokes so he could shout that name at them. Susana! His daughter! The one decent thing in this city of corpses! . . . And what comes next? So many little things left (go on, keep drinking your Coca-Cola) . . . tomorrow's the last little thing, the payoff . . . with someone still expecting me, someone crying over me . . . over me . . . oh this crazy life. . . .

The man with the briefcase was eying him in the mirror.

"Ana, I won't be home tonight." He spoke quickly. "I've got to be in San José tomorrow. It means a sale."

Her voice hesitated a few seconds.

"Well, that's how it goes."

"Sure, Ana."

"Do you want to say hello to the baby?"

His face stared at him from the mirror. It didn't seem to belong to him.

"No, don't bother her. There are people waiting."

Her voice hesitated again.

"Well, take care of yourself."

She always said the same thing.

"Sure, sure. . . ."

He always said the same thing too.

"Chau, Ana!"

And he hung up quickly, without waiting for her voice.

"Well, I didn't say what was on my mind. . . . I never could."

He walked through the bar and into the street.

It was still the same city. And the same night.

They had worked out the plan to the smallest detail, but the chances of pulling it off were remote. They didn't kid themselves about it.

What they were really out for was the effect. The immediate result would be ten or twelve guys riddled with bullets. But they were figuring beyond that. In something like this, the guys shot didn't matter. He liked thinking about the plan. They got started on it in March, six months ago. It worked like a precision instrument. Four guys had gotten theirs ready. But the cost turned out lower than what they'd figured.

Allende's group was just a cog. There were others. Bigger and smaller cogs. Most of them he didn't even know. A Mr. Farkas, for instance, whom he'd met just once and who looked more like an industrialist or a banker or something, acted as their contact with the outside, with the men higher up, whoever, wherever they were. Tomorrow those men would be speculating with their blood, from a distance. *They* wouldn't have to die. That would have been too simple. Garrido, another cog, ran arms over the border. Avila, Catalano, the "Kid" . . . Lalo Marchesi who got knocked off in a bar . . . couldn't be sure where he fit in exactly. There must have been others too whose names he didn't even know. Others who had gotten killed so he could have his turn tomorrow. Now all those cogs were quiet. They had had their turns. The orders came from Allende, but he must have gotten them from somewhere else.

Tomorrow.

For four months they'd been setting it up. Roca's group (which he didn't know directly) had started to move a little before them. Roca must have had an "in" at the Palace. He did a good job; supplied them with floor plans, photos, time schedules, etc. After that they really started moving. Garrido delivered the guns. Allende handed them out and explained how they worked. He wound up with a 9-mm. Pam. It was the first time he'd ever held a gun. Small and black, more like a toy than anything else. But when he gripped it, he could feel it tremble and contract. It was like a living thing.

"You do it like this, like this, like this. . . ."

He loaded and unloaded it over and over again. By now it was part of him, like a foot or a hand. Twice he'd gone to the country, to the home of another cog whom he didn't know either, and had practiced shooting. Stationary target, moving target, shooting on the run.

"You hold it like this, you fire it like this. . . ."

Suddenly the word came: tomorrow.

"Today is tomorrow," he thought.

The people were piling out of the movies after the late show. Midnight. Enormous figures kissing and fighting on billboards. A gigantic John Wayne straddling the void with a Winchester cocked in one hand.

Allende had said to them: "Don't be careless. You don't have the right to. Eat a good meal. Get some sleep. Think about the essentials." Was it really so easy for him? For his own part— whether he had the right to or not didn't matter—he wanted to throw himself down on the ground and start screaming: "Someone have pity on me. Have pity on me for everything I can't say. I'm an open sore from head to foot."

Later, Allende the "indestructible" had told them: "Think it over carefully, boys. You've still got time until tomorrow. If someone isn't sure, don't come. We can't expect all of you to feel sure. Particularly those of us who are only responsible to ourselves. There are other things you can do for the Cause. If you think this is what you ought to do, do it. But only if you think so."

He laughed inside. Maybe he shouldn't after all. "Listen, you people, it isn't that I'm afraid. I'm having trouble understanding. I've just woken up and nothing makes sense . . . anyway, I really am afraid . . . a basic kind of fear . . . a dark water that's churning around in my stomach, that's making my legs weak . . . and something else, two terrible flesh-and-bone arguments . . . but when I think of that I'm not afraid any more . . . then there's only this immense compassion. . . ."

He had stopped in front of a restaurant window and was staring stupidly at the menu.

"Crazy or not, I know damn well that it's too late to pull out. . . . How did I get here in the first place? . . . I'd have to go over my whole life to figure it out. You're on the move already when you think you're only setting out. In '46 everything was possible. All the roads were open where I was. At what point did I start moving? . . . what chances did I let slip by? what action did I forget to take? what word didn't I say? . . . I remember Carlitos Avendano. A nothing. But one day he put on steam and began to pull ahead. . . . When he hears about this tomorrow he's going to say: 'Grieben? Grieben? Sounds familiar . . . oh sure, Pablo! Now, who would ever have thought it?'"

Allende had said between eight and eight-thirty. But the way it turned out, they were all there by eight. Every last one of them.

Now he had to wait.

They all looked so sure of themselves. "I must too," he thought and stared a long time at Hernán's face.

He had never gone much for Hernán. He was a misfit. But now he saw him in a different light. He no longer laughed at his awkwardnesses.

Hernán was talking with Allende. He looked really rugged with the tommy gun under his arm and his voice calm and his face tightened and stubbornly defiant.

The way they had it figured, the attack would take place late in the evening. That would give the survivors more of a chance to escape. Even so, Allende had decided to get them together early in the morning. Any change and they'd have to move fast.

Or call it off: it all depended on what happened. Was there any real hope of that? Forget it: it might be better to have it over with right then.

Every time the phone rang, they stopped speaking.

At noon, Di Salvo brought them something to eat. He felt a horrible emptiness in his stomach, only it wasn't hunger. It was something like the start of an exam. He took a bite and felt like throwing up.

Here was the plan. One ten-man group was going in Allende's truck. Its mission was to seize the north gate. A second group of six would take a van up to the south gate, which was less well guarded. He was with that one. Roca's group, another ten men, would lend support. They decided on that near the end. The idea was to cover the two main groups without joining the attack on the palace. This group had set out already from another part of the city. Finally, four cars would be stationed on the parkway east of the palace. All they had to do was get them out of there, once the job was done.

At least they could hope.

A week before, they'd taken the four cars to the park. It was nice thinking back to that part of it.

The phone rang for the last time. Something told them that this was it.

Di Salvo crossed the room and picked up the receiver.

"Yeah . . . Di Salvo."

As he listened, he motioned to Allende.

Allende took the phone and listened in silence.

The street noises that reached them were muffled by the metal walls and the dimly lit office. A radio chattered in the distance. A woman shouted something to another woman.

Allende hung up the receiver; for an instant he faced them, his hand still holding the phone.

He seemed to be thinking what he would tell them.

Then he put the phone on the table and said simply:

"Let's go."

Allende's group climbed into the truck. Hernán was with them. When all of them were inside, Allende raised the gate and slipped the peg in.

Hernán sat motionless, the tommy gun under his arm, thinking of God knows what. He seemed very far away and lonely.

While Allende was locking the gate, he stuck his head in and stared at Hernán. For a brief moment he smiled. But who could say what he meant by it?

The truck started up and pulled out into the light of the streets.

Pablo waved to Hernán, although he could no longer see him.

The others were climbing into the van. The professor was dressed like a Berber and looked really comic. He was the most relaxed one there. He spoke and smiled and smoked as if this were a meeting of some literary club or, more to the point, some kind of student boat ride. Before getting in, he went up to Di Salvo who was watching them, dark and silent as ever, from the door of his office. He wasn't going with them, having done enough without that.

The professor slapped him on the back and shook his hand. Maybe he thanked him too. It was impossible to hear them.

When they were all in the van, the door swung shut behind them. Swallowed by the darkness, he felt the car move off.

The truck was fifty yards in front, the men inside it hidden by the canvas.

They lost sight of it in midtown, but it reappeared two blocks before the palace.

The professor smoked slowly and without letup; once he asked for the time. Everything was going on schedule.

When they reached the palace, the driver tapped on the window.

The only thing left of Pablo was an enormous emptiness in his stomach. He had lost the rest of his body.

They felt the van stop and one of the men pushed the door open a little.

Their orders were to jump out at the first shot from the truck and attack the gate from the left. The van had drawn up at the opposite curb.

The truck, meanwhile, circled the plaza and stopped at the north gate. Allende jammed on the brakes and began pumping the gas pedal.

Some cars behind them started honking their horns. Allende jumped out of the truck and raised the hood. He had a .45 under his field jacket and two grenades hanging from his belt. He had opened the hood from the side opposite the palace and seemed to be checking the motor.

The noise from the horns was hellish. It was the first signal.

Where there were two guards at the gate to start with, a third one now appeared, an officer. Just as he was starting down the stairway, toward the truck, the men opened fire through the railing.

The officer spread out his arms and tumbled down the stairway like a doll. The other two guards dropped at their posts, without having taken a step.

The men in the van heard the shots and sprang to the ground. But, just at that moment, an enormous bus full of passengers blocked their way.

In the instant Pablo jumped out, the guards opened fire. He saw the professor fall in front of him, in the middle of the street. He rose momentarily on his elbows, then his head struck the pavement. Pablo still hadn't moved. He was near the van, the Pam in his hands, staring at what was happening around him as if trying to wake up.

One of Roca's men started firing at the guards, shouting something to him as he did. But he remained motionless, his legs made of water.

A soldier stepped out on a second-floor balcony, took careful aim, and shot him through the head.

Allende and Hernán got onto the drive through the north gate. The others came up behind.

A man carrying a sheaf of papers cut across their path. He turned toward them with a look of surprise, just as Allende fired at him point blank.

For a second the papers floated in the air like panic-stricken birds. Allende dropped at the foot of the stairs, but got up again.

He fell again on the first landing.

Hernán kept moving ahead.

The noise from below was terrific.

He had to keep moving ahead, open fire on anyone showing his face.

A sudden explosion shook the palace. Allende.

He reached the top of the stairs, quickly pulled the pins out of the grenades, and lobbed them over the railing, one to each side.

He heard them rebound and clatter on the tiles.

They went off at almost the same time.

He sprang into the passageway, the noise behind him, and fired in both directions. Into the smoke and dust that moved slowly toward him.

The office was on the extreme right. He ran toward it, firing the tommy gun.

That was the door. So many times in the past he'd dreamed he was standing there. But, oddly now, the door looked wide open.

He plunged into the lighted room, enormous and triumphant. But it was empty.

For a moment he didn't move.

Then, just as he turned, a burst from a machine gun cut him down.

Some newsboy must have spotted him, or the milkman.

He opened his eyes and saw a few people staring at him with curiosity.

He was seated on the sidewalk, propped up against a wall, partly hidden by the angle of the neighboring house, which jutted out a little. Still, half his legs stuck out into the light.

He tried raising his head, but he couldn't even do that.

He was one of the few who got away from the palace. They had wounded him at the foot of the stairs, but he tried at least to cover Hernán.

When he got back to the street, he didn't think he was so badly hurt. Some of the boys were running to the cars, but a patrol car saw what was happening and cut them off. Two of them dropped in the middle of the street. A third one kept running, but the cops got him in the back as he reached the park.

He gave up on the cars and mingled with the crowd leaving one of the buses that was stuck in the traffic jam.

Those who noticed him at all moved quickly away. A kid followed him for three blocks until he ducked into a bar. He thought of calling Di Salvo, but it wasn't worth the trouble. He was done for.

The bartender gave him a weird look. Allende went into the men's room and sat down for a minute on the toilet. It felt good to be there! But by now the bartender was probably talking to the cops. He went back inside. The man, in fact, was on the phone.

It had started getting dark. The plan was working. That would help some, for all the difference it made. He was still done for.

He kept going for a while, in the direction of the port. Then he couldn't any more and dropped on that deserted street.

As soon as it got light, the people showed up. They came over to get a look at him and watched him with suspicion, from a safe distance.

Allende would fall asleep or blank out from time to time. Every time he opened his eyes, he saw someone eying him with curiosity.

About the middle of the morning, he heard the police sirens. The onlookers moved quickly away. He heard the car door slamming. Then there was a long silence.

A cop appeared.

First his head, steel-helmeted, from around a corner. Then he leaped forward, planting himself in front of Allende.

He crouched in the middle of the street, motionless and tense, examining him with curiosity, as one would an animal.

Finally, he aimed at Allende's chest and killed him.

XXV

The boys went on strike anyway.

They had booted him out but, in the course of time, had come to agree with him. For all the good that would do them now. They were right back where they'd started.

He asked himself who would hire them once this was over.

And yet, when it came to talking strike, Salamanca got to his feet and said what they expected from him.

"Our struggle is the struggle of the entire working class. We do not stand alone. The People stand behind us. With their support, we will triumph! . . ."

But even he didn't believe that now. He had heard the same things said by others: the same gestures too, and the same voice, and maybe the same anger. The literature of rallies and mass meetings. The literature of starvation.

They went on strike.

XXVI

Slowly and laboriously, with the perseverance of a hunter or, better yet, of an angler when he feels a bite; through long-winded, idiotic, expensive conversations at the Naval Club or on the windy terrace of the Amerinda Yacht Club or in the Regidor Grill or, still more often, in the crest-lined dining salon of the Military Club, the colonel (ret.) had thus far succeeded in having his name placed on one of the two lists of candidates for the forthcoming elections to the Board of Governors of the last-mentioned club.

The election campaign was one great round of personal appearances and intricate character readings, millions of smiles, thousands of bows, hundreds of intimate chats, and those abominable M.C. cocktails names after heroes and battles and regiments (he had to put away no less than one "Seventh Artillery Regiment"

daily), all of which nearly destroyed him, with only the vision of
his final triumph keeping him afloat.

The situation was blastedly complicated. You had to be on
the "in" to see just how complicated it really was. The truth was
that the colonel could easily have lived without it. But his wife—
that indomitable war horse, that genuine Valkyrie—had applied
the screws to him and after a lot of clucking and head shaking
in their bathroom and in their Imperial-style double bed, had
finally broken him down.

It would have been easier, and a damn sight less complicated,
to have strangled or poisoned her, but at this point that was only
a pleasant idea to comfort him in the pursuit of his dream.

He had said yes and now he was stuck with it. The first thing
he had to do (with his wife's assistance, as always) was to go over
the lists with great care and thoroughly weigh their chances, before deciding between them.

The "pink" list was headed by Palomeque. Now, Palomeque
had both his pros and cons. And that was where the complications
began. First general pros and cons. Then personal pros and cons.
Among the personal cons was his own long-standing resentment,
to say nothing of the "renovation" project, which had been Palomeque's to begin with, before it ended up completely in his lap.

The "green" list had fewer complications, or, more properly
stated, it all boiled down to a single, frantic one. General Nuevas
headed it. The name itself was an enigma. The only more or
less concrete facts that one could go on were his reputed friendship with J., certain unpleasant favors he'd done for the regime,
and his love affair with a prima ballerina who'd collapsed during
the *pas d'action* of "The Wedding of Aurora." That last gave
him a rather special tone.

If Nuevas was really close to J., he could forget about the
"green" list *a priori*. But, on the other hand, opposing J., although he had no way out, could get him in a lot more trouble
in this instance than opposing K. Palomeque was K.'s pupil, but
K., because of his remote position, wasn't as likely to take things
to heart as J., who was in fact occupied, and preoccupied, with
all these internecine squabbles.

All that aside, Nuevas was an enigma from the start, an enigma full of uncertainty, confusion, and forebodings. . . . Goddamn his wife!

Seeing that he had to decide under any circumstances, and that Nuevas' presumed closeness to J. (and J., somehow, was the point of reference, no matter what he did) killed that possibility from the start, the colonel lined himself up with the "pink" list, which in the long run offered the greatest apparent guarantees.

The decision itself was enough to exhaust all the colonel's reserves. But his wife stood over him.

The process of getting sponsored and inscribed on the list was something so inherently diabolical that it would have driven the cleverest and most resourceful C.I.A. man out of his mind. And when he finally saw his name on the list, he realized that he had only just begun to fight.

Attended by his wife, he established his G.H.Q. in the Princess Room, which was a rather poor copy of the Princess Room in the Hotel Soubise, with a monstrous reproduction of Fragonard's *"L'Escarpolette"* where a mirror should really have gone.

From then on, it was all his wife's: he became a mere spectator, who would agree to everything with a glass of "Seventh Artillery" poised in his hand. Eagerly and joyously, flanked by four or five lower-echelon Valkyries, she intrigued her way through countless appointments, through meetings and concerts and teas and parties and cocktail hours and rummage sales and folk dances, through patriotic and civic and just plain affairs.

Then, unexpectedly and only three days before the election, their prospects brightened in a really spectacular way.

The inscrutable General Nuevas was implicated in what looked like a far-reaching, open-and-shut traffic in auto supplies and had his head on the block.

Whatever the truth of it, he demonstrated his unmistakable lack of competence just two days later (one day before the election), when, in the anachronous style of General Boulanger, he shot himself at his mistress's graveside.

J. (assuming Nuevas had been a disciple of his, and if he

hadn't, the fact that he seemed to have been, involved him any-
how) could do little else but grin and bear it.

So that Palomeque and the "pink" list and, riding their coat-
tails, the neglected, humiliated, and (almost posthumously) vin-
dicated colonel (ret.) had nailed down the victory.

At last!

(A month later, the colonel (ret.), disguised as a priest, sought
asylum in the Venezuelan Embassy. The Eighty-Fifth National
Revolution had triumphed in Amerinda. Or, in terms of personalities, J. had liquidated K.)

XXVII

The strangers from Piedrabuena came back to Rinconcito. Probably they weren't the same ones. But seeing what happened,
they might just as well have been.

They reached town a little before dawn, in a black four-door
Ford with the lights out. Some of the townspeople were wakened
by the motor as the car raced through the deserted streets and
stopped in front of *The Voice*.

They forced open the metal grill, emptied several gasoline cans
on the furniture, the presses and the walls, and set the place on
fire.

Some of the townspeople heard the car doors slam, like four
shots off in the distance, and the roar of the engine tearing
through the night. For a long time they were kept awake by the
brightness of the fire, which could be seen from very far.

The Voice had come out against the Cause. But Romita swore
that this wasn't the Cause's doing.

"It was a bunch of thugs who thought they were doing us a
favor."

He suffered for it too, of course, because with one blow it had
knocked over the structure he had sacrificed so much to build.
But he didn't say any more than that, because he was tired of
talking to the walls and was wrapping himself in a bitter silence.

He had to keep hoping.

But all his hope brought him was the blackest sort of disillusionment.

The Land Reform Law turned out to be a swindle. It gave the tenant the right to purchase up to half the land he was leasing, which sounded pretty good on its face, only the major part of the land was in the hands of phony tenants who had cornered the choicest sites through a special Homesteading Act. In any case, the genuine tenants had to pay for their land at six per cent annual interest on the market value plus ten per cent amortization.

Juana was right. It would always be Whites and Yellows. It would always be one or the other. And the ones who were on the bottom would change their names and again climb over the ones on top.

XXVIII

The officer walked up to the gate with slow and somewhat solemn movements. He kept his gloved hands behind him, paying no attention to the faces that were raised above the wall.

"You've got twenty minutes to clear out," he said, his voice cold and calm, looking first at his wrist watch and then high above them at the row of chimneys like cannons aiming at the sky.

The man didn't answer.

The officer made a smart turn and went back.

Twenty minutes later, the dark line of soldiers came somberly to life.

The faces above the wall started shouting.

But the soldiers kept advancing behind the grotesque armored gun carrier, which was pitching like a boat.

Above his head, Salamanca heard the shouts and, soon after, the explosions; then other, different shouts.

From the gate, he could just make out the officer, standing motionless behind the line of soldiers. He seemed so terribly remote, his hands still clasped behind him.

The gun carrier stopped a few yards from the wall; the turret swung around, its 75-mm. cannon pointing at the gate.

Salamanca took hold of the bars, closed his eyes tight, and tried not to think.

XXIX

Romita traded in the pickup, hitched up his wagon, and headed back into the country, more lonely than ever.

But he wasn't beaten.

He was going to begin again, from scratch, with no one behind him to justify and then betray him. He wasn't going to speak in the name of someone far off. He was going to speak in his own name, to become the voice of the land.

The men were still there. They were the Cause. They weren't going to cast him out, because deep down where it counted he was one of them. No, sir; they would rejoice the more because he had opened their eyes, and because their faith was greater than their pride.

The road was long and hard. Longer and harder than ever. But the little he would do would be done well and would endure for all time; because he was going to begin where he had to begin. On the land itself.

He was returning from the south, rocked to sleep by the jogging of the wagon. The horse changed pace and he awoke.

Rinconcito was in sight.

But a ways back he had passed a black four-door Ford with its motor idling at the side of the road.

It was getting toward evening.

While one of the men stayed at the wheel, the other three came toward him in their slouch hats and dark raincoats and signaled him to stop. It didn't matter, because the horse couldn't go any farther.

When they were closer, he got a look at their faces.

They were coming for him.

One of them took the horse's reins and another motioned him to climb down.

He got to his feet and, standing on top of the cart, looked at Rinconcito. To the right of the tower, between the tower and the silos, was his house.

When he'd climbed down, they told him to head for the car. He did what they told him.

The men followed a little behind him.

The one at the wheel held a door open. He bent over to get in and as he did, they struck him on the head.

He fell over.

When he tried to sit up, they beat him again.

The men said nothing. They simply beat him. And he could barely cry out, with falling and trying to pick himself up. Finally they finished him off with a single blow that had been late in coming because they were looking for the exact spot.

They got into the car and drove off toward Piedrabuena.

Behind them, sprawled out on the road, in the middle of all that land, was Romita.

xxx

North, south, east, and west: they came from all over.

They came with their flags and their placards and their cries.

They were on the go day and night. In tin lizzies, in battered old trucks, in freight trains. By foot.

They camped on the roads and kept coming, driven by hunger and hope and ignorance. With their flags and their placards and their cries multiplied by ten, by a hundred, by a thousand.

XXXI

General J. appeared on the balcony. He looked small and remote.

The flags and the placards came savagely to life.

Then that great voice was heard, like a turbulent outburst of thunder.

The distant figure leaned slightly forward, stared for a moment at the flags and the placards that beat the air like horrible wings, then suddenly stood on his tiptoes, took hold of the microphone, and intoned the old formula of betrayal:

"YOU ARE THE PEOPLE. . . ."

XXXII

The old man said, staring off in the distance with his small, empty eyes:

"Well, son, I believe that after all we're going to have to work it out on our own."

"I reckon so."

"Maybe after this crop. . . ."

"Maybe."

The old man was quiet for a while.

Then he asked, looking at that silent being by his side, as if he saw him for the first time:

"I would sure like to know what you think about all this, providing that you ever think about anything."

"Just that, Pa. That we have to work it out on our own."

—Translated by JEROME ROTHENBERG

JACOB AND THE OTHER
by Juan Carlos Onetti

JUAN CARLOS ONETTI, of Uruguay, has written a number of novels and prize-winning stories. In preparation at present is his book, *El infierno tan temido* (*A Hell So Feared*), to be published by *Editorial Asir* (Uruguay); his earlier novel, *El Astillero* (*The Shipyard*) was published by *Editorial Compañía General Fabril Editora* (Argentina). In 1961 he received the *Premio Nacional de Literatura* (National Prize for Literature). He is the present director of the Montevideo Municipal Library.

I. THE DOCTOR'S STORY

Half the town must have been present last night at the Apollo Cinema, seeing the thing and participating in the tumultuous finale. I was having a boring time at the club's poker table and intervened only when the porter gave me an urgent message from the hospital. The club has only one telephone line; but by the time I left the booth everybody knew more about the news than I. I returned to the table to cash my chips and to pay my losses.

Burmestein hadn't moved. He sucked at his cigar a little more and told me in his smooth and unctuous voice:

"Forgive me, but if I were you, I'd stay and exploit your lucky streak. After all, you can just as well sign the death certificate here!"

"Not yet, it seems," I replied and tried to laugh. I looked at my hands as they handled the chips and the money: they were calm, rather tired. I had slept barely a couple of hours the previous night, but that had already become almost a habit; I had drunk two cognacs tonight and mineral water with my dinner.

The people at the hospital knew my car and remembered all its diseases. And so an ambulance was waiting for me at the club entrance. I sat down next to the Galician[1] driver and heard only his greeting: he remained silent—out of respect or emotion— and waited for me to begin the conversation. I started smoking and did not speak until we turned the Tabarez curve and the ambulance entered the spring night of the cement highway, white and windy, cool and mild, with disorderly clouds grazing the mill and the high trees.

"Herminio," I asked him, "what is the diagnosis?"

I saw the joy the Galician was trying to conceal and imagined the inward sigh with which he celebrated this return to the habitual, to the old sacred rites. He started talking, in his most humble and astute tones. I realized that the case was serious or lost.

"I barely saw him, doctor. I lifted him from the theater into the ambulance and took him to the hospital at ninety or a hundred because young Fernández was telling me to hurry and also because it was my duty. I helped to take him out, and right away they ordered me to fetch you at the club."

"Fernández, hm. But who is on duty?"

"Doctor Rius, doctor."

"Why doesn't Rius operate?" I asked him, raising my voice.

"Well," Herminio replied and took his time avoiding a puddle full of bright water, "he must have got ready to operate at once, I say. But if he has you at his side. . . ."

"You loaded and unloaded him. That's enough. What's the diagnosis?"

"What a doctor!" the Galician exclaimed with an affectionate smile. We were beginning to see the lights of the hospital, the whiteness of its walls under the moon. "He didn't move or moan, he started to swell like a balloon, ribs in the lung, a shinbone laid bare, almost certain concussion. But he hit a couple of chairs with his back when he fell and, if you forgive my opinion, it's the backbone that'll decide. Whether it's broken or not."

"Will he die or won't he? You've never been wrong, Herminio." (He had been wrong many times, but always with some good excuse.)

[1] Galician: native of Galicia, the northwest corner of Spain, from which many people emigrated to Latin America. Tr.

"This time I won't talk," he said, shaking his head as he braked.

I changed clothes and was starting to wash my hands when Rius came in.

"If you want to operate," he said, "I'll have everything ready in two minutes. I've done little or nothing so far because there's nothing to be done. Morphine, of course, to keep him—and us—quiet. And if you want to know where to start, I'd advise you to toss a coin."

"Is there that much?"

"Multiple trauma, deep coma, pallor, filiform, pulse, great polypnoea, cyanosis. The right hemithorax doesn't breathe. Collapsed. Crepitation and angulation of the sixth rib on the right. Dullness in the right pulmonary base with hypersonority in the pulmonary apex. The coma is getting deeper all the time, and the syndrome of acute anemia is becoming accentuated. Is that enough? I would leave him in peace."

It was then that I resorted to my worn-out phrase of mediocre heroicity, to the legend that surrounds me as the lettering of a coin or medal encircles a portrait, and which may possibly stick to my name some years after my death. But that night I was no longer twenty-five or thirty; I was old and tired, and the phrase so often repeated was, to Rius, no more than a familiar joke. I said it with a nostalgia for my lost faith, as I was putting on my gloves. I repeated it and heard myself saying it, like a child that pronounces an absurd magical formula that gives him permission to enter a game or stay in it:

"My patients die on the table."

Rius laughed as usual, gave my arm a friendly squeeze, and left. But almost immediately, as I was trying to locate a damaged pipe that leaked into the washbasins, he looked in again to tell me:

"There's a piece missing in the picture I gave you, my friend. I didn't tell you about the woman. I don't know who she is, she kicked or tried to kick "the corpse-to-be" in the movie theater and then pushed her way to the ambulance to spit at him as the Galician and Fernández were putting him in. I was on duty there and had her thrown out; but she swore she'd come back tomorrow because she had a right to see the dead man—maybe to spit on him at leisure."

I worked with Rius till five in the morning and then sent out for a container of coffee to help us wait. At seven, Fernández came into the office with the suspicious face that God makes him put on to confront important events. On such occasions, his narrow and childish face turns his eyes into slits, leans forward a little, and says through his watchful mouth: "Somebody's robbing me and life is nothing but a conspiracy to cheat me."

He moved toward the table and remained there standing, white and twisted, without a word.

Rius stopped tinkering with the grafts, did not look at him, and grabbed the last sandwich from the plate. Then he wiped his lips with a napkin and asked of the iron inkpot, with its eagle and its two dried-up inkholes:

"Already?"

Fernández breathed audibly and put a hand on the table. We turned our heads and saw his suspicion and his confusion, his thinness and his weariness. Idiotized by lack of food and sleep, the boy drew himself up to remain true to his mania for changing the order of things, of the world in which we can understand one another.

"The woman is in the corridor, sitting on a bench, with a thermos and a maté gourd. They forgot all about her and let her in. She says she doesn't mind waiting, she must see him. That man."

"Yes, my boy," Rius said slowly, and I recognized in his voice the malignity that comes of nights of fatigue, the needling that he administers so skillfully. "Did she bring flowers, at least? Winter is over and every ditch of Santa Maria must be full of *yuyos*. I'd like to push her face in, and I'll ask the chief's permission in a moment for a trip around the corridors. But meanwhile that mare of a woman can visit the body, throw it a flower, spit on it, and throw it another flower."

I was the chief, and so I asked:

"What happened?"

Fernández gave a fleeting caress to his lean face, discovered without too much exertion that it contained all the bones promised him by his reading of Testut, and then looked at me as if I were responsible for all the tricks and deceits that jumped out of nowhere to surprise him with mysterious regularity. He discarded Rius without hatred and without violence, kept his suspicious eyes glued to my face and recited:

"Improved pulse, respiration, and cyanosis. Sporadically recovers consciousness."

This was much better than I had expected to hear at seven in the morning. But I couldn't be quite sure yet, and so I just thanked him with a nod and took my turn looking at the bronzed eagle of the inkstand.

"Dimas arrived a while ago," Fernández said. "I gave him all the details. May I go?"

"Yes, of course." Rius had thrown himself against the back of his armchair and looked at me with the beginning of a smile. Perhaps he had never seen me so old, perhaps he had never loved me as much as he did that spring morning—or maybe he was trying to find out who I was and why he loved me.

"No, my friend," he said when we were alone again. "With me you can play any farce you like—but not the farce of modesty, of indifference, the kind of garbage that's put into sober words like: 'I have once again only done my duty.' Well, chief, you did it. If that animal hasn't croaked yet, it won't. They advised you at the club to do nothing but sign his death certificate—that's what I would have done, with a lot of morphine, of course, if you hadn't happened to be in Santa Maria—and now I advise you to give that character a certificate of immortality. With a quiet conscience and with a signature endorsed by Doctor Rius. Do it, chief. And then steal yourself a sleeping-pill cocktail from the lab and go to sleep for twenty-four hours. I'll take care of the judge and the police. I also promise you to take care of the spitting sessions of the lady who's stoking up on maté in the corridor."

He got up and shook my hand, only once but pausing to transmit the weight and the warmth of his own.

"Okay," I told him. "You'll decide if it's necessary to wake me."

While removing my surgical gown, with a slowness and dignity not entirely produced by weariness, I admitted to myself that the success of the operation, of all operations for that matter, mattered to me as much as the fulfillment of an old and unrealizable dream of mine: to repair my old car with my own hands—and forever. But I couldn't tell this to Rius because he would understand without effort and with enthusiasm; nor could I tell it to Fernández because, fortunately, he could never believe me.

So I kept my mouth shut and, on the way back in the ambulance, heard out with equanimity the clumsily put praises of the Galician Herminio. With my silence, I accepted before history that the resurrection that had just occurred at the Santa Maria Hospital could not have been achieved by the doctors of the capital itself.

I decided that my car could spend another night outside the club and made the ambulance take me home. The morning, furiously white, smelled of honeysuckle, and there was already a breath of the river in the air.

"They threw stones and said they'd burn the theater down," the Galician said when we reached the plaza. "But the police came and they only threw stones, as I've already told you."

Before taking my pills I realized that I could never know the whole truth of that story. With patience and luck on my side I might find out half of it, the half that concerned the people of the town. But I had to resign myself to the fact that the other half would remain forever out of my reach. It was brought here by the two strangers who would, in their different ways, carry it out again, forever unknown.

At that very moment, with the glass of water in my hand, I recalled that I had first got involved in this story a week earlier, on a warm and cloudy Sunday, while I was watching people coming and going on the plaza from a window of the hotel bar.

The lively, charming man and the moribund giant made their way diagonally across the plaza and the first yellowish sunlight of spring. The smaller of the two was carrying a wreath, the little wreath of a distant relative for a modest wake. They advanced indifferent to the curiosity aroused by the slow beast nearly six and a half feet tall: unhurried but resolved, the lively one marched along with an inherent dignity, as if he were flanked by soldiers in gala uniform and some high personage and a stand, decorated with flags and filled with solemn men and old women, were expecting him. The word spread that they had laid the wreath at the foot of the Brausen monument, to the accompaniment of children's jeers and a few stones.

From then on the tracks became somewhat tangled. The smaller man, the ambassador, went into the Berne to rent a room, to take an *apéritif,* and to discuss prices without passion, lifting his hat to anyone in sight and offering deep bows and cheap invitations. He was about forty to forty-five, of medium height, broad-chested; he had been born to convince, to create the mild and humid climate in which friendship flourishes and hopes are born. He had also been born for happiness, or at least for obstinately believing in happiness, against all odds, against life itself and its errors. He had been born, above all and most important of all, to impose quotas of happiness on all possible kinds of people. And all this with a natural and invincible shrewdness, never neglecting his personal purposes or worrying unduly over the uncontrollable future of others.

At noon he called at the editorial offices of *El Liberal.* He returned in the afternoon to see the people from the sports section and get some free publicity. He unwrapped a scrapbook of yellowing photographs and newspaper cuttings, with big headlines in foreign languages, and exhibited diplomas and documents reinforced at the edges with Scotch tape. He made his smile, his unwearying and uncompromising love, float above the ancient memories, the passing years, melancholy, and failure.

"Right now he's better than ever. Maybe he weighs a kilo or two more. This is, of course, why we're on this grand tour of South America. Next year, at the Palais de Glace, he'll regain his title. Nobody can beat him, in Europe or in America. And how could we possibly skip Santa Maria on a tour that is a

prologue to a world championship? Ah, Santa Maria! What a
coast, what a beach, what air, what culture!"

His voice had an Italian tone, but not exactly. There was always, in his vowels and his *s*'s, a sound that could not be localized,
a friendly contact with the complicated surface of the globe. He
traversed the newspaper building from top to bottom, played with
the linotypes, hugged the typesetters, improvised astonishment
while standing under the rotary press. The next day he obtained
his first headline, cool but unpaid: FORMER WORLD WRES-
TLING CHAMPION IN SANTA MARIA. He called at the editorial office every night of the week, and the space devoted to
Jacob van Oppen grew bigger every day, until the Saturday of
the challenge and the fight.

At noon that Sunday when I saw them parading across the
plaza, the moribund giant spent half an hour in church, kneeling
before the new altar of the Immaculate Conception. They say he
went to confession, and some people swear they saw him beating his chest—presumably before he emerged and hesitatingly
pushed his enormous baby face, wet with tears, into the gilded
light outside the church.

II. THE NARRATOR'S STORY

The visiting cards read: "Comendatore Orsini," and the restless and talkative man handed them out, generously, all over
town. A few are still preserved, some decorated with autographs
and adjectives.

From that first—and last—Sunday, Orsini rented the hall of
the Apollo Cinema for training sessions, with a peso admission
charged on Monday and Tuesday, half a peso on Wednesday,
and two pesos on Thursday and Friday, when the challenge was
picked up and the curiosity and the local patriotism of Santa
Maria began to fill the Apollo. It was that Sunday, too, that
the announcement of the challenge was posted on the new plaza,
with proper permission from the municipal authorities. On an old
photograph, the former World Wrestling Champion of All Weights

exhibited his biceps and his gold belt, while aggressive red letters spelled out the challenge: 500 PESOS 500 to whoever enters the ring and is not pinned by Jacob van Oppen in three minutes.

Just a line below the challenge was forgotten; an announcement promised exhibition bouts of Graeço-Roman wrestling between the world champion—he would regain his title within a year—and the best athletes of Santa Maria.

Orsini and the giant had entered South America through Colombia and were now descending it by way of Peru, Ecuador, and Bolivia. The challenge had been picked up in only a few places, and the giant could always dispose of it in a matter of seconds, with the first clinch.

The posters evoked nights of heat and noise, theaters and big tents, audiences composed mostly of Indians and drunks, shouts of admiration, and laughter. The referee lifted his arm, van Oppen went back to his sadness and thought anxiously of the bottle of rotgut waiting in his hotel room, as Orsini was making his smiling progress under the white lights of the ring, drying his forehead with a handkerchief that was even whiter.

"Ladies and gentlemen. . . ."—this was the moment for giving thanks, for talking of unforgettable memories, for shouting *vivas!* to the country and to the city. For months now these memories were forming for the two of them an image of South America: sometime, some night, within a year, when they already would be far away, they would be able to recall it without difficulty, with the aid of only three or four repeated moments of devotion.

On Tuesday or Wednesday Orsini took the champion in his car to the Berne, after an almost deserted training session. The tour had become a routine, and estimates of pesos to be earned differed little from pesos actually earned. But Orsini still felt he had to keep the giant under his wing, for mutual benefit. Van Oppen sat down on the bed and drank from the bottle; Orsini gently took it away from him and fetched from the bathroom the plastic glass he used to give his dentures a morning rinse. And he repeated, in friendship, the old cliché:

"No morality without discipline." He spoke French as he spoke

Spanish; his accent was never definitely Italian. "The bottle is here and nobody wants to steal it from you. But drinking with a glass makes all the difference. There is discipline, there is chivalry."

The giant turned his head to look at him: his blue eyes were turbid and he seemed to see instead with his half-opened mouth. "Dysnoea again, black anguish," thought Orsini. "Best for him to get drunk and sleep it off till tomorrow." He filled the glass with rum, took a swallow, and stretched out his hand to van Oppen. But the beast bent down to take off his shoes and then— second symptom—got up and examined the room. First, with his hands in his belt, he looked at the beds, the useless floor rug, the table, and the ceiling; then he walked around to test with his shoulder the resistance of the doors leading to the corridor and the bathroom, and of the window with the blocked view.

"Now it's starting all over again," Orsini continued. "Last time it was in Guayaquil. It must be a cyclical affair, but I don't understand the cycle. Some night he'll strangle me and not because he hates me—but just because I happen to be at hand. He knows, surely he knows, that I am his only friend."

The barefoot giant slowly returned to the center of the room. His shoulders were bent slightly forward and his face wore a sneering and contemptuous smile. Orsini sat down at the flimsy table and dipped his tongue into the glass of rum.

"*Gott,*" said van Oppen and began to sway as if he were listening to some distant and interrupted music. He wore the black knitted shirt, too tight for him, and the *vaquero* pants Orsini had bought him in Quito. "No. Where am I? What am I doing here?" With his enormous feet gripping the floor, he moved his body and stared at the wall above Orsini's head.

"I'm waiting. Always I find myself in a hotel room in a land of stinking niggers and always waiting. Gimme the glass. I'm not afraid; for that's the worst thing about it—nobody ever comes."

Orsini filled the glass and rose to give it to him. He examined his face, the hysteria in his voice, touched his moving shoulder. "Not yet," he thought. "But almost."

The giant emptied the glass and coughed without bending his head.

"Nobody," he said. "Footwork. Flexions. Holds. Lewis. To Lewis!—at least he was a man and lived like one. Gymnastics is not a man, wrestling is not a man, all this is not a man. A hotel room, a gymnasium, filthy Indians. It's pure hell, Orsini."

Orsini made another calculation and rose again with the rum bottle. He filled the glass van Oppen was clutching to his belly and passed his hand over the giant's shoulder and cheek.

"Nobody," said van Oppen. "Nobody!" he shouted. His eyes turned desperate, then raging. But he emptied the glass with a wise and merry smile.

"Now," thought Orsini. He grabbed the bottle and started pushing against the giant's thigh with his hip, to guide him toward the bath.

"A few more months, a few weeks," thought Orsini. "And then it's over. They'll all come later and we will be with them. We'll go to the other side."

Sprawling on the bed, the giant drank from the bottle and snorted, shaking his head. Orsini lit the table lamp and turned off the ceiling light. He sat down again at the table, adjusted his voice, and sang gently:

> *"Vor der Kaserne*
> *vor dem grossen Tor*
> *steht eine Laterne*
> *Und steht sie noch davor*
> *wenn wir uns einmal wierdersehen,*
> *bei der Laterne wollen wir stehen*
> *wie einst, Lilli Marlene*
> *wie einst, Lilli Marlen."*

He sang the whole song and was halfway through it again when van Oppen put the bottle on the floor and started crying. Then Orsini got up with a sigh and an affectionate insult and walked on tiptoe to the door and the passage. And as on nights of glory he descended the Berne staircase, drying his forehead with a spotless handkerchief.

III

He walked downstairs without meeting anyone on whom he could bestow a smile or a lift of his hat; but his face remained affable, on guard. The woman, who had waited for hours with determination and without impatience, was sunk in the leather armchair of the lobby, paying no attention to the magazines on the low table and smoking one cigarette after another. She got up and confronted him. Prince Orsini had no escape; nor was he looking for one. He heard his name, raised his hat to the lady, and bent down to kiss her hand. He wondered what favor he could grant her and was ready to grant her whatever she requested. She was small, intrepid, and young. Her complexion was quite dark, her small nose hooked, her eyes very bright and cold. "Jewish or something like that," thought Orsini. "She's pretty." Suddenly the prince heard a language so concise as to be almost incomprehensible, unheard of.

"That poster in the plaza, the ads in the paper. Five hundred pesos. My fiancé will fight the champion. But today or tomorrow, that's Wednesday, you'll have to deposit the money at the Bank or *El Liberal*."

"Signorina," the prince said with a smile and swayed with a disconsolate gesture, "fight the champion? You'll lose your fiancé. And I would be so sad to see a pretty young lady like you. . . ."

But she, looking even smaller and more determined, effortlessly defied the gallantry of a man in his fifties.

"Tonight I'll go to *El Liberal* to take up the challenge. I saw the champion at mass. He's old. We need the five hundred pesos to get married. My fiancé is twenty and I'm twenty-two. He owns the Porfilio store. Come and see him."

"But *señorita,*" said the prince with a wider smile. "Your fiancé, a fortunate man if you'll permit me to say so, is twenty. What has he done so far? Buying and selling."

"He has also lived in the country."

"The country," the prince hummed the word with ecstasy. "But the champion has dedicated his whole life to this, to fighting. What if he is a few years older than your fiancé? I fully agree, *señorita*."

"Thirty, at least," she said. She felt no need to smile, relying on the coldness of her eyes. "I saw him."

"But these were the years he devoted to learning how to break, without an effort, arms and ribs, how to remove, gently, a collar-bone from its proper place, how to dislocate a leg. And since you have a fiancé of twenty, and healthy. . . ."

"You issued a challenge. Five hundred pesos for three minutes. I'll go to *El Liberal* tonight, Mr. . . ."

"Prince Orsini," said the prince.

She nodded her head, without wasting any time for sneers. She was small, compact, pretty, and hard as iron.

"I am happy for Santa Maria," the prince smiled and bowed. "It will be a great sporting spectacle. But you, *señorita*, are you going to the newspaper in the name of your fiancé?"

"Yes, he gave me a paper. Go and see him. The Porfilio store. They call him the Turk. But he's a Syrian. He has the document."

The prince understood that it wouldn't be right to kiss her hand again.

"Well," he joked. "First a spinster, then a widow. After Saturday. A very sad destiny, *señorita*."

She offered him her hand and walked toward the hotel door. She was hard as a lance and had barely enough charm to make the prince look at her back. Suddenly she stopped and returned.

"A spinster, no, because with these five hundred pesos we'll get married. A widow neither, because that champion of yours is very old. He's bigger than Mario but could never beat him. I saw him."

"Agreed. You saw him leaving the church after mass. But I assure you that when things really get going he becomes a wild beast and I swear to you that he knows his trade. World Champion of All Weights, *señorita*."

"Well," she repeated with a sudden weariness. "As I told you, the Porfilio Brothers store. Tonight I'll go to *El Liberal;* but you will find me tomorrow, as always, at the store."

"Señorita. . . ." He kissed her hand again.

The woman was clearly looking for a deal. And so Orsini went to the restaurant and ordered a dish of meat and spaghetti. Later he worked on his accounts and, sucking at his gold-ringed cigarette mouthpiece, kept a watch on the sleep, grunts, and movements of Jacob van Oppen.

About to fall asleep above the silence of the plaza, he granted himself a twenty-four hours' vacation. It wasn't advisable to hurry his visit to the Turk. Moreover, as he put it to himself while turning off the light and interpreting the snores of the giant: "I have suffered enough, oh Lord; we have suffered enough. I see no reason for hurry."

The next day Orsini took care of the champion's awakening, brought him aspirins and hot water. He listened with satisfaction to van Oppen's curses under the shower and observed with joy the transformation of his rude noises into an almost submarine version of *Ich hatte einen Kameraden.* Like all other men, he decided to lie, to lie to himself and to trust his luck. He organized van Oppen's morning, the slow walk through the town, his enormous torso covered by the knitted woolen sweater bearing in front a giant blue *C,* the letter which spelled out—in all alphabets and in all languages—the words WORLD WRESTLING CHAMPION OF ALL WEIGHTS. Orsini accompanied him, at a lively step, as far as the streets that descended toward the Promenade. There, for the benefit of the few curious onlookers of eight o'clock in the morning, he repeated a scene from the old farce. He stopped to raise his hat and wipe his forehead, to smile like a good loser, and to give Jacob van Oppen a pat on the back.

"What a man!" he murmured to no one in particular. His head turned away, his arms lowered, his mouth snapping for air, repeated for the benefit of all of Santa Maria: "What a man!"

Van Oppen kept walking toward the Promenade at the same moderate speed, his shoulders hunched toward the future, his jaw hanging. Then he took the street to the cannery and braved the astonishment of fishermen, loafers, and ferry employees: he was too big for anyone to make fun of him.

But the sneers, though never spoken aloud, hovered all around

Orsini that day, around his clothes, his manners, his inadequate education. However, he had made a bet with himself to be happy that day, and so only good and pleasant things could get through to him. He held what he would later call press conferences at the offices of *El Liberal,* at the Berne, and at the Plaza; he drank and chatted with the curious and the idle, told anecdotes and atrocious lies, exhibited once again his yellowing and fragile press cuttings. There had been a time, no doubt about it, when things really were that way: van Oppen, world champion, young, with an irresistible bolt grip, with tours that were not exiles, besieged by offers that could be rejected. The words and pictures in the newspapers, though discolored and outdated, tenaciously refused to become ashes and offered irrefutable proofs. Never quite drunk, Orsini believed after the fifth or sixth glass that the testimonies of the past were a guarantee of the future. He needed no change of personality to dwell comfortably in an impossible paradise. He had been born a man of fifty, cynical, kindly, a friend of life, waiting for things to happen to him. All that was needed for the miracle was a transformation of van Oppen, his return to the years before the war, to his bulgeless stomach, sparkling skin, and needle-cold shower in the mornings.

Yes, the future Mrs. Turk—a charming and obstinate woman, with all due respect—had been at *El Liberal* to pick up the challenge. The head of the Sports Section already had photos of Mario doing his gymnastics, but only by paying for them with a speech on democracy, free press, and freedom of information. On patriotism, too, Sports Section added.

"And the Turk would have knocked our heads off, mine and the photographer's, if his bride hadn't intervened and calmed him with a couple of words. They had been muttering to each other in the rear of the store, and then the Turk came out, not so big, I think, as van Oppen, but much more of a brute, more danger- ous. Well, you know more about these things than I."

"I understand," smiled the prince. "Poor boy. He's not the first." And he let his sadness float over the olives and potato chips of the Berne.

"The man was fighting mad but got himself under control, put

on his short fishing pants, and started doing his gymnastics out
in the open. He did everything that Humberto, our photographer,
asked of him or invented for him, and all this only to get his
revenge and get even for the shock we had given him. And she
was there too, sitting on a barrel like his mother or his teacher,
smoking, not saying a word, but watching him all the time. And
when one thinks that she's less than five feet tall and weighs less
than ninety pounds. . . ."

"I know the lady," Orsini agreed nostalgically. "And I have
seen so many cases. . . . Ah, human personality is a mysterious
thing; it doesn't come from muscles."

"It's not for publication, of course," said Sports Section. "But
will you make the deposit?"

"The deposit?" the prince opened his hands in a pious gesture.
"This afternoon or tomorrow morning. It depends on the bank.
How do you feel about tomorrow morning at your office? It'll be
good publicity and free at that. To hold van Oppen for three
minutes. . . . As I always say"—and here he showed his golden
molars and called the waiter—"sport is one thing and business
another. What can one do, what can we do when a candidate for
suicide suddenly appears at the end of our training tour. And
when—what's worse—he gets help."

IV

Life had always been difficult and beautiful and unique, and
Prince Orsini did not have the five hundred pesos. He understood the woman and there was an adjective at the tip of his
tongue to define her and to enshrine her in his past; but then he
began to think of the man whom the woman represented and
fronted for, the Turk who had accepted the challenge. And so
he said good-by to happiness and the easy life. He checked the
champion's mood and pulse, then told him a lie and, at nightfall,
started walking toward the Porfilio Brothers store with the yellow
scrapbook under his arm.

First the worm-eaten ombu tree, then the lamp that hung from it and produced a circle of intimidated light. Suddenly, barking dogs and contending shouts: "Go away!" "Quiet!" "Down!" Orsini crossed the first light, saw the round and watery moon, reached the store sign, and made a respectful entry. A man wearing rope sandals and ballooned country pants was finishing his gin by the counter. He left and they were alone: he—Prince Orsini—the Turk and the woman.

"Good evening, *señorita*," Orsini smiled and bowed. The woman was sitting on a straw-backed chair, knitting; she withdrew her eyes from the needles to look at him and—perhaps— to smile. "Baby clothes," Orsini thought indignantly. "She's pregnant, she's preparing her baby's layette, that's why she wants to get married, that's why she wants to rob me of five hundred pesos."

He walked straight toward the man who had stopped filling paper bags with maté and was waiting for him stolidly across the counter.

"That's the one I told you about," the woman stated. "The manager."

"Manager and friend," Orsini corrected. "After so many years. . . ."

He shook the man's stiffly opened hand and raised his arm to pat him on the back.

"At your orders," said the storekeeper and lifted his thick black whiskers to show his teeth.

"Pleased to meet you, very pleased to meet you." But he had already breathed the sour and deathly smell of defeat, had calculated the Turk's unspent youth, the perfect manner in which his hundred kilos were distributed over his body. "There isn't one surplus gram of fat here, not one gram of intelligence or sensitivity; there is no hope. Three minutes: poor Jacob van Oppen!"

"I've come about these five hundred pesos," Orsini started, testing the density of the air, the poorness of the light, the hostility of the couple. "It's not against me; it's against life," he thought. "I have come here to set your minds at rest. Tomorrow, as soon as I receive a money order from the capital, I'll make the deposit at *El Liberal*. But I'd also like to talk of other things."

"Haven't we already talked about everything?" the woman asked. She was too small for the shaky straw-backed chair; her shiny knitting needles were too big for her. She could be good or evil; now she had chosen to be implacable, to make up for some long and obscure delay, to take revenge. In the light of the lamp, the shape of her nose was perfect and her bright eyes shone like glass.

"That's quite true, *señorita*. I don't want to say anything I haven't already said before. But I thought it my duty to say it directly. To tell the truth to *señor* Mario." He smiled while repeating his greeting with his head; his truculence barely vibrated, deep and muted. "And that's why, *patrón*, I'd like you to serve drinks for three. It's on me of course; have whatever you like."

"He doesn't drink," said the woman without hurry and without lifting her eyes from her knitting, nestling in her aura of ice and irony.

The hairy beast behind the counter finished sealing a package of maté and turned around slowly to look at the woman. "Gorilla chest; two centimeters of forehead; never had any expression in his eyes," Orsini noted. "Never really thought, suffered, or imagined that tomorrow might bring a surprise or not come at all."

"Adriana," the Turk muttered and remained motionless until she turned her eyes toward him. "Adriana, vermouth I do take."

She gave him a rapid smile and shrugged her shoulders. The Turk pursed his lips to drink the vermouth in small swallows. The prince, his heavy green hat tilted backward, was leaning over the counter, touching the wrapping of his scrapbook. Looking for inspiration and sympathy, he talked of crops, rains, and droughts, of farming methods and means of transport, of Europe's aging beauty and of America's youth. He improvised, distributing prophecies and hopes, while the Turk nodded silent agreement.

"The Apollo was full this afternoon," the prince launched a sudden attack. "As soon as it became known that you've picked

up the challenge, everybody wanted to see the champion training. I don't want him bothered too much so I raised the entrance
price; but the public still insists on paying it. And now," he said
while starting to unwrap the scrapbook, "I'd like you to take a
little look at this." He caressed the leather cover and lifted it.
"It's almost all words, but the photographs help. Look, it's quite
clear: world champion, gold belt."

"Former world champion," the woman corrected out of the
crackling of her straw-backed chair.

"But *señorita*," Orsini said without turning, exclusively for the
Turk's benefit, as he flipped the pages of decaying clippings,
"he'll be champion again before six months are out. A false decision, the International Wrestling Federation has already intervened. . . . Look at the headlines, eight columns, front pages,
look at the photographs. See, that's a world champion: nobody
in this world can beat him. Nobody can hold him for three minutes
and not be pinned. Why! One minute against him would be a
miracle. The champion of Europe couldn't do it; the champion
of the United States couldn't do it either. I'm talking to you
seriously, man to man; I've come to see you because, as soon as
I spoke to the *señorita*, I understood the problem, the situation."

"Adriana," the Turk reminded him.

"That's it," said the prince. "I understood everything. But there
is always a solution. If you climb into the Apollo ring on Saturday . . . Jacob van Oppen is my friend, and his friendship has
only one limit: it disappears when the bell rings and he starts
fighting. Then he is no longer my friend, no longer an ordinary
man: he is the world champion, he has to win and he knows
how."

Dozens of salesmen had stopped their Fords outside the Porfilio
Brothers store, to smile at its late owners or at Mario, to have a
drink, to show samples, catalogues, and lists, to sell sugar,
rice, wine, and maize. But what Orsini was trying to sell to the
Turk between smiles, friendly pats on the back, and compassionate pleas, was a strange and difficult merchandise: fear. Alerted
by the presence of the woman and counseled by his memories

and instincts, he limited himself to selling prudence and tried to make a deal.

The Turk still had half a glass of vermouth left; he lifted it to wet his small pink lips, without drinking.

"It's five hundred pesos," said Adriana from her chair. "And it's time to close."

"You said. . . ." the Turk started. His voice and thought tried to understand, to be calm, to free themselves from three generations of stupidity and greed. "Adriana, I'll have to take down the maté first. You said that if I climb into the ring at the Apollo on Saturday. . . ."

"I said this: if you get into the ring, the champion will break you some ribs or other bones; he'll have you pinned in half a minute. There'll be no five hundred pesos then—though you may well have to spend more than that on doctors. And who'll take care of your business while you're at the hospital? And on top of it all, you'll lose your reputation and the whole town will laugh at you." Orsini felt that the time had come for pause and meditation; he asked for another gin, tried to fathom the Turk's stolid face and anxious movements, and heard a sardonic little laugh from the woman, who had dropped her knitting on her thighs.

Orsini took a sip of gin and started to wrap up the rickety scrapbook. The Turk was smelling the vermouth and trying to think.

"I don't mean to say," the prince murmured in a low distracted voice, whose tone was that of an epilogue accepted by both parties, "I don't mean to say that you may not be stronger than Jacob van Oppen. I know much about these things; I have dedicated my life and my money to the discovery of strong men. Moreover, as *señorita* Adriana so intelligently reminded me, you are much younger than the champion. More youth, more vigor: I'm prepared to put this in writing. If the champion—just to take an example—bought this store, he'd be out begging in the streets in six months. While you, on the other hand, will be a rich man in less than two years. Because you, my friend Mario, know about business and the champion doesn't." The scrapbook was already wrapped, he put it on the counter and leaned on it to get on with his drink and the conversation. "In exactly the same way, the champion knows how to break bones, how to bend your knees and your waist backward so he can pin you on the 'mat.' That's how it's put—or, at least, that's how they used to put it. On the rug. Everybody to his trade."

The woman had risen to put out a lamp in the corner; she was now standing with her knitting between her stomach and the counter, small and hard, not looking at either man.

The Turk examined her face and then grunted:

"You said that if I didn't climb into the ring at the Apollo on Saturday. . . ."

"I said?" Orsini asked with surprise. "I think that I offered you some advice. But, in any case, if you withdraw your acceptance of the challenge, we might agree on something, a compensation. We could talk."

"How much?" asked the Turk.

The woman lifted a hand and dug her nails into the beast's hairy arm; when the man turned his face to look at her, she said:

"Five hundred pesos, no more and no less, right? And we're not going to lose them. If you don't show up on Saturday, all Santa Maria will know that you're a coward. I'll tell them, house by house and person by person."

She spoke without passion. Still sticking her nails into the Turk's arms, she spoke to him with patience and good humor, as a mother speaks to the child she reprimands and threatens.

"One moment," said Orsini. He raised a hand and used the other to lift the glass of gin to his mouth until it was empty. "I have thought of that, too. The comments that people, that the town will make if you don't turn up on Saturday." He smiled at the two hostile faces and his tone became more cautious. "For example . . . let us suppose that you do turn up and climb into the ring. Don't try to provoke the champion: that would be fatal for what we're planning. You climb into the ring, realize with the first clinch that the champion knows his job and let him pin you, cleanly, without a scratch."

The woman was again digging her nails into the giant hairy arm; the Turk removed her with a bark.

"I understand," he said then. "I go in and I lose. How much?"

Suddenly Orsini accepted what he had suspected from the beginning of the meeting: whatever agreement he might reach with the Turk, the stubborn little woman would wipe it out before the night was over. He realized without any room for doubt that Jacob van Oppen was doomed to fight the Turk on Saturday.

"How much?" he murmured while adjusting the scrapbook under his arm. "Let's say a hundred, a hundred and fifty pesos. You climb into the ring. . . ."

The woman moved a step away from the counter and stuck the needles into the ball of wool. She was looking at the earth and cement floor and her voice sounded tranquil and drowsy:

"We need five hundred pesos and he will win them for us on Saturday, with no tricks and no deals. There's nobody stronger, nobody can bend him backward. Least of all that exhausted old man, whatever champion he may have been in his day. Shall we close?"

"I've got to take down the maté," the Turk said again.

"Well, so that's that. Take out what I owe you and give me a last glass." He put a ten-peso note on the counter and lit a cigarette. "We'll celebrate, and you'll be my guests."

But the woman relit the corner lamp and sat down again in the straw-backed chair, picked up her knitting, and smoked a cigarette; and Turk served only one glass of gin. Then he started with a yawn to carry the bags of maté, piled up against the wall, toward the cellar trap door.

Without knowing why, Orsini tossed a visiting card on the counter. He stayed in the store ten minutes more, watching with clouded eyes, perspiring, the Turk's methodical handling of the maté bags. He saw him moving them with the same ease, with as much visible effort as he, Prince Orsini, would use to move a box of cigarettes or a bottle.

"Poor Jacob van Oppen," Orsini meditated. "To grow old is all right for me. But he was born to be always twenty; and it's not he who is twenty now but that giant son of a bitch who is wrapped round the little finger of the fetus in her belly. He's twenty, the animal, nobody can take it away from him to give it back afterward, and he'll be twenty on Saturday night at the Apollo."

V

From the editorial office of *El Liberal,* almost elbow to elbow with the Sports Section, Orsini made a telephone call to the capital to ask for an urgent remittance of a thousand pesos. To escape the operator's curiosity, he used the direct line; he told loud lies for the benefit of the editorial office, now occupied by thin and bewhiskered youths and a girl smoking through a cigarette holder. It was seven in the evening; he almost made some coarse comments in reply to the obvious hesitation of the man who was listening to him from a distant telephone in some room that couldn't be imagined, making grimaces of disagreement in some cubicle of the capital, on an October evening.

He broke off the conversation with a weary and tolerant smile.

"At last," he said, and blew his nose into a linen handkerchief. "Tomorrow morning we'll have the money. Troubles. Tomorrow noon I'll make the deposit in the managing editor's office. The managing editor's office sounds businesslike, right? . . . Ah, there's the boy. If any of you would like some refreshment. . . ."

They thanked him, and one typewriter or another stopped its noise, but no one accepted his invitation. Sports Section, with his thick glasses, was bending over a table marking some photographs.

Leaning against a table and smoking a cigarette, Orsini looked at the men bent over their machines and their jobs. He knew that he no longer existed for them, was no longer in the editorial office. "And I won't exist for them tomorrow either," he thought with a touch of sadness and a smile of resignation. Because everything had been postponed until Friday night and Friday night was just beginning to bud in the fade-out of the sweet and rosy dusk beyond the windows of *El Liberal,* on the river, above the first shadow that wrapped the deep sirens of the barges.

He bridged mistrust and indifference and made Sports Section shake hands with him.

"I hope that tomorrow will be a great night for Santa Maria; I hope that the best man wins."

But this phrase would not be printed in the newspaper to serve as support for his smiling and benevolent face. From the lobby of the Apollo—Jacob van Oppen, World Champion, Trains Here from 6 to 8 P.M. Entrance: 3 pesos—he heard the murmurs of the public and the thumping of van Oppen's feet on the improvised ring. Van Oppen could no longer fight, break bones, or risk having them broken. But he could skip a rope, indefinitely, without tiring.

Seated in the narrow ticket office, Orsini checked the statement of receipts and expenditures and tallied his accounts. Even without the triumphant Saturday night, seats at five pesos, the visit to Santa Maria showed some profit. Orsini offered the other man a coffee, counted the money, and put his signature at the foot of the lists.

He remained alone in the dark and smelly office. The rhythmical tapping of van Oppen's feet on the boards could be heard.

"One hundred and ten animals sitting there openmouthed because the champion skips a rope, the way all schoolgirls skip in the playground—and they probably do it better."

He remembered van Oppen as a young man, or at least not yet grown old; he thought of Europe and the United States, of the true Lost World; tried to convince himself that van Oppen was responsible for the passing of the years, his decline, and his repugnant old age, as if these were vices he had freely acquired and accepted. He tried to hate van Oppen in order to protect himself.

"I should have spoken to him before, maybe yesterday or this morning on those walks of his on the Promenade where he minces along like an old woman. Maybe I should have spoken to him out in the open, facing the river, the trees, the sky, all that these Germans call nature. But Friday has come; it is now Friday night."

He gently felt the bank notes in his pocket and got up. Outside,

Friday night was waiting for him, punctual and mild. The hundred and ten imbeciles were shouting inside the movie house; the champion had started his last number, the gymnastics session in which all his muscles swelled and overflowed.

Orsini walked slowly toward the hotel, his hands clasped behind his back, looking for details of the town to dismiss and to remember, to mingle them with details of other distant towns, to join them all into a whole and to keep on living.

The hotel bar stretched out till it became the receptionist's counter. Over a drink with much soda the prince planned his battle. To occupy a hill may prove more important than to lose an ammunition dump. He put some money on the counter and asked for his hotel bill.

"It's for tomorrow really, excuse me, but I'd rather have it now and avoid the rush. Tomorrow, as soon as the fight is over, we have to leave by car, at midnight or at dawn. I phoned from *El Liberal* today and they mentioned some new contracts. Everybody wants to see the champion, naturally, before the Antwerp tournament."

He paid the bill with an outsize tip and went up to his room with a bottle of gin under his arm to pack the suitcases. One, old and black, belonged to Jacob and could not be touched; there was also, an impressive heap of his belongings on the stage of the Apollo: robes, sweaters, stretcher springs, ropes, fleece-lined boots. But all this could be picked up later on any pretext. He packed his suitcases and those of Jacob's that had not been proclaimed sacred; he was taking a shower, potbellied and determined, when he heard the room door bang. Beyond the noise of the water he heard steps and silence. "It's Friday night," he thought, "and I don't even know whether it's best to get him drunk before or after talking to him. Or maybe before *and* after."

Jacob was sitting on the bed, cross-legged, contemplating with childish joy the trademark on the sole of his shoe: CHAMPION. Somebody, maybe Orsini himself, had once told him as a joke that those shoes were manufactured for the exclusive benefit of van Oppen, to remind people of him and to make thousands upon thousands of strangers pay homage to him with their feet.

Wrapped in his bathrobe, and dripping water, Orsini entered the room, jovial and shrewd. The champion had grabbed the gin bottle and, after taking a drink, continued to contemplate his shoe without listening to Orsini.

"Why did you pack the suitcases? The fight is tomorrow."

"To gain time," said Orsini. "That's why I began to pack them. But afterward. . . ."

"Is it at nine? But it always starts late. And after the three minutes I still have to swing the clubs and lift the weights. And also to celebrate."

"All right," Orsini said, looking at the bottle tilted against the champion's mouth, counting the drinks, calculating.

The champion had put away the bottle and was now massaging the white crepe sole of his shoe. He was smiling a mysterious and incredulous smile, as if he were listening to some distant music that he hadn't heard since childhood. Suddenly he became serious, took in both hands the foot bearing the allusive trademark, and lowered it slowly until the sole was resting on the narrow rug by the bed. Orsini saw the short, dry grimace that had replaced the vanished smile; he hesitatingly moved toward the champion's bed and lifted the bottle. While pretending to drink, he could estimate that there were still two thirds of a liter of gin left.

Motionless, collapsed, with his elbows leaning on his knees, the champion prayed:

"*Verdammt, verdammt, verdammt.*"

Without making a noise, Orsini moved his feet from the ground and with his back to the champion, yawning, took out a gun from his jacket hanging from a chair and put it in a pocket of his bathrobe. Then he sat on his bed and waited. He had never needed the gun, not even to threaten Jacob. But the years had taught him to anticipate the champion's actions and reactions, to estimate his violence, his degree of madness, and also the exact point of the compass at which madness began.

"*Verdammt,*" Jacob kept praying. He filled his lungs with air and rose to his feet. He joined his hands at the nape of his neck

and dipped from the waist, hard, bending his chest first right,
then left toward the midriff.

"Verdammt!" he shouted as if looking at somebody who challenged him, then remade his distrustful smile and began to undress. Orsini lit a cigarette and put a hand into his bathrobe
pocket, his knuckles resting against the coolness of the gun. The
champion took off his sweater, his undershirt, his pants, and the
shoes with his trademark; he threw them all into the corner between the wall and the closet, where they formed a pile on the
floor.

Leaning against the bed and the pillow, Orsini tried to remember other outbursts, other prologues, and match them against
what he saw. "Nobody said we should go. Who told you we must
go tonight?"

Jacob was wearing only his wrestling trunks. He lifted the
bottle and drank half its remaining contents. Then, keeping up
his smile of mystery, allusions, and memories, began to do gymnastic exercises, stretching and bending his arms while bending
his knees to squat.

"All this flesh," Orsini thought with his finger on the trigger of
the gun, "the same muscles, or bigger, as twenty years ago; a
little more fat on the belly, the loins, the midriff. White, timid
enemy of the sun, gringo and womanish. But these arms and
these legs are as strong as ever, maybe stronger. The years didn't
pass him by; but they always come, search, and find a place to
enter and to stay. We were all promised old age and death, sudden or by inches. This poor devil didn't believe these promises;
and to that extent the result is unjust."

Illuminated by Friday's last light and by the lamp Orsini had
lit in the bathroom, the giant was shining with sweat. He finished
his gymnastics session by lying down flat on his back and lifting
himself up on his arms. Then he gave a short and slow salute
with his head to the pile of clothes by the closet. Panting, he took
another drink from the bottle, lifted it into the ash-colored air,
and moved toward Orsini's bed without stopping to look at it.
He remained standing, enormous and sweating, breathing with
much effort and noise, with an openmouthed expression of fury

from end to end. He kept looking at the bottle, looking for explanations from its label, rounded and secret.

"Champion," Orsini said, withdrawing but not touching the wall, raising a leg to get an easier grip on his gun. "Champion, we must order another bottle. We must start celebrating right away."

"Celebrating? But I always win."

"Yes, the champion always wins. And he'll also win in Europe."

Orsini raised himself from the bed and maneuvered his legs until he was seated, his hand still in his bathrobe pocket.

In front of him, Jacob's enormous contracted muscles were expanding. "There have never been better legs than his," Orsini thought with fear and sadness. "All he needs to knock me out is to bring down the bottle; it takes a lot less than a minute to crush a man's head with the bottom of a bottle." He got up slowly and limped away, showing a bland paternal smile all the way to the opposite corner of the room. He leaned against the table and remained for a moment with his eyes ajar, muttering to himself a Catholic and magical formula.

Jacob hadn't moved. He remained standing by the bed, now with his back toward it, the bottle still in the air. The room was almost dusky now, and the bathroom light was weak and yellowish.

Maneuvering with his left hand, Orsini lit a cigarette. "I have never pushed him that far," he thought.

"We can celebrate now, champion. We'll celebrate till dawn and at four we'll take the bus. Good-by, Santa Maria. Good-by and thanks, you didn't treat us too badly."

White, magnified by the shadow, Jacob slowly put down the arm with the bottle and clinked the glass against his knee.

"We're going away, champion," Orsini added. "He's thinking about it now, and let's hope he'll understand it in less than three minutes."

Jacob turned his body around as if he were in a salt-water pool and doubled up to sit on the bed. His hair, scanty but still untouched by gray, showed through the dark the tilt of his head.

"We have contracts, genuine contracts," Orsini continued "if we go south. But it must be at once, it must be by the four-o'clock bus. I made a phone call from the newspaper office this afternoon, champion. I called a manager in the capital."

"Today. Today is Friday," said Jacob slowly and without drunkenness in his voice. "So the fight is tomorrow night. We can't leave at four."

"There is no fight, champion. There are no problems. We go at four; but first we celebrate. I'll order another bottle right away."

"No," said Jacob.

Again Orsini leaned motionless against the table. His pity for the champion, so exacerbated and long-suffering in the last few months, turned into pity for Prince Orsini, condemned to a nurse's life of coddling, lying, and boredom with this creature whom fate assigned him to earn a living. Then his pity became depersonalized, almost universal. "Here, in a South American hole that has a name only because someone wanted to comply with the local custom of baptizing any heap of houses. He, more lost and exhausted than I; I, older, gayer, and more intelligent than he, watching him with a gun that may or may not shoot, determined to threaten him with it but certain that I'll never pull the trigger. Pity human existence, pity whoever arranges things in this clumsy and absurd manner. Pity the people I have had to cheat so that I could keep alive. Pity the Turk of the store and his fiancée, all those who don't really have the privilege of choice."

From far away, disjointed, the sound of the conservatory piano reached them; in spite of the hour, one could feel the heat rising in the room, in the tree-lined streets.

"I don't understand," said Jacob. "Today is Friday. If that lunatic no longer wants to accept the challenge I still have to do my exhibition, seats at five pesos."

"That lunatic. . . ." Orsini started, passing from pity to fury and anger. "No, it's us. We aren't interested in the challenge. We leave at four."

"The man wants to fight? He hasn't backed out?"

"The man wants to fight and he won't be allowed to back out. But we go away."

"Without a fight, before tomorrow?"

"Champion," said Orsini. Jacob's bent head moved in a negative gesture.

"I'm staying. Tomorrow at nine I'll be waiting in the ring. Will I wait alone?"

"Champion," Orsini repeated while approaching the bed; he affectionately touched Jacob's shoulder and lifted the bottle for a small drink. "We leave."

"Not me," said the giant and began to rise, to grow. "I'll be alone in the ring. Give me half the money and go. Tell me why you want to run away and why you want me to run away, too."

Forgetting about the gun without ceasing to grip it, Orsini spoke against the arch formed by the champion's ribs.

"Because there are contracts waiting for us. And that business tomorrow is not a fight; it's only a silly challenge."

Without betraying his uneasiness, Orsini moved away toward the window, toward Jacob's bed. He didn't dare turn on the light; he had no fight in him to win with smiles and gestures.

He preferred the shadow and persuasion by tones of voice. "Maybe it would be best to end it all here and now. I have always been lucky; something has always turned up and it was often better than what I lost. Don't look behind you; just leave him like an elephant without a master."

"But the challenge was ours," Jacob's voice was saying, surprised, almost laughing. "We always issue it. Three minutes. In the newspapers, in the plazas. Money for holding out three minutes. And I always won. Jacob van Oppen always wins."

"Always," Orsini repeated. He suddenly felt weak and weary; he put the gun on the bed and put his hands together between his naked knees. "The champion always wins. But also always, every single time, I first take a look at the man who accepts the challenge. Three minutes without being pinned to the carpet," he recited. "And nobody lasted more than half a minute and I knew it in advance." He thought while saying this: "And, of course, I can't tell him that I sometimes made successful threats to some contenders and that I bribed others to last less than thirty seconds. But maybe I'll have to tell him after all." Aloud he went on: "And now, too, I have done my duty. I went to see the man who picked up the challenge, I weighed him and measured him. With my eyes. That's why I packed the suitcases and that's why I think we should take the four-o'clock bus."

Van Oppen had stretched himself out on the floor, his head leaning against the wall, between the night table and the bathroom light.

"I don't understand it. You mean that he, that small-town storekeeper who never saw a real fight, will beat Jacob van Oppen?"

"Nobody can beat the champion in a fight," said Orsini patiently. "But this is not a fight."

"Ah, it's a challenge!" Jacob exclaimed.

"That's it. A challenge. Five hundred pesos to whoever will remain on his feet for three minutes. I've seen the man." Here Orsini paused and lit another cigarette. He was calm and disinterested: this was like telling a story to a child to make him go to sleep, or like singing "Lilli Marlene."

"And that one will hold me three minutes?" van Oppen sneered.

"Yes, he will. He's a beast. Twenty years, hundred and ten kilos—it's only my estimate, but I'm never wrong."

Jacob doubled up his feet till he was sitting on the floor. Orsini heard him breathe.

"Twenty," said the champion. "I, too, was twenty one day and not as strong as now; I knew less."

"Twenty," repeated the prince, turning his yawn into a sigh.

"And that's all? That's all there is to it? And how many men of twenty have I pinned in less than twenty seconds? And why should that hick last three minutes?"

"It's like this," Orsini thought with the cigarette in his mouth, "it's as simple and terrible as to discover all of a sudden that a woman doesn't rouse us, to remain impotent and to know that explanations won't do any good, won't even provide relief; as simple and terrible as to tell the truth to a sick man. Everything is simple when it happens to others, when we remain alien to it and can understand, sympathize, and repeat advice."

The conservatory piano had disappeared into the heat of the inky night; there was the chirping of crickets, and, much farther away, a jazz record was turning.

"He'll hold me for three minutes?" Jacob insisted. "I saw him too. I saw his picture in the paper. A good body to move barrels."

"No," Orsini replied with sincerity and serenity. "No one can resist the world champion for three minutes."

"I don't understand," said Jacob. "Then I don't understand. Is there anything more to it?"

"Yes." Orsini was speaking smoothly and indifferently as if the matter were unimportant. "When we finish this training tour, it'll be all different. It will also be necessary to give up alcohol. But today, tomorrow, Saturday night in Santa Maria—or whatever the name of this hole—Jacob van Oppen cannot clinch and hold a clinch for more than a minute. Van Oppen's chest cannot; his lungs cannot. And that beast won't be thrown in a minute. That's why we have to take the four-o'clock bus. The suitcases are packed and I've paid the hotel bill. It's all settled."

Orsini heard the grunt and the cough to his left and was measuring the silence in the room. He picked up the gun again and warmed it against his knees.

"After all," he thought, "it is strange that I should make so many evasions, take so many precautions. He knows it better than I and for some time now. But maybe this is why I chose the evasions and looked for precautions. And here I am, at my age, as pitiable and ridiculous as if I had told a woman that we were through and was waiting for her reaction, her tears, and her threats."

Jacob had moved back; but the band of light from the bathroom revealed, on his backward-tilted head, the shine of tears. Orsini, still gripping the gun, walked to the phone to order another bottle. He grazed in passing the champion's closely cropped hair and returned to the bed. Raising his legs, he could feel the heavy roundness of his belly against his thighs. A panting noise reached him from the seated man, as if van Oppen had come to the aftermath of a long training session or the end of a very long and difficult fight.

"It's not his heart," Orsini reminded himself, "nor his lungs. It's everything: a six foot six of a man who has begun to grow old."

"No, no," he said aloud. "Only a rest on the road. In a matter of months, it'll all be like before again. Quality, that is what really matters, what can never be lost. Even if one wants to lose it, or tries to. Because there are periods of suicide in every man's life. But they are overcome, forgotten." The dance music had grown louder as the night advanced. Orsini's voice vibrated with satisfaction and lingered in his throat and palate.

There was a knock on the door and the prince moved silently to receive the tray with the bottle, glasses, and ice. He put it down on the table and chose to sit down on a chair to continue the vigil and the lesson of optimism.

The champion had sat down in the shadow, on the floor, leaning against the wall; his breathing could no longer be heard and he existed for Orsini only by virtue of his undoubted and enormous crouching presence.

"Ah yes, quality," the prince resumed his theme. "Who has it? One is born with it or dies without it. It's not for nothing that everybody finds himself a nickname, stupid and comical, a few funny words to be put on the posters. THE BUFFALO OF ARKANSAS, THE GRINDER OF LIEGE, THE MIURA BULL OF GRANADA. But Jacob van Oppen is simply called 'World Champion.' That's all. That's quality."

Orsini's speech faded into silence and weariness.

The prince filled a glass, tasted it with his tongue, and rose to carry it to the champion.

"Orsini," said Jacob. "My friend Prince Orsini."

Van Oppen's big hands lay heavily on his knees, like the teeth of a trap; the knees supported his bent head. Orsini put the glass on the floor after touching the giant's neck and back with it.

He was adjusting his position with a grimace, weariness attacking his midriff, when he suddenly felt fingers encircling his ankle and nailing him to the floor. He heard Jacob's voice, slow and gay, lazy and serene:

"And now the prince will drink the whole glass at one go."

Orsini threw himself back to keep his balance. "That's all I needed: that the beast should think I want to drug him or poison him." He stooped slowly, picked up the glass, and drank it rapidly, feeling the grip of Jacob's fingers weakening on his ankle.

"All right, champion?" he asked. Now he could see the other's eye, a scrap of his lifted smile.

"All right, prince. Now a full glass for me."

With his legs apart and trying not to stumble, Orsini returned to the table and refilled the glass. He leaned against it to light a cigarette and saw, with the small flame of the lighter, that his fingers were trembling with hate. He came back with the glass, the cigarette in his mouth, a finger on the trigger of the gun concealed in his bathrobe. He crossed the yellow band of light and saw Jacob on his feet, white and enormous, swaying gently.

"Your health, champion," said Orsini, offering the drink with his left hand.

"Your health," Jacob's voice repeated from above, with a trace of excitement. "I knew they would come. I went to the church to pray that they would come."

"Yes," said Orsini.

There was a pause, the champion sighed, the night brought them shouts and applause from the distant dance hall, a tug sounded its siren thrice on the river.

"And now," Jacob pronounced the words with some difficulty, "the prince will take another drink at one go. We're both drunk. But I don't drink tonight because it's Friday. The prince has a gun."

For a second, with the glass in the air and contemplating Jacob's navel, the prince invented for himself a life story of perpetual humiliation, savored the taste of disgust, and knew that the giant wasn't even challenging him but was only offering him a target for the gun in his pocket.

"Yes," he said a second later, spat out the cigarette, and took another drink of gin. His stomach rose to his chest as he threw the empty glass on the bed and laboriously moved back to place the gun on the table.

Van Oppen hadn't moved; he was still swaying in the dusk, with a sneering slowness, as if he were performing the classical gymnastic exercises to strengthen his waist muscles.

"We must both be crazy," said Orsini. His memories, the weak heat of the summer's night pressing against the window, his plans for the future were all of no use to him.

" 'Lilli Marlene,' please," Jacob advised.

Leaning on the table, Orsini put away the cigarette he was about to light. He sang with a muted voice, with one last hope, as if he had never done anything but hum those imbecile lyrics, that easy tune, as if he had never done anything else to earn a living. He felt older than ever, shrunk and potbellied, a stranger to himself.

There was a silence and then the champion said, "Thanks!" Feeling sleepy and weak, fumbling with the cigarette he had left on the table by the gun, Orsini saw the big whitish body approach him, relieved of its age by the dusk.

"Thanks," van Oppen repeated, almost touching him. "Another time."

Stunned and indifferent, Orsini thought to himself: "It's no longer a cradle song, it no longer makes him get drunk, weep, and sleep." He cleared his voice again and started:

"Vor der Kaserne, vor dem grossen Tor. . . ."

Without needing to move his body, the champion lifted an arm from his hip and struck Orsini's jaw with his open hand. An old tradition stopped him from using his fists, except in desperate circumstances. He held up the prince's body with his other arm and stretched him out on the bed.

The heat of the night and of the fiesta had made people open their windows. The jazz for dancing now seemed to originate from the hotel itself, from the center of the darkened room.

VI. THE PRINCE'S STORY

It was a town rising from the river in September, give or take five inches south of the equator. I woke up, with no pain, in the hotel-room morning filled with light and heat. Jacob was massaging my stomach and laughing to speed on its way a stream of insults that culminated in a single one that he repeated until I could no longer pretend to be asleep and drew myself up.

"Old pig," he was saying in his purest German, maybe in Prussian.

The sun was already licking the leg of the table and I thought sadly that nothing could be saved from the wreck. At least—I began to remember—that's what I should think, and my expression and my words should adjust themselves to this sadness. Van Oppen must have foreseen something of this because he made me drink a glass of orange juice and put a lighted cigarette in my mouth.

"Old pig," he said, as he filled his lungs with smoke.

It was Saturday morning and we were still in Santa Maria. I moved my head, looked at him, and made a rapid balance sheet of his smile, his gaiety, and his friendship. He had put on his expensive gray suit and his antelope-skin shoes; a Stetson hat was tilted against the nape of his neck. I suddenly thought that he was right, that life was always right in the end, that defeats and victories didn't matter.

"Yes," I said, withdrawing my hand from his, "I am an old pig. The years pass and things get worse and worse. Is there a fight today?"

"Yes," he nodded enthusiastically. "I told you they would come back and they did."

I sucked at my cigarette and stretched myself out on the bed. It was enough to see the smile to realize that Jacob had won, even if he had his spine broken that hot Saturday night, as anyone could foresee. He had to win in three minutes; but I was getting more money. I sat up in the bed and kneaded my jaw.

"The fight is on," I said, "the champion decides. Unfortunately, the manager no longer has anything to say. But neither a bottle nor a blow can abolish facts."

Van Oppen began to laugh and his hat fell on the bed.

"Neither a bottle nor a blow," I insisted. "The fact still remains that, as of now, the champion hasn't enough wind to support a fight, a real effort, for more than a minute. That's a fact. The champion won't be able to throw the Turk. The champion will die a mysterious death at the fifty-ninth second. The autopsy will tell. I believe we agree, at least, on that."

"Yes, we agree on that. No more than one minute," van Oppen assented, sounding young and gay again. The morning was now filling the entire room, and I felt humiliated by my sleepiness, by my objections, by my bathrobe weighed down by the unloaded gun.

"And the fact is," I said slowly, as if trying to take revenge, "that we haven't got the five hundred pesos. Of course, everybody agrees, the Turk can't win. But we still have to deposit the five hundred and it's already Saturday. All we have left is the bus money and enough for a week in the capital. After that, we're in God's hands."

Jacob picked up his hat and started to laugh again. He was shaking his head like a father sitting on a park bench with his diffident little son.

"Money," he said without asking. "Money for the deposit? Five hundred pesos?"

He passed me another lighted cigarette and put his left foot, the more sensitive one, on the little table. He undid the knot of the gray shoe, took it off, and came over to show me a roll of green bank notes. It was real money. He gave me five ten-dollar bills and could not resist showing off:

"More?"

"No," I said. "It's more than enough."

A lot of money went back to the shoe: between three and five hundred dollars.

And so I changed the money at noon. Since the champion had disappeared—his initialed sweater did not show up that morning

for the trot down the Promenade—I went to the Plaza Restaurant
and ate like a gentleman, something I hadn't done for a long
time. I had a coffee, prepared on my table, the appropriate liqueurs and a cigar, very dry but smokable.

I finished off the luncheon with a tip usually lavished by drunkards or crooks and called the hotel. The champion wasn't there;
the rest of the afternoon was cool and gay; Santa Maria was
going to have a great evening. I left the newspaper's telephone
number with the receptionist so that Jacob could call me about
our going to the Apollo together and a little while later sat down
at the *El Liberal* morgue with Sports Section and two more faces.
I showed them the money.

"So that there should be no doubt. But I'd prefer to hand it out
in the ring—whether van Oppen dies of a syncope or has to
make a contribution to the Turk's wake."

We played poker—I lost and won—until they informed me
that van Oppen was already at the Apollo. It was still more than
half an hour before nine; but we put on our jackets and piled into
some old cars to drive the few town blocks that separated us from
the cinema, giving the occasion an accent of carnival, of the
ridiculous.

I went in through the back door and made my way to the room,
littered with newspapers and photographs and furiously invaded
by smells of urine and rancid paste. There I found Jacob. Wearing
his sky-blue trunks—the color chosen in honor of Santa Maria—
and his world championship belt that glittered like gold, he was
doing setting-up exercises. One look at him, at his childish, clean,
and expressionless eyes, at the short curve of his smile, was enough
to convince me that he didn't want to talk to me, that he wanted
no prologues, nothing that would separate him from what he was
determined to be and to remember.

I sat down on a bench, without bothering to listen whether or
not he answered my greeting, and lit a cigarette. Now, at this
moment, in a few minutes, the story would reach its grand finale.
The story of the world's wrestling champion. But there would be
other stories, too—and an explanation for *El Liberal,* for Santa
Maria, for the neighboring towns.

"A passing physical indisposition": looked better to me than "excessive training blamed for Champion's failure." But they wouldn't print the capital *C* tomorrow, nor the ambiguous headline. Van Oppen was still doing his setting-up exercises, and I lit another cigarette from the first to neutralize the odor of ammonia, no forgetting that clean air is the first condition of a gymnasium.

Jacob was bobbing up and down as if he were alone in the room. He moved his arms horizontally and seemed both thinner and heavier. Through the loathsome smell, to which his sweat added its contribution, I tried to hear him breathe. The noises from the theater also penetrated into the stinking room. Maybe the champion had wind for a minute and a half, but never for two or three. The Turk would remain standing until the bell rang, with his furious black mustache, with the chaste knee-length pants that I expected him to wear (and I wasn't wrong), with his small, hard fiancée howling with triumph and rage near the Apollo stage and its threadbare rug that I insisted on calling "the mat." There was no hope left, we would never rescue the five hundred pesos. The noises of the impatient mob that filled the theater grew louder and louder.

"We must go now," I said to the corpse doing its calisthenics. It was exactly nine by my watch; I left the bad smell behind me and walked through darkened corridors to the ticket office. By quarter past nine I had checked and signed the accounts. I returned to the smelly room—the roar indicated that van Oppen was already in the ring—and took off my jacket, after depositing the money in a pocket of my trousers. Then I made my way back through the corridors, reached the theater, and went up on the stage. They showered me with applause and insults, which I acknowledged with nods and smiles, knowing that at least seventy of those present hadn't paid for their ticket. In any case, I would never get my fifty per cent from them.

I took off Jacob's robe, crossed the ring to salute the Turk, and had time for only two more clown's tricks.

The bell rang and it became impossible not to breathe and understand the odor of the crowd that filled the Apollo. The bell rang and I left Jacob alone, much more alone and forever than I had left him at so many other daybreaks, on street corners, and in bars, when I began to feel sleepy or bored. The bad thing was that when I left him to occupy my special seat that night I felt neither sleepy nor bored. The first bell was to clear the ring; the second to start the fight. Greased, almost young, without showing his weary weight, Jacob circled, crouching, until he reached the center of the ring and waited with an expectant smile.

Jacob opened his arms and waited for the Turk, who seemed to have grown bigger in the meantime. He waited with a smile until he came close, then made a step back and advanced again for the clinch. Against all rules, he kept his arms up for ten seconds. Then he steadied his legs and turned; he put one hand on the challenger's back and the other, and his forearm as well, against a thigh. I didn't understand this and never understood it for the exact half a minute that the fight lasted. Then I saw that the Turk was flying from the ring, sailing with an effort through the howls of the people of Santa Maria and disappearing into the darkness of the back rows.

He had flown with his big mustache, with his legs flexing absurdly to find support and stability in the dirty air. I saw him sail close to the roof, among the search lights, maneuvering with his arms. The fight hadn't lasted fifty seconds yet and the champion had won—or hadn't, depending on the way you looked at it. I climbed into the ring to help him with the robe. Jacob was smiling like a child; he didn't hear the shouts and the insults of the public, the growing clamor. He was sweating, but not much, and as soon as I heard him breathe I knew that his fatigue came from nerves, not from physical weariness.

Pieces of wood and empty bottles were now thrown into the ring; I had my speech ready and the exaggerated smile for foreigners. But the missiles kept flying and I couldn't be heard above the din.

Then the cops moved in with enthusiasm, as if they had never done anything else from the day they got their jobs. Directed or not, they scattered and organized themselves properly and started knocking heads with their flashing nightsticks until all that were

left in the Apollo were the champion, the referee, and I in the
ring; the cops in the hall; and the poor half-dead boy of twenty,
hanging over two chairs. It was then that the little woman, the
financée, appeared from God knows where—I know even less
than others—at the side of the Turk. She started to spit on the
loser and to kick him, while I congratulated Jacob with all due
modesty and the nurses or doctors carrying the stretcher appeared
in the doorway.

—Translated by IZAAK A. LANGNAS

DREAM WITH NO NAME
by Ramón Ferreira López

RAMÓN FERREIRA LÓPEZ is a citizen of Cuba. He was born in
Spain and came to Cuba at the age of eight. He has written
many short stories and plays, some of which have won prizes
and been performed in Cuba, Mexico, Puerto Rico, and New
York. A collection, *Tiburón y otros cuentos* (*Shark, and
Other Stories*) received an award as the best book of 1951 in
a contest sponsored by the Ministry of Education in Cuba, and
was published the following year. Awaiting publication is a
new volume entitled *Un color para este miedo, y otros cuentos*
(*A Color for this Fear, and Other Stories*).

He awoke upon feeling the sun, sat up on the bench and looked
at the morning. A policeman was coming toward him through the
park making a noise with his stick. It was the fat policeman who
had at times treated him well and one day had given him a peseta.
On another day he had not given him anything and had told him
to beat it. Today he was coming unhurriedly clacking his stick
against the ground and saying let's go. Probably he was going to
give him another peseta. For that reason he waited for him. When
he came close he looked at the ground and crossed one bare
foot on the other. He put his hands between his knees and continued waiting. Let's go he heard him say and then the sound as
he knocked his stick on the walk. He got up to leave. But first he
looked at him. He stood unmoving and looked at him asking for a
peseta. That was what he wanted to ask him with the look. But
the policeman did not understand him and went back to saying
let's go. He walked a few steps and then he turned. He looked behind him and waited to tell him I'm hungry. He looked up at his
face and told him. I'm hungry. The policeman stopped and said
not even if I were your father. And then he said let's go and went
back to knocking his stick against the walk. Of course he wasn't
his father. He knew that well enough. His father was his uncle.

Or his uncle was his father. It was the same thing. He hit him if
he didn't bring any money and if he brought some he'd take it off
him. Then he gave him something so he could go eat at the
lodging-house. If he didn't bring him any money today then he
wouldn't give him any. People were not giving to him as they
used to. Because now he was bigger. So big that they wanted him
to go to school. Or to work. Some of them even looked at him
meanly. It was bad to go on growing like this. Someday they
wouldn't give him any more and his uncle would hit him with the
belt. That was what he told him when he got tired of hitting him
with his hand. But if no money came in today he wouldn't go
back home either. Yesterday there hadn't been any and because
of that he had stayed in the park and had had to eat leftovers
stolen from the cooks and to run off when the policeman arrived.
Some policemen treated him well and others treated him badly.
The thin policeman had threatened to take him in. But he was not
on this beat today and the fat one treated him well. He hadn't
given him money but he treated him well. And he let him beg
and let him walk behind the tourists. The tourists were different.
Sometimes they gave you money if you just looked at them. But
if you touched them then they would not give you anything. He
knew that already. You had to pay attention when they started
drinking. And not do anything until they asked for another drink.
Then one could look. He leaned against the column and looked
at them without begging. Sometimes they took two drinks and did
not pay any attention to him. They saw him but pretended to
look in the other direction. Those were the ones who gave most.
At first they did not want to give and then they gave more. But
today there weren't many tourists. The situation and the heat
the chauffeurs said who drove rented cars. And they sat about
swapping comments with the whores that things were bad. The
whores were odd. Sometimes they treated him well and wanted
to put their arms around him. One time one of them kissed him.
And then brought him to the lodging-house and told the cook to
give him something to eat. The cook didn't want to and so she
took money out of her wallet and began to scream at him and the
cook had to give him beans and rice. The whore watched him

eat and called him *mijito*. But when he finished eating she told
him to beat it. And now it had happened that she did not remember him. Because she didn't want to continue giving to him. They
were all the same. They only gave once. It was because of that
that you had to walk so much. But that was not important. It
didn't bother him to walk. He liked it. Because only by walking
would he be able to meet her. That woman who covered him up
in his dreams. Sometimes she passed without stopping and did not
notice him. Although he shouted she did not pay any attention to
him. Because he didn't know what her name was. Dreaming he
would set himself to find out her name in order to call her. But he
could not find it. Today he hadn't dreamt with her. Nor yesterday.
When he wanted to dream of her he did not dream. But when he
dreamed it was easier to look for her. At the end of the dream he
remembered her. Her face no because he always saw her in
shadows. But when he met her he was going to recognize her. He
knew it. Someday he was going to meet her. And when he met
her she was going to speak to him. In the dreams she did not
speak to him. She looked at him very seriously and said nothing.
She only looked. And if he was cold she covered him up. But
if he were hungry then she went away and if he began to cry he
started to run covering her ears with her hands. For that reason
he did not cry. Even if he were hungry he did not cry. And he let
her come close to the bed. It was a different bed. Not like the
bench in the park or the stone step of a doorway. It was a real
bed like those they advertised in the display windows of the
stores. Even bigger than those they advertised in the windows.
Only he never had anything to cover himself with and had to
wait until the woman came. If he were cold she would come and
cover him. Then he would wake up. The heat of the blankets
woke him up. Today it had been the sun. But in the dream it was
the heat of the blankets that woke him up. It was still early. Some
cafés were already open but it was still early and he had to wait.
There were no tourists at that hour. And the whores had already
gone to bed. In the morning it was more difficult to find a meal
because in the morning people were in a bad mood and it wasn't
worth-while to begin to look from the doorway. The waiters clean-

ing up told him get out and if he did not go threw water at him
with a bucket. He was tired and he leaned against the wall. He
had just gotten up and he was already tired. But the sun took
the cold off him. The hunger no but the cold yes. He could close
his eyes and think of whatever he wanted to. Except food. If he
thought about food he felt sick. So he thought about the woman
in the dream. And this time he saw her as though she were coming walking out of the sun. It seemed true. She came walking
from the sun and he stood quietly and immediately thought of
what he could do. He would make himself sleep and that would
let her come. It was the first time that he had seen her awake and
this time he would not let her get away. He had to speak to her.
And afterward touch her. And later let her touch him. Something
like the whore. But not like the whore. Who would touch him
and call him *mijito*. For this reason he was not going to think
about wanting to eat. He went on feeling hunger and not thinking about food. Only about the woman who was coming nearer.
And when she was close he would open his eyes even though the
sun bothered him and he would see her face and call her by her
name. Yes now. Now she was going to know him. She was going
to know him as soon as the sun stopped concealing her. She
was so close. She was so close that he opened his eyes wide
to see her. But she was going to pass by without saying anything to him. And she was passing without saying anything to
him. He stretched out his hand to touch her. And he touched her.
The woman yelled and gave him a hard slap. Then she gave
him another and called him fresh. When a woman yells everyone
starts to look. And if he did not begin to run she would call the
police. He began to run. The woman stood yelling on the corner
and pointing with her finger. But he kept on running. He crossed
the park and then the street. He dashed in by one archway and
came out by another. Until he was tired and leaned against a
column. Then he saw these two guys. One looked at him and took
a sip of coffee. He said something and then the other one looked.
He was also drinking coffee and then both of them were looking
at him. He put on his begging expression and played the innocent.
One looked at him again. Then the other looked. And then they

both kept looking at him. He continued playing the innocent and let his head fall on one shoulder. From time to time they took pity on him and said poor little thing. And once an old woman had given him a peso seeing him like that. Afterward he had kept on doing that but no one gave him anything. But now it could happen again. While he rolled his head down on his shoulder one of the guys called him. The one who had seen him first was the one who called him. He told him come over here. So he had to look at him. Come here he said to him and he came up. Sit down he told him and he sat down. One of them continued looking at him and said no he's very little. But the other told him to be quiet. You must be crazy he began to say. The other guy paid no attention to him. Then he asked him if he were hungry and he said yes. The waiter brought him coffee with cream and toasted bread with butter. And when he had finished he brought him more. The two men watched him eat saying things that he did not understand. One took him by one hand and looked at it and the other said to be quiet. How do you feel he asked him. He said that he felt fine. And when he asked him what his name was he told him Raúl. And then that he lived with his uncle. And that he was not going home because he hit him if there wasn't any money. And that there hadn't been any money because things were bad. And that the tourists were not coming and were not going to come. Both of them looked at him and then they asked him if he wanted more. He said no. Come said the other one. He got up and they stopped. One put a hand on his head and looked at the other as if he were going to hit him. See how thin he is he said and placed it on his waist. But the other one shoved him by the shoulder and said that he was no baby. Then he squeezed his shoulder and he liked that. They left the café and walked along the sidewalk. Where are we going he asked and they told him you'll see. They continued walking and crossed a park. Then they continued past the gates and reaching a doorway one of them stopped and said it's impossible. The other called him an imbecile and said he should get out of the way and he moved. Upstairs one kept standing in front of him and said you'd better think about it carefully. And then the other one pushed him and said

if he were afraid he could leave. You're the one who's afraid said
the first one and they began to argue. Go on in and don't pay any
attention said the other and he went in. Immediately they were
in a corner and continued arguing. He sat down on the bed and
waited. Finally they agreed and one came and told him that
everything was all right. And he answered that he was not afraid.
The other laughed and told him to take off his clothes. He asked
why and the other said to him to clean you up. He helped him
take off his clothes and asked him if he never bathed. Then he
led him to the door of the bathroom and began to laugh. As he
passed him the other gave him a whack on the tail. And before
opening the door the first one gave him another. Presently he
heard them laughing together. At first the water was cold but
then he liked it. The other came and gave him some soap. He began to look at him and said that he didn't know. He took the soap
away from him and told him what he had to do. The first one
brought him a towel and began to dry him. Then he asked if he
felt all right and he said yes. Good said the first one. The thing
is said the other. And the two of them were silent. Well the first
one started to say. Look said the other. Leave me alone said the
first one and the other withdrew. He asked him how old he was
and he said he didn't know. But you're already a big boy and he
said yes. Grown and blown and he said yes again. And you want
to earn money and he said sure. And not see your uncle any
more and he said no. Then he went to the table and took the
newspapers from on top. Everything was in disorder. There were
bottles and cans and nuts. And screws. And pieces of metal. And
little boxes and big boxes. And words in American. Look at this
he said to him and showed him a metal tube. Then he talked
about the big store where they sold mattresses. And of its doorway where he sometimes tried to sleep. He asked him if they let
him sleep there and he said that the guard always threw him out.
That is where you're going to put it. He asked put what. And he
showed him the fuse. The other came and explained to him.
Because they're lousy and won't let you sleep in the doorway.
Because they won't let you go into the store. Because we're going
to give you a peso, and if you do a good job another. And prob-

ably afterward we will let you live here. He looked at the bed
and he liked it. It was mussed up but he liked it. And one of
them liked him. And the other liked him. Now both of them
liked him. They had given him something to eat and they put
their hands on him all the time. But now said the first one you
have to be careful. You have to carry it like this said the other
and he fastened the fuse in his belt. When you get to the doorway
sit down as though you were going to sleep. Stay quiet until there
is no one passing by. Make sure that no one is passing and turn
it the other way around. Then. Then one started to say something
and shut up. Then said the other you get up and you go. Without
worrying said the first one. Nor running said the other. And don't
get nervous or look behind you. Wait said one and went and got
the fuse. He gave it to him and he said that he would do it. He
put it inside the belt and asked like this. Yes said the first one.
Perfect said the other. Now he walked as if the window were this
corner. He walked to the corner of the room with the fuse fastened in the belt. Imagine that this is the window and sit down
to wait. He sat down. Now look and see that no one's coming.
And he looked. Now no one is coming and you take it from the
belt and you put it next to the glass. Now you turn it the other
way around. Now you get up. Now you go away. Without being
afraid and without looking back. And you come back here. Just
like that. Come straight here. Then they came running over and
the two of them embraced him. They squeezed him hard and
passed their hands through his hair. Then they asked him to do
it another time and he did it again. He put the fuse in his belt
and started again to walk toward the corner. He sat down beside
the pretend window and put the fuse on the floor and then he
turned it around the other way. He got up and started walking
again. He did it one time and then once more. And that took a
long time. Until he got tired and said that he was hungry again.
The first one went out and brought in some food. Later they made
a telephone call and a woman came. When he saw her come in
he thought that she was the woman from the dream. He looked
at her wishing that she were the woman from the dream but the
woman did not look at him. She only looked at the first one. She

looked at one and then she looked at him. The other guy walked out. He said he was coming back but he walked out. Then the woman asked him if she couldn't carry it. But the first one said it was impossible. He explained it to her in a low voice and the woman looked at him again. Then she came close to him and said to him baby. But she did not touch him. The person she touched was the first one. But he told her be quiet. Then she asked him to send him out and the first one said again impossible. She threw herself on the bed and lifted up her clothes and showed her legs. The first one went and pulled her dress down and she lifted it again. Then she grabbed the first one by the arm and he sat down on the bed and he looked at him angrily and said that he should look the other way. The woman from the dream was not like that. The woman from the dream was no whore. The woman from the dream would embrace him but she would not throw herself on the bed. Nor show her legs. And she would not whisper with another man while he was looking the other way. He wanted to know what they were doing. And if he looked from the corner of his eye he would be able to know. He was certain that it was the same thing as the thin policeman with the whore on the staircase. He had watched and seen them doing things. It was because of that the thin policeman threw him out of the park. And now if they saw him looking probably they would also throw him out. And they would not give him the money. Or let him sleep in the room. But he wanted very much to look and if he turned his head a little he could see. And he began to turn his head. Till he saw them. But when he saw them they were already not doing anything and she came over exhausted and gave him a kiss on the face. Then she went into the bathroom and began to sing. The first one ran his fingers through his hair and came over and said to him comrade. Then he searched through his pocket and brought out a handful of money. He gave him a peseta and a reál. But that didn't come out to a peso. He said to him that they would give the peso to him later. When he did the business in the doorway. At this point the other arrived. He came in and said that everything was okay. He opened his shirt and showed them the fuse which he carried attached to the belt.

He took off the belt and put it on top of the table. At this the woman came out of the bathroom and came over to him. She looked at one and she looked at the other and immediately said that it was no good. She had another face now. Not how she was when he had thought that she was the woman from the dream and she wasn't. Now it was possible. She looked like the woman in the dream washed like this and without any make-up. Only she was younger and her hair was another color. But she looked at him with her face serious. She gazed at him just like the woman from the dream. As though she wanted to cover him up. And she said again that it was no good and the two guys looked at her. Tough titty one said you didn't come here to screw. The other said that it was his fault for getting women mixed up in this business. She said I'm going to do it and went and picked up the real fuse. Put it down said the first one and planted himself in front of her so that she would not be able to. Then he grabbed her by the wrist and they began to struggle. Leave her alone said the other and see if she gets to the corner. And then he asked her if she wanted to wake up with her mouth full of ants. She said okay but it's no work for a kid. Just for that reason said one. He doesn't run any risk said the other. Then they looked at him and one asked him if he were afraid and he said no. And you know how to do it the other one said and he said yes. Then they gave him the false fuse so that she would see that he knew how. They put it in his belt and he went back again to do it. She began to tremble and then she said I can do it myself and once again wanted to pick up the real fuse. He's already good said the first one. There's no other solution said the other. She went over and turned the light out and then went to the window. They stayed there looking at the real fuse and for a while they said nothing. I would do it said the first one. But that's no good said the other. Then don't do it she said and kept looking away. Then she said again that that was bad. And that it would be better to let it go until it was possible. Then everyone was silent. The first one got up and went to where she was at the window. The other came close to him and told him listen to what I'm saying to you. He looked at him so that he would say it. He said you're not afraid and he said no. And you're going to go straight there and he nodded yes. All right said the woman and took her purse and went to the door. What are you going to do said the first one and she did not answer. What are you going to do he asked again and she still did not answer. I'm not saying anything right now and she went out slamming the door. It was better now. The three of them were alone and it was better. They would give him the money. And if he did it well they would give him more. Probably later they would send him to put more fuses someplace. If people wouldn't give him money any more because he was big now he was able to earn it. One came and loosened his belt. He put the false fuse in it and then he tightened it. You have to be sure he told him and tightened it more. You're going to confuse the kid said the other and came and took out the false fuse. Let's go it's time he said to him. And he went to the table and got the real fuse. When they got downstairs one went out of the doorway. The other stayed with him fastening the fuse with the belt. He tightened it until he said it's good. Very straight and carefully he told him and he said okay. The first one looked at them and motioned with his head that they could go out. The other shoved him by the shoulder and said let's go. Remember come back slowly and without confusion. And without looking behind. He said yes and went out the doorway. When he walked the fuse pressed against his belly and after a little while begun to hurt him. With his shirttail out no one noticed but if he touched his belly he could feel it. He walked more and it kept on hurting. But the store was not very far and he wasn't going to split. No one looked at him. And if anyone looked at him he looked in the other direction. Because now he ought not to beg. Nor amuse himself. Nor go looking for the woman from the dream. That he would do later. When he had money he would look for her in other places. Probably he would find her in the stores where they wouldn't let him go in. When he had new clothes and was clean they would let him go in. And if he did not find her there he would look for her in some other place. Because now surely he was going to find her. And she would ask him where he had been keeping himself. Because she also was looking for him. The pain in his belly began to make him slip and he had to stop to overcome it. He pulled his trousers up and raised its position. And then he went on walking. At the beginning it did not hurt him and later yes. But there wasn't much further to go. And when he had crossed the street he would go into the doorway. And now there was only half a block to go. At that point the kids saw him. They saw him and they began to call him. He played the dummy and went on walking. Then they broke into a run and caught up to him. How's it going the negro boy said and the white boy pushed him. Then the negro boy pushed him. He defended himself with his foot and told them to leave him alone. But they wanted to go on playing and went back to shoving him. The fuse hurt him in the belly button and he had to put up with it. The little negro looked at him seriously and then he said he was hungry. Same as me said the white boy. We're going to rob the Polack said the negro and crossed the doorway and sat down at the café. The white boy followed him. And he took advantage of this move to keep on walking. There was not far to go now and he couldn't lose time. Only that now the Polack began to yell in the café and the little negro and the white boy passed him like a flash. And he stopped so they would not think that he was going to run too. And he was standing there when the Polish woman arrived all choked up and yelling stop. Coming up to him she stopped screaming and looked at him. Then she grabbed him by one hand and called thief. I wasn't there he began to say and she said you'll see. And without letting go of his hand she began to yell for the police. People began to stop. Some were laughing others not. Some said let him go and others for shame. One woman came up and said to the Polack that she had to let him loose. But the Polack paid no attention and kept yelling police. The policeman did not come. And more and more people began to gather. Then the woman also grabbed him by the other hand. She hauled at him and told the Polack that she had to let go. Don't mix into this said the Polack and tugged from her side. That made the fuse begin to hurt him again. Every time they pulled him this way and that it began to hurt again. He wasn't there said the woman and began to pull very hard. But the Polack did not let go and the fuse began to slip. I'm going to lodge a complaint against you said the woman for beating up a baby. And the Polack said she had not hurt him. Yes you did you hit him said the woman and I'm going to lodge a complaint against you. Then the Polack let go of him. Then she said in this world there's no justice and went off talking to herself. But the woman did not let go. He pulled at his hand but the woman did not let go. Come and eat something she kept on saying but he did not want to eat. He was hungry but he did not want to eat. He wanted the woman to leave him alone and the woman would not leave him alone. She grasped him more firmly and she said ungrateful and that boys of your age ought not to be out alone at this hour. Let me loose he said and she got angry. And then that she was going to take him to the station to see why he was out alone. Now he was scared. He was frightened because now the policeman was coming. She saw him too and held on tight with both hands. Then he had to bite her. As soon as she felt his teeth she let go. She gave a cry and let go. And again he had to run. To run and to run stopping the pressure of the fuse with both hands. Until he arrived at the doorway. There were still a lot of people in the doorway. It was like when the movies were out. People were walking little by little looking in the windows. And he always took advantage of that to beg. Only that now he was not able to. And there were so many people looking in the windows. It was the best hour for begging. He went up to one and began to look. Sometimes if he only looked they would give to him so he would go away. But now he had to go straight up and sit down beside the window. When he got there he met a man and a woman who were looking at the suits. Then they looked at him. The woman said poor thing and looked through her purse. Here take said the woman. But he did not move. Take it she kept on saying and he took one hand away from the belt and held it out. Poor thing the woman said again and the man said to him beat it. When he was alone he sat down. He leaned back against the window and the fuse began to hurt again. But he could not take it out yet. There were still people looking at the windows. Some of them went that way and some of them went this. But the fuse hurt more and he had to take it out. He lifted his shirt and

got a hold of it. Right away like they had shown him. And he put
it between his legs. He stayed that way for a while. Leaning back
against the window and letting people pass. Until no one was
going by and then he could do it. He grasped it by one hand and
leaned it against the wall. Then in a single motion he turned it
around. He turned the fuse around the other way and he stood
there. There were still people looking in the windows. But they
were going off. And in that direction he began to walk. He passed
the first window and then the second. Then the third and then
alongside the people who were going that way. Until he arrived
at the corner. When he was turning the corner he saw the other
policeman. And he began to be afraid. And to tremble. And to
want to run. And to get back to the room and hide. Where there
would be no policemen. Or people looking. Or anyone who would
say that what he had done was wrong. That was what he wanted
to do. Although he knew that he ought not to be afraid or run. He
was about to run when it happened. It happened that there was an
explosion like the nine-o'clock cannon. And the earth shook. But
it wasn't the nine-o'clock cannon because the glass of the show
windows began to rain. After the explosion it began to rain slivers
of glass. And someone cried out. Cried out once more and then
was quiet. People began to run toward the sound of the explosion.
Then he saw smoke coming out of the window and some who
were running in that direction. Not him. He began to walk. Because there was something on the ground that he wanted to investigate. Something that everyone looked at. When he got to the
group they would not let him see. They only said what a horror
and did not let him see. And then a policeman kept striking his
stick against the pavement. No one drew back until the ambulance
arrived. Then everyone began to run. Except the policeman with
the stick. And he could not move. Because he had seen the woman.
Thrown mouth down and covered with slivers of glass. And one
arm bent backward and the other did not have a hand. The blood
that poured out seemed to be the other hand. The flow grew
larger and ran along the ground. Until it ran so far that it could
not be the other hand. At that point more police arrived. They
ran up to the woman and began to get the glass off from on top of

her. They swept the glass off with their sticks. One caught her by the arm which had a hand and turned her over face up. And then he saw her face. Because of that he did not understand what the policeman was saying. Nor feel the whack that another gave him. Nor the threatening signs they were all beginning to make at him with their hands. The woman's face yes he understood that. And what the wide open eyes were saying to him. They looked at him very wide and said to him *mijito*. The same as the woman from the dream. Because she had found him and did not want to lose him. Only now it was she who was cold. Because of that he tried to come close to cover her and so that they wouldn't carry her off. But another slap would not let him. Because this time he felt the pain in his face. And the pain of being pushed against the wall. And the other blow they gave him because he hadn't yet gone away. But he still kept back the urge to cry. Until he saw that they were really taking her away. And how the arm without a hand was streaking the glass with blood. Then he could cry. Because he hurt everywhere. The shoulders. The legs. The face. Where the fuse had hurt him. And then all together when the police car screeched off at top speed. It was running behind the ambulance that he began to scream. Because of everything that hurt him. And because of something that hurt him more the more he felt it waken. The woman's name. Finally he had remembered it and could call to her. And as long as he ran and ran behind the ambulance the name he had looked for for so long was torn from him between sobs.

—Translated by PAUL BLACKBURN

SUNDAY FOR AN ARCHITECT
by Rolando Venturini

ROLANDO VENTURINI was born in La Plata, capital of the province of Buenos Aires in Argentina. He showed literary leanings from an early age, appearing in print sporadically with short stories and poems and helping to found a number of literary magazines. He makes his living as a lawyer and notary public. In addition to literary and theatrical pursuits, he confesses to a strong interest in the raising of horses in his native country.

The choir of little city noises started formally at six in the morning, when the first cart passing along the avenue finally woke me up. After that I lay quietly, with my eyes closed, waiting every few minutes for the distant tremolo of the streetcar. My fingers began indolently to trace the linen thread design on the bedsheet and I could suddenly identify a sensation: the surprise of luxury. Many things had surprised me since my return from Italy; but the specific cause of my present surprise was the start of the day, the edge of a different bed at the moment one leaves sleep to make one's first contact with the world. This enormous four-poster was substituting, perhaps to no advantage, for my simple white iron bed. And the day, too, prepared itself to be different, only I did not know what its difference would consist in.

When I opened my eyes, the brief striations of the window light were already dividing the half dusk of the bedroom into long parallel bands, and when I turned over to lie on my side the long and svelte body of my wife was left uncovered amid the tumbled bedclothes. Vicky was sleeping deeply, with that calm that only a very healthy organism can impose on sleep, though always with some intimation of an intense vitality. For Vicky was a beautiful woman. During the night the sheets formed new folds at my flank, and her gradual renunciation of covering, favored

by heat and humidity, revealed to me an extensive and downward
view of her long, smooth, and tawny limbs, while the upper opening of her silk nightgown announced, as if by design, a white and
firm bosom, singularly powerful within the brevity of its lines.
"You are like the world in your attitude of surrender. . . ." the
old line of verse I used to recite to her came back to me in a
flash of clarity. "White thighs, hills of white. . . ." My memory
was beginning to return to me intact a part of my life that I had
lived with intensity. But not only that. Now that I had returned,
it was forcing me to re-examine my entire approach to the situation. Although I knew that recapitulations served no useful purpose, there was something in me that made me frequently link
together faces, landscapes, certain external facts, peculiar states
of emotion that have sometimes to be repeated. For suddenly it
is no longer memory, or conscience, with its power to wound us,
that makes us relive a reality; but rather it is as if a dark force
insisted that we face up to certain facts that are like the basic
words of a language that we have to know if we are to keep on
living.

I had married, six years ago, the woman I loved. I had suc-
cessfully pursued my career as an architect without ever com-
promising, at any time, my true vocation. The municipal prize
I had just won—and I would like to emphasize that I had sent
in my design from Rome so that I had won it without even being
here—nourished my *amour propre*. And yet, at the very moment of returning to my country and my wife after almost two
years, I could see myself only as an undecided and unsatisfied
man. And just as I could not find myself, so I could not find in
my city, even after lingering long in my favorite corners, that old
peculiar atmosphere that made me feel I belonged to it, that I
was somehow part and parcel of its definition as a city. And could
it be that the same thing was happening to me with my wife?

The moods of depression did not, fortunately, last long. It is
only that they occasionally descended on me with such an intensity that I felt completely baffled. On such occasions I either passively let the course of events take charge of me or lavished an

unusual display of physical passion on my wife. I realize, of course, that I indulged in the latter course in a deep expectation that Vicky would once more assert her domination over me, as she did in the old days, simply by her overwhelming gaiety and vitality. And since it is sometimes good to believe that some portion of distributive justice proceeds not from the powers that be but from a mere tendency toward equilibrium inherent in the nature of things, I cherished for a few moments a hope, founded only on the color of the morning, that this would turn out to be at last that different kind of day for which I had been waiting so long.

It was past seven when I got up, moving carefully so as not to wake her. In my morning reflections I had been considering various contrasting modes of behavior. I now chose—just as one chooses a suit—a mood of good-natured passivity for the party I had to face this Sunday, the party in the country. Vicky had lately been visiting the Solanos, and I knew they were having a barbecue today on their ranch. Maybe it really was—as Vicky suggested—in my honor: but more likely it was—as I was inclined to think—merely an excuse for a party. I didn't know who was likely to be there; but I suspected I wouldn't meet any intimate friends. And though I already knew the Solano ranch, whose countryside mused on amid the array of urban comforts, this did not help me to guess in advance what kind of a party it would turn out to be. Unwilling to worry unduly over so indefinite a future, I went to do my waiting under the bushy *araucarias* of the avenue where, at this hour, the benches were still greedily competing for the first playful caresses of the sun. There are people whom the morning links with childhood, and noon with maturity. But the early hour did not take me very far back in years; rather it gradually brought back sweet and bitter memories of the time before my departure: of my engagement and my married life.

I believe that Vicky was superior to me physically. Thus although she wasn't taller than I, I liked to think of her as taller.

And she was not only willing to understand that I actually preferred this silly fiction; she agreed to share it with me and to act
accordingly. She thus set the style of our conjugal life—which I,
in turn, willingly permitted her to impose—and wisely distributed her doses of pinches and caresses, irritations and concessions.
That is why our game of love depended so many times on our
mutual recognition, in the fraction of a glance, that we were
both willing and eager. Then I conscientiously played the part of
an adolescent excessively spoiled by a more mature and vigorous
teacher, a part that she, in turn, was willing to act. And so the
lie of a reprimand was followed by a bolder caress and then by a
fictitious struggle or a little vaudeville chase through the rooms.
We imposed silence on ourselves with urgent gestures, hid from
the servants, and finally took refuge in the bedroom, acting as if
we had no right to do so. Right to the end we kept up an exchange
of fictitious reproaches as if we were doing something really
naughty and could be surprised at it by the grownups at any moment. And on many occasions, when everything was already over
for me and I was gradually reassuming my identity, with those
confused misgivings with which a reflective man watches his departing biological and animal self, Vicky was still scattering
around my neck her joyful squeals, the uncontrolled fruits of an
intensity that was at once fiction and love.

However, now, on my return, Vicky no longer exhibited this
spontaneity. Or maybe that isn't quite what I want to say. Maybe
it is that I myself no longer seemed to be that young and inex-
perienced animal that effortlessly lent life to the fiction. There
were times when I believed that the only thing wrong with me
was a lack of adaptation to my surroundings. It was as if my
movements were no longer the same, or the actual flexings of my
body had not yet refitted themselves to the old folds that they
had made in clothes that were later, and unexpectedly, withdrawn from use for an indefinite time. But even so my wife's
behavior remained outwardly one of flattery, so that I could convince myself that the fault lay with me and that time would correct it.

On the other hand, my initial difficulty in approaching Vicky was of long standing. I had suffered from it when our courtship culminated in our engagement and even more when circumstances, dances, conversations largely confined to discussions of future possibilities, and kisses stolen in the elevator, finally established between us a relationship with clearly sexual implications. The fact is that she waited for my reactions with an expectant smile, and I for my part could perceive in her expectations and her consents only a strange contradiction, as if she were simultaneously exhibiting innocence and experience. This disconcerted me so much that at any given moment I could only retire into an irritating timidity. This kind of thing also happens, I know, to the novice card player. While he tries to remember the rules, he enjoys the game only so long as the other players do not observe him too closely. Then he is dealt a certain card, makes a move that suddenly makes him conspicuous and attracts the attention of the whole table. It is then that his intense fear of humiliation—a possibility that perhaps only he foresees—makes him take too many chances and stake all he has. To come back to love, who says that we are not under observation while engaged in it? Can we isolate ourselves so securely that we are sure the eyes of our fiancée, those small affectionate lights we adore on a park bench, are not the eyes of a judge? Or that the eyes of our mistress, half-opened, are not scrutinizing our attitude in bed? I believe it is because each of these situations ended with me in a position of dependency that the day came when I decided to launch an all-out attack.

One afternoon toward the end of the summer, after working out a plot to the last detail, I took Vicky for a drive in the family Pontiac on the shore road that goes southward to Magdalena. Under a roof of matched clouds that tempered the afternoon heat, we passed, in succession, the outskirts of the city, the stream, the zone of intensely cultivated farms—whose varied shades of green seemed always grouped in defense of some geometry—and finally reached the country, that open country which, flat as it is, offers only the occasional minute variation of a clump of blackthorn or poplars. We hadn't gone far into the country when I stopped the car, after working the engine feed in a way that produced the impression that the motor was going to give out at any moment. I muttered some fictitious curses, and Vicky easily accepted my suggestion that we should watch for a truck driver, for someone who would rescue us by lending us a pump that would restore the free flow of gasoline in a matter of seconds. In the meantime there was nothing for us to do but wait. For a long while things went the way I had expected and wanted. Only I was actually too scared to follow up, and I reached a new decision well after an hour's waiting, which we spent lying on the scanty vegetation of the roadside, with not a soul visible on the highway. But Vicky showed no sign of preoccupation even then: she was as gay as the robins that twittered in the treetops, leaned over my forehead, and repeatedly assured me that this world was, in some way, ours. I could not proceed with my maneuvers, and it all ended in humiliation, in my confessing the plot to her. She smiled at first, while trying to guess what I would come out with next, and then helped me to unfasten her bra. However, while we were both submitting to the growing urgency of mutual caresses, something inside me told me that I should feel wretched, wretched and chastened. And that something must have triumphed that afternoon, inasmuch as I believe I did not possess her then because I was frightened by the easy progress of the adventure or perhaps because I suddenly came to dread—without admitting it to myself—the prospect of finding her to be wiser than I and again, as on previous occasions, calmer and more powerful in her expectation. Her final reproach of "After all, Aldo dear, one doesn't do such things" was shorter than my own confusion. I didn't recover from this bungle for a long time; not, I believe, until well after our marriage when the habit of intimacy finally turned the failure into an innocent and forgiven jest.

It was about ten in the morning when, after putting on some sports clothes and completing the brief preparations for the trip, I went to look for my wife. Her happy "Good morning, darling!"

shouted from the thick atmosphere of the bathroom, charged
with steam, suggested to me with utmost clarity that we would
be late.

"Vicky, are you ready?"

"I'm never ready."

"Be serious for once."

A minute later she emerged, wrapped in a kind of cotton cloud,
her gay clean face crowned by a stiff white cone that I identified
as the towel with which she held up her hair. I tried to match
her optimism:

"Can I witness the Birth of Venus?"

"Don't be silly."

"Then I'll tell you that I have an idea about bathrooms that
will help you not to underestimate my professional capacity. But,
meanwhile, may I ask you at what hour we are expected?"

"Don't worry about the time. You haven't dressed for the
country. Look, I want you to behave like a civilized person. I
don't know, Aldo, but since your return, I have noticed you
sullen sometimes with people, reserved. . . ."

"Give me a kiss and I'll be good."

"Of course, they don't know enough to be able to argue with
you. But they don't like you to lecture them either. They are
almost all of them people of good social position, but quite simple
really. I'll go further than that. You may be shocked sometimes
by their superficiality, their frivolity; but let me tell you that
they often act this way only to be in the swim, socially speaking.
And besides, if only for a change, don't you like to meet people
now and then who are not intellectuals, who can offer you nothing
but goodness? Oh, you really have made me lose time!" She
turned around to give me a kiss and stayed on to look into my
eyes for a moment and to say, with a gesture of feigned desperation: "You haven't become a Communist by any chance?"

We left at eleven, at last. And I'll confess that, during the drive,
I played with the idea of putting on a show. Social conventions
appeal, like constitutional preambles, to bores of good will. Tired
in advance, I foresaw that someone would inevitably want to

engage me in a completely affected conversation, of the kind that certain people prefer because it makes them feel as if they had paid a tax—a levy on boredom—that gives them an apparent right to indulge afterward in any kind of triviality. I have seen it so many times, at so many latitudes. "Do you know, professor," a woman told a friend of mine, a few days ago, at a chaotic party, "do you know that I have discovered that Paul Klee's painting justifies me to myself? Because, you see, the irony that his fine drawing reflects actually helps express a very indescribable thing, my own infra-reality. . . ." I made a gesture of weariness and concentrated on the driving.

When we reached the residential part of the ranch, and I finally stopped the car under the tufted trees that face the main building on the north, a heterogeneous group of people, who seemed to have dedicated themselves noisily to cocktails, solemnly interrupted their activity to come out and greet us. And, immediately, the circle of faces I had to confront for the introductions offered me the first deception. Apart from the host, there were only two men—young lawyers whom my memory failed to connect with any particular court—with whom I had previously been in some vaguely friendly and cordial contact. There are situations that force one to sport a stereotyped smile. One shakes, one after another, various strange hands. This unusual and nervous flexing motion tires out one's right arm (as if its strenuous physical contribution were an indispensable preliminary to the birth of a new affection) and there is nothing left for one to do but to bear in mind the ephemeral duration of all this effusion. Three or four days later, in a station waiting room, affection would already be reduced to a greeting; a month later, it would be a mere nod. There are times when three steps are enough to determine the character of a social function. One takes them toward a group of young people and votes to become one of them; or else, as I did on that particular occasion, one moves toward the older ones, being equally the victim of a voluntary deception. Actually, it was my deep and confident hope that Vicky would attract the general attention; this would permit me to pass unnoticed and, besides, it immediately made her euphoric. And, indeed, it seemed as if the trend of my thought had taken on the importance of an order and obtained an immediate compliance from the "extras" peopling the stage. Within two minutes, the unanimous buzzing of voices around my wife reached that appropriate crescendo that only generous alcohol can maintain indefinitely. Within my own group, however, just as I had expected, two respectable gentlemen began to show an undue interest in the postwar development of Italian architecture. My explanation, given in the patient tone required by this sacrifice to one's profession, had barely got over the necessary preliminaries about European reconstruction when Vicky—who obviously captained the noisiest group of the party —warned me not to count on her for the next hour as they had decided to refresh their appetites with a ride.

I honestly believe that one never feels more painfully empty and lonely than when one has to talk, in an inexcusably trivial manner, about the most cherished aspects of one's vocation. *Señor* Barrie, for example, a stiff and bony old man whose main occupation was to repeat, constantly and from memory, the latest quotations on the Smithfield Meat Market, proclaimed that only the Gothic cathedrals and a few public buildings of the eighteenth century were worthy of his respect. *Señor* Tellechea, on the other hand, whose deafness was even more pronounced than his Basque origin, ventured the opinion that Michelangelo was the great architect *par excellence,* so that, from his day to ours, architectural creativity was reduced to the hope of producing an acceptable gloss to his work. And how could I, a spirited young man, heady with a recently acquired list of impressive names, dare to dispute his opinion? And dare it, moreover, on this flattest of plains, which God probably included in his world for the sole purpose of breeding the cattle necessary to feed the rest of mankind? *Señor* Tellechea hastened, however, to emerge once more from his deafness to tell me that his exaltation of Michelangelo was not made for any personal reason—he couldn't very well have any—and that I shouldn't take offense at a point of view that he derived exclusively from a solid spiritual foundation.

While I accepted his explanations with all kinds of suitable gestures and did not use any number of arguments because they would have been futile, a series of cordial and imperious announcements made us move to occupy our seats at the great barbecue table, judiciously placed at a good distance from the house, under the refreshing shade of the eucalyptus trees.

I have always been inclined to think that Magdalena Solano, nervous and friendly, constituted a worthy exception within her group. And so it was with a sigh of relief that I let her lead me away. Together we crossed the rest of the spruced-up terrace of glass and flagstone to where the ground suddenly became natural and gentle, and where presently we could smell an appetizing smoke in the air. Magdalena is one of those women who, when we have a chance to think of them as Argentine, arouse in us a certain kind of pride lightly chastened by falsehood. I sometimes think that I could not validly accuse her of turning her back on her country because to accept suddenly a divorce between the soil that nourished her and the kind of sensibility that makes us compatible would be as painful as to admit that our own historical determinism is stronger and more important than all hopes of escape. In any case, Magdalena, who frequently quotes Simone de Beauvoir, would evade all such accusations, aided merely by her sense of humor. Perhaps by contrast with my recent endeavors with regard to Messrs. Barrie and Tellechea, her unconstrained laughter aroused my sudden sympathy. Although there was nobody present on that ranch whom Magdalena could not view with ridicule, it was when she proudly confessed to me the secret of her true citizenship—she told me in her own language what amounts to the same thing, that she felt a stranger on her husband's estate —that we both felt entitled to laugh conveniently at the weird cattle barons. A few minutes later, the majority of the guests joined the barbecue.

"Come, Aldo," Magdalena told me, "come and look at them. Can you remember one open-air barbecue, just one, without this stampede for roast meat?"

"Well, to tell the truth, *I* prefer meat pies."

"Ah, but they turn it into some kind of ritual and that's what makes it so hateful. A ceremonial rite to show off an instinct that they may or may not have. Soon they'll be waving strings of gut from their forks as if they were battle trophies. It's horrible, don't you think?"

"I wouldn't go as far as that. I'd say it's just ill-mannered behavior."

"Maybe so, but the worst thing about it is that they indulge in it as if it were an Argentine characteristic, an affirmation of our nationality."

"A rather beefy affirmation, don't you think?"

Magdalena's laughter accompanied me until we were close to the head of the table.

"Very well, Aldo, I'll go to look for Vicky and bring her back right away."

I have seldom thanked anybody so much, without saying a word, as I then thanked Magdalena for her intention to return my wife to me. I suddenly felt that Vicky was my only point of support, and I started a ceaseless and strenuous search for her, scanning one after another of the young and vaguely irresponsible faces I had seen close to her on their boisterous progress to the stables. But more than a big glass of native wine had to be my only confidant.

When Vicky finally came back and sat down on a chair facing mine, I thought that the most unpleasant part of the day was behind me. I had no idea that I could be so mistaken, all the more so since my wife favored me immediately with a small demonstration of solicitude.

"Look, Magdalena," I told our hostess, "in spite of what we said before, I still maintain that the only good way to eat barbecued beef is with one's own knife. And I haven't brought mine."

"Well, that's easily remedied. I'll bring you one at once."

"Oh no, how horrible!" Vicky detained her. "I'm the one who forgot." And, quickly rising to her feet, she stayed us:

"Don't you move, Magdalena, I'll get it. Wait for me."

Magdalena wanted to recall her: "But, Vicky, dear. . . ." My wife wasn't listening. She made a commanding gesture from a distance and then disappeared running. Shortly afterward she returned triumphantly with a small, sharp horn-handled knife. Its two initials, set in gold, seemed to declare that this was not a knife for daily use, but the dull and much-worn blade denied it.

"Where did you find that?"

"That's my secret," she replied. "Don't you worry." Her tone, at once comical and enigmatic, put an end to the incident.

If I say that the lunch went normally I only mean that, like everyone else, I ate till I almost burst, though I did not participate in the extremes of the general merriment except by passive consent. And when the numerous toasts of the "bottoms up!" variety were over, Solano's figure rose at the head of the table and made a good-natured plea for silence; I guessed it was time for the speech. Vicky gave me a smiling wink, as if to say, "Now you'll see!" and tried to silence with a gesture Señor Tellechea, who had been so busy enumerating the virtues of the Hereford steer that he seemed to be taking no notice of the announcement.

"My friends," Solano said in a voice not untinged by alcohol, "we who love our country and all its products can calmly risk all we have on the success of an Argentine who goes to Europe to lecture when that Argentine—who graces our table on this joyous occasion—is called Aldo Vicenzi." At this point, Solano's emphatic manner produced the inevitable burst of applause; he raised his hand to stop it and resumed his search for inspiration, his eyes firmly fixed on the tablecloth. "Because the Argentines used to go to Europe only to waste senselessly the money earned by the sweat of our generous soil; but now—and I'll soon offer you proofs—we have Argentines who do better: they go there to display the glories of a legitimate triumph, the fruits of an intellectual effort, and the rewards of diligent toil." Another try at applause. "And if Vicenzi obtained over there the approval of the experts, as abundantly proved by his numerous articles in the Milanese review *L'Architettura Italiana* and in other academic

and specialized publications, his work has never become sterile or
alien to us, as shown by his recently won municipal prize, a victory which, I am sure, will be but the prelude to many others.
And now, while he is still paving the way for these coming successes, I gather from your lips the warm congratulations that you
all want to lavish on him, and I want the toast I am about to offer
him to include an affectionate endorsement of his future tri-
umphs." He did offer me a toast and made me toast him in turn,
amid new applause; he then sat down to thank, with a lamentable
dignity, his immediate neighbors. I had no alternative but to offer
my thanks, too. I did it confusedly since I had a very clear feeling that I was more and more alone, and I experienced the bitter
certainty that only a foreigner can have of being abandoned by
all.

"Wait a minute, I'll take your knife back before everybody goes
away," said Vicky, rising to her feet. "And you know how they
are," Solano went on. "Not one ranch hand is to be found here
on Sunday, for love or money." The gin that was now served
helped to re-establish a capacity for connected speech, and I
could again submerge myself passively in the circle of jovial faces,
now engaged in going over anecdotal memories of the ranch. It
was then that Magdalena began to recruit volunteers for a trip
to a neighboring ranch, *La Enramada,* where a furiously con-
tested *pato*[1] game was due to be played at three in the afternoon.

"Why don't you come with us, Aldo?" Magdalena invited me.

"Don't you remember any more what *pato* is like?"

"How could I forget! I need only tell you that, as a boy, I saw
it played by genuine sons of the soil."

"Ah, but surely it wasn't as well organized as this one. The
best thing about it is a combination of our primitive elements,
wild and anarchical, with the spirit of 'fair play' that is the essence
of sport and that we learned so well from the English. There are
very strict rules."

"You won't be annoyed with me, Magdalena, if I don't go?"

---

[1] *Pato:* rough Argentine country game, played on horseback, with a duck
(*pato*) as prize. Today a combination of polo and basketball.

"Well, since the party is in your honor, you do what you like. Would you like to take a little nap?"

After that other solitude, physical solitude would hurt me least. I accepted.

The guest room was a first-floor bedroom, large and silent, with a cool atmosphere that anticipated somewhat the relief of the siesta. Vicky accompanied me.

"Are you staying with me?" I asked, beginning to undress.

"I don't know. You got up so early today that you're sure to fall asleep. I think I'd rather go and come back soon."

"Listen, dear," I told her. "Everybody has either gone to *La Enramada* or is about to go. What are you going to do here?"

"I'd rather they all went, because I'd just love to stay here and play the lady of the house. To walk around, without going anywhere in particular, to stop at any place that hasn't been put on exhibition, I mean prepared for a visit. That's the good thing about the country: you can just poke around and commune with the primitive."

"Ah well, if you lay down with me now, it wouldn't exactly be in search of the primitive, would it?" I said, giving way to an unreasonable fit of jealousy.

"Stupid. Or maybe Solano's speech has annoyed you."

"I am not annoyed."

"All right, be a good boy and go to sleep. Look, I'll draw the curtains for you."

I watched her as she carefully knotted her silk scarf, darkened the room, and left. My boots weighed as heavily as the leg irons of a feudal dungeon. I took them off with some difficulty and plunged into the softness of the sheets. The noise of some departing cars sounded ever more distant to me. Then I must have fallen asleep.

I don't know how much time passed, but it must have been the silence itself that pushed me back to reality. I should have explained that my sleep is a guarded sleep, of the kind that has to be periodically fed by external noises to be confirmed in its

calm. A moment came when the sonorous void finally startled
me out of my sleep. I didn't know where my watch was and felt
too lazy to look for it. The residual effect of the local wine was
threatening my throat every minute. I dressed at last and, watching out for the other people in the house, went out on the porch.
Nobody else seemed to be there. "And Vicky?" I asked myself.
My wife must be walking on the grounds, she may have gone to
the corrals, to the ruins, or heaven knows where. The sun was
still so vertical as to suggest that time had no power to move it to
one side of the sky. The heat turned the air into that static thing
it is in summer, with that sudden trembling that shows up even
sometimes in Fader's paintings.[2] I walked slowly toward the
stables.

And I was lucky. Out there in the shade, tied by the halter
and looking like the gentlest and best-groomed animal of the
entire ranch, a saddled chestnut horse was waiting for me. Whoever took care of him had not unsaddled him to give him relief
from the afternoon heat, but had merely loosened the cinch of
the broad saddle he bore. I worried but briefly about not telling
anyone that I was taking somebody else's horse. I mounted it
and, without looking back, rode the gravel paths, trying to find
an exit from the labyrinthine park. At first, well-tended greenery
showed the marks of an almost city-like care.

But then, quite unexpectedly, the row of plane trees that
served as border came to a sudden end in the parenthesis of a
palisade, and the true countryside, authentically disheveled for
all the seven shining wires of the fences, stretched away unim-
peded except for a mill or two and some flattened woods in the
distance.

I had no fixed itinerary. An alternation of long and short
gallops brought me to a small rise behind which I could see the
remains of a ruined ranch. The locals called it *La Rosada,* possibly in traditional ironic allusion to the presidential palace, *La*

---

[2] Fader: Fernando Fader (1882–1935), Argentine painter of the impres-
sionist school. Tr.

Casa Rosada. However, there was nobody around, nobody meaning, of course, Vicky. Nonetheless, I moved closer and, resting
my elbows on the horse's withers, stayed awhile to trace the
foundations of the walls, the deep cracks, and some imbedded
relics of lime, with its original pink coloring miraculously preserved. And this, I thought, is what Vicky means when she talks
about the rough surface of the pampa. But it was a poor and
agonizing spectacle. After all, this ruin could barely be as old as
an old man. And even if it were older, could I possibly respect
something like this and raise it to the category of a true historical
relic? I remembered other ruins that my recent memory tried
avariciously to preserve. And, usually, when circumstances indicate a choice, it becomes a political vote: a vote for the party of
the just, of course, for the Apollonians and the noble-hearted. I
suddenly tried to think whether it was something valid—something like the two Argentine generations of my family or the
principles of May 25 or Monte Caseros[3]—that pushed me toward
a compulsory identification with these walls that my other heart
disdainfully refused to recognize. I knew that I could suspend
judgment in the meantime—the choice becomes all the more difficult the more sincere one wishes it to be—but I had to take into
account the testimony of these walls, which seemed to be aware
of the shame of their improvised style. Actually, the pampa had
not delayed long in giving its answer: it obliterated them, it was
obliterating them.

I took a short cut toward some haystacks at the far end of the
corral. Two dogs got up to receive me, but their hostility proved
as transitory as the alert that they were, no doubt, accustomed
to give, since they must have recognized my horse immediately.
Vicky wasn't there either. I turned back and started on my re-
luctant return trip, at the horse's own pace. I still couldn't explain
to myself why my wife should want to lie to me. Human con-

[3] May 25, 1810, marks the beginning of Argentine independence; the battle
of Monte Caseros, in 1852, brought about the end of the dictatorship of
Rosas and the restoration of Argentine democracy. Tr.

duct, like physical facts, can be explained as a relation between cause and effect. And was the cause, the explanation, about to come to the surface?

By the time I returned to the group of buildings that composed the home farm, I was getting an ever-clearer idea of the situation. And jealousy, the green-eyed monster that had that day become my solicitous companion, whispered to me at great and repetitious length that my wife had given up the *pato* game at *La Enramada,* that she wasn't in the main house, which looked silent and deserted, and, finally, that she wasn't wandering about the corrals, the ruins, or the haystacks. There remained one peremptory possibility: she was *there*. There in the shed where the ranch hands lived, a building of ample and simple design. At the rear it probably communicated with a lower building, the residence of the foreman, hidden in a kind of brick-floored patio, almost completely covered by grapevines arranged in rectangular patterns. I cursed silently because no one was in sight and entered the shed by the front door.

Inside, the double tier of beds left room for a kind of corridor. At its end, in the half dusk, a locked door beckoned. Some big and angry fly used the narrow crack of light that my passage had left in the doorway to fly out in freedom. Rage and shame grew jointly in me as I walked on tiptoe the brief trail of my spying expedition. As if I were a blind and absurd gamecock, something in me obliged me to experience, in one gulp, all the successive stages of ridicule: mild, warm, hot, very hot, burning! . . . Yes, there she was, there they were. Vicky's quick unmistakable laughter had just stopped short, evidently suffocated by an avidly opened mouth that pretended to devour her. I heard a brief smacking noise, an obscence announcement that those two tongues were reveling in their filth. And then I could not but identify carefully the little creaks, the labored breathing, the disordered sequence of the sounds of love. And finally silence.

I strained my ears for a long time, clinging to the wall in the belief that I would hear better this way, or putting my head to the dark keyhole, vaguely fearing that I was the one to be discovered, to be surprised. I don't remember how many times I anxiously glanced at the distant shed door. The harsh taste of deceit, that merciless taste which I had never known and with which I had just become acquainted, mingled indistinctly the words I tried to but could not pronounce—death, gun, filth—with the wounding and half-heard sounds, feigned denials, and the animal crushing of the bodies.

It was then that I realized that things were not like that. That I didn't belong to this world any more. That I was nothing but an uprooted man. The insult of the soil and the insult of my unfaithful wife could only appear to hurt me. I shook with mad joy when I made this discovery. And that's why I started listening again and, strangely enough, did not feel contempt for Vicky. The game of love seemed to have ceased, and I heard steps in the room. Barefoot steps that caressed the floor. I heard the harsh sound of a match, as if it had struck fire only after the fourth or fifth try. And then, clearly, the voice of my wife: "It's like this, Gómez, you don't know what the city is like. . . ." The man cut her off in mid-sentence: "You should come here more often. This is what you really want. . . ." A slow and heavy voice. It sounded so sure of itself in its slowness that I could not but forecast a long and thorough caress that would bring on a resumption of love play. Now they were joined again. She, lying on the bed, was smoking lazily, trying to shape the smoke into prolonged and voluptuous shapes. And the man began by sitting down at her side, and I knew that his words would soon become more and more incoherent. I could guess that he was carefully scrutinizing in the dusk the naked body of my wife. For I myself had gone through so many such uncontrolled studies, imagining biological approval bestowed on her firm and delicate limbs, and even on that zone of hard and specially naked flesh that sheer stockings, however stretched, would never manage to cover. What's more, the cold and intellectual phrases I used to murmur

to her—like "O Actité, Supreme Dancer!" must have deployed
themselves impertinently over her sweet belly, while all that this
fleshly and innocent woman really wanted was the response of
the earth, a man as plain as the pampa, the man who was now
caressing her, some poor devil named Gómez.

"No, Gómez, no. Please, that's enough. I tell you it's late." I
don't know how much time had passed but Vicky spoke rapidly
and in an ever-louder tone, so as to convey a note of urgency.
"Seriously, it's very late," she repeated herself.

"Come!" Gómez displayed an imperious manner, wanted to
be suggestive, to force her down again.

"No. Go now, please." It was almost like a plea. "I'd better
dress alone. Maybe Aldo is already awake and looking for me."

"Tell me when you'll come back!"

"I don't know. How can I know?"

"When?"

"But how can I know, Thursday. . . ."

I didn't want to hear any more. The mention of my name had
suddenly returned me to my initial state of resentment. There
should be a law in this game, some rule to concentrate the ridicule
on the institution of "husband" instead of on my name "Aldo."
Aldo. And it was obviously not I; it is not a name, it's a word.
There are words which, no matter how lightly pronounced, bear
a heavy load of imputation. It's just the opposite of what they
were trying to teach us in language lessons. I'll never forget the
weary voice of my English teacher saying: "But look, you must
put the stress *on that word*. . . ." Otherwise they wouldn't understand us. But yes, yes, one does understand when one is the
defendant. And then there is nothing left but to deceive oneself
gradually, to decide that the drama wasn't really a drama, only a
farce. It's easy to do it, it's like lowering the volume of a radio.
So that the voice of our Conscience, the conscience of Socrates,
is no longer heard but vanishes like a murmur into the false foli-
age of the sets. And it seems easy to explain things to oneself that
way, only it wasn't easy that time. But I managed it. I agreed it
would be a good thing to play my part in the comedy.

I sneaked away quickly to return to my room and, wherever I could, I clung to the walls on my return trip. I dreaded meeting anybody and giving myself away with a gesture. I'll admit I was lucky. The patios were empty, and no one moved on the porch. The thick shadow seemed to be doomed to wait a long time until the sun got tired of oppressing the afternoon. I was, of course, the first to reach the guest room. I locked the door with a key to ensure privacy and took a leisurely bath. The dilatoriness with which the water lent me its elemental coolness restored some of the calm I needed for a further readjustment to my situation. Without any urgency, and with the apparent laziness of someone drawing on the smooth sand of a beach, I started outlining to myself the scheme of this new freedom. For it was, indeed, a freedom, a disconcerting kind of freedom that carried no apparent benefit and, moreover, scared me. The successive symbols that would keep intersecting, the contacts, the disengagements and the new meetings, the hot vicinity under the bedsheets—all this had just died there, in the birth of this absurd freedom. And it was then that I remembered Bompiani, or rather what Bompiani had told me jokingly or dramatically in Rome, some three years ago: "And you, Aldo. Do you really believe that I'll let my honor hide indefinitely under my wife's petticoats? Wouldn't it be like submitting it to the law of gravity?" Well, the apple had, at last, fallen. To estimate when it became loose seemed as improper to me as to dilute a drama artificially with anecdotes. The fact itself, insolent and lewd, rasped on my ears every now and then. And each time I imagined a succession of acts of violence, interminable scars on the face, deformities and revenges. And yet none of these fantasies outlasted the enactment of animality they expressed. The animality to which I succumed now, merely by recalling those silent duels to the death, with cloak and knife, with which legends were able to fill this very pampa. Their inevitable cause was—except for occasional affronts to the vanity of courage—a primitive and ragged woman, the most ridiculous of all causes. And what had happened to me was, ultimately, that I lost to Nature a battle in which the odds were stacked heavily against me. No. The idea of my own complicity grew in me as a thing that could not be delayed. And I had to let it come.

I lay down and lit a cigarette. Then another. The silence conspired with me, while the convolutions of smoke ceaselessly pursued their leisurely course toward their final destination, the open air. Then someone—Vicky—tried to open the door; but I resisted the impulse to get up and take out the key. I supposed she would be relieved to think that I was asleep, and I imagined the explanation she would think up for Magdalena when she went to use her bathroom. After a long while I decided to dress.

I left the bedroom, finally, when I felt that my defenses were ready for any eventuality. First the armchairs of the hall, then the furniture of the spacious dining room and all the objects on the table laid for tea, each and all assumed personalities of their own and became a scattering of mocking witnesses. There was a moment when I wasn't sure that I could withstand the successive impacts of reality. Because there were still the people to be faced. That group of tired, self-satisfied people whose very sight hurt me. For most of them the party would become by tomorrow merely another Sunday, perhaps slightly marred by the need to make a business call: some tenant with rent in arrears—a particularly negative and disagreeable occasion—or a mortgage payment to be collected. But the balance sheet of the day would be, in any case, so favorable as to make the temptation to repeat it irresistible. Not only hadn't they lost a peso at the Palermo races; they merely had to look at their forearms to see the lasting pink pigmentation, the healthy caress of the sun. There was, moreover, something very important that only I could now estimate at its true worth: none of them had been adorned with horns, none of them found his wife lying with a ranch hand.

Magdalena and my wife came together to receive me. Vicky's face shone like a toothpaste ad, like a flag, with colors as beautiful and false as only the artificial hues of publicity can be. Magdalena said to me:

"Well, Aldo, you seem to have had a truly provincial siesta."

"Yes," I agreed. "I'm afraid the 'sixth hour' stretched into the seventh and even into the eighth. And how did it go at *La Enramada?*"

"You don't know what you missed, Aldo. It was really magnificent."

Vicky took my arm. "And I, too, feel guilty, you know. I could have woken you up. But I actually walked about all afternoon and behaved as if the ranch were my home."

"As if you had to stand on ceremony here," Magdalena scolded her. "You know very well that this really is your home."

And although it was hardly necessary the way things were going—the door she had found locked an hour earlier should have convinced her—Vicky slipped in a little cover-up story.

"Come, Solano," she called our host. "When you've heard what I have to say you'll have to make me an inspector of your ranch." Solano approached us with a look of surprised and pleased solicitude.

"An honorary inspector, of course. Don't worry. Aldo is becoming so successful that I'll hardly need the wages. Well, let me tell you that one stretch of your wire fence is quite useless. Over there"—she pointed vaguely—"on your boundary with *La Concepción,* I think."

"Wonderful, Vicky. I congratulate you. Gómez told me about it early today. Tomorrow, when I have my ranch hands back, we'll go and repair it. But you know, of course, that the post of lady foreman is yours whenever you want it."

They all laughed amiably. I, too, smiled. I thought that if Magdalena knew the whole story she might have approved the procedure. Only she would have used the word "alibi" instead of "cover-up." I entertained myself for a while by looking at Magdalena, studying her. The tailored riding breeches she was still wearing failed to Americanize the classic shape of her hips, smaller than my wife's, but equally firm and feminine. I was amused to recall a kind of dance we have in our crowd, which generally makes us experts in the art of quickly judging the couple next to us. At the first handclap, the agreed signal, all men immediately drop their partners and start dancing with another woman. At the first signal, or the second, the change-over occurs

with relative sobriety. There is always someone who will attempt
a bow, an unusual and Mozartian gesture, like that fake porcelain
painted with motifs from Watteau. But the successive changes
become more and more lively. The band's music becomes ever
more frenzied, with parodies of military marches, "Valencia."
The last changes are really collisions, direct embraces. And I
asked myself: how would this farce turn out if I now tried another switch, an embrace with Magdalena?

But circumstances forced me to postpone the diversion that my
imagination had begun to work out. *Señor* Tellechea joined our
group, and the second editions of the intelligible phrases that keep
conversation going—sounding as if they were loud and portentous
recriminations—were now all directed at him. The usual triviali-
ties filled the air. First, the evident successes of Duggan, the im-
pulsive manager of *Los Teros,* the *pato* playing field, and then
the happy repaving of the road to the Ranelagh golf course at
last reduced the conversation to the languid stage for which I
was waiting to take my leave. And if they did not applaud me to
endorse my final salutation, it may have been simple forgetfulness; but I remember that I felt thankful for it, as if it were a
most honest act of omission. When I turned the steering wheel
toward the asphalt highway I seemed to enjoy the comfort of a
physical liberation, as if the distant little hands still waving their
farewells were the last muddy claws of a swamp from which one
manages to escape at last, but only at the cost of exhaustion
and pain.

The return journey was almost silent. Vicky, leaning her head
against the back of her seat, kept her eyes half-closed, to observe
the various stages of a rosy sunset that had begun gently to dilute
the sky. Then she closed her eyes because, she said, it was so
wonderful to be carried lightly over the smooth highway, the
motion consuming the tiredness of the day, the physical residue
of the strain of a Sunday in the country. She must have slept—
unless she fooled me—as calmly as I saw her sleep this morning

on our bed. She woke up with a start when the traffic suddenly became heavy and nerve-wracking at the approach to the city, and we talked.

"I was thinking, Aldo," she said. "I didn't really expect you to have much fun, but at least I hope you weren't too annoyed. With the party, I mean, the people."

My reply was deliberately tortuous:

"Look, Vicky, I wouldn't be lying if I told you that I felt this time, as I have felt few other times in my life, the urgency of certain fundamental questions, the kind of questions one doesn't ask oneself every day."

But my wife decided to ignore completely any dangerous implications, and when she spoke to me a few moments later it was in a rather light tone:

"Oh, I forgot to tell you the funniest thing that happened to me this morning. You remember the youngest of the Silvestres, that tall boy who plays polo and has recently grown a tremendous mustache to look two or three years older?"

"Yes, I believe I do. I mean I can't really say. I know quite a few Silvestres."

"Yes, but surely you remember the Silvestre who went out riding with me this morning. You must have seen him."

"All right, so I know him. What about him?"

"I'll come straight out with it, and please don't be annoyed: he propositioned me."

"What?"

"Of course, it's nothing serious. You know the boys of this generation: if they don't do it at least once with every woman they meet they're afraid they'll get the reputation of being homosexuals. Oh, but it was really funny how he gesticulated while trying to keep up with my horse, in a gallop. And his vehemence, shouting even! I was really afraid the others might hear us."

"Maybe . . . maybe you shouldn't have refused him outright." She gave me a look of mingled surprise and intrigue. "What I mean to say is this, and I'm really serious about it: I believe I'll go back to Italy."

"What? But, darling, you never told me. . . ."

"Yes, Vicky, I believe I'll go back." And, immediately, I added a lie, prompted by a shame I couldn't overcome: "Maybe you'll join me there soon. I'm sure you've worthily played your part of Penelope these last few years. . . ."

We now reached the belt highway and crossed it. The night was becoming ever darker and more uniform, and the lights multiplied dazzlingly at our sides. When we drove onto the main highway, its asphalt, alternately lit and darkened, suddenly seemed to me like the twistings of an immensely long reptilian tongue. And when the night finally descended upon us, black and viscous, it seemed as if the road had finally acquired a moist palate of flesh and bone. And then, gradually, the city swallowed us.

—Translated by Izaak A. Langnas

E